THE WATER DIAMONDS

Dennis Bowen

The Water Diamonds is a work of fiction. Names, characters, places, and incidents are the products of the author's imagination or are used fictitiously. Any resemblance to actual events, locales, or persons, living or dead, is entirely coincidental.

ISBN: 978-0-9881841-0-7

FIRST EDITION

www.DennisBowen.com

www.twitter.com/DBowenThrillers

www.facebook.com/Dennis.Bowen.90

Book Interior Design by 52Novels

ACKNOWLEDGEMENTS

I would like to thank the readers of *The Water Diamonds*. Readers cause writers to thrive, and for that gift I am grateful. Numerous people offered suggestions and encouragement during the writing of *The Water Diamonds*, and they also deserve my appreciation.

In particular, I wish to thank Laura Taylor, my mentor, editorial consultant, and colleague, for her guidance during my journey to publication. Any errors or omissions in *The Water Diamonds*, I claim as my own.

—Dennis Bowen

CHAPTER 1

The look on his face appeared as determined as it was pleasured. What he had accomplished at the behest of his government was monumental. Never before had anyone created a road map for national conquest. And he had done it not once, but twice.

The high-powered sports roadster streaked up the Pacific Coast Highway north of Malibu—some of Southern California's most beautiful coastline. The driver had sea waves crashing on his left, a mountain barrier on his right, and a curving two-lane blacktop ahead. Add the thunder of a *built* V8 engine, and he was zoned-in.

A quick stop for lunch at Neptune's Net was all that had interrupted the drive. This was the same drive he took anytime he needed to reflect on a task he had just completed. He'd accomplished the unimaginable. He had been the Sun Tzu, not of bloody battle, but of bloodless political conquest.

• • •

Three miles ahead, beyond the north end of an incoming fog bank, two extended-cab pickup trucks blocked the roadway. Between them, a six-foot square electronic sign surrounded by red pylons informed oncoming vehicles that the highway south was blocked due to a major accident. There would be a one-hour delay.

Men in identical trucks blocked the roadway a few miles to the south.

• • •

The driver tensed his jaw and dropped the transmission a gear. He fueled the fire with his right foot. The RPM jumped. The wind whistled through the sports car roll hoops. Its high pitch brought melody to the V8's rhythm. A name painted on the driver's door said *Nirvana.*

• • •

Two miles ahead, a rented Ford Explorer with a roof-rack sat parked alongside the road. The two passengers had already unloaded a ten-foot plastic toboggan. They struggled to drag it up the 60-degree slope of blown sand pressed against the hillside. They had learned from prior recon that vacationers slid down the sand bank for an adrenaline rush, since the slope was very fast and terminated at the highway edge.

They stood atop it now, and the roadway below resembled a narrow black ribbon. They felt the moisture of the incoming fog and worried their effort would be scrapped. But as they watched the white puffy mass inch across the road, they heard a sound in the distance that inspired hope.

Now they could see it. With just the right timing …

The engine roar grew louder as the sound waves compressed toward them. A phone text 'Now!' was all they needed. They pushed off.

The driver saw them at the last moment. He knew the authorities kept people off the slope the best they could, but there would always be crazies.

The collision was seconds away.

The driver swerved.

Over an embankment.

The men in the pickups heard the crash. One man made an anonymous call to the California Highway Patrol. They packed up their gear.

The men on the toboggan slid across the road and dragged to a stop. They walked to the road edge to look down. They glanced at each other and nodded the affirmative. No one could survive such a crash. They, too, packed up and left the scene.

The man in the sports car felt the first impact. In that instant, his mind snapped to black.

CHAPTER 2

It was his last day. He had planned everything down to the final detail. He had learned a great deal in the past fifteen years with the company. Now, he was putting it to work. He'd stepped into the elevator before 4:30—before the rush. Alone.

In his excitement, he had mashed his index finger onto the rectangular glass pane, and a voice had queried his floor selection. "Zero," had been his response. Voice recognition software verified that 'he' had answered and that the last-day floor had been enunciated. Security had been alerted.

It was tough. He was still trying to get his emotions under control from yesterday. His colleagues had stood up at his going away luncheon—some he had considered friends. Making fun of his size. Making fun of his sense of humor. Tonight, he would show his 'friends.' And he would show the rest of them.

The ride down began in absolute quiet. His focus narrowed to the dead silence. The silence began to pound his brain like a jackhammer.

"Make a fucking noise!" escaped his clenched teeth.

It did.

Without warning, the elevator slammed to a halt. Between floors.

He tumbled to the floor—his precious cardboard carton, too.

"Oh, my God!" His breathing ramped. "No!" he wailed at the ceiling. An hour in a stuck elevator would destroy him. He grabbed his head with both hands. He squeezed his eyes shut to hold back the tears. What to do? The emergency phones had gone in a budget cut. *Wait! Of course!* The elevators were sigh-quiet so as not to interfere with the eavesdropping. *That's it!* He yelled out the emergency code word for 'stuck.' "*Tarbaby!*"

Instead of the security staff, he heard a harmonious chorus.

"G-O-T-C-H-A: Gotcha!"

Some of his colleagues were ingenious. They had to be to survive. A freakin' practical joke. A perfect freakin' practical joke. He felt like a smile, but he couldn't even force one. In utter silence, the elevator resumed its descent. He wiped his forehead with his sleeve. Close. Too close. The elevator continued down to Zero.

The man, whose stature pushed upward of five-foot-five on a tall day, exited the elevator. He moved at a controlled pace across the floor, carrying only his cardboard carton. Machine Parts it said—they all did.

He looked down at the sound of his new leather Florsheims on the whisper smooth granite floors; they felt and looked good. He walked as if mentally determining each step. He forced himself to breathe easier. That is, until he looked up and saw the new security box. No one just walked out the front door. Not here. Not ever.

The old airline-like setup had allowed twenty-eight employees and visitors to be killed—the consequence of a paradise-designated Arab. The man with the carton had helped to specify the new ingress/egress security. The enclosure had a formal name, but he had nicknamed it BOB for Big Ol' Box. The little man had helped to create the BOB. It could become his enemy in a heartbeat.

The crystal clear box appeared innocuous. One-at-a-time you were buzzed in. You remained inside—alone—until security processed you with a *negative*; then you were buzzed out. Should you be deemed a security risk by, say, pulling a weapon, grenade, or if the security czar was having another of her 'happy 28th' effusions, a button would be pushed. No ordinary button, this.

The specialized glass would turn milky white. The captive could not see out. It would contain any bullets or shrapnel the captive wished to deploy. They had gone over budget to include a gassing option. The injection of an inhalable, atomized version of the date-rape drug had its merits.

With that in mind, the man entered the line for outbound security, trying to look normal. Then, he sneezed. *Damn!* A tell. He always sneezed when his nerves got to him. It was probably in his profile. He glanced at the button pusher.

When his turn came, he placed his carton in front of the On-Duty Security Operative. On request, he handed his badge to the ODSO and stepped inside the BOB. The door hissed shut. It was close inside. He sneezed.

The ODSO stripped the tape ends from the pre-securified carton. He removed the lid and looked inside.

Even a less-than-astute observer could see the man in the BOB was petrified. They know, he thought. They freakin' know. Then, it got worse.

The ODSO reached in and picked up—of all things—*the toy*. It was an action coin bank that allowed its owner to fire coins inside. That's all. The guard shook it and heard the few coins inside rattle.

Don't open it! the man-inside-the-BOB prayed. *Please!*

"You might want to reconsider retirement," the ODSO quipped into the short-range intercom.

The small pear-shaped man sneezed again.

The ODSO replaced the carton lid. Then, he smiled. "You going to slow down now?"

The little man formed his hand into a stroking form and moved it up and down. "Wife's gone—nothing changes."

Laughter.

It was closing time with other people in line. Small talk was kept small. The man focused his gaze on the little green and the large red lights. Whole seconds passed. And … *green!*

The ODSO placed a sticker on the man's ID badge, then buzzed him out. The little man took his badge and his carton—the violated security tape ends flapping. He stepped outside through the building's final set of doors. The wind had picked up enough to blow the ambient leaves through the air like aimless, variegated butterflies. As he made his way down the steps into the parking lot, he sneezed again. *Damn!* His hold on the carton escalated to a death grip. It was *that* important.

His clock was ticking. It was approaching dusk, and he was on his way—away. Away from work—away from other things, as well.

A day filled with bright Autumn sunshine at lunchtime had morphed into a cotton gray. He didn't care. His heart began to surge. He stopped. He knew better than to look back. But, he had to. He had put in some serious time here. He turned to glance up at the seven-story building—at the director's office. *Just go ahead and shoot* ran through his mind. No shots were fired.

His eyes swept all of the tinted windows, seeing the shapes and shadows that moved back and forth. They had used a blend of LED and nano technologies to create the effect. No one inside ever matched up with the images. Even the shadows lied here.

He gave a nod. A final farewell. A single tear ran down his cheek.

He'd never been a spy. Not really. But, things were different now. Just this once. Tonight.

He had forced himself to breathe normally just to exit the building. Now, his respiration accelerated. He sneezed again.

If they were watching, all they could see was a dumpy little man whose stomach continuously tested the buttons of his wrinkle-free white shirt. A man whose tie was out-of-date, tied too short, and whose curled profile resembled a ski jump viewed from the side. He appeared a threat to no one. His physical attributes had finally become an asset. *Who knew?*

He continued across the parking lot. He drew closer to his car. Fifteen more feet. Almost there. Then, someone clicked a remote. A car locked. Its horn honked.

His heart jumped into his throat.

He tripped.

He dropped the carton.

All of the crap he had collected from his desk on his final day now lay strewn at his feet. He could have thrown it all away. He could have left with just the clothes on his back. Except for *the toy*.

For Christ's sake! Don't blow it now! He fell to his knees, scraping everything back into the box with the lid. He froze.

It was not there! He sneezed as if in a death rattle. And then again.

He was frantic. He jerked his head left. Nothing. To the right. *There!*

It had bounced against his left rear tire. *It* lay there looking up at him. Taunting him. *It* was painted in bright yellow, red, and green. He had dubbed *it* rasta-toy. A kid's toy. When he'd first discovered *it*, he had cocked the thing and fired in several coins. Fun. Until he discovered *its* secret. Now *it* was his life. His new life.

He clamped his hand to his chest as if to stave off a heart attack … or another of those dreaded panic attacks. He caught his breath. He placed all the remaining items back in the box—the toy last. Gently. With respect. He did not look around for watchers. They always watched. Just let them see the klutz they had grown to expect. Act normal.

He opened the rear door. Unlocked. No need to lock anything here. He placed the carton in the back seat, closed the door, and, for a moment, caught his reflection in the window. Even without the fun house effect, he was shorter, rounder, and sported more wrinkles than just a few years ago.

He drove to the outbound security gate, pressing his right hand to his cheek, holding a finger hard against his upper lip as he struggled not to sneeze. The gate guard approached. He knew the guard. Maybe, just maybe, he'd get a pass this time.

"Take that out," commanded the guard, pointing at the carton.

The little man in the car started to shake—inside. He withdrew the carton, placing it on the pavement. He stepped back. The guard lifted the lid and made a cursory check of the desk items. He seemed satisfied. Then—he picked up *the toy*. Sweat spotted the man's white shirt. Odd for an afternoon like this.

"You better have shot a whole bunch of coins you think you can retire in this economy, Yo," said the Philadelphia native. "Have a nice day Mr.—wait!"

Oh, Christ!

"You been promoted to civilian. Yo, have a nice day, Sammy."

Sammy smiled at the guard, who returned the carton to the back seat. He surrendered his badge, the last vestige of his employment. And then, the man with a mission—the little man named Sammy—exited Langley for good.

• • •

Sammy caught *Dolley Madison*'s boulevard and headed east. Inside, he felt the uncontrollable urge to weep. He thought of his wife. His kids. But this was no time for sadness. It was time for resolve. For courage. For spunk. Chutzpah.

He turned onto Highway 495 toward the capitol, Washington, D.C.—the epicenter of the free world. The final battle of good versus evil would take place there. He was sure of that. But he digressed. Focus was critical.

Sammy fed gas to his prize black Buick and merged into the evening traffic flow. As forecasted, rain began to fall, drops detonating like tiny bomblets on the windshield, slopping into puddles on the over-waxed hood. He should have hated it. The darkness. The grayness. The portent of gloom and doom. He should have hated it. Instead, he embraced it. Perfection. Rain was the juice that made it all work. It set the mood. He could not have dialed it up better. It was the exact backdrop he needed. The prescient night expressed itself to him.

His mind switched to thoughts of the two kids he kept buried in his heart. He would travel to see them. Make amends. It had been a long time. Too long.

Done with that thought, he noticed something else. The lights playing through his field of vision moved the shadows, casting them this way and that like an infestation of spies lurking amok. *How freakin' appropriate.* His mind began to merge with the night. The oh-so-somber bleakness, gray in the distance, seemed to provide cover for whatever went on behind. And the lights—the lights of moving cars at once alone and ensemble. They interacted to produce erratic shadows that cast about like insane little secrets. He imagined spies darting from place to place, using the shadows as cover. His vision of future paradise was hard to see on a night like this, but it was out there, just the same, on the other side of the muck. And he was on his way.

His mind bounced all over the place. He needed control. He needed calm. Breathe and release. Ah, there … he calmed.

Then, "Fuck!"

His heart raced. Flashes. Red and blue flashes. Not from ahead—from his mirror. His heart raced. Something was wrong.

"Well, shit!" he screamed at the mirror. "Not me! Not tonight!" Some asshole cop was lighting him up. He didn't have time for this. God, he hated Virginians.

"Shit! Shit! Shit! This is the luck I have?" His adrenaline spiked. He prepared for the worst.

"Christ!" He had a date with destiny and, tonight, destiny closed up shop at six p.m. sharp. Six or never. Should he rabbit? Should he pull over and just shoot the bastard? No. He'd need a gun for that. Some spy *he* turned out to be.

"Okay," he said. "I will stop. I will beg forgiveness, promise a blow job, whatever it takes." He would persuade the trooper to back off. "Whatever it takes." But, as he drifted in submission toward the side of the highway, the flashing Christmas tree on wheels sped by. It was another one of those boner-head, dufus locals with a totally legal, Let's-Pretend-I'm-The-Man light bar attached to the top of a trashed red Ford F-150 pickup. God, he hated Virginians.

Realization struck. "Jesus Christ! I'm goin' to the bonus round!" *Breathe and release. Under control, Sammy. Focus.*

The rain settled down into more of a nuisance. The wind pushed it across the highway in wafts of light gray mist, tapping an irregular beat on his pride and joy. It had been a present to himself for being promoted to the Inspector General's office—he and the other deadwood. Okay, fine. The new job had set him up for tonight's big score—$12.5 million U.S.

• • •

Sammy reached the Tysons Corner Mall just west of D.C. at 5:15. The rain-soaked Autumn sun had decamped, done for the day. Darkness cloaked the landscape. He had allowed for heavy Friday night traffic, but it had been light. He had some time to kill.

Further instructions awaited at the American Grill. By coincidence, one of his favorite haunts. He was excited. He yanked open the door so hard, he whacked a man standing in front. Lithe and athletic, he looked to be half Sammy's age and taller by a few inches. He had a cell phone to his ear, and Sammy almost knocked him down. Sammy noticed the cartoon-like, oversized jaw on the man tense. As the man spoke into the phone, his beady dark eyes tracked Sammy.

The language sounded foreign—Sammy didn't catch a word. Might be one of those short-fuse types, he thought. When times were hard, like now, some fuses got cut in half. Sammy threw a quick, insincere, "Sorry about that." over his shoulder. You had to be careful, he considered. Everyone in this state carried a gun. God, he hated Virginians.

The Grill was having its Friday Night Big Band Swing Night, and the drummer pounded out, Gene-Krupa-like, the intro to Benny Goodman's *Sing Sing Sing*. Sammy liked the old stuff, but was no match for the twenty-something jitterbuggers who tore up the dance floor. He had brought his wife here often. Now, with her in God's hands, he did not get out much.

He found a stool at the bar. With practiced accuracy, he informed the bartender, "Bond .... James Bond."

"Yeah, and I'm Trump Donald Trump and this is Happy fucking Hour," the bartender shot back, unimpressed.

"Uh, the martini. The one spies drink. Lillet Blanc and the other stuff."

The bartender moved off to re-create the historic drink. Sammy smiled to himself. He felt good. After all, this was his night. Until 4:30, he had been stuck in the IG's office in the world's greatest spy company. It was Internal Affairs to covert operatives who dealt out extreme prejudice for a living.

Just a job. Now, he was playing for real. He was one of them. Sammy Spy. Ha. He blew through his drink. Then, as he set down his glass, he noticed writing on the napkin. Directions. Spies really did this shit, he realized, and not just in crappy movies. He paid his tab and headed outside for his clandestine phone meet to set up the exchange. *His* evidence; *their* money. Sweet.

As he exited the Grill, he followed the wall of store-fronts that curved off to his right. No perpendicular intersecting walkways at Tysons. Maybe the builders had decided to cater to drunks.

He quickly found a place where a pie-shaped section gaped open. He turned into the empty wedge as instructed by the napkin and found the phone bank. The lighting was poor, affording him the requisite privacy. He located the money phone. It had a little green garage-sale dot on the side, per the napkin.

He was so ready for this to be over. His heart pounded like a tympani drum on Rockstar squared. The martini should have helped more, but 100% booze just wasn't enough. Sammy felt himself bending—hoping not to break.

He saw 5:59 p.m. on the Citizen his mother had given him. Make his call precisely on time or the deal was off. So he had been told.

"Tonight changes everything," he muttered to the inanimate telephone.

At 6 o'clock straight up, he lifted the receiver with a trembling hand and punched in the numbers he'd been given. He carefully dialed from memory, getting it right the first time.

It rang twice.

He hung up.

He knew the penalty for a screw up at this level would be severe. And final. His forehead dripped sweat.

All Sammy needed to do was make his connection and listen. A drop site would be specified and a lifetime of paradise—heretofore denied—would be his. As he waited for his call-back, a figure stepped out from one of the many shadows in the alcove and stole up behind his left shoulder.

The phone rang.

Sammy jumped.

He grabbed the receiver on the third ring. Instructions. Control your breathing, he told himself. Don't let them hear you sweat.

But before he pressed the receiver to his ear, there was a quick movement by the figure behind him. Sammy's head snapped back, a hand clamped hard over his mouth. Then, a pinch. It felt like the sharp muscle twitch men his age got all the time. It was not.

A voice. An accented voice next to his ear, speaking slowly. "So ze tail was goeeng to wak ze dok? As you haf sed, my leetle frand, *zeece* … shanges averyseeng."

In no more time than it took for the assailant to lower Sammy to the cold pavement, Samuel Walter Silberweiss was dead. Paradise denied.

The killer's free hand moved to his victim's throat, verifying that Sammy would enjoy no tomorrow. He checked the pants pockets and then the jacket. *Nothing.* Nothing but a wallet and some papers. He put them back.

The little man had been told to have *it* with him. Nothing.

Control was not the killer's strong suit. He flew into a rage. He kicked the dead man in the groin.

Again. And again.

Nothing.

What he sought was hidden inside *the toy*. Not the coins, but an encrypted memory card concealed in the plug. The fate of his beloved country, and perhaps the world, depended upon its destruction.

In his haste, he missed the valet ticket. He could not have read it anyway. He wanted to return home, but tonight's bad fortune meant he would have to finish business here in America. In California.

It was raining. It was Happy Hour. It would be a while before anyone noticed Sammy's corpse. And, with that in mind, the assassin with the evil-looking face disappeared into the gray of the night.

• • •

The detective called to the scene three hours later was Harry Blackstock. His colleagues called him Hap. Short for Happy—his nickname's nickname. He found it hard to be happy tonight. Uniformed police and an impatient coroner's office representative loitered at the scene; none of them were happy either.

As he walked in, Maglight in hand, his foot crunched on some plastic bits on the cement. Instead of looking down, he looked up. Whoever had killed the little man had used an air gun—or something similar—to take out one of the two overhead lights. That explained the shadows. He observed it could have been a while since the murder. On a rainy Friday afternoon, people were either at Happy Hour or at home—precisely where a going-off-duty detective should be found.

One of the uniforms, a sergeant, handed him the wallet found in the man's pocket. Hap flipped it open. He squatted on his haunches, lifted the black plastic someone had used to cover the body, and verified that the man identified in the wallet as one Samuel Walter Silberweiss was, indeed, dead.

He saw no blood on the man's clothing and none on the ground. Nor did he see the small slit on the back of the dead man's dark jacket. It didn't matter. The Medical Examiner would determine cause-of-death. He glanced around, knowing it would be impossible to find witnesses, reliable or otherwise, on a dreary Friday night. This one was pretty much a write-off.

Hap allowed that deaths by crime were somewhat of a regular occurrence in the D.C. environs. Given the large number of criminals, it was the victims who were in short supply. He laughed to himself and headed back to the station to write a brief report. It was getting to be family time.

The following Monday, Detective Harry "Hap" Blackstock received a call from the M.E. Death had been due to a single stab wound in the heart, entering from the rear, but without the usual exsanguination or bleed out. A narrow knife, probably a commando stiletto like the WWII Fairbairn-Sykes, had been thrust through a small rubber sleeve, or 'plug', prior to the stabbing. The killer buried the knife to the hilt with deadly precision, held the plug in place with the fingertips of his free hand, and slid the knife out with the other. The nature of the rubber plug caused it to seal itself when the knife was withdrawn. No blood spill. No spatter.

He thought it an ingenious way to commit a murder. It gave the killer plenty of time to get away clean. It hit the detective that this killer was too clever by a lot. This was no act of revenge or anger. And the man who'd committed the crime was nowhere near the same as the one who'd wanted it done. This had been a hit, pure and simple, but not by an angry husband or the mob. Experience told him this was special—a conspiracy.

That evening, he called a friend who had achieved intimate knowledge of this kind of thing in the service of the government. Not the FBI. Not the CIA. Just, *the government.* His friend took less than five minutes to get back to him.

"This is Charleroi," came the Cajun drawl. "Hap, you've got something. Your vic is *company.*" He sang the last word *sotto voce.*

The caller clicked off. The detective was left with a blank stare. He was certain this was above his pay grade in the extreme. He did not know the vic's car and contents had already been picked up by *company* employees. He could not know that the answers to the questions he hadn't even had time to ask himself were taking shape on the West Coast. All he could say was, "This changes everything."

CHAPTER 3

The sun played into the northern foothills of the San Bernardino Mountains like a mammoth spotlight. In the Fall, it did not produce the ninety-degrees-plus temperatures of Summer. At 4 p.m., it began to cast shadows onto several huge piles of gravel and sand in an open area surrounded by fingers of hillside, which gave way to the flat expanse of the broad high-desert valley. The lights blinked on in a distant four-corner town in the middle of the valley. To the east, the sun gave last light to the Bullion Mountains and, farther east, the giant Marine Corps Air Ground Combat Center known by locals as Twentynine Palms.

The sounds of the quarry had played out for the day, the workers who had begun work at daybreak now en route home. They all lived in the Southern California valley called Lucerne, which bore no resemblance to its Swiss namesake. They all knew the icy cold Winter days and nights would soon stake their claim to the desert floor.

But all was not yet done at the quarry. A heavy rolling door to one of the large, corrugated garages trundled and squeaked its way open to allow the departure of one special vehicle. Had anyone been observing, it would have seemed odd to see an ambulance with paramedic livery crunching across the rock-strewn drive to the blacktop two-lane. The remote road ran from the Lucerne Valley floor uphill in twists and turns to a resort area known to the entirety of Southern California as Big Bear.

The driver looked tired. Well past 40 years of age, his face resembled a roadmap history of the many places he had been. Tough places. His passenger, however, was a short distance past 30 and provided little unprompted conversation. Neither of them had anything to do with paramedics, ambulances, or medicine. The man they were transporting was their current reason for being. He was attended by a well-qualified male nurse, who kept the IV drip stable as the encased entourage proceeded southbound and uphill.

"I wouldn't cover this again and again if it wasn't that important," the driver began. "It takes one hell of a case to get someone with your qualifications detailed to this kind of assignment. Your employer is down with this all the way. But remember, you report directly to me and only to me for the duration. Every aspect is TS—Top Secret SI. Do you understand?"

"It was made exceptionally clear to me, Mr. Sommers," said the athletic-looking, but shapely blonde passenger. She wore a blue denim pants suit which, blended with the blonde hair and her tanned complexion, could easily have, in other circumstances, turned the man's head.

She continued. "I am, by your direction, to keep *the subject* alive at all costs, including my life."

"That you were the best available is a concern to me, Agent Bransfield. A grave concern. Failure on this assignment is not an option. Clear?" said the man as a father admonishing his daughter, but not daring to take his eyes from the often treacherous road.

"I shoot straight; I don't miss. But you know that," the blonde retorted.

"When someone tells me I'm getting a sharpshooter ace, I'm not impressed. If and when you engage, I want to be hearing about two or three taps to the chest. Each target. It's in the Bureau manual."

"I know the manual. I've stood bodyguard duty before. I have engaged successfully. I'm the best available now, because I'm the best available period." She needed to put her foot down here so that Mr. Sommers would not get in her way. Sometimes a man did that to a woman. Not on purpose—it was gender genetics.

The driver maintained a safe speed …

"Black ice!" he yelled as the ambulance made an abrupt turn sideways, throwing the nurse to the floor and banging the blonde woman's head hard against the door glass.

The ambulance slid across the invisible ice totally out of control. The driver tried to steer into the skid, but to no avail. They picked up speed on a surface like polished glass.

The road curved to the right ahead. The ambulance sailed toward the edge, facing an imminent in-flight experience. They had noticed the topography on the way up—the drop would be several hundred feet.

They hit dry pavement. The front wheels, with force supplied by the still-driven rear wheels, gained traction. The driver straightened out the vehicle and slammed to a stop.

The man and woman released their held breaths ensemble. They stared entranced through the windshield at nothing but space. Several heartbeats passed.

"Everyone okay?" The driver threw the words into the back.

"We'll live," the nurse said. "The patient is sedated next to comatose—didn't feel a thing."

The woman rubbed her head. Pain from the serious head-banging she had taken had just surpassed the fright of the moment. She turned to the driver. "Patient? Didn't they call him *the subject* at the hospital? I thought—"

"Don't think. He's recovered out of any medical danger. He's now going into a therapy process that is part of a study—a classified study. Like I said … Top Secret SI. Not your problem," he finished in an end-of-topic tone.

Ignoring the tone, the nurse finished, "Until he's *in* there," meaning the destination, "and I'm *outta* there, he's my *patient.* After that, he becomes the subject of the study."

With that, Jack Sommers smiled and continued the drive uphill, albeit at a slower, less heart-attack-inducing pace.

After what must have been the 100th left-then-right turn, the ambulance reached the mountain plateau and changed direction from southbound to westbound. The sun was almost down as they neared their destination. It glared into their faces, blossoming like hundreds of tiny sparkles through the pitted windshield.

They circumnavigated the dry lake known as Baldwin and skirted the shoreline of Big Bear Lake on a winding dry road appropriately named North Shore Drive.

Surrounded by hills, Big Bear Lake was as storybook as anywhere on the planet. Looking across the expanse of lake to the mountains on the south side, the passenger saw the swaths of thirty-foot pine trees subordinated only to their fifty-foot brethren, their green hues broken only by a number of ski runs. And the lake. The late afternoon sun sent water sparkles her way. The lake glistened.

The blonde said, "Oh, yeah, this is a place to retire. A mere two hours by Porsche from the big mama city of Los Angeles. Perhaps a little longer by Beemer." She played with a short braid that swung, pendulum-style, next to her left temple.

It was easy to see why the locale was touted as *the* Summer and Winter playground for Southern Californians.

Another twenty minutes wiggling along the ragged north shore, they turned left off the two-lane into a fifty foot long driveway. The passenger spotted three structures: a large log house to the right, a small log cabin to the left, and what appeared to be a three-car garage of matching construction between.

The driver brought the ambulance to a gentle stop beside a large sedan and a small coupe.

The nurse riding in the back expressed relief that all the rocking and rolling was done. He removed his patient from the ambulance, rolling the gurney with some difficulty over the gravel driveway and along a pathway that led to the smaller cabin's front door. The driver opened the door. Once the nurse rolled the patient-*subject* inside, he and the passenger stepped into the cabin. The driver immediately entered a code into a security pad mounted on the wall. Unknown to everyone but him, the standard-looking keypad enabled or disabled a state-of-the-art, highly-classified security system.

"This place doesn't look lived-in at all," the passenger observed.

Everything was in its proper place. A small living room was dead ahead of the entry with the kitchen to her right. The passenger observed a doorway on the lake-facing wall and, to its right, ten feet of orange-and-black curtains. She entered the living room, turning right to face the kitchen. Beyond the fridge, she saw a door that could provide a third entry or exit point—duly noted. She retraced her path to the southside wall and brushed aside the curtains to reveal a picture window and approximately fifty feet of flat land that separated the cabin from the lake. There was a small dock, but no boat.

"You know, it's gonna take an army larger than one to protect your, uh, *subject*, Mr. Sommers. It would be quite easy to surround this cabin with just a few bad guys."

"There won't be any bad guys, Agent Bransfield. You were a check box to enable the study situation to take place, that's all."

"Fine. But it would make me happy if you just called me Phoebe."

Jack had a retort ready, but he decided to soldier on.

"Phoebe, I'd like you to meet someone. You will be working with him."

She turned and there, standing next to Jack, was a diminutive man that she just knew would get in her way.

"This is Lenny Lipschitz," Jack said, pushing the man toward her.

She burst into laughter. It was not like her. She just could not help herself. "You have got to be majorly shitting me. Lenny Lipschitz?" Her laughter intensified.

Neither Jack nor Lenny smiled. In fact, Lenny cocked his head back like a banty rooster ready to do serious repartee.

"I'm sorry, Lenny Lipschitz," she said as she approached him and extended her right hand. "It's been a long ride."

"Whether you have been ridden long and hard is not my concern," the little man responded. "You can probably run along; I'm used to working alone."

Agent Phoebe Bransfield gave him an are-you-serious look and slowly shook her head. She glanced over at Jack. "We need to talk."

"The two who need to talk are the two of you. Get to know each other—first name basis. I have spoken separately to each of you about why you are here. Get clear about your two distinct roles in this assignment. Oh, and you'll have to feed *the subject* the first couple of days—the yum-yums are stowed in the fridge. You've got my number if there's a problem. I'd love to stay and chat, but I've got to get back down the hill. That road is even more deadly after dusk."

The nurse had just taken one of the drips out of *the subject*'s arm and, without looking back, said "Pull out the other drip in the morning. He should be fine. You can expect him to be pretty docile. And, he won't remember much, so take that into account." Then they were through the door and gone.

Phoebe Bransfield and Lenny Lipschitz just looked at each other with the most nonplussed of expressions, walked to the couch, and sat down. They both grasped that this was no normal task, assumed it would be much harder than Jack had let on, and each had better mark his and her own territories before things got out of hand.

They retired early that night. Lenny decided to spend the night on the long couch. He was lights out in short order. Phoebe, still wound up, kept an eye on the man on the gurney she had never even heard speak. She wondered what his story was. It took her a while to drift off as she slouched on the loveseat. She slept in her clothes—her weapon still attached.

CHAPTER 4

The next morning, Lenny and Phoebe faced their first full day of duty. They sat once again on the couch and loveseat, staring at each other for several minutes. Then, Lenny decided to check out the place. After all, he was a California-certified Private Investigator.

Lenny Lipschitz had grown up in an East Coast city. He had never been in a real log cabin before. It was actually nice in a rustic way. The round side of the peeled cedar timbers had been fully varnished and, to a lesser extent than the outside, had yellowed with time. It exuded warmth.

He stood and walked to the front door. Then he turned and observed, his usual routine in a new place. As would a CSI who had entered a crime scene, he got his bearings from the main point-of-entry.

"Good lake view through large back window," he pronounced as if dictating to a recorder. "Kitchen on other side of wall to the right. Bathroom and bedroom to the left with single entryway in middle. The rest is for living and loving. But what the hell is that?" He pointed to some kind of artistic metal sculpture straight ahead. It looked like one of the first American space capsules painted blood red.

"It's a Swedish stove, city boy," came Phoebe's husky, yet still feminine voice. She motioned from the cordwood stacked against the living room wall to the stove. "You put that stuff in there and light it up. Keeps you warm. It's chilly in here," she said, embracing herself and rubbing her arms. "Think you can make a fire, city boy?"

Lenny, in his typical abrupt manner, walked to where she sat on the loveseat.

"Cold, huh? Stand up."

Trying to make nice, she did.

"Ever heard of Mike Hammer? No? Famous TV private eye—tough and smart. And a man with the ladies. He and me are cut from the same scrap. Let me show you how *I* keep warm."

Before he could get his hands on her, Phoebe stepped forward, raising her left fist as a feint. Lenny's head followed. The lady agent clocked him with a solid right. Down he went. She turned and walked toward the bedroom, throwing over her shoulder, "Oh. We're the softer sex, Mike—make a note."

Lenny sat on the floor, holding his jaw. "Yeah. Note to self. Watch out for soft right cross."

Phoebe returned with a photograph in her hand. She handed it to Lenny. What Lenny saw answered a few questions.

"It was taken right after a bout. Sorry I didn't have the gloves on for you. It would have softened it up a little. Hard to tell, but I was an Army brat. Moving around, you didn't have time to make friends. Things got boring. So I took up the sport and competed in the women's boxing tournaments on base. Kinda puts what just happened in perspective, huh?"

"Yeah. My eyes are starting to refocus on perspective."

Lenny regained his feet and stepped back to the center of the cabin to continue his recon.

"The couch and loveseat are positioned at right angles to each other so heat from the stove is unobstructed," he reasoned. His experience with this kind of thing did not extend beyond gas logs.

"Curiously, all the walls are hung with collector-edition plates. Thirty or forty of them. They portray normal-looking people doing normal-looking things." Lenny drew from this a desire on Jack's part to set a calming mood. "The ambience is *sans souci*—not-a-care-in-the-world in French," he informed Phoebe. To be honest, Lenny's French was minimal. His teacher had tossed him from the class after he made a move on her at break time. She had decked him, too. He hoped it was not some kind of trend.

To the east side of the cabin had to be the sleep and wash up facilities. He proceeded through a doorless doorway and stopped. On his left was the bathroom—good to know—and to the right, the sole bedroom. He stepped inside and observed what he took to be cabin-typical bedroom furniture. Something odd about the bed, though. His P.I. training caused him to look for the unusual. The high-sided wooden bedframe could mean only one thing—a born-of-the-60s waterbed. Hmmm, he thought. Lenny and the blonde doing a little wave bucking. Possibilities, he thought. If only she could lose the attitude.

He turned on his heel and proceeded back to the center of the cabin. The last item of note was the half-height partition separating the living room from the kitchen. The wide counter top on the partition and three barstools suggested a place to have drinks with a food back.

Just then, their patient released a severe groan. Phoebe jumped up to check his monitor. All the numbers looked good. No flat lines on the screen.

"Oh, he must be hungry." She turned on the feeding drip. "Steak and eggs."

"Liquid MREs, huh?" said Len. "Meals Ready to Eject." He laughed at his joke.

Phoebe just smiled while fondling her weapon. Had Lenny been able to read minds, he would have read thoughts like friendly fire and the positive karma she would generate should that come to pass.

Just then, there was a crash. Both heads snapped toward *the subject.* Lenny ran to the gurney just as their ward jumped up and yanked out the drip line. Before the P.I. could do anything, the man grabbed him by the throat.

Phoebe dashed forward to help, but the man, who had been in bed all those weeks and who should have been too weak to move, hit her chest high with his left arm. The force of his elbow smashing into her sternum slammed her into the nearest wall, nearly knocking her out.

Across the room, Lenny gagged like the end was near. Phoebe struggled to her feet. In spite of the choking, Lenny saw her open her mouth about an inch and purse her lips. Full-on attack mode.

The agent-protector charged full tilt, hitting *the subject* with the force of an NFL linebacker. The three catapulted over the couch, landing in a heap.

That was it. The battle concluded—exhaustion claimed them all.

"Looks like a three-way tie," Lenny gasped when he regained his ability to speak. "Why didn't you take him down with one of those punches?"

Phoebe started to laugh. "If he got seriously damaged, Mr. Sommers would so have our butts in a permanent sling."

The subject sat up, his head wobbling like a stuporous bobble-head. He could barely crack a smile.

Phoebe and Lenny helped him back onto the gurney. This time, they parked it against a wall, reducing the likelihood of a recurrence by half. They both sagged onto the couch shoulder-to-shoulder and fell asleep.

• • •

The man in the gurney did not sleep. Not at first. His eyes searched the ceiling shadows as he tried to remember. Something. Anything.

He remembered nothing.

He whispered into the darkness, "I feel … empty. Emptied. I feel what seems to be defined by what I do not feel … cannot feel. No urges, no desires, no anger, no fear … and no connection to this place or to these people."

Closing his eyes, he drifted off.

He did not know what he could not know. Absent any points of reference, he couldn't know that the man he would have recognized in a mirror twenty-nine days earlier … was Magus Crayle.

• • •

Only an hour later, Lenny woke up. He decided to check out the kitchen contents while he waited for the agent to rise from her much-needed sleep.

In short order, Phoebe awoke to the noises of Lenny rifling through the kitchen cupboards and drawers. After a couple of minutes of letting her clear some cobwebs, he walked to the living room. He needed to make peace. Things might go better with her if he removed his handgun, he thought. Less of a worry for her.

As he reached back for it, he heard a sudden snap. He looked up and there stood the blonde. Three feet away. Legs spread apart for balance. And a two-handed combat grip on a weapon bigger than his.

"Hey, do you suppose we can just 'Rodney King' get along," he said. "The guy on the gurney will have major concerns if he wakes up and we're both dead."

"Both of us won't be dead," Phoebe corrected. Round one of who could piss the farthest went to her.

After the rest of what seemed like an extra long day, it grew late and both were tired.

"I'll take the couch," Lenny said in a less than chivalrous manner.

"Yeah," was all he got in return. "Probably makes into a bed."

And so it did. Phoebe slept in the waterbed room, and Lenny passed the night in the living room with *the subject*. The night became quiet.

Tomorrow would be different.

CHAPTER 5

The next day typified late Autumn days in the Big Bear valley: bright, cool, and crisp. The sun was out, the sky a clear blue. The persistent chill indicated the cold and snow of Winter were near.

The unlikely pair had risen with the chickens since there were a few of them in the vicinity. Phoebe tossed on her clothes and ambled into the living room. Lenny had fired up a pot of coffee in an old blue pot with white speckles. The altitude—at 6,827 feet—made the gas-fired coffee-smell waft through the living room like a scent of heaven. It was one of the few things they both could agree on.

"So, Phoebe the Fibbee, what can you do that a seasoned P.I. like myself can't?"

"You can call me Agent Bransfield, for one, and don't piss me off—I'm armed and dangerous," she responded. "And cut the jokes, okay? I need some quiet time."

Lenny took another stab at humor. He did not notice the heel of her right hand again move atop her holstered weapon. And he did not notice her fingers glide up and down the length of the gun's receiver.

To her, there was something sexual about it. Her mind drifted into her recent past as he droned on.

Phoebe had several wins under her belt, but her last gig had not gone well. She had been assigned a caretaker-bodyguard role. No one would deny she possessed the experience—and the chops—for the job. As far as the Bureau was concerned, she kept her man alive—another win. But, it did not play that way in her heart.

She'd bodyguarded a rock singer, who had turned for the FBI on an interstate, under-age prostitution beef. The rocker got wound up on drugs and alcohol one night after a concert and decided to sample her like a groupie. She lost the fight but, instead of taking him down hard and trashing a major government case, she'd let it slide. She tried to wear the episode inside like her own personal Purple Heart, but the experience had damaged her. She learned later that the toasted-up rock star remembered nothing the next day.

Phoebe had not been *with* anyone since that night. But if and when she ever did, she reckoned he'd better wear glasses with TRUST and RESPECT taped to the inside of the lenses so he did not forget. Her mind was made up. The next man who wronged her would pick up the tab for himself *and* the rock star.

As if on cue, Lenny said, "You ever have a boyfriend?"

Phoebe realized she did not know how to deal with this guy. He knew how to get under her skin—like a self-perpetuating ingrown toenail. She told herself to stay calm and professional, just answer the question. Her response came out personable and casual.

"Dated a *company* man once. A Central Intelligence guy. Got tired of the lies." She fully expected a "Well, duh. That's what they do," from the P.I. Instead, he said, "I'm sorry," his eyes compassionate.

She could see her grief struck something inside him—a personal loss, perhaps. She almost asked him his question back, but let it go. People will always surprise you, she thought. Perhaps little Lenny Lipschitz had a heart after all.

The look on Lenny's face said he felt it time to change the subject. He sat back, his hands resting in a safe place atop his thighs. "I've been a P.I. for seventeen years. Out here in Southern California for the past three. I'm contracted for this gig because my specialty is background reconstruction, especially for amnesia cases like his," he said, gesturing toward *the subject*.

"Yeah, there must have been a bunch of those."

"You catch on quick. It's especially old folks. They forget relatives, what they own, and who they owe. A lot of them hire me to help make up a who-gets-what list."

"And they want that because …" Phoebe asked, dragging out the last word.

"So they can list stuff to go to certain individuals after their own expiration date comes due. The list stays outside the Will, so it's easy to change when they get pissed off. I would have counseled 'em to give stuff away before they died so the probate people wouldn't take it, except it would cost *me* money."

She feigned genuine interest. "Are you a legal expert in addition to being a compassionate man?"

"Ha. No. I have a lawyer friend who helps with that stuff. And the long Winter nights, too. But—and you need to know this—Alona really doesn't like to share. We would have to be careful if anything, you know, happened between us. The first word Alona learned as a child was emasculate, " he said with a nervous smile.

CHAPTER 6

The remainder of the afternoon passed without incident. That evening, Lenny fixed dinner for the three of them. Phoebe did the dishes while Crayle, now able to move about, sat on the couch and watched the sun slide down over the mountains at the west end of the lake. The rest of the evening could have been just rest and relaxation for the three of them, but the P.I. had other ideas.

Though Crayle was still shaky on his feet, Lenny was in a hurry to make progress. Sitting around in the cabin would not get it done. He decided it best to get *the subject* out in a social atmosphere and cheer him up at the same time. They were going out. He got the other two ready by being a nuisance and then hustled them out to his car. The large sedan afforded comfortable transportation for all.

The night was quite cold and all were bundled up in the special gear Jack had left for them in the cabin. Sweaters and jackets in all the right sizes hinted at some degree of preparation prior to their arrival.

Lenny drove east, the route the ambulance must have taken to get back down the hill to the quarry. His passengers appeared enraptured by the beauty of the night, brightly lit by the moon and stars. The light reflected unevenly on the breeze-undulated water. Across the lake, the lights of the town known as Big Bear Lake summoned a dreamy, village-on-the-water effect.

After about ten minutes, Lenny made a right turn onto Stanfield Cutoff. They heard a hum that seemed far away, but then began to grow to a crescendo as a single-engine plane screamed over their car. The Cutoff not only ended the lake on its east end, but also marked the west end of Big Bear's recreational airport. It got their blood pumping.

Several turns later they headed east, away from the major town and its ambient glow. The darkness began to surround them. Each felt uneasy in his or her own way. It was Phoebe's first time out with *the subject*, and she needed to go light on the booze. One more right turn, a little uphill jaunt, and they arrived at the remote mini-civilization away from downtown—a sign called it Sugarloaf. The area contained several hundred cabins, mostly vacation and weekend getaways for city people. Ahead at an intersection stood two old wooden buildings, which constituted downtown.

Lenny pulled up in front of the second of the two buildings and parked diagonally in front, along with several other cars and a few Harleys. The place was a bar and diner with neon beer signs in the windows and a sign that read: 'Fried Chicken Dinner … $7.95.' All of the eating and drinking went down in a suitably rustic single-story place, perhaps 100-feet long and half as wide. The carved and painted wooden sign outside proclaimed it The Sugarloafer, as well as the presence of live music to go along with the food and booze.

"I don't know about dead music—other than disco, so live music will do," Lenny said.

"Way up there on the funny meter, Lipschitz," Phoebe observed with justifiable sarcasm.

Inside the door and straight ahead was a bar with seating for about twelve people. This night, four women sat atop the stools and six men stood beside them, each holding a bottle of beer. All had the same red and white label.

Lenny turned his entourage to the right, and they passed a dozen or so square dining tables. Just a few couples there. All were drinking the same beer. Past the dining tables they ascended three wooden steps to what appeared to be a dance floor. Ahead of them at the far wall was a setup of band instruments. On either side of the dance floor were bar-height round drink tables and stools.

A barmaid approached their table. The tattoos on her arms were barely visible and the undulating lines on her face resembled the craggy topography of a Shar Pei.

"You know what the frig you want?" she drawled with a voice that sounded like she'd just gargled with gravel.

"What you got for us, honey?" Lenny asked.

She looked at him like he had just asked to be cornholed. Then at the ceiling. Without losing a beat with her chewing gum, she spat out "Bud and Bud Light." She looked back down at the lead loser.

"I want a Newcastle," Lenny said. "It's the brown ale."

"Bud and Bud Light." The intonation of her voice spoke volumes: 'pick one or I will personally break your legs.'

Phoebe came to the rescue. "A pitcher of Bud Light, please."

The waitress returned with a pitcher and three glasses plus a spare, pulled out a pack of cigarettes, and proceeded out a side door. Break time.

A number of disconnected noises emanated from the bandstand. Then, the band began its first set. The apparent leader, a well-constructed man in his thirties and just shy of six feet tall, gave an opening statement. "We're Hot *Rod!*" They launched into a blues tune cover called River Runs Deep by someone named Cale.

"I know the lead guy." Lenny pointed at the singer as if to claim secondary celebrity status. "Jack introduced him to me. He's a Mister Fixit if there ever was one. The music thing is just extra."

The guitar player, handsome with close-cut red hair, abundant freckles, and a red day-beard, looked the guitar-god part.

Lenny continued, "He comes with some baggage though, but who the hell doesn't?"

Phoebe was into her second glass of beer and feeling good. "Yeah. I'm likin' the way that baggage hangs."

"Be nice and I'll introduce you," Lenny admonished. "Y'know, it's great here when they have a country band. The ladies have a few, and they just gotta dance. Hook up with one and, I swear, they'll run across the street to the general store and buy the condoms themselves—on their dime, too. What's not to like?"

Phoebe and Crayle looked around at the ladies, wondering how few drinks it would take.

After 45-minutes of decent renditions of rock and blues covers, the band announced a break and stepped out from the bandstand. The leader walked directly over to Lenny, extending his hand. Lenny had a friend, after all.

"This is my good friend, Mick MacKay," Lenny said. "I call him Micmac, for short."

He introduced Crayle first and then Phoebe, who did a convincing impression of a woman feeling lust in her heart. MacKay pulled out a chair and sat down.

"Have some of our Bud Light," Lenny pushed a glass in front of the musician and sent a glower Phoebe's way.

"Jees," MacKay said, pushing it back. "That stuff ought to be served in a specimen jar."

The trio's eyes homed in on the half-empty pitcher, trying to combat any sort of preparation visual.

"You like our stuff?" MacKay asked, looking at his guests one at a time.

"Uh-huh," dreamed Phoebe. Her beer-induced stupor seemed to have fogged-up her rock star memories.

"Me, too," said Crayle. "But tell me about that song right after the Blues Image's Ride Captain Ride. I felt that one. Did you write that yourself?"

"Oh, you mean *Life Is Just A Game.* No, I didn't write it. Wish I did. It was written by a pretty much unknown songwriter, who used to live up here. We became friends and I play some of his tunes in with the rest. What did you like about it?"

"The beginning: *Life is just a game where nothing is certain. It is such a shame not knowing who you are.* It hit close to home," Crayle explained.

Lenny helped.

"I forgot to tell you: Mr. Crayle here was in a severe accident over on the coast highway, the PCH as we natives like to say, above Malibu. You know, just south of Mugu Rock. He has amnesia from it. I'm helping him get back memories." Then, turning to Crayle, "Blues Image? Ride Captain Ride? One gold memory point. Way to go, MC."

"Yeah. The song you mentioned before only has two verses, but they get inside you, memory loss or no," MacKay finished the thought. "Then, the chorus tells you not to take things too serious. Something like that."

"If you don't mind," said Crayle, "I'd like a copy of the lyrics."

"Sure," returned MacKay. He scribbled the words on a napkin for Crayle. At the bottom, he printed a 'C' with a circle around it. "There. That makes it legal."

While Phoebe tried to stretch her foot to within calf-rubbing range, Lenny recited Mick MacKay's curriculum vitae to Crayle.

"Besides his obvious talent for music, Micmac likes to fabricate things and fix stuff. And that includes everything." He glanced over at Phoebe. He could guess what she wanted fixed. "That is his day job. He is a former Seal or something like that—"

"Underwater demolition and weapons specialist," MacKay corrected. Then he gave a little laugh. "Sorry."

"Hey, I knew water was involved," Lenny retorted. He turned to Phoebe. "Always dresses his 5' 10", 185-pound, rock-hard body in green cargo pants and skin-tight pullover shirts, as you can see. Oh, yes, and he's gay."

"No he's not," she said, running the words together, not taking her eyes off the prize beef. "Five bucks if you take off the shirt." Phoebe smiled, batting her eyelashes.

MacKay laughed. "It hides the sweat." Then quickly added, "From the stage lights."

Phoebe was starting to breathe hard. Drool would soon follow.

The band members had reassembled on the stage, having consumed all twenty minutes of their fifteen minute break.

"Time's up. I wish they paid me to talk. Nice meeting you all," he said with a slight wave of his hand and a quick glance into Phoebe's eyes.

MacKay strapped on his blonde-on-blonde Les Paul Custom, and the band fired up the crowd with the Stones' *You Can't Always Get What You Want.* Indeed.

After a few more songs, the eclectic trio headed back to the cabin. It was sleepy time. They all dropped into their respective beds and slept off the buzz. Lenny had been right: they all needed the club atmosphere—each for his or her own reasons—and Lenny had delivered. It was good for him to score positive points. It made the score seem less lopsided.

• • •

The next morning, the nominal private investigator awoke first. The FBI's deadliest agent remained fast asleep. Lenny rose slowly and without a sound. He walked over to the gurney to check on the so-called *subject.*

To his surprise, Magus Crayle was wide awake and staring at the ceiling. He did not notice Lenny's arrival.

"I'm here to help you get it back," Lenny said.

"Get what back?"

"Your memory. Your life. The whole enchilada."

Crayle turned his head to look into Lenny's eyes. "I remember so little," he moaned.

"Hey, we know you worked for the government—they're paying for all this. And I found a slide rule in your box of stuff from work. A mathematician, maybe."

Crayle looked dazed.

"Look. Getting memories back is what I do. A lot of the stuff I can track down on the Web. But some of it will include field trips into the wilds of civilization, and we may come across something to jog the memories back."

"Like the Sugarloafer. Yes. That sounds great. I will ask people. Who *am* I?" Crayle closed his eyes.

"Hey, you gotta keep your chin up, MC. We'll establish a baseline. You know, the stuff you already know. I'll need you out of bed for that, though."

Crayle sat up and twisted so his legs hung over the side. He seemed a bit dizzy, but he continued until he stood on the floor.

"I feel a bit woozy," Crayle observed. "Anything else we can do?"

"Well, there is one more thing. Your doctor, Pirmin Rorschach, has left instructions. It's something he says you need to do—by yourself. Would you like to hear what he said?"

Crayle looked around the room as if seeking some sort of structure. It did not come. "Tell me what this Doctor Rorschach said. Please. I need any kind of start on this. It's starting to drive me crazy."

Lenny recognized a voice close to pleading. He had worked in the past with a number of amnesia cases, a couple of which had ended in suicide.

"Okay, here it is. He says in this note …" Lenny unfolded a piece of what looked like parchment. "… there are three things you must do in order to make progress.

1. Detect and record a baseline of current memories.

2. Interact—under supervision—in social and physical circumstances.
3. Hold—in the complete absence of others—internal dialogs in which you express your observations and your feelings about them.

An electronic method of recording these spoken dialogs has been provided."

"That's it?" Crayle asked, looking betrayed. "Writing down my current memories will take five minutes. Number two I can see doing, but I wouldn't even know where to start on those dialogs. Or how."

"Here." Lenny handed him a silver device, approximately one inch by four inches by half-an-inch thick. "The doctor said to give you this." He spent a few seconds reading the note, before he paraphrased its contents.

"It's a Sony. It records everything you say, so keep it in your pocket at all times. It will pick up and record only *your* voice based on a stored voice-recognition pattern. The batteries last for years, it says, so don't turn it off. Even a fart could be important."

Crayle looked doubtful about the last notion.

"Oh, and its purpose is to reassure you that your new, and any recollected memories, are correct. And so's he can log old memories as they come back. Later, he'll analyze it and see how you're doing. He'll track your progress in addition to talking directly with you at some future date, it says."

"Pattern recognition? Only *my* voice? Analyze?" The questions were rhetorical in tone and nature. Crayle seemed out of touch with the grand scheme for his recovery. Perhaps the answers would come in time.

Crayle tried to consume and net out what he had just been told. It sounded good. An expert could guide him back to normalcy. It seemed to be a lot of attention for a government functionary to receive. For that, he was grateful. Right now, he felt the need to acknowledge the P.I.'s help.

"Okay. I will keep this close, Lenny. Thank you. I mean it."

"You are surely welcome, MC. The next first order of business: the Fibbee and I get out of your way for a while so's you can get started on the dialogs. Doc says the best intel is when you are alone, so express yourself out loud, okay?"

Lenny walked to the sofa. He thought about picking up the snoozing Phoebe. He knew, however, if he touched her, the gun would come out and he would be shot dead. If he tried to remove the gun first … same end. He moved back three steps and called her name.

Phoebe lurched up, wiped her eyes, and stood as if by command. Good so far. Lenny stepped to her side and led her into the bedroom. No thoughts of a physical repartee this time, he helped her onto the waterbed. She resumed her sleep without incident.

Behind him, he heard Crayle in the living room, starting to mumble. Lenny concluded the man was a self-starter and gently lowered himself down onto the waterbed beside Phoebe, making as few waves as possible. Lenny knew nothing about the rock star.

• • •

The surrounds of Crayle's environment caused a reverberation when he spoke.

"I … I don't know what to say. I mean, I don't even know how to begin. I don't know if I have a beginning …

"I woke up on a gurney in a log cabin somewhere. How I got here—I don't know. Where I was before—same."

He walked to the bedroom. Slowly. Without sound. The P.I. and the Fibbee both slept. Good. He returned to the living room. He felt he could speak his feelings now. He felt alone.

Before he could continue, the man they called *the subject* noticed a painting on the wall. He walked to it.

It was oddly shaped, like something from Salvador Dali, but he recognized the symbol. It depicted the interrelationship between *Yin* and *Yang*—female and male qualities and characteristics considered by Oriental cultures to be present to various degrees in all humans. It also inferred a co-existence—perhaps a concordance—to be struck between the two. And a balance.

The artist's rendering portrayed two stylized figures—one white and one black—one inverted, yet juxtaposed to the other. The normally curved boundary between them was jagged, like shark teeth, as if each part was attacking or devouring the other. Somehow, *subject* Crayle felt the meaning more than he saw it.

"I feel this painting is somehow about me. In some way, it stylizes my being. I feel I have travelled to the Orient, perhaps to live. I do not know why I feel this."

His speech was methodical. It was measured and based on knowledge perhaps lost forever. Then he noticed two red characters to the side, one above the other.

"Those characters are a *chop*—a Chinese artist's signature. They say Yao-wu. And the picture's name was the same—*Apply Violence*. It is strange. I feel I know this man … he is brilliant and twisted. But this is Jack's painting. I am just confused."

He turned away and walked to the big window.

"I see a lake—rather big—its far shore is covered with tall green trees—pine trees," he said. "I have remembered that they are pine trees. The water is deep blue, its surface ruffled by a breeze. I can see the breeze in the tree-tops."

And then he saw motion on the lake.

"There are small black birds with little white patches on their heads. Like racing stripes. They run from their foreheads down to their beaks. There is a patch of brown soil running from this cabin to the water's edge, and the land is bordered on the left and right by bushes and trees. The bushes are ironwood, but I do not know why

I am sure of that. The view to the lake is framed by the land, the greenery, and the sky.

"There is a wooden dock in the middle of the shoreline, perhaps fifteen feet long. No boat—just a dock. Midway between this cabin and the dock is a picnic table with benches. They are made of redwood. Heart redwood."

He stopped. "Heart redwood? How do I know the specific cut of the wood? Tell me, Doctor, how can I remember these details and not remember who the hell I am?"

Crayle felt he had done enough for the day. Just moving about after being hospitalized tired him. He returned to the gurney. He felt hope. Only a little. He resolved to work the regimen prescribed by Doctor Rorschach; he resolved to find himself once again. And then he slept.

CHAPTER 7

The man descending the jetway was not happy. It was not the trip that upset him. His ride across the country to Dulles International Airport in the French Dassault Falcon 7X was smooth. The plane had a tall fuselage—he could walk to the bathroom or bedroom without stooping over. The food had been good, the flight attendant the beck-and-call type.

What was not to like about it was the reason for the trip. He had no desire to be anywhere near Washington, D.C., especially not for the purpose of meeting his boss. Jack always lost these encounters. His boss had called the business jet a perk. Jack knew better. It was so he could call Jack in on short notice for these briefing-cum-lecture events his boss loved.

What Jack did like to do was his job. He was truly at home organizing and operating projects that ranged through varying degrees of deadly—but always for a good cause. Meeting with bosses and other functionaries was, to him, as much a waste of time and energy as a desert monsoon. Jack believed these meetings contained only negative potential.

The pickup car was a hardened Lincoln Town Car in basic midnight blue metallic. Its tags made it appear to be a limousine service. The driver was the usual five-ten, thick-bodied individual, who could steal a heart with his looks or steal a life with his honed skills. No weapon was visible but, given the more than thirty means of concealing a handgun, Jack knew the man carried one or more on his person.

The driver popped the trunk for luggage, but Jack waved him off. No luggage. This was going to be downtown and turnaround. He had advised the pilot to be ready for their return flight in two hours.

The car headed south on 28 out of Dulles. It blew by the little burgs of Herndon and Chantilly. The driver turned west onto 29—Lee's Highway. Jack caught a glimpse of his favorite restaurant ever in Centreville—the Shade Tree. At Jack's request, his boss, Neil, had taken him there for lunch and complained about the plebeian fare the entire time. Neil did not know Jack had developed an addiction to Campbell's Chicken Noodle Soup as a child. The *Tree* served up a steaming hot exact replica.

The Lincoln crossed the Bull Run river and turned right into the Civil War battlefield at Manassas—now a national park. The twenty-eight-minute ride had been long enough for Jack to stew about the current non-op he was stuck with in California. Babysitting was a better description. He was determined to stand up on his hind legs and convey his displeasure to Neil.

Jack's man-of-breeding boss was, in fact, one Neil Patrick Wohlford, a man of serious patrician lineage who naturally fell into the class demarcation philosophy. By appearance, Neil looked taller than his moderate five-foot-eight-and-a-half actual height. His custom Swiss shoes made him appear five-nine and his *über*-expensive three-piece suits distracted attention from his slender build and reinforced his oversized head and good looks.

Wohlford commanded the Strategic Solutions Office within the CIA's operations entity, the National Clandestine Service. Its standard rules of engagement: break all the laws of other nations, but break none of your own. For Neil, it meant: don't use agency resources if breaking American laws becomes necessary. That was where Jack's International Operations Unit—IOU—came in.

Jack, unlike Neil, had no desire to elevate himself into America's quasi-aristocracy—the so-called *Elite*. He just wanted to take down some of the country's serious international enemies. But, since Neil had asked for a full, in-person update on *the subject* under Jack's care, Magus Crayle, here he was.

The driver pulled into the public parking lot of the Bull Run battlefield of Civil War fame. Jack new the ingress drill. He walked through the tourist information building and started down the path tourists followed. Fifty feet along, he made an oblique turn left and headed for a set of construction site porta-potties. There were six potties surrounded by an eight-foot high cinder block wall, ostensibly to protect them from any belated grape-shot blasts. He passed through an opening in the wall and checked the 'busy' indicators of the potties. All green but the last. Good. Red on any of the first five meant one or more were occupied. Green on the last one would mean: *boogie now!*

As he stepped into range, the proximity card within his coat unlatched the door. Inside, the door closed automatically and relatched. He pressed his right hand against the shined steel mirror. The magneto-thermology scan complete, he stepped to the plastic urinal and provided a sample. The DNA comparison done, the white urinal turned green. He sat down for the ride. He noted that the mirror showed no handprint residual. Attention to detail could mean life or death in Jack's business.

The inside shell of the porta-potty descended 312 feet to an underground complex. It was one of the special kinds of non-government operations, NGOs, the CIA needed to accomplish its mission. Jack reasoned it would be difficult for an attacking force to squeeze into a single porta-potty. That must have been the characteristic justifying such arcane ridiculousness. He thought the simulated potty smell to be Neil's idea of a joke. Ah, but Neil did not have a sense of humor, did he?

Jack made his way down a two tone hallway of surplus eggshell and green paint—reminiscent of most VA hospitals—to Neil's office. The low-end feel of the hallway ended at Neil's polished Brazilian mahogany door. Jack waved his pass at the six-square-inch plaque next to the door. Neil buzzed him in.

The office had not changed since Jack's previous visits. Neil was a traditional man of class and bearing. Quite predictable. The room was not like other government entities. No gray steel desks or file cabinets. And no administrative assistant polishing nails and watching the clock.

Jack had heard the story of Neil's pre-French Revolution ancestry before. Neil fit the part well with his beyond *GQ* bespoke suits and his handmade *Bass* shoes. The walls of select mahogany were adorned with French artistry and the bar provided the best *pastis* from the south of France. There was a unanimous feeling among colleagues that Neil was 'too too', but his success rate was as immaculate as he was. Hence, those above left him alone.

"*Bonjour*, Jack. How are things in the valley of the *large* bear?"

Jack saw Neil size up his rumpled, oversize gray suit. He should have worn the blue jeans and western belt. And the cowboy boots and shirt.

"It's the *big* bear, and I wish I were there. I'd like to hop over the pleasantries, sir, and get this done. I don't feel at all comfortable this far away from such a—how did you put it—*crucial* operation." Jack really leaned on *crucial*. He felt better now.

The sarcasm was not lost on Neil. He chose to rise above it.

"It is of huge importance, Jack. *The subject*, Mr. Crayle, survived an assassination attempt. They ran his car off a coastal roadway. He was left in bad enough shape we could no longer keep him operational."

"I've been read-in to the background, sir. Then you decided—or higher ups decided—to engage him in some serious mind-fucking. Enter Doctor Ink Blot."

Wohlford winced at the intimation of *higher ups*, but did not lose his train of thought.

"Jack. Being able to express the human memory as text and pictures, as can our esteemed Doctor Rorschach, is a monumental achievement. My God. Think of being able to retrieve and re-implant memories of amnesia victims like Mr. Crayle. Think of the value to us of being able to display selected regions of the mind and, with cursor selection, merely hit the *delete* key and those memories are gone. Or the *copy* key. Or the *move* key. Or *drag and drop*, as they say. And to insert, as legitimate and naturally-acquired, memories such as the specialized knowledge necessary for one of your operations. Linguistic knowledge, cultural knowledge, *intimate* knowledge—by merely positioning a cursor and touching the *insert* key. Instant read-in. So simple. So elegant."

"Heart attacks are simple and elegant. What I am babysitting is an extension of the old brainwashing experimentation championed by one Doctor Gottlieb, one-time head of the *company's* Technical Services Branch, and his operational minion at that medieval, pardon me, medical institute in Montreal. A Doctor Cameron, I believe. 'Oh, what's your specialty, doctor?' " Jack said in a gay-impressionistic tone. " 'Oh, computerized mind-fucking taken to the extreme. Isn't it special?' "

Neil Wohlford, who himself had a little more *yin* than *yang*, did not appreciate the effeminate mockery in Jack's voice. Sadly, he needed Jack.

"Maybe it's time to retire," Jack mused, as if trying to irritate Neil. "A boat, a hammock, a beach."

It was usual for Neil to refrain from religious references, but this called for an exception.

"It's come-to-Jesus time, Jack. Every organization has a mantra. If Central Intelligence has one, it is *you can retire any time you like, but you can never leave*, as the song says." He watched the effect of his words on Jack's face. Neil prided himself on owning tidbits of knowledge that could trigger desired connections with his commoner underlings. He continued. "How do you know of this … this Dr. Gottlieb and the other … uh … Dr. Cameron, Jack?" He feigned ignorance.

"I read it somewhere. We operational types can read," replied Jack with indignation. He also got in a dig with respect to Neil's lack of operational experience.

Neil breathed deeply—he was not amused. "When I can tell you the rest of the story, Jack, you will embrace these scientific breakthroughs as I have." Neil noted silently that, if Jack's attitude got in the way, he could be the next to be mind-fucked. He smiled. "So, please, fill me in."

Jack took a deep breath, held it for the five seconds the *company* doctor had prescribed to settle his nerves, and then proceeded to tell his boss what he wanted to know.

"As planned, the doctor at the quarry's underground medical facility handed *the subject*, Magus Crayle, over to me, and I transported him to the Big Bear safe-house."

Highly classified operation and high profile to boot, Jack knew he needed to be careful. He was not in a position where high project visibility was a good thing. When functionaries at the top did not believe things were going well, the shit would roll downhill in his direction. Like a Jack-seeking missile.

Jack waved his hands out to the side. "IOU does not guard bodies. So, I called in a marker at the FBI. You would not believe who they sent," he said in dramatized disbelief. "I'm not kidding. The U.S. government equivalent of the famous cowgirl sharpshooter. Phoebe 'Annie Oakley' Bransfield. She was the best they had, I was told, and had done high-profile protection before."

"And that protection was satisfactory?" Neil asked.

"Yeah, well she protected this rock star asshole alright. But, the dude got loaded up and jumped her. And she took it. Why she didn't blow his brains out the window I don't know. She took one for the team."

"And the Oakley tag?"

"Oh, that. Their agents have standing rules of engagement. Single target: boom, boom—two taps to the chest minimum. But, not Miss Oakley. *Nooooo*. Twice she's had to draw down and both times: one shot—right between the eyes. Instant end-of-life experience for the perps and a dressing-down for the lady."

"That is loose cannon stuff, Jack. She is to see that Mr. Crayle does not go off the reservation. On his own or any other way, right? And you need to be more respectful of Doctor Rorschach. It is true he is descended from the famous originator of the ink blot, but he has taken the science of mind manipulation to the outer limits.

"You must also be mindful that he reports not to me, but to Dr. Rikki. Since she and I both report to the head of operations, we are caused to cooperate. The good Doctor Rikki is connected in ways you would not understand, and Dr. Rorschach is, in a sense, her fair-haired boy. And he seems to have *his* end under control." Neil supplied another subtle dig.

Jack started to retort, but Neil preempted with a hand gesture.

"Just yesterday, he advised me it is too early to tell if the relevant data has been *completely* extracted from *the subject*'s memory. The doctor is pursuing a new theory. He believes memories can exist in multiple places as some sort of safety precaution taken by the brain. Backup storage. He mentioned the words RAID and mirroring and striping, for some reason. I should not need to tell you that some of Mr. Crayle's knowledge would be uncomfortable for us should he be able to reconstruct it and be caused by our enemies to share. But please, continue with your report."

The more things change, the more they remain the same, thought Jack. The energy and effort being expended on some messed-up dude had a whole lot more back-story than Neil was letting on.

"Neil, the girl's fine. I've been around enough to tell she is the focused-to-the-max type. I think she could take down Godzilla. The other one's a bit iffy. I know you said he's gotta be there, and I'm sure he's going to use those P.I. skills just fine." Jack stopped. "But, why the hell do you remove specific memories from an ops guy and then hire a private detective-type to help him get the memories back the hard way?"

Neil only smiled. *Pay grade, my boy, pay grade.*

CHAPTER 8

Neil saw Jack out. He laughed inside about the small world of most people. The ones a British oil company chairman had referred to as 'the small people.' The regular people of no major consequence. They were best kept herded in the right direction. Neil was certain he and his ilk were, by natural selection, the ones to do the herding.

As the notion applied to Neil's project manager underling, he knew Jack was happy to survive the meeting and return to his comfort zone away from authority and in charge of something he could mentally grasp. Neil, with his innate ability to comprehend high-level concepts as well as critical details, would have taken a moment to admire himself had not his phone rang. His special phone.

He looked around, but no one had spirited themselves into his office. He pulled the phone from his inner jacket pocket and slid it open. The phone was, as appropriate, blue, white, and red—the French tricolor.

Although Neil was a calm and controlled man under even the most pressing exigencies, he knew the ultimate personal risk he took each time he received this particular telephone call. His body would tighten in anticipation. Should he put any word wrong or convey the wrong perception, things could turn on him in a most disparaging way.

He gave his head a quick shake. He had to catch himself thinking in the negative and turn it around. Should he get the words right and convey exactly the correct sense of confidence, the future would be his to define. He pressed his hand to his breast to calm himself.

He answered the call. The voice he heard was deep and strong, the accent foreign. It was calm and casual without being languid.

"Neil. It is the appointed time. May I have your status report?"

Neil was sure he could hear the random sounds of encryption. It was an encryption unknown to the intelligence communities.

"It is good to hear your voice, sir. I realize I have said this before, but still I look forward to the day when we may finally meet. I—"

"That day may … or may not … come, Neil," the older man interrupted. "Regardless, we shall carry on as strangers. You are writing your own ticket, as you Americans like to say. There may well come a day when I can welcome you into the Echelon of the Enlightened—the top of the new global order. But you must keep your eye on the ball, for now, Neil. Your report?"

The man at the other end displayed no anger or frustration with Neil's suggestion that they meet. The man was never ruffled. Never.

Neil began.

"*The subject* has been relieved of certain memories, sir. We have been successful in relocating him for observation. At this point, he has *some* prior memories, but indicates no remembrances related to the Blackstone affair. I have selected operatives to protect him and help him probe his past to see if his mind can indeed resurrect them. He is the perfect specimen for this most important study."

"This *experiment,*" the Elder corrected, "is beyond any importance you may be aware of, Neil. None of the players here, especially the good doctor, can be allowed to learn the true purpose of this exercise. Exposure is not an option. You are on track to be drawn into the

Echelon should this project conclude as hoped. Remember that Mr. Crayle put together for us what has to be the most diabolical global subterfuge in the history of mankind. Of course, he knows nothing of my existence nor of your relationship to me. Remember this too, Neil: the downside risk may only be contained and put to bed if, at the conclusion of the experiment, all knowledgeable parties are dispatched to the hereafter, present company excluded, of course."

"Yes, sir. That will not be a problem," Neil confirmed in a monotone.

Neil had deduced that his *external* boss was not in the United States. But where on the planet the Elder resided, he did not know. The accent seemed European, but he could not place it. And using Central Intelligence resources to satisfy his own curiosity was out of the question. He did, however, recognize in the man's verbal mannerisms an ultra-high degree of sophistication, class, and wisdom. He was dying to meet him.

"The big picture is coming along nicely, Neil. You will have to prepare. There has been no movement yet in Asia or Europe, but it will commence soon. You will receive the particulars in due time. Until next time, *adieu*, Neil."

Neil's shadow boss rang off.

Neil knew the history of Magus Crayle. He knew about France and China. And about Switzerland. Whether Mr. Crayle would come to recall those projects was the matter in question and under investigation by Doctor Rorschach. Some latitude would be given Jack. Opportunities to reconstruct Crayle's highly classified memories, from what the doctor had left behind, would be given every chance to produce fruit.

Unknown to Jack, Neil had personally given instructions to Agent Bransfield. Protect *the subject* and private investigator during the rediscovery process. Beyond that, protect Neil if things went wrong. Whether she would, in fact, take out Messieurs Crayle and Lipschitz and Sommers, if the need arose, remained the question.

Regardless, Neil would need a Plan B to ensure the tying up of loose ends. Perhaps someone French.

Enough of that, he thought. His mind shifted to loftier goals. His next step would be to become not just an underling to his foreign boss, but his recognized successor. To achieve that end, he would need to determine his competitors for that honor, then eliminate them. This he *could* do with Central Intelligence resources, but at the appropriate time. Then he would be able to see for himself the transformation of lands and societies to a new world, as delineated by the Elder.

An end to wars. An end to deaths from famine and preventable disease. An end to conflicts borne of religious faith, ethnicity, or national pride. These goals, he believed, humanity had the capacity to reach, but only with truly enlightened leadership. And the greedy, self-serving bastards, who now pretended to lead, would be replaced by people such as himself—ordained, not by some god, but by breeding and intellect, to wrest the reins of leadership from the incompetent, the corrupt, and the religious.

And the solution would be half-born in Neil's beloved France.

CHAPTER 9

It was in the late hours three evenings earlier when Jean-Marc had made the phone connection with Wolfram. They did not exchange pleasantries even though they knew each other quite well.

The next morning, Jean-Marc drove up to Antwerp in northern Belgium from his home in eastern France. He'd left his Peugeot 508 coupe in a long-term parking garage. His two days of browsing and shopping in Antwerp were uneventful and he was careful to look for any hint of a tail. His sampling of world-renowned Belgian chocolate was confined to a Mozambique transplant, who was exotically beautiful with exceptional eyes and a dark bronze fleshtone that had attracted both his eye and his libido.

He did not lose sight, however, that this trip was what the Americans would call mission-critical. His father had advised him of its pivotal importance in the grand scheme of things. The grand scheme, of course, was his father's, but that was good enough; he had become a most willing accomplice.

When he felt certain he travelled solo, he boarded the Thalys 9351 express train in the late afternoon. 16:31, to be exact. He arrived precisely one hour and twelve minutes later at Amsterdam's central station. His father had used the American version of time, calling it 4:31 P.M. Jean-Marc still wondered why his father would, from time to time, say things the Americans would.

On his previous visit to Amsterdam, his assumed cover as a middle class student had caused him to travel second class instead of first. He had loathed the stench of evil lower class tobacco associated with evil lower class bodies. This time, he utilized Premier First Class with meal and lounge access, the $146 price tag well worth it.

The train pulled into Amsterdam central at 5:43 and, of course, no one greeted him. He made his way from the station to the infamous Canal Street area and easily found Warmoesstraat. As he walked along the side of the canal, he could not help but check out the window displays.

People from around the world came here to walk and gawk as each row house in the red light district used its front window for salacious advertizing.

The Dutch girls on display were 'to die for' types that caused many a man to seek pleasures inside. The no-haggle price tag of fifty Euros per half hour was standardized by the government. The big surprise, however, was that what you saw was not what you got. Once inside, the high anticipation was dampened when the substitute lady proved to be a category or two below what was advertized to the spectators outside—a classic bait and switch.

Jean-Marc had no time for any more frolic this trip. Upon reaching house number 39, he turned and walked up the stairs to the front door. He made a point not to look at the woman in the window, although she made a point to look directly at him. He could not see her press a button on the underside of her armchair. Neither did he see the Chinese Fire Drill reaction at the receiving end of the signal.

Before the European Union, his father had brought him here to celebrate his sixteenth birthday. The price was twenty-eight Dutch Guilders at that time—around $7 U.S.—and his father had made sure he received prime meat. The girl had been the usual cute'ish blonde with straight bangs and full lips. He had learned well. But that was then and this was now.

Jean-Marc gave the doorbell three short rings. A young blonde answered, and he could swear she resembled his first one. Cute young blondes who performed as students or prostitutes were ubiquitous to Amsterdam. This one had cute, dimpled cheeks and puffy lips accented by lavender gloss. She wore a black silk robe with burgundy-red lapels that covered little. She led him upstairs without a word. They stopped at the end of the hall. She smiled. He smiled, took a fifty Euro note, and slipped his hand into the top of her robe to tuck it into her bra. She was not wearing one. He dropped the note and then tried to find it.

"Allow me," she said in perfect unaccented French. She found the note, and then turned and walked back down the hall. Jean-Marc's gaze followed her. He was not sure what *je ne sais quoi* was, but he was sure she had it.

Inside the room, Jean-Marc found a man sitting on modern Dutch furniture. He recognized his friend at once. Wolfram Silberweiss. He had met Wolf at the University of Leiden where they were both finishing university studies. Jean-Marc had moved on to graduate school in Paris, followed by a career in Private Wealth Management in Antwerp. Wolf had opted for the diamond industry, proving to be a worthy contact for Jean-Marc's rich clients as well as for making the secret transactions Jean-Marc's father required from time to time.

Jean-Marc never really understood how Wolf, an American, had come to be taking university in the Netherlands. The topic had never come up. But, his friend had been twelve years at a diamond brokerage and seemed to like the work.

"John Mark of the Rocks!" Wolf exclaimed in English, happy to see his friend once again. "*Comment ça va, mon ami*?" he added in French.

Jean-Marc laughed at the Anglicization of his name, including the rendering of his last name, Desrochers. "*Très bien. Et vous*?" Jean-Marc posited the traditional reply.

"*Bof!*" exclaimed Wolf. "I have had a severe personal tragedy."

"We can discuss it another time." Never one for small talk, he handed over his satchel to Wolf.

"It is in 500 and 100 Euro notes as you requested. Do you have my Christmas present?"

Jean-Marc knew Wolf was not much into Christian religious holidays. So Christmas was a little code word each used to indicate they were not compromised either with video or audio surveillance. Wolf took the elegant Louis Vuitton case from his friend and set it on the table.

"I must look inside," he said apologetically, but Jean-Marc knew this transaction was by far their biggest and he did not take offense. "It is better to not create interest in this town by carrying such an expensive bag, my friend."

"It is the cheapest one I had," replied Jean-Marc.

They both laughed.

Wolf turned up the 6-inch sides on a two foot by two foot table covered in black velvet. He then produced a bag of purple velvet, the top secured by a thin, yellow length of rope. He lifted the bag over the table. The two men's eyes stayed riveted as Wolf poured out its contents onto the table. The mere sound of so many D-flawless clear diamonds flowing like a waterfall, each at one carat or slightly more, was incredible. Jean-Marc felt a definite tingle inside.

"Ah. A waterfall of diamonds," Jean-Marc observed.

"Yes, my friend, for your water project. Then these we shall dub the, uh, the *Water Diamonds*," said Wolf, sounding much like a philosopher.

Jean-Marc remembered his friend's way with words during school. Too bad these water diamonds would be used as a down payment for goods to be delivered half a world away. There were several European properties he would like to buy, but he knew the money was not his. He sighed.

But then he returned from fantasy mode and smiled. Wolf smiled in return. Jean-Marc scooped the diamonds back into the bag, tucked it in his inside jacket pocket, and zipped the pocket shut. They shook hands, and he left the way he had come.

Wolf, out of respect for the young French aristocrat wannabe, did not count the currency until his long-time friend had left. Opening the case, he carefully counted the packets of fresh Euros. He also made a random check of the watermarks and found no suspicious notes. Everything looked fine. As he closed the case, the petite Dutch girl re-entered the room. She smiled as she walked over to him, her blue eyes sparkling like champagne. She looked up at him as she took his hips in her hands and pulled him against her. She could feel him already becoming hard.

"Your friend left some time on the clock," she said in trademark perfect English. She undid his pants and slid them to the floor as she descended slowly to her knees. She began to stroke him with her left hand as she slid her right hand between her thighs. It really was not for herself, but it turned men on big time.

"Oh, I see you are Jewish," she exclaimed in mock surprise. "Jewish men are my favorite." Those were the last words she was able to speak.

Five minutes later, Wolfram left the whorehouse with his newly-acquired Louis Vuitton case. He was already planning a recreational trip after all was done. He was sure he liked Angel best when she was unable to speak. He did not know her pretty Dutch name, pronounced with a hard *g*, meant *messenger* to the Americans.

CHAPTER 10

The previous night, Sylvain Lalumière had driven the back roads from his home in the Vosges region of eastern France to the city of Metz. He checked his rearview mirror the entire distance, even pulling off onto side roads to observe other travelers. Confident he was not being followed, he drove the A31 main road the rest of the distance north to Luxembourg City. He checked in to his favorite haunt, the Hotel Kravat, and concluded an evening of fine Letzebourgish cuisine in a one-night affair. The young blonde woman he had met in the bar intrigued him. Born in Slovakia, she worked as a script girl in New York. She had provided ample conversation and subsequent sex. She was cute, young, innocent, and delicious. The dimples on her cheeks had made her seem angelic. The encounter had eased his tension, making him quite ready for today.

The Kravat had an outdoor patio that opened onto a public square. Men, women, and children sauntered here and there like artwork in motion. It lacked only an Impressionist painter for completion. As he sat at the outdoor table he had reserved for its view and intimate size, he inspected each face he saw in the square. He could not shake the fear that his son, Jean-Marc, returning with so massive an amount of diamonds first by train to Antwerp, then by car the remaining 265 kilometers, could have run into bad people. But he wasted the worry. At last, he saw his son cross toward him. Despite his youth, the son's 6' 6" height and Gallic nose made him look quite like the great French general and leader, Charles De Gaulle. With a wave, the young man took the seat opposite his father. Lalumière was relieved to see him safe and sound.

Lalumière had no son by his only marriage. Like many Frenchmen, he had sought solace—and completion—outside of marriage when the creation of his family of two daughters indicated a male heir by his wife was unlikely. As luck would have it, his mistress straightaway bore him the son he had longed for. Alas, Jean-Marc was *le fils bâtard,* his bastard son, and did not yet share his last name. For many years, Lalumière had waited to see how the young man would turn out, desperately hoping he would make a suitable and capable successor to a new dynasty.

Lalumière saw that Jean-Marc had a youth-ubiquitous iPod tucked into his jacket pocket. He motioned for him to remove the ear buds; he needed his son's full attention on the conversation they were about to have.

Jean-Marc took out the ear buds and, as an ice breaker, remarked, "It is *Téléphone*. They are French. My favorite of theirs is called *Argent Trop Cher*. It is on the *Rappels* CD.

"Money Most Dear," Lalumière translated. "I like that. Yes, we must follow your lead and speak in English. Our comfort in speaking and hearing it is most valuable, *non*?"

"You bet, Dad," came the reply.

Lalumière leaned closer to his son. "You do have the prize?"

"Of course." Jean-Marc reached inside his jacket.

His father seized the offending arm. "Not here. Not now. You must deliver them to Chin. He will meet you in Taiwan." He handed over a packet of instructions. "You will spend the night here. I have made arrangements for your entertainment."

Just then, a very pretty brunette walked by and Jean-Marc exchanged smiles with her.

"No, Jean-Marc. Not for a while. You must use the working girls until it is time for you to marry. I have a very strict plan and a timeline that must be followed to the letter. It will lead us to the glory that we both deserve."

"Why do we deserve glory? And where did all of these dia—"

"Shhhhh! Do not say the word. They are the currency that makes the plan work. Jean-Marc, I must tell you some things now. I have been saving them for this moment."

"Dad, you don't need—"

"Shhhhh! Only listen. You know that I went to work for the large French company Veolia Environnement many years ago. It was just to make ends meet. I was assigned to the Middle Eastern territory to dig tunnels, lay pipe, and bring to the Arabs and Persians a commodity rare to the desert. Far more precious than gold or oil. Water. Those flush with petrodollars could purchase priority and extent with what was, to them, pocket change.

"My talents were noticed, and I moved quickly up the ladder. But then something unforeseen happened. While home between projects, I travelled to Nancy. It had been the capital of the Duchy of Lorraine before the revolution. I searched the archives for the genealogy of our family. What I found changed my life. And, in an indirect way, yours."

"What did you find that was so remarkable, Dad?"

"Our ancestors were aristocrats before the revolution. They had a château and grounds in the Vosges and treated the peasants well. But with the Reign of Terror in the early 1790's, the family was decimated by decapitation. Only one, Jean-Claude Lalumière, survived. Jean-Marc, I located the château. I became obsessed. I had to have it."

"But father, I remember growing up there. It was overgrown with weeds, in total disrepair, and damaged by the Germans and the Americans who used it during the war. I saw the passion with which you began renovations, seeking out only guildsmen who brought their specialties to bear. But where did all the money come from? Surely the water company did not pay that well."

"As soon as I was back in the field, I was approached by sheikhs and others, wanting to move up in line for water resources. With oil money spilling from their pockets, bribes were the way business was done. Their pocket change swelled the coffers of one *Directeur* Sylvain Lalumière."

Jean-Marc looked shocked. "You took bribes?"

His father inclined his head in admission. "I was obsessed. I invented goals for myself. The first to create a massive fortune, which I stashed in Switzerland. It is still guarded and maintained by Herr Kobler. He is my personal banker, and you will meet him some day. The second goal was the restoration, not only of the château and its lands, but the restoration of the previous prominence of our country. The château work is nearly complete. And I am now important enough to be invited to parties by the most prominent political and social forces in all France. But there is a third and final goal, my son."

"Father, we are doing well. What could possibly be missing?"

Lalumière looked around before leaning even closer. He lowered his voice, aiming his words at his son's left ear. "I have joined an organization. A very secret organization. Its members are at the top of their game in almost all countries of the world. They are the A-list of A-lists. With these contacts, I can see my way, our way, to the achievement of the third goal. It is the glory goal. It is the restoration of France."

Lalumière sat back in his seat to watch the effect of the words on his son. It took Jean-Marc several seconds to respond.

"Are you crazy, Father? France sits geographically atop Greece, Italy, Spain, and Portugal. The geography mirrors the economic state of affairs. They are falling one-by-one and then, as the Americans say, we French are toast."

"Through the society, my contacts brought a man to me to solve that problem. He was a brilliant man. Learned through high-level mathematics and science in solving the most daunting, complex, and impossible problems. Exactly the kind faced by France. I know what you are thinking. Anyone can make a plan. His plan is viable and actionable—I have studied it from every angle."

"If what you say is true, he is also a very serious threat. He knows everything. He knows what you will do next and after that."

"Yes, and he is also a highly skilled operative in America's intelligence community. Quite deadly, in fact, but I am confident we can mitigate the risk."

"So your plan will solve the business problems we learned about at the HEC?"

"I used some of the water money to send you to the *École des Haute Études Commerciales de Paris*, because the 130-year-old graduate business school is top notch. I knew that your studies there would ready you for the work to be done. But business and economics are not enough. Our return to glory requires a first class military, a permanent energy solution, and the resolution to the biggest problem of all. We must remake France for the French."

Jean-Marc looked deep into his father's eyes. "You mean the immigrant problem, don't you?"

"They come here in droves, and they are not like us. They gather in ghettoes and speak their North African language. They maintain their old ways of life. Bringing them, like nationalizing industries, was part of the grand socialist plan. As you have learned, the government-run industries became noncompetitive and had to be reprivatized. The immigrants, however, are still with us."

"What can we do, father? We can't just kill them all. And we can't just ship them back to Africa. Did your genius American spy supply an answer for that?"

"It is good that you are skeptical, my son. The short answer is yes. A resounding yes. Which brings us back to the prize secreted inside your jacket. The prize is the currency to commence the rebirth of France. In just a few major steps, it will be restored to glory. France will transform from just a name on a map, as it is now, and will become once again a superpower."

Jean-Marc was speechless.

"You must take the prize to the island of Taiwan, and deliver it to Chin. You may be unaware, but his country is in a similar state of affairs. The only difference is that his country hides that fact quite well—ours does not. Chin and I will move on from there. I will keep you informed as need be, but without placing you in unnecessary danger."

"Well, I have done as you asked. Without knowing why, I arranged for a week off from my work. I hope this courier trip will be complete within that time frame."

"Indeed, Jean-Marc. You will travel there with several stops, the first being the Azores. I have included instructions for detecting anyone who may attempt to follow you, even by private jet. You should be in Taiwan and conclude the delivery in three days. You will leave tomorrow from the Luxembourg airport, a private jet identified in the packet awaits you there. Oh, and one final thing. Be prepared. Mr. Chin is a bit eccentric."

With that, Sylvain Lalumière stood. His son followed suit. Jean-Marc, the one pound prize zipped safely inside his jacket pocket and armed with his packet of instructions, hugged his father. Both turned away from the small table.

Jean-Marc paused mid-stride. "We forgot to pay."

"They know me well here, my son. It all goes automatically on a tab. Some day it will be that way everywhere."

Jean-Marc fashioned a smile. His future was no longer in his hands. The good news, however, was he knew his father's tastes. Jean-Marc would have someone delicious tonight. He would begin his journey without stress. And that was good.

As they left, they did not see the Slovakian script girl rise from a table at the other end of the patio. She had been facing away, so neither father nor son had spotted her. She reached under her now red hair, pulled a device from her ear, and placed it in a clutch purse. She walked to the Lalumière table, leaned over, and smiled as she plucked the listening device from the table's flower arrangement. She was not a Slovakian script girl who worked in New York. And last night's blonde hair and innocence had been fake, too. The dimples, however, were real.

CHAPTER 11

Chin Yao-wu did not look or sound like the average Chinese male. His countenance displayed a thin, pointed nose reminiscent of a hornet, and his voice sounded shrill and high-pitched. None of these characteristics, while memorable, had impeded his rise to great wealth and influence in Hong Kong society. Not unattractive, he presented himself as charismatic with strong leadership qualities.

At age sixty-two, he was still considered in the prime of his life. Those who encountered him would forever remember the implied callousness of his dark brown eyes. He was, to those who knew him, a man with an insatiable lust for power over his destiny.

It was evening now in Hong Kong. The sun had made its dispassionate departure and the city glowed with lights. Chin indeed felt fortunate to have selected what he considered the world's greatest city as his home. He felt destiny had willed him here from the remote village of his birth—at the headwaters of the Yangtze—and the memories best left behind.

He closed his special cell phone with a smile. The Frenchman's son would arrive in a few days with the diamonds. Chin planned to make certain purchases that would initiate the process of ascendancy for both men. He still could not fathom the degree of good fortune that had brought the two of them together in the rough interior of Scotland. Most often, he had found, good fortune could not be explained. The ball, as the Americans said, had been lobbed into his court.

Chin entered the spacious Room of Learning through theater-like burgundy curtains and stepped onto a foot-high stage. All walls were gold in color, as was an arc of ceiling directly above the stage. The rest of the ceiling was decorated with chrome, foot-long, rod-shaped objects pointed downward. It gave the effect of a large, dense version of the Indian bed-of-nails, only upside down.

He sat on the ornate gold and red throne like a king. He looked out at his twelve daughters, who stood arrayed before him in an arc of lesser chairs. They bowed deeply to his presence. He motioned for them to sit. They obeyed, as always. He gestured for the two oversized guards to take their places beside the huge red double doors. A virtual keyboard embedded in the stage rotated to a position just above his lap. He pressed the sinogram for *Isolate* so that no sounds could enter and, more important, none could leave the room.

The young women ranged in age from thirteen to nineteen. Each wore a traditional cheongsam dress of her assigned color. Chin brought them to this room as part of their education, which he oversaw with great personal involvement. When he lectured, he spoke his mind freely to them, a means of venting. However, a daughter became, over time, a weapon that could be used against him. Each one had been told that, upon her twentieth birthday, she would achieve freedom and have the advantage of an extensive education and Chin's high-level contacts. In fact, none of them would go free. A graduation celebration kept the remaining daughters as true believers. Then, those celebrated were led away and executed.

"Today's lecture describes the past greatness of our country and the necessary moves to regain it. All discussion is of highest confidentiality, and punishment for violation shall be dramatic and permanent. I see you all nod your understanding. We will proceed.

"My motives for achieving wealth include remaking China to its former greatness under the Ch'in Dynasty. The original Ch'in unified the separately-ruled kingdoms to create his namesake empire—the first China. This you know.

"Since that time, China provided governmental administration over territories like Tibet, Taiwan, and the northern districts of Vietnam. Tibet has been brought back into the fold. Taiwan has been a struggle. But, with the clever inclusion of capitalism into the People's Republic, China can reel the Taiwan Chinese back into the empire.

"The northern territories of Vietnam will be more difficult. Vietnam was lost to us just before 1000 AD by the T'ang dynasty after 1500 years of rule. The political and martial fighting between territories in China had taken away the T'ang rulers' attention. The Vietnamese built a new capital at Dai-la, and the indigenous people achieved independence."

At this point, Beige daughter spoke up.

"Was not this original capital later abandoned, to be reinstituted as Thang-long—today known as Ha'noi?"

"You have learned your history well, Beige." He concealed his feeling that this one needed to be watched. "I will continue. All future attempts by our country to regain the territory were rebuffed by the Vietnamese and, in the long conflict known as the Vietnam War, North Vietnam relied on the Russians for aid much to the chagrin of its former master, our nation, right next door."

Beige interrupted again. This time she stood up. "You did not mention, Father, that the Vietnamese chose the Soviets because they did not trust the Chinese to not master them once again."

That was the final straw. Chin pressed 12 on the keyboard. There was a whoosh of air from the high-pressure pneumatic system in the ceiling. Then, a whining zip and a crunch as a crossbow bolt fired straight down into the skull of Beige. She wobbled. She sank back into the chair, her hair now dripping red. She was allowed to expire before the two giants carried her away.

The remaining daughters kept their faces straight forward the entire time and their gazes to the floor. An event of this nature had been anticipated by the older ones. Order and respect must be maintained.

Instead of watching Beige's demise, Chin had observed the others for reaction. Good, he thought. They understand well. He continued.

"You may think the Vietnam war was lost by the Americans due to an inferior army. It is not true. Theirs was one of the best in all history. The American government *threw in the towel*—as they themselves say—when they were winning. It was unbelievable. This sole failure reinforced in my mind that there is suicidal folly in electing a leadership based on the rantings and emotional meanderings of the masses. What fools the Americans were. China may not be able to outpower America, but it certainly will be able to outsmart it—with the correct leadership."

His eyes panned the arc of remaining girls. "Are there any questions or comments?"

There were none.

With that, Chin waved dismissal to them. As they filed out through the now open doors, Chin exited through his private portal.

• • •

Back in his office, Chin sat at his desk and began to focus, not on his ultimate goal, but on the first necessary step. He had realized early that he could not use local currency for his plans. He needed something universal. It had to be viable anywhere in the world. Gold and diamonds fit the bill like nothing else. Gold, however, possessed the problem of size, weight, and detectability. One million dollars in gold weighed in at about 666 ounces—a devilish amount. The same value in twenty-five supra-carat D flawless diamonds weighed only five grams—.01 lbs. It made so much sense. But, he could not take delivery in China. At least, not this China. He would travel soon.

Yes, his deal with the Frenchman would bring him the diamonds. With a portion of them, he would procure what the Frenchman needed. The first step demanded by destiny.

• • •

Chin's primary daughter entered the room and, without a word, pressed the control to close the window shades. Miraculously, the directional transparency shades kept out prying eyes, but still maintained the spectacular view.

The Black daughter was dressed in a Chinese cocktail dress with slits up both legs and a high, close collar. As he had with all of his daughters, he had acquired her when she was new to the physical manifestations of womanhood. He had seen to her training in his needs and, for the next five years, she had learned each aspect to perfection. At age seventeen, Chin had personally exchanged her plain black dress for this one. The gold embellishments signified mastery of sexuality and inner strength.

She moved to him in an effortless flow. She took the red and gold pillow from his lap and placed it at his feet. She moved slowly to her knees, looking downward in deference the entire time. When she was fully at rest on the pillow, she reached out and ran her long slender fingers along the tops of his thighs. Her mastery of the art of creating uncontrollable sexual tension was second to none. And Chin had experienced many.

She eased his knees apart. The hinged chair complied with neither noise nor resistance. She parted his robe and when her hands reached the gold and black satin underwear, she released the Velcro attachments. She performed the only kind of sex he could allow himself. He would never defile the female sex organ—his long ago promise in his mother's memory. He saw this self-constraint as honorable rather than as a kind of neurotic psychosis as lesser men might conclude. The memory of his mother long gone was soon interrupted by an explosion in his loins. In just a few seconds, this young woman caused him to feel like an emperor.

CHAPTER 12

The new day produced a balmy afternoon in Hong Kong. Balmy for Autumn. The man looking out the floor-to-ceiling window marveled at the view he alone owned. The skyline of Hong Kong had remained the same for decades—there was no more land on which to build. Later, he would view the sunset. And after, the real beauty of the most important Asian city would be created yet again for his pleasure.

The man named Chin had achieved a great deal. He likened himself to a nuclear missile that had taken a great deal of preparation and effort to create, but whose real impact could only be felt after a successful launch and eventual display of its immense power.

Chin had a grand plan. The plan would first require a cleansing of China. He would rid his beloved country of its encumbrances. For his first step, Chin needed to utilize the Muslim entity, Iran. He required someone who could intrude on its weapons program, but had no resource at hand. And he could not go to his many contacts in the Beijing government and ask questions.

Iran was on the highest priority list of the government. China received critical oil supplies in return for weapons and nuclear technology. And at the same time, Iran stuck its thumb in both eyes of the post-capitalist West. Any inquiries by Chin, no matter how benign, would be referred to the Communist Party leadership with serious consequences. He had to try something different.

General Li Ya-fei, a longtime friend of an uncle, had come to mind. Chin knew that Li commanded the supply of nuclear technology to Iran. It made him a perfect match. And Li, like Chin, had come from humble beginnings, but his superior knowledge of wartime and peacetime strategies had moved him up to a general-ship. Still, Chin knew, without the contacts and the *in vogue* family history, Li had reached his azimuth. Chin felt confident only he could offer Li a lift up into the rarefied air reserved for the *crème de la crème*.

Chin had contacted the uncle. He persuaded Uncle to recommend the two get together so that Chin would not be perceived as initiating the meeting. A wary Chin knew that Uncle, an aged man, would not last long under Li's interrogation, should that come to pass. He kept Uncle in the dark as to the purpose of the meeting, which took place at the Dragon structure Chin owned in Hong Kong's Wan Chai district.

• • •

"Good evening, General. I am happy we could finally meet. Please take a seat and allow me to offer you something to drink," Chin began. He could see that Li was at least fifty, closer to sixty.

He motioned General Li to a beautiful black lacquer chair with padding of deep red and gold. Those colors would give Li a feeling that an association with Chin could lead to prosperity and wealth.

"I will defer to your taste, Chin," Li responded, "but I prefer something strong at this hour. I have had a quite challenging day."

Chin turned to his right and signaled a male aide. No words were spoken, the communication complete. The aide turned and left the room. Chin had made sure that his male aides would not speak.

He had also made sure that they would pose no sexual threat to his daughters. The young men had been altered.

"I am sure you are, in the least, curious regarding my request to speak with you. I will tell you up front that our relationship, should it develop to that, will be worth every second of your time should you agree to continue. I will understand if you choose to respectfully disengage at any time."

Chin had learned at an early age how to use language deftly to secure his wishes. He also knew, if Li remained through tonight's dialog, the only way Li could disengage would be if his heart ceased to function.

Chin eased himself into a larger more elaborately padded chair behind his hand-carved desk. "My concern has to do with something that is bigger than us both, but that is of substantial concern to each of us. That concern is the future of our great country. We are now the inhabitants of a country with thousands of years of most significant history. We Chinese have created some of the world's most important inventions. We have been involved in no wars of our choosing, but have been victimized numerous times."

General Li nodded. If this was going to be a drawn out soliloquy, he would politely listen, and then graciously excuse himself. Or was this going to be the relationship, as Chin called it, that would propel Li to the top of the heap? In either case, the drink relaxed him. He settled back to listen.

"Nationalism is at a peak. The people demand severe action with regard to Taiwan and Japan. Beijing does nothing. Beijing utilizes the pent-up frustrations only to cover up government ineptitude and corruption. They take no real action. Government-enabled protests are like opening a valve on a pressure cooker. When it is closed, the pressure rebuilds until the whole of it could explode."

"Yes. The deflection of public emotions away from the government is, I suppose, necessary at times," replied Li.

"Li, at times, the deflection is all that keeps the table of power from tipping away from Beijing and into the hands of the people it governs."

"I have not observed it to be as tenuous as that," said Li. "After all, the government has one of the greatest militaries in the world. We have tanks, we have nuclear missiles. Our armies have incredible morale and devotion to the country. We are both unassailable and unbeatable."

Chin smiled. "General, what you have observed has not gone unnoticed by me. I have seen our strength displayed at parades and in our foreign policy positions. But consider these few inconvenient facts. It took but one man to stop the tanks of our friends, the Russians. That single nonviolent act began the demise of the seminal bastion of Communism, the Soviet Union. Seventy years were destroyed in an instant.

"Their hundreds of nuclear warheads, thousands of armored vehicles, and a highly-trained military were useless in the face of a population that had endured long and painful years awaiting the socialist promises to bear fruit. There, but for several self-preservative moves by our government, go we."

Red daughter entered the room with a tray of glasses, a fresh bottle of Scotch whisky, Norwegian water, and a lead crystal ice bucket. She poured a perfect three-finger drink for each man. Then she added a dot of the artesian water to release the whisky essence. Backing away, she left the room again. Li's gaze followed this beautiful young woman.

"She is quite capable as are the others," Chin said, correctly estimating Li's lustful intentions. "In fact, they are all quite capable and are not to be underestimated."

"I am pleased that she has left us to our discussion. I do not want to be distracted as important as our dialogs might become," said Li.

"Li, a sole young man stopped our tanks at Tiananmen Square. These events are not lost on the West. They are encouraged to probe and poke at us diplomatically to find a weakness they can exploit. We must never forget that the people of the West believe they can choose their leaders and replace them at will. They are deceived in this, of course. Democracy assures that the existing corrupt, incompetent bastards can only be replaced by other corrupt, incompetent bastards."

To this, Li gave a chuckle. Chin was right on the money with the seriousness he found in their situation, but able to poke some humor at the same time. "Please continue."

"There is, however, an incredible possibility that I have discovered. It would remove any threat of an overthrow of our government."

Li really wanted to hear this. An overthrow would pull the rug out from under his personal ambitions.

Chin saw that Li was taking the bait, but thought it wise to bide his time and to set the hook patiently, but thoroughly.

"How do you like the malt Scotch, General?"

"It is wonderful. Please, continue."

"It is getting late," sighed Chin. "If you don't mind, I would like to call it a night. Perhaps we can continue our discussion in a few days. I have some business to see to and have more information to confirm. I will have it ready when we reconvene."

"Certainly," replied Li, hiding his disappointment. "Please, call me at the same unlisted, direct number your staff used to contact me this time. I will keep our conversations private unless you instruct otherwise. I look forward to our next meeting." With that, Li stood. As if by magic, Red daughter reappeared to escort him from the room and the building.

Chin felt good. It was not the rare 16-year-old *Isle of Jura* single malt that gave him calm. It was his successful manipulations, which soothed the frustrations of his mind. This evening's *tête-à-tête* with Li had placed and set the hook. His wildest and fondest dreams had never been more within reach.

From their exchange, he could tell that the good General Li would become a major pawn, just like the Frenchman, in his master plan. Chin would take the lead. As the American had said, there would be no stopping him.

CHAPTER 13

In the fifty-six days since the crash on the Pacific Coast Highway, Crayle had recovered well. He had come to be tolerant of Lenny and actually liked the FBI agent. She had been nice enough to move to the big house so Crayle could have the waterbed. There had not been any protecting to do, and he knew she was bored.

And there had been a first snow. He had run outside to shovel it before it melted—for the exercise. He was now able to do everything for himself. Still, he tended to sleep in every day, but that was about to change.

"*Reveille! Reveille!*" Lenny yelled at Crayle from three feet away. "C'mon, get up. You're obviously stressed out and that is not conducive to getting your memory back. The Chinese say, 'If you give a man a fish, he'll be pissed at you the next day if you don't give him another one. But, if you *teach* a man to fish, then he'll be pissed at you for a lifetime.' Something like that. *I* am going to teach you to *fish*."

Crayle mumbled something that sounded like "If … kill him … use memory loss … extenuating circumstances. Better … jury … who knows him."

But complaining would do no good. He shuffled into the bathroom to brush out the mold he felt growing in his mouth. He finished the teeth and then peered at his image in the mirror. A two-inch slash on his right cheek looked healed.

He pulled off his green hospital nightshirt. More scars. He touched a sore rib and swore. He wondered what had hit him there. Then, he stepped back and dropped the green pants.

A scar covered his left knee, but it had healed. His private parts looked intact, but his muscles lacked the tightness he wanted. He would get back in shape, he told himself. He dressed in a few minutes, and the two headed out the back door toward the lake.

They covered the distance to the dock of about fifty feet in short order, despite Lenny trying to carry two poles, a tackle box, a kreel to store their catch, and a bag of bait. The appearance was of someone ready to jump full force into no-win situations. An accurate appearance.

The sight of bushy-tailed squirrels hustling around in search of pine nuts for their winter stash reminded Crayle that life existed outside the human experience. With or without humans around, the squirrels and their brethren faced life in exactly the same way. He wondered whether squirrels ever suffered amnesia.

At least his senses were intact. He felt the light breeze against his flesh and observed it undulating the water as it passed across the lake. The early glow of the sun rising in the east added mood to the image. Too, the smell of Autumn pine was thick on the crisp air. Crayle breathed it in deeply. However, Lenny did not have time for scents. A man on a mission, he made a beeline for the dock.

While the wind could blow the lake water into a rough chop on occasion, the breeze was light and the lake was calm on this particular morning. They could see fishermen loading gear, flush with optimism, across the lake at the upscale settlement, Boulder Bay. Most wore plaid flannel overshirts for warmth. Crayle was just fine in his short sleeve shirt and fisherman's vest. He figured those across the way to be city types here for a weekend and a brief taste of nature.

Meanwhile, a crew of five fishermen approached a water craft up the north shore from the cabin. The five fishermen intended to launch from a point past the prominent white-domed space observatory building far beyond the sightline of Crayle and Lenny.

Along with their poles, the fishermen loaded a large black tackle box and a large black duffel bag into a Zodiac. They had chosen an eighty-horsepower Mercury marine engine for power. For reasons known only to them, they had opted for the black woven turtleneck sweaters and lightweight European-style waterproof pants. They pulled on matching knit watch caps and looked like quintuplets. Their boots were light weight, crepe soled, and waterproof as well. Today was practice.

Lenny had actually never caught a fish, but there he was. Never mind that he absolutely loathed fishing every bit as much as its land-bound corollary, golf. Upon reaching the dock, Lenny gazed out over one of the most beautiful mountain lakes in Southern California. He hoped not to be helpless against the wily fish as he felt the calm of a dozen natural tranquilizers. He stood next to a man who had nothing to do, nowhere to go, and barely knew himself. Compared to Crayle, Lenny realized he was in good shape.

Lenny lowered the gear to the dock and handed a pole to Crayle. It was all ready to go, he said, all Crayle needed to do was catch something.

"Now, have a seat on the dock, and we can proceed with the lecture," Lenny instructed.

Crayle complied, sat cross-legged, and looked up at the supposed fishing savant.

"Sometimes I feel the need to employ what we intellectuals call *contrarian insight*. In order to help you find the truth about your past, we must first teach you about untruth. Listen carefully."

Crayle studied him like a four-year-old trying to understand why grown-ups got to make all the decisions.

"There is no reason in the world why any rational person should actually try to catch a fish for the fun of it. Fishing is like golf. Golfers talk about their lie. To improve their lie means they come up with ever better fabrications to be delivered to even greater fools."

"What does this have to do with me? I don't know if I've lied. Or to whom I might have told lies."

"Fishermen lie about their ability to outthink and outmaneuver a dumb fish. Both golfers and fishermen lie in every aspect of their lives. In their professional lives, in their personal lives. In this respect, they are quite similar to politicians and spies—liars do not just do it *sometimes.* We need to catch a fish in a totally honest way. It is much more difficult, but worth every bit."

With that, Crayle got up, took the pole, and turned to let fly.

"You'll need to cast way out there," Lenny said, pointing somewhere out in the lake. "The tide's out, and you don't want to be pulling in my used *raincoats* from the bottom."

As old as the Lenny-isms were getting, Crayle decided to play. "You been out here screwing the fish, Lipschitz?"

This time, *Lenny* ignored *Crayle.* Instead, he pulled a bright yellow and black book out of the kreel that bore the title, *Fishing for Dummies.*

"I thought you were an expert at this. I think you are a dummy at this, too. Have you ever caught a fish? And what does it matter? What I need is to know something about my father."

Lenny flashed a smile.

"It is not in the least funny. Do not make a joke about it."

"Who's your daddy?" Lenny howled.

Crayle grabbed the closest thing—a filet knife.

Lenny's eyes opened wide. Just as Crayle lunged at him, he sprang backward off the dock, cannonballing some ten feet away. Crayle stopped short of going after him with the knife.

"Help!" Lenny cried, looking up at Crayle and splashing wildly with both arms. "I can't swim! I can't swim!"

Crayle dropped the knife on the dock and jumped in—feet first. It was a quick swim to the drowning man. Crayle summoned enough extra strength to turn the P.I. around—facing away—and drag them both to the shore and safety.

"You saved my ass. You're a hero, MC," panted a water-logged Lenny. "I owe you one. Say, how did you know you could swim?"

Crayle shrugged. He had no idea.

They made it back inside the cabin, Crayle half carrying the lake-soaked Lenny. He dumped him into the bathtub, then sat down on the stool to catch his breath. He scowled at the hapless P.I.

"Get yourself changed," Crayle told him. "It's nap-time."

Lenny struggled out of the tub and put on some dry clothes. Then, a light went on. "Wait! There is something way cool I need to show you. You gotta check this out."

Lenny led Crayle into the kitchen, stopped at the thermostat on the wall, and punched in a four-digit code. Nothing happened. He punched in another code. Nothing.

As the P.I. continued to punch in codes, Crayle commented, "I hope whatever this way cool thing is, it doesn't have a use by date." Damn, he thought. Lenny's pitiful and annoying sense of humor was communicable.

The fourth code did the trick. The heater and air conditioning duct cover on the wall slid sideways to reveal a black hole in the wall. Crayle walked over and saw stairs that led down into a tunnel. Before Lenny could speak, Crayle descended into the blackness.

A light, triggered by a motion sensor, came on. The illumination revealed the extent of the tunnel. Lenny joined Crayle at the base of the stairs.

It was clear to Crayle that someone—or some people—had worked quite hard to cut through the granite bedrock and then shore the walls and ceiling with mining-grade timbers. A few burlap bags full of dirt made it clear that it had been done without alerting anyone of the activity. A secret tunnel? Why?

In his time at the cabin and its environs, Crayle had concluded that nearby Fawnskin was far from the epitome of a nest of spies and other malcontents. It was peaceful, calm—everything nice families could want for a getaway or even permanent residence. So, why the intrigue? Why a secret tunnel?

Seeing the puzzled look on Crayle's face, Lenny supplied an answer.

"It was built so people could get from the garage to the cabin without getting cold. Jack didn't want to wade through waist-deep snow carrying loads of groceries. See, it's simple."

Simple? Because of his affliction, it seemed to Crayle that everything was at once simple and complex. As for Lenny's explanation, he only half-believed anything Lenny said to him, but he accepted the answer—for now.

They walked down the tunnel. Crayle counted twenty paces before reaching another stairway, which they ascended to a small landing and another door. Next to this one, at chest height, was another code input pad, only this one did not look like a thermostat. This time, Lenny punched in the code correctly—the same code, Crayle noted. The door opened.

As they stepped into the garage, fluorescent lights powered on to reveal a garage capable of containing three cars and perhaps a motorcycle or ATV. The garage was empty save something covered by what appeared to Crayle to be a gray parachute.

Lenny noticed the object of Crayle's attention. "Hey, whatever you do, don't touch that. That is Jack's baby and, knowing him, it's rigged to blow."

With that admonition, Crayle stepped forward, pulled the chute free, and sucked in a sharp breath. Before him sat a deep red sports car with twin white racing stripes front to back and an open cockpit. It looked to him like an artistic incarnation of pure mechanical muscle.

"It belongs to Jack," Lenny reminded. "He really wanted a full-blown Shelby, but didn't have the bucks. He settled for a replica with Shelby badging. Not exactly legal, but who's gonna know? Everyone calls 'em Cobras, anyways."

"You ever ride in it?" Crayle asked.

"Oh, yeah. Me and Jack go back a long way. We're buds," came Lenny's smartass reply.

Crayle walked around to the driver's side, popped open the door, and eased himself inside.

Lenny started to speak, but he knew Crayle wouldn't listen. So, instead, he observed, "You look natural in there. In fact, most people would not know the door latch pulls are inside. How …"

Crayle reached across and opened the glove box. Inside, he found a document detailing the major components of the car. He read them off:

1. Superformance Cobra Mark III
2. Engine: 351 Cleveland V8
3. Brake Horsepower: 450+
4. Transmission: Manual 6-speed with close ratio gears
5. Fully triangulated roll cage
6. Simpson 6-point racing belts

The list went on to include the few other components.

"Look at this. There's no radio on the list," Crayle observed.

"The entertainment is right here," Lenny said. He raised the hood to reveal the engine. "C'mere—check it out."

Crayle got out of the car and walked quickly to the front. The V8 was there, alright, but attached was something looking like a large, silver snail.

"It's a turbocharger, MC. Jack needed this thing to go faster than instant."

Crayle said, "Let's go back."

They buttoned up the hood, re-covered the Cobra, and returned to the cabin. It had been a full day, especially for Crayle. He was still recovering from his severe crash—he needed rest. Both slept well.

CHAPTER 14

Lenny got up with the chickens the next day, careful not to wake Crayle. He grabbed a can of liquid breakfast from the refrigerator and was out the door and headed across town in a couple of minutes. He needed to get his head straight, and Alona excelled at getting things straight.

Phoebe spent most of her time in the big house. Crayle did not expect Lenny back for awhile given his propensity to entertain wherever he went. It gave Crayle a chance to continue his self-dialogs without interruption. He lingered in the waterbed and gazed at the ceiling, the recording device still in his pocket from the day before.

He began, "My name is Magus Crayle. I know that because I have been told. I have awakened to a world I do not remember. I look about at my surroundings as I suppose does a baby, but a baby, I am not. My private investigator has recovered that I was a government functionary—perhaps a mathematician. Also my university. But no parents, siblings, wife, children, friends—nothing. I have myself discovered familiarity with an Oriental philosophy … and an artist, Yao-wu. I recall one rock and roll song. I am a grown man of … I don't know the years. There are healed bruises and gashes on my body. I am rehabilitating from a near-fatal automobile crash in which I should have died. 'Should' was Jack's word. He seemed an honest man—so, I *am* Magus Crayle."

Crayle walked into the kitchen to fix himself breakfast. He found a note Lenny had written, which instructed Crayle to go to the big house. With the P.I. gone, he would be under Phoebe's protective wing. It seemed like a good idea. And with Lenny gone, Crayle decided to use the opportunity to obtain some answers from Phoebe. He felt certain she knew things the P.I. didn't. Somehow, he sensed that talking to people one-on-one produced better results.

When he stepped outside through the back door, the brightness of the mountain sun forced his eyes shut. He stumbled and almost fell to the ground. Once his eyes adjusted to the light, he looked around.

From the south-facing lake side of the cabin, he saw the expanse of blue water. On the other side, an eclectic collection of cabins nestled among huge pale gray and tan boulders. The partly cloudy sky above transformed the environment into a living picture. A beautiful living picture. But Crayle had more important things to do than admire scenery.

He turned right and followed the path to the big log house. At least twice as large as Crayle's new home, its logwork matched that of the smaller cabin and garage in diameter and in its yellowed-varnish appearance. Crayle concluded all three had been built at the same time. It was an expensive place for a government servant like Jack, he realized.

The lake side of the main cabin was fronted by a deck that extended the length of the house and protruded about twenty feet toward the lake. There was no railing. Two pairs of teak lawn chairs with small teak tables for drinks and snacks sat on the deck. The house itself boasted boat-prow windows that ran from the floor to a roof line he estimated at twenty-five feet high with a projection toward the lake of fifteen feet.

When he entered the doorway to the right of the prow, he felt compelled to turn around and look out through the giant windows. The view from this vantage point was magnificent. The panorama available through all of the windows was somewhat greater than that of the cabin, but the height of them drew in the sky as well. It was at once relaxing and astounding.

"Don't move!" came an order from behind. "Turn the fuck around!"

Crayle knew not to move suddenly and to keep both hands in sight. He turned slowly.

He faced the blonde woman. She held her Glock and obviously knew what to do with it, if the need arose.

When she recognized him as her ward, she holstered her weapon. She bade Crayle, with a motion of her hand, to take a seat on the couch.

"Habit," was all she said.

Crayle knew he had been about two-tenths of a second from being dead. He wondered how he knew.

When Phoebe had seated herself at the other end of the couch, Crayle began with, "Why are you here?"

"Nice foreplay." Phoebe looked down as she reminded herself that she could assume Crayle did not know what she knew. Or that nothing was as it seemed. She continued. "I was told about your amnesia. Not much else. I am an agent with the Federal Bureau of Investigation. My job here is to protect you." Phoebe did not know how to mince words.

"From whom?"

"Good question. I don't know. They only said 'Protect *the subject* with your life, if necessary.' Knowing why is apparently above my pay grade. The good news: I've never failed to protect. The bad news: we always say 'never' until the first time."

He sized her up. Well built. Attractive in a masculine way. Almost pretty. He started to feel a chemical urge inside.

Phoebe noticed the pregnant pause in the conversation. She knew he must have a million questions, but she sensed something else was in play at the moment.

"It's been a while, huh?" she observed as much as she asked.

"I don't know," was his response.

"Well, save those feelings for a more likely prospect, okay? We agents are trained not to get involved with our charges. It causes problems that can be fatal. So what happened to you, Mister Crayle? How did you get all banged up and forgetful?"

He thought about the question and then answered.

"It was an accident, I guess. That's what the doctor at the hospital said. It happened on the coast road north of Los Angeles. The doctor called it PCH. He said the road is a basic two-lane blacktop and that there are some nasty wrecks whenever the fog comes in. Cars go wide around the corners and take someone out coming the other way. He said my long-term memory was affected. It was weird. I felt like I'd gone through a time warp. One of the nurses came in and called him Dr. Rorschach. You know, like the psychiatrist who did the ink blots. Maybe he was a brain doctor or something."

"Did he say anything about Lenny or me? I mean, why we are here?"

"Jack told me someone was tasked to probe into past records on the Internet to help me fill in the blanks. He said the government was paying for him, not to worry. But you. Why does a man who served in the government and who can't remember much need protection?"

"I don't know either. Jack told me it was critical to see that you were *unimpeded* in your search for your past. You and your lost memories seem quite important to the government. Who knows, maybe you'll start finding pathways back to memories they want to know about."

Animation and emotion suffused Crayle. "Did Jack say if I was driving or if anyone was in the car with me? Was there another car? Is there a police report or a news article?"

Phoebe saw the pain in Crayle's face and heard it resonate in his voice. She moved closer to him, placing her hand on his arm. Her voice softened. "Mister Crayle, I bet the private investigator can help you track down the answers. That's what he does. Try to be patient. He's just getting started. Give him a chance."

She noticed that Crayle twisted his head around from side to side while they talked. He seemed still to be sore from the accident. She stood and circled around the couch. Behind him now, she stroked his soft dark brown hair. "This helps me connect. It makes the person real to me—not just a job," she said.

In no more than five minutes, they were pounding into each other in the master bedroom. Crayle created a memory as much as she lost one. He felt the tremendous heat of her body, when she suddenly flung him off the side of the bed. He slammed into the log wall, surprised by her strength. He internalized the pain, his face expressionless. He stood, his back against the horizontal timbers.

Phoebe cast a glance at her backup weapon on the nightstand, then she jumped up. She moved quickly to him. Standing on tiptoes, she converged with him again until she exploded inside. She let the feeling surge through every cell of her being, then decoupled, backed away, and collapsed cross-wise on the bed.

"So, how do you like life in Fawnskin?" she asked, once her heavy breathing subsided.

"I don't know. Not a lot to do. Boring comes to mind."

"Boring?" She sat up. "Sex with me is boring? Where's my weapon?" she said, feeling around on the bed.

"No, no. That was incredible. Perhaps your silent weapon." And then, "Phoebe, I don't know what questions to ask." A plaintive statement.

"Well, you have me as your first sex memory. C'm'ere. You won't be forgetting *me*."

Crayle moved to her. He stretched out beside her.

She rolled onto her side and gently sampled his flesh with her lips and tongue and teeth. In a few minutes, they made love again, this time with slow, enduring passion.

Their love-making complete, an exhausted and satisfied Phoebe fell asleep. Fully content. Renewed inside. Crayle dressed and left the bedroom, careful not to wake her. One last look at her, and Crayle realized that she was a straight up human being—everything was real—even the blonde hair.

Crossing the living room, he leaned against one of the large window panes and began to speak.

"It was so good, I can't imagine not having done it before. But when? With whom? I feel like a man buried alive who, in a brief moment, has found a cool, moist pocket of air. And the man has breathed in the cool, moist air as if it were a god-send. But, in the next instant, it's gone. Now what? I want her again and again and again. I want my life to return. Please, doctor, if you can hear me, help me."

With that, he dropped his face into his hands. He wanted to cry, but tears needed a basis for their existence. As it stood—like Crayle—they had none.

CHAPTER 15

"Holy Crap!" shouted Lenny, "It's a brand new day! Rise and shine, MC, before this fine fucking day gives up on you."

Crayle massaged his eyes open to the visage of one Leonard Dennis Lipschitz. He had slept off the stupor from another long, late night at the Sugarloafer, but he needed a few more hours to get right.

But, no. Lipschitz was holding a glass of water in his hand and marching to Crayle's bedside. Crayle did not need a glass of water and—

"Ah!" he cried as the water splashed down on his head. "Ah!"

In the next instant he was on his feet and chasing. Lenny had started to run, but was overcome by the humor in it all. In other words, he had a laugh attack. Crayle hit him high, and they both landed on the living room floor.

Crayle jumped on top and began to choke the little P.I., who simultaneously laughed and gagged.

Then, Crayle stopped. He jumped up, dragging Lenny up with him. There would be other opportunities to end everyone's misery. Nothing could stand in the way of Crayle getting his life back.

"I guess that was a bit drastic, but my intentions were noble," Lenny blurted. "Hope you don't hold a grudge."

Crayle did not know if he held grudges, but considered taking up the practice soon.

"I'm up. Why?" Crayle asked.

"Because ole Doc Rorschach said you need to get out, you know, do regular human stuff. We're goin' out."

"What about Phoebe? She'll want to go."

"She's still counting perps," he said, providing a job-appropriate substitute for sheep. "We'll be done and back before her pretty blonde brain decides she's hungry and wakes her up. But, let me put your worries to rest, my dear Mr. Crayle. I do think of everything. It's why Jack picked me. To be sure, all bases are covered. I already left her a message on her cell. She'll be fine with it. C'mon, let's go have some fun."

"I like that. How about getting a boat—a fast one? Feel the cool air and the wind in our faces. A very fast boat. Let's go." It was the first time Crayle had experienced the thrum of exhilaration. It felt good.

"Actually, that will have to wait. We need groceries." With that, Lenny handed a list to Crayle.

"Groceries?" said a crestfallen Crayle.

"Yeah, groceries. I'll drop you off so you can re-experience for the first time the fine art of buying vittles. You'll be on your own 'til I get back, so don't mess up. And who knows—you may make some new friends."

Crayle glanced out the back window just in time to see a speedboat fly across the water, its inhabitants obviously having an incredible time. Clearly, Lenny was the ultimate buzzkill. His list of faults grew by the day.

• • •

Lenny and Crayle crossed the lake at the Stanfield Cutoff and headed east on the two-lane. The trees on both sides flashed past to create a strobe-like effect from the morning sun. Lenny had the windows down, and the clean chill air stimulated Crayle to a state of full awakeness. Not bad if you can't have the speedboat.

After barely two miles, Lenny turned left into a large dirt parking lot almost devoid of cars. He dropped off Crayle with, "I gotta go back and see the attorney about something relating to your case. I'll be back in no more …" Lenny looked at his watch, "… than fifteen, twenty minutes, or so. Try to stay out of trouble."

Crayle had gotten out of Lenny's car, and he turned to look at him. "Alona."

"Hey, hey, hey!" Lenny chortled. "Short-term mem is off the charts."

With that, the P.I. jammed the gas and sped out of the lot, heading right toward the village of Big Bear Lake. Crayle swore at the dust cloud and entered the store.

Crayle realized this was his first real post-trauma chance to accomplish something without the guidance and shepherding of Phoebe and Lenny. Pressing his case long and hard with them the previous night, he insisted he needed to absorb life without handlers and nursemaids in attendance. Phoebe protested, but finally relented—as long as Lenny stayed nearby.

Crayle walked past a customer standing at an up-front counter who was examining a large hunting knife. As he passed, he registered the customer as a woman—a rather beautiful woman with smooth, butterscotch skin and straight silky black hair down to her waist. Her five-foot-six'ish stature enhanced her loveliness. She was dressed in brown buckskins with matching moccasins on her feet.

She looked up for a moment, and their eyes met. For a couple of stop-motion seconds, neither could disengage. The encounter ended as quickly as it started. Crayle continued down a row of dry good shelves to a wall of coolers at the back of the store. Lenny's list told him they needed some milk and beer—his two basic food groups—and where they could be found.

Before Crayle could open the cooler door for the milk, a man burst out from behind a beef jerky display without warning. The man, shorter than Crayle by a few inches, had a strong, stocky build. Crayle reacted without thought. He blocked a knife thrust and knocked the man backwards. The back of his head hit the freezer door handle just below the skull. In just three seconds, the incident ended with the man dead on the floor.

In the wake of what had just happened, Crayle did not appear to be shaken. His mouth was closed and his breathing was rapid, but controlled. He was more than a mathematician—he knew that much.

Now, he needed to tell someone—he needed to alert Lenny. He flipped open his cell, but it showed no signal. He started toward the storefront, but stopped short. Another man stood at the front end of the aisle, aiming a silenced pistol right at him. Before he could shoot, the girl who had been looking at knives, darted behind him.

She jumped to her tiptoes and plunged the ten-inch knife hard into the back of the man's neck, missing the spinal column and thrusting through his esophagus and windpipe. In an uncontrolled reaction, Crayle's would-be attacker dropped his gun and grabbed for his throat, impaling his hands as he did so. He collapsed to the floor, writhing in pain, gasping for a next breath.

Crayle witnessed everything. The only words he could muster were, "My God!"

He collected himself in the next instant, and ran full speed down the aisle toward the woman. Looking past her through the large front window, he saw two men jump out of a sleek black sedan. Weapons drawn, they dashed for the store.

Crayle, by instinct, grabbed her by the hand, yanked her behind him, and ran back down the aisle toward the back.

The two men outside fired at them through the large front window, shattering it into at least a thousand pieces, but missing their targets. Crayle and the woman raced out the back door.

By the time the two men had made it through the store, jumping over their fallen comrades without so much as a look, Crayle and the woman were gone.

• • •

The sleek black car contained five men as it sped away from the Tack Store after the assassination-attempt gone way wrong. The driver was a pro and had never left the car. The two backup assassins sat in back with the two bodies. The knife was still embedded in the one body and, even to the untrained eye, one could see the bloody finger imprint of the woman, who had so deftly wielded it and then run off with the target. These men had resources, and those resources could put a name and location to the woman, which could lead them back to the target. They would not miss a second time. Their employer had a three-strikes rule. Three strikes and you're dead.

• • •

The woman urged Crayle across the small back parking lot to the only car there. Both jumped into her blood orange Bronco and fled the scene. They heard law enforcement sirens, but Crayle knew he could not explain and did not want the woman, who had saved his life, to have to deal with them.

She drove east as fast as possible without attracting unwanted attention. "What just happened?" the woman shouted above the wind noise.

"You saved my life," Crayle responded.

"No. Why did two men come into the Tack Store and try to murder you?"

"Murder? Maybe they wanted to rob the place."

"With a silenced automatic? I watch TV—that's an assassination tool." The woman swerved around a slower car.

"I don't know … I have no way of knowing." Crayle shook his head.

She swerved around another car, being sure to signal the lane changes.

"How did you react that way? How did you know how to … to kill him?" he asked.

The woman glanced at him. "I run a ranch. I make instant life or death decisions with the animals. And you. You killed the other one. With no weapon."

She reached over and placed her hand on his arm. Each felt the chemistry.

"Look. I am taking you to my home. It's a ranch not far from here. Here is what you must do. My dad is at home, and you must not say anything about this. He is upset enough about the life of the ambient people, as he calls you. I will make something up—you were interested in quarter horses or something like that. Just follow along. And one other thing, if it appears he does not like you, it is a good thing. Okay?"

Crayle just shook his head. 'Is this what happens to mathematicians?' played the enigma of it all in his head.

They turned onto a long drive, parking just outside the ranch house door. The woman led him up to it, paused just outside, and looked directly into his eyes.

"Remember."

Crayle nodded.

CHAPTER 16

Hekka Poppi was beautiful by any standard. Her perfect high cheekbones and flawless butterscotch skin caused men to stare wherever she went. The Native American side of her heritage provided her not only the beauty, but also the athleticism, determination, and strength her heritage demanded.

But rather than be bounded by the confines of a reservation, she and her aging father lived and worked a small 120-acre ranch at the east end of Big Bear Valley. As their ancestors had done, they raised quarter horses, some of the best in the region.

But her usual straightforward and predictable regimen on the ranch had, in an instant, been turned upside down. Thrown together with this man, she had brought him with her to her only refuge, her home. Yet, he was a total stranger—a not-one-of-us stranger. That, and the violence at the Tack Store, unsettled her, to say the least.

When she brought him inside the home, she introduced her father, who sat in a rocking chair and whittled on a piece of wood. She guided Crayle to a couch made of rough-hewn timber with cushions of Serrano coloring and pattern.

Since her father said nothing—his normal response to strangers—she began to speak to Crayle. Her voice was soft so as not to disturb her father.

"Our ranch house is rather large for just the two of us. Since my mother passed away five years ago and my two older brothers packed away to war, I and my father keep things going here on the ranch. Wrangling horses is not supposed to be a woman's work, but these are modern times."

Hekka looked to her father, who glowered his disapproval of modern times. That, and the fact his sons had chosen duty to the country of the white people before duty to family and their tribe. She decided silence was called for, and she fell silent.

The trio sat for what seemed to Crayle like an eternity. He looked around at the colorful hand-woven blankets adorning the wall. He wondered if Hekka's mother had made them.

There were no words, no physical expression until Hekka thought of an ice breaker. She knew her father to be quite proud. She asked him to give Crayle a bit of history of their tribe and what had led them to where they were today.

Reluctantly, her father complied. He spoke, his voice deep and smoky. She translated.

"Our tribe, the Serrano, has a recorded history in this place for over 2500 years. In earlier times, the tribe would Winter to the north in the valley of the antelope. And in the Spring, they would travel to the south up the steep slopes to the valley of the big bear. In those days, there were plenty of bear coming out of hibernation to provide for my people. We thanked their spirits for giving us life."

"Where are all of the people of your tribe now?" Crayle wanted to know, his current mental state turning him into a knowledge sponge. When he realized that interrupting an elder was not acceptable in their culture, he apologized and bade Hekka's father continue.

"When the settlers to the south heard that gold had been discovered in the Holcomb Valley just over the hills on the north side of the lake ..." Her father made direct eye contact now. "... the white men came up here in numbers. In the process of developing their mines and taking their precious gold from the ground, they drove away all of the bear that they did not slaughter."

Crayle wanted to ask questions to add to his meager memory base, but he could sense the feelings starting to well up. It was clear Hekka's father needed to complete his story first.

"Our people were pushed aside. Our entire lifestyle changed forever. Our only revenge had not been the taking of many lives as our sacred spirits would have demanded. Instead, it has become the taking of many wallets at our casinos."

Though the old man showed little outward emotion, it was clear to Crayle that the current plight of the Serrano was embedded in the hearts of its people as a sadness.

And then her father turned to Hekka, saying, "Taqt, taamit, nuht, muat. Taqt, nuht, pat." With that, he excused himself and left the room. He walked down a hall and turned into what Crayle suspected was a bedroom.

Crayle felt nonplussed. "What was that last part about? I didn't understand what he said."

"Ah, yes. You would not understand the words of Takic that he spoke. It is rare today that anyone speaks our ancient language. The last speaker that outsiders knew about died in the 1990's."

"But your father speaks—"

Hekka lifted her hand to stop Crayle. "Only here … only with me."

"What did he say?"

"Man, sun, woman, moon," she answered.

"But I counted seven words."

She drew a breath, then exhaled.

"The last were 'man, woman, … water.' He says things like that. I do not understand their meaning sometimes."

Crayle nodded an understanding he knew he did not possess.

"It's alright," she said. Their eyes then came together as if pulled to each other by an unstoppable force. Then she spoke again, softly, "Give me one second."

Hekka left the room and checked on her dad. He had decided to go to bed early this night instead of his usual 9 p.m. He was in his room, and the light was out. She closed his door.

She came back into the living room, whispering to Crayle, "Come with me. I have something I want to show you."

• • •

She took Crayle by the hand and led him out the back door. Across the yard he saw a man-made waterfall—its sound the only sound.

He looked up to a sky devoid of clouds. It had gotten dark and, with little ambient light, the crisp, clean air posed no impediment to a clear view of the heavens. His mouth dropped open at the awesome sight.

"A panorama of a thousand stars on a pitch black canvas under the luminescence of a wolf moon," were her words, softly spoken.

"A wolf moon?"

"A sliver of a moon casting just enough light for the wolf to hunt, but not enough for his prey to be aware," she explained.

"This is a beautiful place," he said, still gazing heavenward.

"I was born on this ranch," she said.

"Someday I may have memories from before—of beauty like this," he said. "But, if I don't, then tonight will begin the beautiful memories I will have."

She looked up at him—his head was still tilted skyward—and she sensed that he was a good man.

He turned away from her to scan the rest of the sky, listening as she made her way to the waterfall. When he heard a splash, he looked around, but could barely see her shape at the base of the fall. She was right. The wolf moon only provided an inkling of what was there.

He walked toward her. It was only when he was at the edge of the waterfall's pond, perhaps fifteen feet, that he stepped on something. He stopped and reached down. When he straightened, he held her buckskins. He looked again, now able to see that the wolf moon hinted at her feminine curves. And it added gentle highlights to her figure. An iridescent hue from the splash of the water on the rocks made it all seem natural, yet surreal.

Crayle removed his pullover shirt, never taking his eyes from her.

She turned her head, peering back at him over her water-speckled shoulder.

He searched for an expression, but there was none.

He waited for a word, but there was none.

He stepped into the pond and walked toward her. The water slowed his steps as he approached, wicking up his pantlegs. The icy coldness stimulated him inside.

She stepped closer to the fall. With her back still to him, she bent over and placed her hands on one of the flat stones of the fall. It had been put there by her father about three feet off the water basin's surface. It splashed enough water to provide a soothing sound.

Crayle moved up behind her. He reached out and touched the curves of her hips. Her flesh was smooth and soft, and the warmth he felt inside made notable contrast with the crispness of the evening. Then, the sound of an owl in the distance.

His pants dropped to the water. He pulled their bodies together and, as he did, her eyes closed and she let out a wisp of air. He began to move with her to a slow sexual rhythm. He could hear her breathing as though he had shut out all other sounds. She dropped her head so that her long black hair touched the stone and made a luminescence as it carved the waterflow into glistening streams.

He slid both hands around and down her belly. His finger movements were precise and, by her response, were doing all the right things. Both knew he had done this before. A few seconds later, she moaned and threw back her head. The ice cold water droplets hit his flesh like a hundred frozen needles.

They both experienced the special moment. They did not move apart right away, but rather savored the deep sensual dénouement.

• • •

The night-vision binoculars, held in normally rock steady hands, began to shake. The green-tinted view of the intense, passionate intercourse had an unintended and undesired effect.

Phoebe threw them down hard on the car seat next to her. The man she thought might be different was giving the same intense, not-found-in-this-world pleasures to this—this Indian bitch. She spat out her feelings between clenched teeth.

She wanted to cry. Her face screwed up with the extreme emotional pain.

Furious, she slammed her hands again onto the top of the steering wheel. Her pulse raced. Her heart pounded. Her head bobbed up and down in the fury of it all.

She was the woman scorned on steroids. Her right hand went to her gun, the cold steel always ready to console her.

"No!" she cried. "Fuck!" she screamed into the windshield.

She had awakened to find both Lenny and Crayle missing. She was forced to activate tracking via the Vestige chip embedded in one of Crayle's shoulder wounds. Being too small to hold all tracking data, it stored location information to surrounding metal structures as vestiges of where he had been. She used it to follow him to the Tack Store, and then here. A mistake.

After a few minutes, her rage began to subside. First, her pursed lips began to unfurl. She unclenched her jaw.

She slowed her breathing and regained her composure. She picked up the binoculars from the seat. And she looked again.

Still they went on, like animals in slow motion, every thrusting moment pleasuring the girl and driving poor Phoebe stark raving mad.

Phoebe closed her eyes. She counted her heartbeats to ten. Then, she opened a dialog with herself.

"I am a professional," she told herself. Then a pause, "I will protect him with my life."

At that point, her tears could not be restrained. She sobbed for several minutes before her emotions began to subside and her heat began to cool. Her father had taught her not to cry—he would be upset with her. With her thumbs, she brushed the tears from her eyes. Sitting up straight, she brought up the binoculars.

One more look, but they were gone. As she panned from the waterfall to the rear of the ranch house, all she could see was the closing screen door.

The impulse to go in and finish the bastard came next. She shattered the dome light with the binoculars. Exiting the car in the scant moonlight, she stepped with care down a cut-across path to the back door. Her Glock was in her hands now. She reached for the door. It would be over soon.

No. What was her mind doing to her? She had to leave. She needed to get away before she did the unthinkable.

Phoebe re-holstered her weapon and retraced the path to the car. She spun it around and headed back toward Fawnskin. More away from here than towards there. Her once resolute and focused mind was now divided neatly into two opposing camps.

"God help me," she wailed. "God fucking help me!"

• • •

After Crayle and Hekka finished at the waterfall, they moved the party inside. She admonished him to be quiet. She did not want to wake up her father, especially under the current circumstance. She led him to her room and shut the door, quietly but secure.

"Here, let me pull up this Indian blanket to cover us."

They continued on for another full round of sex, Hekka reminding him at sporadic intervals to keep quiet.

"What happens if he wakes up and finds us making love?" Crayle wanted to know.

"It will not go well," was her terse answer.

"I've already lost my memory, I'd hate to loose my scalp," he provided between heavy breaths.

"My father still speaks to me of the value of scalping. For you, he would find something with an old and rusted blade. He would prefer an unhoned edge," she replied in a most convincing serious voice.

Crayle carried on the pretense, "Has this happened before?"

"It is why I must continually seek new boyfriends," she replied somber-voiced.

"And what does he do with all of these scalps?"

"He makes them into Indian blankets," was her answer.

At this point, her stoic demeanor broke down. A quick gush of laughter escaped. She quickly regained control, however, and slid down under the blanket to take him again.

When all was done, Crayle felt like a man found. He wondered if there had been times like this—a woman like this—before. If there had been, what had become of her? Was she somewhere waiting for some word of him? Was she now alone and devastated with the knowledge that he was somehow gone from her? Or was it the worst possible situation—one he could not stand to even imagine, but he did imagine. Had a former lover and soul mate died in the wreckage of a crash he may have caused? He did not know, and he wondered if he ever would.

He snapped back to the present. What had happened with Hekka had been incredible, but he knew she was right. It would not go well if her father woke up to find him there. He told her his concern.

"Yes. You are right. It would be good for you to leave now. Please, I will take you to your home."

They dressed and quietly made their way outside. She slid something into her purse.

Hekka drove him back to the cabin in her Bronco. He leaned back and looked at the stars as he felt the Autumn breeze's splashing chill on his face. He resisted the questions that swarmed into his mind.

Had her father actually seen a vision of what had happened at the waterfall? Was the 'man, woman, water' a portent of the most incredible pleasure they had experienced there? Or was it something else? His only conclusion was that these people were an enigma that mere knowledge could not explain.

The Bronco arrived at the Fawnskin cabin thirty minutes later. Hekka turned to see him staring at her. She reached into her purse and withdrew a leather bracelet. It had three narrow ribbons of leather, woven from end to end. On each brown strip, several flying birds were embossed in white. She fastened it around his wrist.

"It is old—from the 1800's. It is a Serrano amulet. It will protect you until we are together again." She kissed him goodbye. Crayle had trouble reading the look she gave him before she drove away. It implied she knew him better than he knew himself. The memory of her, he knew, even if he never saw her again, was indelible.

As he walked to the cabin, he did not notice the glint of the wolf moon off the binoculars inside the big house's upstairs window. Phoebe's window.

And neither he nor Hekka had noticed the sleek black sedan that had followed them. Like Phoebe, they had access to artifacts from the Vestige chip she had activated. They had been held up near the Tack Store, waiting for the sheriffs to leave. The car and its crew parked several hundred feet down the road from the cabin, and the three men inside observed the whole scene. One of them was on the phone. He gave a situation report, the man on the other end not at all happy with what he was hearing.

CHAPTER 17

It was a new day in Hong Kong, and Chin had it booked solid. He had given Green daughter orders to schedule Li for the next evening. It gave the General time to ponder their first dialog, and it gave Chin time for a strategic trip to Taiwan on his private jet. This particular jet was exactly the same model as was that of Jack Sommers, but Chin's had been a treasured gift from someone quite special in his life. He had personally designed the interior in the red, gold, and black themes so prevalent in Chinese opulence, although the inclusion of solid gold *objets d'art* slowed the plane.

As the jet soared through its northeast trajectory, Chin smiled at the relationship between the People's Republic and Taiwan.

The island of some 14,000 square miles had been independent for thousands of years. Only after first Emperor Ch'in had added Tibet, Mongolia, Manchuria, and Xinjiang did Taiwan come within reach of the new empire known as China. But China had gained this strategically and tactically important island only to be lose it to Japan in a war 200 years later. Many heads had rolled as a consequence.

That needed to change. Chin's grand plan would re-unite China to its former self. Today, he travelled to Taiwan to secure the underpinnings of his plan. Those underpinnings would make financing available to the necessary resources worldwide.

Given the distance of only 503 miles between Hong Kong and the capital city of Taiwan, Chin arrived mid-day in Taipei's international airport. He and his small entourage were quickly approved through customs. They climbed into a black Mercedes limousine which transported him and his daughters along the coastal road to his destination 221 miles to the south.

His daughters loved this picturesque road and the luxuriousness of the limousine. That, beside death as the only alternative, was one of the many reasons they would stay with him. He loved to watch them drink of the plentiful alcohol and misbehave. His own youth should have been so frivolous.

Chin kept a downtown penthouse in the west coast port city of Kaohsiung. Security at the residence was first-rate. The floor-to-ceiling windows could be covered in a few seconds with bulletproof metal shades. Without them deployed, the same windows provided a panorama of the myriad city lights and the well-protected natural harbor.

Chin had been here many times since making his fortune on the Chinese stock market, and he knew the town quite well. Kaohsiung was by day a busy harbor city facing west across the straits toward the People's Republic. By night, it was a hotbed of dark secrets and intrigue. The sailor-town bright lights and cacophonic sounds elevated that part of the city to fever pitch, while international plots and schemes hatched and developed in dark rooms. Huge sums of money, in its many and varied incarnations, changed hands.

• • •

Chin reached Kaohsiung as the sun set. His scheduled meeting with gem dealer Xiang was productive. He had seen the skinny, five-foot-five-inch man several times before, but he still started each time he looked into the man's one black eye and one blue eye. And Chin was unnerved that Xiang had a habit of turning his head to one side or the other while speaking or listening. It was an annoyance, but one Chin could tolerate—as long as Xiang performed his duties in a satisfactory manner.

The cultural pleasantries completed, Xiang handed Chin a sealed mailing tube of metal-lined heavy cardboard. He had received the tube on Chin's behalf from a courier named Desrochers. The outside label identified its contents as machine parts. Chin withdrew a special device from his pocket and opened the x-ray proof tube. He poured hundreds of perfect white diamonds onto a black velvet examination cloth, insisting that Xiang have them examined and verified. He would not leave without proof positive.

Although a certified GIA Master Examiner of both colored and white stones, Xiang had brought along a GIA-certified examiner. The examiner would also verify the quality of the stones. Soon after, he would become the apparent victim of a fatal accident. Xiang would, of course, perform the task, which he viewed as an act of professional honor whenever he dealt with Chin.

There were, at final accounting, 300 perfect stones weighing just over one carat each. The perfect unit of currency in the global underworld, Xiang could easily fence them for Chin and receive market pricing rather than the usual deeply discounted valuations from other tangibles. Xiang could also choose the currency denomination and target financial institution for the proceeds. Chin would never be required to take physical possession of the diamonds or the money.

"They are worth a little more than twelve million U.S. dollars through my contacts," Xiang said after interacting on his private, encrypted network.

"How much is the little more?" asked Chin.

"Two hundred forty thousand US," replied Xiang, who kept all manner of possible numbers in his head for instant retrieval upon request.

"Then you may keep the little more," Chin returned. "It should help you to recoup some of your expenses. It is a small number for what lies ahead."

Xiang's razor sharp mind calculated the return. He wanted to tell Chin that a 2% fee constituted an insult, considering Xiang's worldwide network of unsavory yet reliable precious gem functionaries, mules, and bankers. However, discretion remained the better part of valor. Such a confrontational statement would have led to grievous consequences for himself. He smiled, bowed deeply to Chin, and wrote it off to bigger paydays ahead.

It was of no small matter to Xiang that working at Chin's bidding brought not only monetary reward, but also significant perks. His heart would almost stop every time Chin arrived with his gaggle of fine mainland Chinese women—his daughters, as he called them. Adept in all of the services a rich and powerful man like Chin would require, they excelled to the extreme in what Xiang considered one of the lost sexual arts. He knew Chin would see that he, Xiang, was treated once again to such pleasures still unknown or at least forbidden in most parts of the world. He could only imagine the pleasures Chin himself received. He knew Chin would never marry.

When Chin had departed, only one daughter remained—Green. She gave Xiang a sampling of extreme pleasure as many times as he could stand. When she left in the early morning, he was both exhausted and committed. He vowed to stay on Chin's good side.

CHAPTER 18

The man had been sent to Chin three years ago as a consultant from the West. The consultant proved to be an extraordinary, insightful, even brilliant man. He had mastered a formal construct called *Systems Methodology*, and he used it to render the most complex of problems into viable strategic solutions.

The consultant had examined a brief history of China, its current makeup, and its environment on the plane. This environment included all that was not the System of Study, as he had defined China. Chin had been amazed. It was well known all Americans viewed the world outside their borders only from an American perspective. Yet, the consultant, Magus Crayle, had stepped outside the standard American view. He provided Chin with a letter-perfect, infallible strategy, which detailed the need for new leadership and concluded that Chin was the one to do the leading.

Once the strategy had been completed to the minutest detail, an attempt had been made to erase the consultant's knowledge by erasing the consultant. Although a confirming lifeless body would have been preferred, the Frenchman had assured Chin that Mr. Crayle had died in a horrific automobile crash. The explicit photographs from the scene had satisfied Chin.

But then he had received information that Magus Crayle had survived, but suffered from severe memory loss. Chin could not afford the remotest possibility that Crayle could recover, or be caused to recover, his former assignment or its outcome. Or the players involved. He must dispatch his own people to find the man and eliminate him—this time with proof positive.

It would have been difficult to track down the man in America and remove him permanently from the playing field. Mr. Crayle had been good company, and Chin would find a way to enjoy his company again before placing him, once and for all, into the hands of Eternity.

But first, Chin had scheduled a second meeting with General Li. He would set the hook deeper and reel in the military man. Things were falling nicely into place. Destiny would provide him his due. And the people of China theirs.

• • •

When Chin next met with General Li, three days had passed since their seminal meeting. Chin's aide had contacted Li and reported back not only that Li had agreed to meet again, but was looking forward to the meeting.

They convened again at the Dragon Building. The myriad high-definition surveillance cameras installed throughout the mansion recorded Li's every move. Chin took particular pleasure in viewing Li's reaction to the number of beautiful assistants in his employ. It was clear that Li, just like the Taiwanese Xiang, had other needs. Chin could see to those needs if the situation called for it. It did not hurt to hold cards the other players coveted.

Chin and Li went through the usual motions of greetings and repartee before they sat down. Chin offered and Li accepted a different, but likewise excellent, single-malt Scotch to help them both rinse the challenges of the day away and to open up their minds to the possibilities of China's new future. And to enable the fulfillment they both so sincerely desired.

"A peaceful world is something all noble men should perceive as the end game, Li," Chin began as his gaze wandered up to the beautiful ceiling. As if by mental command, the ceiling disappeared to reveal a crystal-clear sky and the brilliance of a thousand stars. "Peace is a noble goal, perhaps the most noble," continued Chin. "But, my dear General Li, balance is a rational goal."

"What part can a humble general play when the force I am trained and able to deploy can only create peace at the *expense* of balance?" replied Li.

"It is not possible for two goals to have one master, General."

"Ah. So you have selected me to be your co-master in this grand plan. Please, go on, Chin."

"I have carefully selected you for your qualities as a general, as a man, and as an honorable citizen of China," Chin responded without showing he did not intend to have Li or anyone else as *co* anything. "We are at a grand beginning, General," he observed. "As such, you can understand that, for me to continue with substantive, detailed information, I must be assured that you are willing to help build a grand country—a Grand Imperial China."

Li wanted to applaud. Instead, he maintained his demeanor, which prohibited him from jumping up and dancing around the room. He merely nodded without expression as someone of his high place was wont to do.

"To the prospect of a Grand Imperial China," the General toasted as he quaffed the remainder of the fine Scotch.

There was a ringing sound. Chin reached into his pocket and withdrew an object in the red and yellow livery of Chinese communism. He spoke briefly and flipped the phone shut.

"Ah, Li, I understand you have a personal computer specialist whom you trust explicitly. Something has arrived from a foreign land that I have every hope will hasten any and all plans we have for our beloved country. It is a very special electronic device with capabilities beyond anything either you or I could ever countenance."

"My expert is quite busy keeping prying eyes from my most secret files, Chin."

It seemed Li was setting his own bait.

"Yes, of course, but I do not exaggerate. This is a critical tool. Could you please evaluate it for me—for us?"

"Of course, Chin."

Chin withdrew a brown paper package from a drawer and handed it to Li. He also handed him what appeared to be a manual.

"This document explains the software application and its use."

"I will have him examine it, Chin. And since the time is late, I must, by your leave, depart." Li felt in a stronger position now and was the first to suggest they conclude the meeting.

"We will continue, then, in the near future, Li?" Chin asked.

"Very soon," was Li's reply.

Chin stood in agreement that tonight's meeting was complete. Next time, Chin would provide strategic details for Li's first assignment. Once the Frenchman said everything was a go, he would meet with Li as his committed associate. Then, the biggest game of Chin's life would be underway.

Chin watched Gold daughter escort Li out and then reviewed the security video. Li did appreciate the ladies. Li's lust for conquest would make the General the long term player Chin needed. He remained unsure about the Frenchman, who just might have to become expendable after fulfilling his part.

• • •

Before leaving the previous night, Li had asked Gold daughter to confirm the subsequent meeting with Chin for the next evening. Apparently, the good General thirsted for more. He wondered whether Li recognized the potential that Chin so easily saw. Perhaps it was time to give the General a little taste, so to speak, of the perks. Perhaps Green or Red or Gold. But not Black.

"Ah, General. It is good to see you once again. I trust your other endeavors have been beneficial to you. Please have a seat. We shall resume."

"Yes, Chin, I have been busy elsewhere, but I am happy that we can meet once again," said the General with less enthusiasm than at their last meeting.

"And did your new electronic toy perform as you expected?" Chin referred to the computer he had given to the General.

"It was in good working order and has been examined. The software seems to be at an experimental stage. I am seeking an appropriate opportunity to try out its mind-processing capabilities. I will report results when I have them."

Li was protective of this new item. Chin was a little more than intrigued. But, he let the issue drop—for now.

"Good. We will have our drink and, by your leave, I will add delicious detail to what have been generalities. We can agree that the Ch'in Dynasty began a process of defining our country's greatness. And we can also agree that acts of stupidity and acts of corruption have caused us to sustain huge losses, both of land and of face. I propose that we embark on a path to restore the integrity of China's lands and, at the same time, position her at the forefront of not only local, but international respect. I am proposing that we take her to the very top of the international order, and we shall do so without firing a shot."

"What you describe, Chin, sounds like a very serious, even well thought out dream. It has been my dream as well, but, in the end, only a dream. What is the substance? There must be substance."

The first round of drinks had arrived. The twenty-nine-year-old Inchmurrin Scotch smelled of marshmallow and apple. Tasting of fern and hazelnut, it was a drink of medium body that freshened the senses and opened the mind.

"Did you know, General, that the north of Vietnam was once a protected and administered territory of China? And did you know that the internal conflicts and animosities of the T'ang Dynasty caused us to lose that territory in the Tenth Century? We must not allow internal strife and bickering to cause us such heavy losses. What I propose will bring all Chinese together once again. It will end the frequent protests *and* it will supplant the tenuous hold of the Beijing regime."

"You are proposing a government change, Chin? You are proposing a government like that of the United States where officials are freely elected by the people? That is preposterous. It would never work." Li looked as if he had just lost all respect for Chin and was ready to depart the presence of this crazy man.

"Relax, General," said Chin with a wry smile. "I believe that our Communist friends in Beijing have begun a government that will provide a much better base for the new China than one mirroring the failures of governance that we see today in the West."

Li settled more comfortably in his chair, but took a long pull on the Scotch just the same.

Chin continued, "The Constitution of the United States has described, brilliantly, I might add, an idyllic yet unachievable state wherein the people choose their governance. Should the government not fulfill its promise and fail to solve problems that arise, the people can choose new leaders to replace the old. On the surface, democracy sounds good. But, the reality, after all these years, is that America suffers from walking the path too long.

"The Constitution provided the path to governance, but as the politicians tread the path over and over, it has become a deep rut from which they cannot escape. With but two parties, the citizenry can only replace bad politicians with other bad politicians. Professional politicians, in case you did not know, have only two masters: a lust for power and a greed for wealth. Notice that I did not mention *the people* in that statement. The people of America have been relegated to the role of keeping the two parties in power and of providing a huge pot of money for them to divide."

"But Chin, how does this apply to China if, as you said before, you do not plan such a system for our country?"

"My dear General, I have observed America, the greatest superpower the world has ever known, and I have observed China, the country with the most potential. We have the resources in our 1.3 billion populace. We have the will. All we lack is a master plan and the correct leadership."

"With all respect, Chin, we have a government that realizes what it must do. The Central Committee knows it needs to uphold its principles against America's attempts to subvert, penetrate, interfere in, and undermine our Communist foundation. What more can they do?"

"My answer to your question is that they are doing all they can do. But is it enough? As you know, the Central Committee engages in an incestuous relationship whereby it elects the top leaders of our country who, in turn, appoint the members of the Central Committee. We can see how well that has worked out, can we not?

"General, my plan does not call for the toppling of this government and its admittedly cumbersome structure. It calls for a select group of true Chinese leaders and patriots to bring about a monumental success for China. Such a success will facilitate an indestructible and self-sustaining process. That process *must* and *will* endure for the next several hundred years. It is a process that will move China to the pinnacle of world leadership. Do you not see? Everyone will view the successes of China's version of Communism and will want to make it theirs. We will show by example, not by force. We will win." Chin finished triumphantly with an enthusiasm that Li could see came from his heart.

General Li released an audible sigh. How many times had he dreamed of collaborating with someone of Chin's stature? How many times had he hoped for a leader to emerge who possessed a vision beyond party rhetoric? He certainly could not count them. He finally nodded several times. "Chin, you have my support. I still want to hear the details for I am a detail man. Let's hope that we can light this fire without getting burned to a cinder ourselves."

"When next we meet, General, I will give you the particulars you need to begin operations. I know you will discern the meat through the fluff. Further, I am completely confident you will give 100% and become a key factor in our collective success—as individuals and as a nation."

General Li stood, but Chin stayed his departure. "General, I know this has been an extremely heady conversation. And I know that your days are typically quite full and challenging. I would like you to stay a little longer and allow my aides to bathe you in my gold Jacuzzi. I believe you will find the experience both exhilarating and fulfilling."

"I would be honored by your generosity, Chin," replied Li.

Three of Chin's finest available daughters—Green, Red, and Gold—escorted Li to the Golden Chamber elegantly decorated with symbols of China's past. As the girls undressed him and guided him into the frothing tub made of solid gold, he could not help but notice the three Chinese ideograms embossed on the wall: Peace—Harmony—Balance. Perhaps these beautiful and talented young women would help him to experience them all. They did that and more. Much more.

• • •

As Chin reflected on this meeting, he knew it had gone well. It was time to give Li some tasks to accomplish. He could let no one get in his way, and he needed to coordinate with the Frenchman or his grandiose plan would fail. And, in that case, he would not become the next emperor of China.

CHAPTER 19

The day that followed the Tack Store close-call passed without further violence. Phoebe called the P.I. to inform him she would spend the day in the big house, unless she was needed. Crayle rested every few hours. He spent the remainder of the day working with Lenny. They made little progress on finding the past. Lenny discovered reports of the Tack Store "robbery gone bad," but there was no mention of the silenced weapon and the hit team stationed outside. Absent answers, Crayle went to bed early and slept well into the next morning.

At ten o'clock, he opened his eyes to the new day and to Lenny. Again. The P.I. was more like a torture therapist than a resource. Still, he had to make every session with the P.I. work. The process of filling in the blanks improved his sense of accomplishment. And it provided a steady, increasing momentum—as in the snowball rolling down hill analogy. Regardless, he still felt poised in the middle of something huge without the perspective to see what it was.

The more he thought about it, he felt he'd been cast into some kind of game. One thing he did remember from his past, every game has rules. Oh, yes, and sanctions for breaking those rules. He needed to figure out the rules everyone else already knew. Then, he could be a player, too.

The professional nature of the Tack Store attack made Crayle feel that someone was running a scam on him. Someone he knew. Was it Jack? Was it Rorschach? Someone else? Were Phoebe and Lenny innocent bystanders? Or were they players? The frustration of it all had taken up residence in Crayle. It was eating him alive.

He needed to get into this game, and the only way was through intelligence: *intel* those in the intelligence community called it. He recalled this from the past. He needed the intel Lenny would extract from the Internet—and from elsewhere. The big question: how to determine the elsewhere? He knew on a gut level that he, Magus Crayle, was an expert in finding every last piece of a puzzle. Any puzzle. And this particular one was *his* puzzle.

He sat up with a start.

He realized for the first time since he had regained consciousness that puzzle-solving was what he had done for the government. That was it. And intense, complex government puzzles required complex mathematics and a discipline known as systems theory. He knew this.

To solve his own complex personal puzzle, he required not only the P.I.'s skills, he required his own. Yes. He had in an instant achieved a clarity that had evaded him for the past weeks. He felt more ready than ever. He needed to get Lenny engaged. He needed Lenny engaged at the same level as himself.

Crayle, still clad in black flannel pajamas, bailed out of the waterbed and ran into the living room.

There he found Lenny at the dining table, eyes intent on his laptop screen. He was muttering to himself in incomprehensible terms as he pressed keys in rapid succession and visually scoured the screen. He was his usual unusual self. It was good to be a little unpredictable, but Lenny made it look like a neurosis.

"Where's the FBI agent, Lenny?" he asked, his senses perked in anticipation of a sight or a sound.

"Man, she was upset about something. I've never seen anyone wound so tight. It's like she just can't wait the full twenty-eight days to be a grouch. She grabbed the rest of her stuff and schlepped it over to the big house."

"Did she say anything?"

"Not a word." Then, he reconsidered. "Oh, she bitched something about the Tack Store. And she said 'fuck' a lot. I suppose she could have been more in the loop on the little groceries trip."

"You mean the one that almost cost me my life?" Crayle's anger spiked as Lenny's screwup came into sharp mental focus.

"Yeah, and something about hating Native fucking Americans."

Crayle did not know how to parse that comment. He let it go as another indecipherable Lenny-ism.

Of course, neither of them could see Agent Bransfield from where they were. If they could, they would have seen her sitting on a couch with a pillow clutched to her torso, shaking, and staring out one of the big house windows at the lake. And they would have seen the tears. And they would have heard the sobs.

As Crayle had been scoring an epiphany, Phoebe had donned sweats and stomped off toward Fawnskin. He could not know that she would buy fifty rounds of .45 caliber +P rounds for her weapon. He could not know that her anger had her buying the overpowered, super lethal bullets that could terminate his quest by ending his life. He could not know the depth of her hurt.

But the boys were not in sensitivity mode—they were in research mode. Lenny took the lead as he pecked at his computer's keys.

"There are some basic bits of self-knowledge you need to have, MC. Do you remember stuff like your schools, childhood chums, team sports you played … any place or anyone I can track down and ask about you? How about parents or hometown?"

"Nothing," replied Crayle, in an instant descending into a funk.

"Well, here's some good news then. I checked out no fewer than eight alumni websites, and I have results you're going to just love. Wanna hear?"

"Tell me, please," Crayle beseeched.

"You're name is unique, so I did not get a ton of multiple hits. You were a Wolverine, MC. You went to the University of Michigan in Ann Arbor. Not only that, you majored in Mathematics, which explains the funky, retro slide rule in your shit box." He motioned to the shipping box, a piece of security tape removed, sitting on a credenza. "And your attendance dates set your current age at around forty-seven, assuming you weren't some kind of prodigy or took a sabbatical."

Crayle consumed the information. Something welled up inside, like he'd broken out of a maximum security prison of his own making.

"Lenny, what the hell is a wolverine?"

"Oh, it's like a big fat hairy rat with rabies on steroids, I think. That's not the technical description. It doesn't matter."

Crayle tried to conjure up a visual, but with no luck.

Lenny continued, "Look, I brought up your senior yearbook. There's your picture. Handsome guy without the scabs and scars. Check out the hair. Is that a pony tail I see?" Lenny tilted his head sideways, as if trying to look around the photo at the back of Crayle's headshot.

"I can't find any participation in sports except you attended physical education classes in Martial Arts. It shows someone presenting you a belt. Maybe to beat the crap out of those tough math problems."

He laughed alone.

"I can't make out the belt color since the photo is black and white. Looks like a shades-of-gray belt, MC." Another laugh.

Crayle was not in the mood.

"How about a girlfriend?"

"You mean your first fuck?" blurted Lenny the romantic, turning the laptop around to face Crayle. "Girlfriend? Check out the 'here's when we looked good' page. The chick on the right seems to be looking at you, but I really think she's looking at the chick on the left. Looks like we'll have to wait on the intimate relations portion of your therapy, MC." He turned the laptop back around, flipping the lid shut.

"Is that it—that's all?" Crayle appeared upset at the paucity of information.

"That, my friend, is quite a lot," Lenny said, wanting to set the expectations bar low. "And how much would you pay for all that? Nineteen-ninety-five?"

He flipped the lid back open. The screen returned.

Then Lenny started. Something had popped up on his screen that woke him up.

"But, wait! I think I actually have something of extreme substance here," Lenny said, checking a virtual private network email marked 'Urgent.'

"Talk to me," Crayle said.

"I got a friend I call the Mad Geek, for obvious reasons."

"So, what does this friend who can't get close to girls, dresses eclectically, and can't carry on a conversation about anything but computers have for me?"

The P.I. tilted his head, giving Crayle a raised eyebrow as if he had violated Lenny's comedic union job description.

"Remember my bud, Micmac? At the 'loafer?"

Crayle nodded.

"He *can* get close to girls, MC. Anyways, he knows a chick who works in the old archaic mainframe world."

"So what?"

"Aw, maybe you don't really want to know what I got," Lenny teased.

"You might want to cut the crap and live to see the sun go down."

Crayle was in a no-nonsense mode—his tone of voice left no doubt. He fondled a butcher knife that had been lying on the table.

"Yeah, well, the sunset, yeah, that would be good," Lenny said nervously.

Had Crayle been able to read the P.I.'s mind, he would have seen that the more intel Lenny picked up on the so-called *subject,* the more concerned he became about his own well-being. Mathematician, indeed. Crayle didn't even know where he had been—what he had done. And Lenny still was not sure of Crayle's temperament. Would he snap over nothing and fly into a deadly rage? What if he touched a nerve in Crayle's past that suddenly imploded? Meltdown time. He wished to hell Phoebe was there.

"The chick pulled up an operation you did in China a couple of years ago. She uses the word *operation* rather than the word *work.* That's significant."

"Why is that a big deal, Lenny?" Crayle had lost parts of his personal dictionary. He wanted—no, needed—them back.

"Work is what folks who *work for the government*, the normal government, do. Operations, on the other hand, are what spooks do."

"Cut the Halloween crap, Lipschitz. What do you mean by spooks?"

"In mathematical terms, spook equals spy."

"That's ridiculous. I'm no spy. I'm ..." Crayle lost his pointer. His mind fogged up. The more that time went on, the less he understood. The emotional ups and downs took their toll.

"Look, tell the girl thanks. And ask her—"

"Hey, by the way," Lenny interrupted. "I need to float some righteous grease her way to keep the info flowing—you know what I mean?" said Lenny.

Crayle leaned toward Lenny for emphasis. "Give me the intel, Lenny, or you won't need to worry whether it flows or not. And how does she know about China?"

"Jesus Christ. Let's keep calm and civil here … oh, and non-violent, okay?" Lenny looked a little shaken, but tried to maintain his SIC, smartass-in-charge, control over the situation. "She knows about China because, *ta-da*, she's Chinese."

Crayle shot him a pursed lips, time-is-running-out glare. Lenny went on.

"But wait! There's more! She has a postscript. Says you spent some time in Hong Kong, buddy boy. You did a gig over there that was classified up the yingyang. She thinks she can drill down, but it's going to take time and it could get risky. She has to be real careful with stuff this sensitive."

"I don't remember Hong Kong at all," Crayle said. He shook his head back and forth, feeling like big chunks of his past had been etch-a-sketched right out of his memory. "Is there any more?"

"Oh, yeah. She did pick up a name. It just could be the name of the op."

"Let's hear it. I doubt that it will ring any bells—all of my bells are silent these days."

He showed Crayle the three Chinese characters.

"*Shui yikuai zuanshi*," Crayle read. "Water Diamonds?"

Lenny's mouth dropped open, but no words emerged.

"Wait," said Crayle. "Why would … are you sure about the name?"

"You … you … you just spoke Chinese."

Crayle's mind was elsewhere. "Why would I be on an op with a Chinese name? And no, I don't speak Chinese and I don't know—or can't remember—anything at all about Hong Kong. It doesn't make sense. Mathematics, martial arts, ops, Hong Kong? Lenny, what does it mean?"

Crayle had picked up a few things about his background, which was nice. But the China connection could well be a new game piece. He needed more, but he needed rest and nourishment.

"Time for a break," Crayle said.

On cue, Lenny said, "You know what, MC? I'm hungry." He stood and headed into the kitchen.

"Yes. And *I'm* thirsty," followed Crayle.

Crayle walked to the bar. Jack kept it fully stocked. He poured each of them a Malibu and coke. Crayle had tried different things since starting his new life in Big Bear, and rum and coke was where he ended up. He wondered what had been *his* drink before. Before the accident.

Lenny had pulled some ham and Swiss sandwiches and potato salad from the refrigerator, tossed it all on two plates, and set them on the bar next to the drinks.

"There," he proclaimed. "All the basic food groups."

He placed forks beside the plates and began to eat.

But, Crayle did not. "I have no idea which hand to eat with," he said as he stared at the setting.

Lenny picked up Crayle's fork and held it out to him. Crayle took it with his right hand.

"There. Right handed. *Ta-da*," he sang. He gave *subject* Magus Crayle a glowing see-how-clever-I-am look.

Crayle—puzzled—transferred the fork to his left hand, and began to eat the potato salad.

"Or not," the P.I. concluded.

When they finished, Lenny tried again for clever.

"You know, my research says you may have been a waiter, so it might help your memory to clean the table and wash the dishes."

Crayle gave him a hard, knowing look.

Lenny did the dishes.

Crayle suddenly recalled a phrase. "Have you heard this, Lenny? 'Those who do not remember the past are doomed to relive it?' I know nearly nothing about my past. It looks like I might have to relive it on purpose. Perhaps survive or die is where my new life is headed."

Lenny did not respond. He was lost in suds and sponges.

Crayle changed the subject. "Why do you work so hard, Lenny? I appreciate it, but you seem to be obsessed with this job. Christian work ethic? How did *that* happen?"

"Look. I'm just the personification of a Christian hard worker stuck with a Jewish dick—the worst of both worlds." Of course, Lenny was 100% Jewish or, at least, born that way. The Christian work ethic had been acquired.

Crayle headed into the bedroom for a nap. He felt quite tired and lacked the energy for today's internal dialog. Just a few words before he dropped off.

"I can't kill him," Crayle whispered. "Not yet."

• • •

Back in the living room, Lenny returned to the computer. There were things he needed to find out. Crayle was an important piece to his own personal puzzle. Crayle would help him to discover those things. Lenny would never tell him. They were that personal.

Finding nothing that helped, Lenny shook his head and curled up on the couch. Tomorrow was another day.

CHAPTER 20

The next day dawned as yet another beautiful day on Big Bear Lake. This beauty was different. Snow had fallen during the night and the light powder had not yet melted. White covered the ground, giving the tall pines a frosted appearance. The visual put to shame the mere postcards tourists bought in the sucker stores.

The *edge* fishermen had been in place for at least a half hour because, at dawn and dusk, the sturdier insects came out to play and the fish surfaced for protein. Of course, all fishermen stayed away from the shores fronting the private cabins. The juxtaposition of land to water seemed to assert that lakefront cabin owners possessed exclusive fishing rights. They didn't.

At the cabin, Crayle and Lenny had come in from a chilly breakfast on the outside deck. They sat down at the computer to work. Lenny searched the Internet for any information about Crayle's past far into the afternoon until *the subject* had finally had enough.

"How about drinks and hors d'oeuvres? I'll fly and Jack'll buy," Crayle offered.

"Deal," Lenny agreed.

Crayle went into the kitchen, made up a plate of crunchies and dip, and conjured a few Malibu and Cokes to help wash down the solid stuff. They had barely seated themselves at the breakfast bar next to the kitchen when they both heard a pop from outside. Something hit the floor-to-ceiling window facing the lake. It sounded like the thud of an errant bird. Then another. And another, the final two striking in quick succession.

They both spun around to see the cause of the noise. In the light of the new day, they made out three men. Each wore dark clothing and had painted his face with black striping. All three were armed with assault weapons pointed right at the two of them.

The redwood picnic table had been turned on its side. One man crouched behind. The second and third used the big pine tree and the wishing well for cover. Crayle and Len caught glimpses of two Zodiac boats pulled up on the lakeshore next to the dock.

Another pop. Another splat hit the window a few inches away.

Lenny reacted first. "The glass is bullet proof! Jack thought of everything!"

He stood and walked toward the window, both hands outstretched at shoulder level as he flipped off the frustrated assassins.

One of the men had switched his weapon to semi-automatic. He fired separate shots now. The first shot hit the window harmlessly. The second shot was down and to the right. Also harmless. Crayle noticed the deliberate pattern and yelled at Lenny to take cover.

The third shot completed the triangle. The outside pane of the dual bulletproof window shattered into tiny pieces before Lenny could move.

Lenny had kept his phone in Phoebe-push-to-talk mode for emergencies like being out of toilet paper. He shouted, "Mayday! Mayday!" as he turned and ran for cover behind the bar, grabbing his computer and Crayle on the way by.

They crouched down, making themselves as small as possible while more splats hit the inside pane. It would shatter any time now, giving the assault team a giant window of opportunity.

Apropos of absolutely nothing, Crayle began to talk as if this were the perfect occasion for the resumption of his self dialog. "We are now under attack from unknown assailants. They are armed with automatic—"

"Jesus Christ! We're under assault by a bunch of heavily armed maniacs, and you're doing play-by-play. Dialog only when alone, okay?"

A heartbeat later, shots rang out from the main house. Two quick booming shots from the Phoebe .45 and two shooters went down—big holes in their foreheads and their brains decorating the landscape in gray and red. The third man turned and emptied a clip in Phoebe's direction.

Crayle and Lenny heard her cry out. Then, no more shots from the main house.

The gunner, well-built physically, ran toward the smashed window, reloading and firing again. Crayle recognized the oversized triangular-shaped jaw on the man. This was the leader he'd spotted at the Tack Store.

He and Lenny remained behind the bar. Bullets whizzed overhead, taking out all of Jack's wall-mounted trophy plates.

Crayle and Lenny heard the screech of car tires on the street side of the cabin. Suddenly, there were slamming sounds from a door crash pole. The barbarians were at all of the gates.

They knew only too well that none of the double bulletproof windows that remained intact, nor the one that was destroyed or the front or rear cabin doors would aid their escape. The passage through the ciphered doorway to the tunnel and garage was now their only way out alive.

The situation left Crayle and Lenny no time to think. They knew Phoebe was probably down hard, and they were outnumbered. Crayle grabbed Lenny by the collar, dragging him along as they traversed the kitchen to the secret passage.

Lenny, out of his element, gasped more than breathed, and the adrenalin approached the red zone. He fumbled with the cipher lock on the thermostat.

Finally, the lock accepted his code input. The two fugitives jumped the stairway. Crayle slammed the door behind. Even as they raced down the tunnel, they heard the assassins crash through the cabin's front door. Shouting in a foreign language followed, as did footsteps on the broken window glass.

Lenny struggled with the garage door cipher lock. "Sorry," he said, repeating it over and over as he fought with the keypad.

The team of assassins had found the locked door behind them and were trying to beat it open.

Lenny achieved compliance from the door. They rushed into the garage. Again, Crayle secured the steel door behind them. He then, much to Lenny's shock, yanked the parachute cover from the Cobra, jammed it against the steel door, and lit it on fire.

Crayle and the P.I. were fast into the Cobra's racing seats. Within thirty seconds, Crayle was tight in his six-point racing harness. It would keep him, the driver, in place against the high G-forces brought about by the hard cornering of a Cobra at full tilt.

The assailants reached the final steel door. Their intended victims heard the banging of metal on metal, and then gunshots, all trying to remove the last physical barrier to accomplishing a most deadly mission.

Crayle's passenger swore. Crayle reached over to help the struggling Lenny connect the race quality shoulder, waist, and emasculation belts.

There.

Now they were in solid.

Now they were good to go.

CHAPTER 21

Lenny grabbed the clicker from the glove box. He hit *open* so hard the button cracked. The large wooden doors slid sideways along the wall as they reached the doorway's edge—a feature Jack had selected for snowy winters.

The open position of the westside garage door blocked the steel door, holding back the attackers. Jack had thought of everything.

"They'll see they can't get us through the door, put it in reverse, and come out the front door in about fifteen seconds!" Crayle yelled, setting expectations for the P.I.

Crayle jammed the 'ON' button on the console. The 351C roared to life. He dropped the clutch on first gear. The Cobra fairly exploded from its stall.

They screamed down the driveway in less than two seconds. Crayle slid the car left onto the two-lane before the attackers could make sense of what was happening. The blast of the big engine's steel sidepipes had them ducking for cover inside the tunnel.

Crayle knew the assassins would be on their tail soon. In the next instant, a black Charger appeared in the rearview about 200 yards back.

"I bet that's the car from the Tack Shop," Crayle guessed. "It's coming on way too fast for a rental. That one's a Hemi."

"You're a fucking mathematician, for Christ's sake! How the hell do you know all this stuff?"

Lenny felt like he'd been played in a major way. If he survived, he intended to have a talk with Jack.

Crayle wigged and wagged through the little town of Fawnskin in fifteen scary seconds. He knew his deadly pursuers would not abide by any traffic laws. And he knew he needed to become a world-class traffic scofflaw if he wanted to survive.

They flew around the west end of the-lake-of-the-big-bear, taking advantage of any stretch of straight road to open the gap. But the straight road only provided a chance for gunfire directed at them. It was the many-curved road—the twisties— that gave them cover.

Each time Crayle came to some twisties, he braked hard going in, his full weight thrown forward against the safety harness. The harness straps cut into his flesh. It hurt, terribly, but the pain ramped him up to an even higher level of intensity. And that was good.

He was sure the short bursts up to 120 miles per hour, the heavy braking, and the rear end of the car sliding precariously out to the left and then right pushed Lenny's heart rate off the charts.

A quick look in Lenny's direction confirmed. His knuckles on the dash ingress-egress bar were as white as the snow. And his face looked close to losing its industrial quality tan.

The snowplows had done their job, but the roads in wet conditions could be slick.

The three black chase cars proved a match on level roads. The nearest one closed on the Cobra.

They reached a point where straight ahead would take them on a treacherous-at-speed road called Rim Of The World to a down-the-mountain stretch and then on to the county seat of San Bernardino.

Lenny shouted, "Turn left!" as if he knew something Crayle didn't.

Crayle obeyed, sliding the Cobra into a lefthand drift that started them over the Big Bear Dam.

The Charger behind them attempted to make the turn. The driver, accelerating to catch the Cobra, braked too late.

At that speed and on the wet pavement, its slide carried it off the pavement and into a high arc over the dam's several hundred foot spillway gorge.

Shocked onlookers heard the car's engine whine to a high pitch as the traction load provided by the roadway disappeared.

The crash at the bottom of the gorge was horrific, the sound and heat of the explosion causing the people to jerk away as if they had been slammed back by the impact themselves.

The second Charger schooled up on the first. It slowed enough to make the turn and continued the chase across the dam.

Crayle realized he was headed east toward the southside of the lake. Toward civilization. Too many people to hurt. He needed to change course.

Midway, Crayle spun the Cobra into cross traffic. There was just enough room. The Charger's driver tried to stop, but broke onto a skid as the Cobra flew past in the opposite direction.

Crayle glanced into the open rear window as the two cars passed. The gunman was looking down, reloading. He glanced up just in time to catch Crayle's eyes. The man with the triangle jaw yelled in frustration.

"*Merde!*"

Crayle reached the end of the dam just as a third Charger, the hitman cleanup crew, approached. No way back to Fawnskin. Crayle cranked the wheel hard left and pointed the Cobra down the hill—to begin a thirty-three mile race on the treacherous road to San Bernardino. The potential for death flooded the air.

The cold mountain air scorched his lungs as he breathed fast and deep. The oncoming vehicles driving between thirty and forty miles per hour produced combined closing speeds nearing 150 miles-per-hour. One wrong move would prove deadly for many.

As Crayle got the feel of the Cobra, he started to forego the braking part.

"I liked it better when you used the brakes!" came Lenny's plaintive cry.

"What does braking do?" Crayle yelled back.

"It's what slows you down!" Lenny screamed.

"We want to go fast, don't we?" came back the rhetorical.

"Yeah, but—"

"No brakes!"

They squiggled back and forth along the rim road, the mountain hillside to their right, a dropoff of several hundred feet on their left. Crayle cut as close as he could to the mountain without molding the Cobra to it.

He prayed no Volkswagen-sized boulders had fallen onto the roadway ahead, not unusual for mountain roads. The drop off to their left looked like a mile down, and sliding that way around the right-hand turns induced turbulence in the P.I.'s stomach.

"I'm gonna throw up!" he crowed.

"Or *die!*" was Crayle's terse response.

The red and white sports car fairly flew around westbound traffic as Crayle tried to keep from sending the eastbound cars over the cliff.

They sped past the hillside road cut where the road turned into a valley area. The drop off was behind them for now and Crayle continued at as high a speed as he could.

They were now flying through an area with some early snow. The ski-lift operators loved early snow. It meant money. To Crayle, it meant crashing out was more likely. Crashing out meant certain death.

On either side of the road, families with their little kids on toboggans and sleds transformed to a blur.

Then it hit Crayle for the first time that whatever there was about him that attracted assassination teams, children could be among the dead innocent bystanders. At that moment, he really wanted to live so he could track down the bastard with the triangle jaw—the leader—and make him suffer in extremis before dying. Mathematician—hell.

Lenny found a brief moment on a left turn to check the wide, five-paned mirror mounted near the top of the windscreen.

"It's called a Wink!" yelled Crayle.

Whatever it was called, it afforded a panoramic view of everything behind them.

"The closest one is about a quarter mile back. TJ's back another quarter!" Lenny advised.

"TJ?" asked Crayle.

"Yeah. The one with the fucking ugly jaw. TJ. Triangle Jaw," Lenny hollered his definition.

The two fugitives from assassination blew through towns with country sounding names like Deer Lick and Running Springs as if they were on a mountain autobahn.

From Running Springs on, it was steep downhill. Twelve miles of some of the most treacherous roadway in the country.

Crayle continued the driving style that had kept the two of them alive so far.

"Yeah. That's it. Save the brakes for later!" complained the P.I.

Lenny was growing hoarse from the yelling. It had no effect on Crayle's driving, but Lenny had to let it go anyway.

Then Crayle slowed just a bit. He checked the Wink, seeing no black-as-night Chargers for a period of several minutes. But the twists and turns were deceptive. From out of nowhere, the third Charger came flying around a corner and closed in.

Ahead Crayle saw a turn ahead that veered sharply to the right, then led to a narrow bridge. And there was a dirt road—no more than a pathway actually—that cut across the turn.

Using his left foot, he laid it lightly on the brake. Just enough to light up the car's brake lights. The pursuit car would see the lights and assume Crayle had jammed on the brakes for the paved turn.

It worked. The driver of the Charger decided he could brake even harder than the Cobra, cut across on the dirtway, and put himself—and the gunmen he carried—in front of the fleeing duo.

Facing backward, the gunmen in the back seat could make short work of the Cobra and its passengers. At these high speeds, the Cobra would likely flip end-over-end over the side of the road and pound itself into a fiery ball as it bounded down the mountain.

When the Cobra blew around the turn, much faster than anticipated, it put the two cars on a high speed collision course.

The Charger driver swerved to the right to avoid the Cobra. He ran head on into the end of the bridge.

The Cobra flew past, never changing course.

The Charger spun onto the bridge banging from side to side and finishing in the middle, a crumpled wreck that blocked passage for whoever got there next.

Who got there next was a still simmering Frenchman with an overpowering countenance and an awareness that he had struck out. Again. That made two.

His driver screeched to a stop at the blocked bridge. TJ exited the vehicle and approached the mangled car of his partners in crime. In the distance, he saw the red sports car riding off into the sunset, as the Americans liked to say.

He heard groans from the wreckage. Jaw clenched tight, he sprayed down the car with bullets. The groaning stopped. He tossed a match to a spreading pool of gasoline and returned to his car as the shredded metal and bodies exploded into flames.

As the remaining gun car turned and headed back up the hill, the Cobra continued down to the bottom, albeit at a much reduced speed and with a more sensible, to Lenny, utilization of its race-bred braking capacity.

Having returned to normal breathing, Lenny called for a potty stop and cleanup at a Wal-Mart at the base of the mountain. As he sat in a bathroom stall, he caught a moment to think.

He could tell from what had just gone on that one Mister Magus Crayle had done some serious driving in his previous life. Way too serious for a mathematician. He remembered his own dad taking him to a car show when he, Lenny, was just a kid.

His dad had caught him eyeing a particular sports car. It was red.

"That's a Cobra, son," his dad explained.

"The man over there said it's just a replica, dad."

"No, this one is real, son. This is the real thing."

"Well, what's a replica, then?"

"There are many kinds, but, in general, it's something that is put together to seem to be what it is not."

Jack Sommers had acquired one just like it. A coincidence? Lenny deduced that there were a number of things going on right now that were not what they seemed. *He* even fit into that description. Was he just a replica?

Lenny figured there were a lot of things, some of them deceptions, that *he* would discover as Crayle discovered them himself. Make no mistake. Lenny intended to stick with this job no matter how dangerous it became. He was officially on an unofficial mission so intensely personal, he wouldn't even consider backing out. In for a penny, in for a pounding.

CHAPTER 22

At the bottom of the mountain, the switchbacks changed to a straight but hilly road. Crayle checked the car's fuel supply, discovering they'd blown half a tank in the chase. Lenny gripped the phone, talking in fits and gasps to Jack. Lenny flipped on the speaker. Crayle shifted up a gear.

Over the reduced roar of the 351C, Crayle heard Jack provide directions to a secluded valley where he claimed they would be safe from any further pursuit.

After about forty minutes, they passed a quarry with a couple of corrugated metal buildings and huge piles of various kinds of rock. A conveyer moved rock from one pile into the bed of a large truck. Other than that, there was no observable activity. Crayle had no idea that his entire life had been altered forever in an elaborate covert hospital housed deep beneath that same quarry.

Arriving at the valley fifteen minutes later, they were surprised to find an airstrip. As they approached, they saw a building and, next to it, a large business jet painted a powder blue color with gold trim.

Crayle parked the car at the building. Before they could climb out, a figure stepped out of the plane and started toward them. Jack.

"From what Lenny said on the horn, Crayle, you went through some real hell up there. What happened?"

"I need a bathroom again. Real bad!" yelped Lenny. "This man drives worse than any maniac. If he hadn't saved my poor miserable life, I'd sue." He figured the vertically-corrugated galvanized steel building next to the runway to have lavatory facilities and, uninvited, headed inside.

Crayle did not buy Jack's surprised demeanor regarding the near lethal attacks. He felt there was a lot more to be known here than his own memories, and he sensed they tied into a much bigger story. He just did not know how. Yet.

"That's twice, Jack. You know who they were, don't you?" There was no humor in Crayle's voice. He had been lucky—very lucky—two times now. And he didn't want to count on the third time being a charm. "Why are they trying to kill me? What do I know?"

Jack put on his best nonplussed expression, but he saw *no sale* on Crayle's hard face. Jack could not betray what he knew: the man who stood before him was probably America's most dangerous weapon. Setting aside the high intellect, Magus Crayle could do serious physical damage if he failed to receive some answers. Jack decided to take a chance. Hell, couching the truth with lies always worked in Washington.

"You've lost your memory, Crayle. You know that. It was a wicked crash you survived. You probably should have died. Look, I am not supposed to tell you this. It turns out you did some work in China. In Hong Kong, actually. That's all I know. If I knew what you knew that was so damn important, I would have already told you. You gotta trust me on this." Well, it was half true.

"What about Phoebe? You knew I needed protection. You knew I was at risk. Somebody wants me dead. You knew that." Crayle spooled up. "You just underestimated the threat by a platoon or so. She took one back there—I'm sure she's dead. Did she have any say about getting into this? Did you level with her about a known threat? I don't think so, Jack. I need to know who they are and why they want me dead. Then I either have to take every one of them out, or I have to remove the reason they want to kill me. Those are my options, aren't they, Jack?"

Neil was right about this guy, Jack realized. The ordeal he'd survived was much more serious than any car crash. Still, Jack could not tell him the truth.

"You had a top clearance, okay? Top Secret in a compartment held by only five people on the planet. Neil ordered me not to tell you because, without the knowledge you lost, it could be fatal for you and a severe security risk to the country."

Jack took a deep breath and looked up at the sky. In his mind, it was blue sky, partly cloudy, and seventy-two degrees. Welcome to Southern California. He breathed out slowly and continued. "We didn't expect anyone to find you. Especially not a hit team. And that's what it was. From what Lenny told me on the phone, it was probably the same team at the Tack Store. They thought you'd be an easy hit. But they had a Plan B, just in case. The cabin assault proves that."

"And they're not going to give up, are they?" Crayle demanded. "You're stalling, Jack. I don't remember how violent I can get when I'm pissed off, but we are going to find out together if you don't cut to the chase *right fucking now!*"

"Don't go off on me, Magus. I'm here to help you." Jack had been taught by Neil you could slow things down by going to first names—something Jack did not do naturally. Neither did he like to lie. Not like the politicians back East, but it was getting ever more necessary by the moment. He empathized with the pols for a split-second.

"All Neil would tell me is that we needed to try and get some of that memory back. There's ..." Oh, boy, he thought. "... there's nukes involved, Magus. And we don't know where, how, or any of that. You had some heavy stuff in there," he said, pointing at Crayle's head, "and we even enlisted a special doctor to try to help you retrieve it."

Crap! Jack did not want to bring Rorschach, the modern day Mengele, into Crayle's shrink-wrapped world. And with good reason.

"You mean I survived a violent crash and you guys put me into some kind of experimental—"

"Whoa! Stop!" Jack pushed his hands, palms up, toward Crayle. He needed to keep the pulse rate down here. "No harm was done. Honestly." The lie became easier, albeit more elaborate. And elaborate was not good in lies.

"Then we brought in Lenny to see if he could help. Since some pretty severe government secrets were involved, I put Phoebe on just to keep you away from any unnecessary public contact and to do some bodyguarding. Sometimes this much memory loss causes guys to get into situations where things get rough, but I honestly didn't expect the full-on threat." Jack looked away into the distance at the mountains as if searching for a well-hidden epiphany. And then he appeared to locate it.

"Magus, the circumstances have changed so drastically, I've got to call Neil. Give me fifteen minutes. Please?"

"Fifteen," Crayle uttered with as hard and cold a look as he could muster.

Jack turned and walked to the jet. As he neared, the ramp came down and he bounded up the stairs and into the plane. He reached Neil on his first try and filled him in. Situation critical. Jack could sense Neil's retention of his usual patrician calm even now. Always in control. The son of a bitch.

"Let's see. It was French—*no*—Chinese thugs who forced his sports car off the road north of Malibu at high speed. He finds this out—from you—and heads off to the land of Chinese thugs. To see the man. You will facilitate this, Jack, and you will spare no expense." The directive articulated, Neil rung off.

Fourteen and a half minutes later, he made his way back to where Crayle and Lenny now stood. No one spoke. Their eyes tracked Jack's every step.

"I told Neil what I wanted to do. He didn't like it at first, but, after some thought, he's down with it. Here goes. The answer, he told me, is not here—it's not even in the states. There's a contact in China. Hong Kong, to be exact."

Crayle started for the plane.

"Hey! Where do you think you are going?" Jack asked, sincerity ringing in his voice.

"Like you said, Jack. Hong Kong is where the *who*, the *what*, and the *why* get answered. That's where I'm going. Lenny can tag along if he likes."

"Lenny works for me, Magus. I'll decide what he can and can't do. Neil said you would react this way. You don't even know what questions to ask. I'd come with you but I can't 'cause I'm tied up here."

Jack looked to be pondering the possibility. Actually, Neil had told him what he wanted said and done. It all came down to finding the right words.

"Alright, alright! You two get the hell out of here. We'll be in contact with anything we can learn in the meantime. Go ahead. Take my personal jet. I'll hitchhike back to D.C. Hell, I needed to catch up on my ass-kissing, anyway."

Crayle felt like he'd breathed in new air. A positive attitude gripped him and overrode his analytical nature. He would get answers, and heaven help anyone who stood in his path. The addition of Lenny was a wild card, but Crayle figured his own will could overcome anything at this point.

"I took the liberty to have some things brought aboard for my next trip, but you will have to buy clothes, et cetera in Hong Kong. Not bad. The shopping place of all shopping places. I'll see you have plenty of spending money. And bring me back some of those iridescent pants—38/34 unhemmed. Now get outta here before I decide to have you both cornholed by Sasquatch," Jack finished from the foot of the boarding stairs.

They boarded the aircraft and cinched in. Jack watched as the plane taxied and lifted off, pulled into a tight arc, and headed west. He closed his eyes, hoping his mom was not feeling the vibes. She would say, "Do unto others as you would have them do unto you." The woman loved to quote the Bible. Jack had never shared his personalized version with her. "Do unto others *before* they do unto you." Such was life in government.

• • •

Inside the aircraft, Crayle and Lenny saw that Jack did not suffer much when he travelled. He had a magnificent private jet, a Dassault Falcon LX custom made for Neil, at his beck and call, and the interior personified luxury in its purest form.

The cabin contained four seats, each one constructed of the most supple, sumptuous gold-trimmed white leather known to man. Work surfaces were placed strategically between them, the remainder of the interior obviously created, not by an interior decorator, but by an interior artist. Gold frame prints of the masters adorned the bulkheads. The usual track-light strings had been replaced by elegant looking gold Syroco sconces. The window curtains were of burgundy velvet.

The only words spoken were by Lenny, "Worthy of a French whore." And then a new voice sounded.

"In case Mr. Sommers did not tell you, I am not a French whore. I am Flori, and I am here to provide you with anything at all that you need. Anything, gentlemen." To make her point, she placed her left hand on her breast and her right hand on her lower abdomen.

The husky voice they had heard belonged to a lovely and well-built young woman. Lenny looked up from her cleavage and noticed the singular beauty of her face. Her not quite brown hair had just hints of light streaks through it. Her dark brown eyes danced above a dusting of small, dark freckles over prominent cheekbones. Add long black eyelashes and full lips—Lenny let out an involuntary sigh.

Crayle ordered a pair of rum and cokes and asked the obvious question, "Where does *anything* end?"

"Gentlemen," Flori continued in her velvet soft tone, "you may think—but only think—of me as your whore. I am, in fact, Mr. Sommers' well-compensated executive flight attendant." She smiled a knowing smile. And then she repeated in her soft, sexual voice, "*Anything*."

Flori bent over to give the men a better look, unbuttoned her top button, and then turned to stroll seductively to the bar at the front of the cabin. Crayle tried to figure out what was really going on here. Jack was upscale blue collar. The sumptuous interior was way out of character. He glanced at Lenny to get his reaction and noticed nothing other than the P.I.'s tear-filled eyes.

The aircraft soon reached cruising altitude. Next stop—Hawaii to refuel in order to complete their journey.

After their drinks, Crayle asked Flori where he could wash up. Flori showed him to the bedroom in the aft section of the plane. She closed the door behind them. Forty minutes later, Crayle emerged sans Flori. Lenny's mouth dropped to the open position.

"She's asking for you," Crayle teased.

Lenny stood and walked trance-like into the bedroom. Flori closed the door.

CHAPTER 23

Jack lingered for a while to watch the jet head toward the western horizon. Then, it hit him.

"Shit! I gotta call Rorschach. Neil wouldn't have done it. Shit! The good doctor is not going to like this turn of events one bit."

Jack strode down the runway to the building, not really wanting to go inside. He did anyway. He knew from experience it was best to get the ugly jobs over with. They could only get worse with time.

He pictured the tall, thin and somewhat older man and his balding head with a surround of snow white berm. And the matching snow white, pointed goatee. And the attendant matching snow white lab coat. Mad Swiss doctor, anyone?

Seldom had Jack been able to get him on the horn—always the voice mail. Lucky for Jack, this time Rorschach picked up on the third ring. The doctor's first reaction was a tirade in his native *Schwyzerduutsch*. Then, realizing Jack could not get the benefit, he succumbed to English.

"You foocking vot?" shrieked the doctor. He was livid. No, he blew past livid in the first ten seconds of the call. "Ve are goink to neet a stronker vort zan *imbecile* for zis von," he yelled into the secure phone, throwing in the French pronunciation as if that country produced even worse imbeciles than the others.

Rorschach caught a quick breath and realized he was most capable of accent-free English. He continued.

"I was given *the subject* Crayle for my studies. Mr. Wohlford made certain promises to my superior, Doctor Rikki. There must be controls in such an experiment, and they must be maintained!" he shouted into the phone. Rorschach, usually in control, startled the others in the underground mind lab. He quickly closed his office door for privacy—this was going to be an indelicate conversation.

"Hold on, Doctor, hold on." Jack needed to mitigate the outrage and put this particular genie back in its box. "We had him isolated and under the strictest observation in the Big Bear safe cabin. Uh … there was a bit of a to do, uh, at a local store. You know, a little violence. Probably, uh, a holdup gone bad. It caused a temporary departure from the, uh, plan."

"Violence!" Rorschach cried. "Holdup? Departure? Temporary? My *subject*, Magus Crayle, has not only left the control structure, he has left the continent!" he shrieked into the receiver. "On a chet plane, no less. Do you haff any idea vot zat koot mean?" His Swiss-German accent returned, full bore. That, along with his pounding of his desk, gave his paced, deliberate tone a Hitleresque quality.

Jack figured he could make a good guess as to Rorschach's lividity index right about now. "Calm down, Doctor, please. Your *subject* is unharmed, and he's safe. The guy won the DNA lottery, Doc. He recovered faster than anyone since Frankenstein."

An extended moment of silence at both ends. Heartbeats slowed just a bit.

"On a jet," the doctor continued unabated, but back into conventional English. "Do you realize the loud noise of a jet engine could melt the cochlear insert circuitry Science and Technology developed and asked us to test? It could turn the devices into little micro-globs of jelly. This is the finest, most sensitive circuitry on the entire planet. It is the latest in the class of devices known as nanocomm. Thirty thousand dollars it cost. Per ear. And you let him near a jet?"

"Cochlear implants? Nanocomm? Jesus. Look, what you did to this guy is between you and the devil, Doc. My purpose in life, with respect to this little gig, is to keep him in one piece. I've done that so far." He regretted the *so far*. "Besides, it was just a little jet."

"Ahhhhh!" yelled Rorschach. "Vile ozzers haff been at za leetink etch, I, Herr Doktor Pirmin Rorschach, haff gone beyont to za bleetink etch!"

"And who did all the bleeding, Doc?"

"Ahhhhh!" wailed Rorschach.

This was not going well, Jack concluded. Time to bring in the big gun.

"Look, Doctor. Neil made the decision, not me. Because of the attack, he went to what he called Plan B. His exact words were *tactical necessity*," lied Jack.

"Attack?!" shrilled the doctor.

"Oh, yeah," Jack responded, "I guess I left that part out. After the store thing, it seems some folks came after our guy at the cabin, but it's okay. He outran all the bullets and lost the assassins somewhere in the downhill twisties."

"Bullets?! Assassins?! Twisties?! You must be insane. Mr. Crayle was given to me as a research *subject* with a work history in planning and execution. Now you have managed, in your casual manner, to tell me someone tried to kill him. *My* subject. This cannot have happened."

"Yeah. Well, it did. Uh, twice, actually," Jack said, raising the information level a bit too much.

"Ahhhhh!" screamed Rorschach.

"First time could have been a coincidence. But the full-on attack at the cabin kinda put that notion to rest."

"Full on?! Kinda?! Twisties?! This is not the English I learned at the *Technische Hochschule*! I need an interpreter! Spare me any more sordid details—where is he now?"

"Well, that's classified—" Jack began.

"Ahhhhh!" gasped Rorschach as his pulse rate surged past 160. Now he was virtually drained of the last modicum of energy. "I must call Mr. Wohlford. He does not keep secrets from me," he huffed into the phone.

Rorschach was about to require a serious dose of defibrillation. Jack realized he needed to better assuage the good doctor. The little white lie about being classified was necessary. Still, he needed to get Rorschach out of the loop. There was a real good chance the good doctor would never see Crayle again—or his precious nanocomm implants.

"From what Neil told me, Doctor, if you start making a bunch of noise from the sanctity of your subterranean lair, Neil could view that as a threat to the bigger mission. Between you and me, I think you are just one part of a much grander strategy. A very important part, mind you, but we seldom get to see the entire picture at our level. You know what I'm saying?" Jack hoped to hell that a we're-in-this-thing-together ploy would produce some traction here.

A brief pause ensued, followed by, "Mr. Wohlford said I was important?" A much calmed voice.

Jack just shook his head and silently mouthed the word, bingo. These doctor types always responded to a little carefully constructed ego therapy. "Yeah, Doc, that's what he said." Okay, so two white lies. Or was it three?

Jack finished with, "Doc, I promise I'll take care of your *subject*, Crayle, and I'll keep you informed, okay?" He rang off without waiting for a reply.

• • •

Rorschach clicked off. The fact that Mr. Wohlford saw his work as important was good news, indeed. When it came time to decide to continue his project, he wanted Jack's boss on his side. Besides, he was not too worried about the *depatterning* memory erasure and relearning experiment. Memory mapping should be fine as long as *the subject* remained alive, he reasoned. Extending the work accomplished by the great Dr. Cameron in Montreal thrilled him. And Doctor Rikki's sponsorship from her high position inside the CIA made it all possible.

The second component of the experiment had been the personal surveillance implants. Surgeons had taken a device the size of a pin head and surgically implanted one into each of *the subject*'s ear canals. After drugging him, they'd kept him in an induced coma for two weeks.

Rorschach had left instructions for *the subject*'s handlers, Lipschitz and Bransfield, to read to him. Soon after, he had received acknowledgement *the subject* had been informed to talk out his feelings, especially when alone.

The device was a development of the U.S. clandestine services' hi-tech surveillance group. It was of the class of devices known as nanocomm. Nano technology was fairly new in this area and took miniaturization to a new level of small. Rorschach was already planning for a second phase using nano-microphones.

Typically, surveillance microphones were planted in rooms. Targets needed to be present and within the operating range of the nearest mic.

But, countersurveillance measures were employed to check for such bugs. Or a radio or stereo was turned up in the room. Listeners could barely tell people in the room were talking, let alone understand what they were saying.

The nano-microphone removed all of the obstacles to audio surveillance. It could not be detected because it was completely invisible. And no bug sniffing devices could detect it and its nanobattery. The device picked up any sounds coming into the target's ear and picked up the target's voice from the ear's natural stirrup, anvil, and bone structure. It was ingenious. Music and other cover sounds were reduced to background and whatever was being spoken to him that he could understand could also be understood by the listening surveillance team. As an added bonus, the device went wherever the target went. The big challenge was the limited range of the device's transmitter. Nano-blue technology connected the implant to a nearby electronic device.

In *the subject*'s case, it was a modified handheld recorder. It received the short range burst transmission from the nanomics and appeared to merely be a personal voice recorder to anyone who saw it.

One in each ear easily caught both sides of any phone calls made or received by the target. The only real weaknesses were battery life and susceptibility of the device to high db noises. Jet planes and rock concerts would fry the little bugger. Still, he could not wait for the next generation. It would be powered by a rechargeable nanobatt which would draw electricity from its human host. *Wunderbar*.

And Mr. Sommers. Rorschach allowed that, impossible as he could be, he was only doing his job. In reality, he needed Mr. Jack Alan Sommers at least as long as *subject* Crayle could be kept alive. Dr. Rorschach decided to take a new tack.

After all, he would soon get his subject back and perform a memory dump. Then he would have his beloved computer compare before-the-crash memory data with the new. An analysis of such comparison by someone as noteworthy as himself would yield any memory progress Mr. Crayle had made. Rorschach knew he could experiment further by going farther afield in the removal of memory links and then let Mr. Crayle loose again. He smiled at his brilliance—a Nobel prize would surely be inadequate.

With that, Rorschach sighed. He did not have much hair left to pull out, so he would from this day forward deploy a positive attitude. Good. And with that he opened his door and walked smiling from his office into the Commons area where his colleagues stared at him—bewildered by the change in demeanor. Perhaps the man was bipolar.

CHAPTER 24

Sylvain Lalumière had been born in the Vosges region of northeastern France into a once aristocratic family. Of that family, eight generations displaced from the present, only Jean-Claude Lalumière had survived. The family lands became public by order of the post-monarchy regime, and were allowed to be overrun by the region's numerous varieties of flora and fauna. The only remnant of the entire family lay in their once elegant, crumbling, but substantial home.

In modern times, Lalumière's father ran a restaurant in a tourist area not far from the town of Dabo, a small village set amongst the forested hills on either side of a two-lane. It was positioned six miles south of the arrondisement seat known as Sarrebourg. The Lalumière home was a four-room cottage less than a kilometer from the town.

His mother had been hard put to produce children at all, let alone a male heir. But, in 1954, she gave birth to Sylvain, a son. As fortune would have it, she gave her life in the process. Sylvain's father, at once elated and devastated, never fully recovered until his death in 1996.

Sylvain discovered the location of his family château and the original document granting possession to lands within the vast timbered expanses of the *Forêt de Rocher*—the Forest of the Rock. He was able to purchase the ruins of his family's estate and begin restoration. For most people, recovering the 247 acres, the château and gardens, and stables for twenty horses would have been sufficient. Not for Sylvain. He had already completed a broad and excellent education. But the breeding—the class and the superior attitude—would be more difficult. He must not only study, but achieve the mindset and feeling of the great pre-revolutionary philosophers and leaders.

And he had learned the bane of the Catholic faith, which he blamed for the destruction of the monarchy. And with it, his family and its position in French society. Sylvain had latched onto the meanderings of the noted Order of the Illuminati founded in Munich on May 1, 1776, by a Jew turned Catholic turned atheist. The founding occurred a mere 34 days before the Americans declared their independence. The Illuminati became a bastion against religion. It became the largest and most secret of secret societies in the world.

While that brotherhood had been well documented, few knew that its principles had been co-opted by a group of enlightened Frenchmen, made even more secret, and made indelibly French. Clearly, they said, the Catholic Church and its appeal to the masses had to go. And some progress had been made. The numbers of churchgoers in his country had been in decline for decades. Soon the masses would require a new highest authority—a new master—to replace the old. Lalumière was convinced beyond any doubt the corrupt and inept government in Paris would pose little resistance.

But the French brotherhood of the enlightened, *Les Illuminés* as they called themselves, disappeared around 1794 and had only recently resurfaced. And, since Lalumière's feelings had been expressed to the right ears, he had been properly embraced by the nouveau *Illuminé* and had risen to appropriate high office within it. Today he would further cement his position and influence by adding his bastard son, Jean-Marc, to the rolls of the *Illuminé* faithful. He sat down beside his private phone and punched in the number.

• • •

"Allo. Qu'est-ce que vous voulez ce matin?" said the voice in a deep, but soothing manner. Sylvain knew the man was not asking what he wanted this morning—this man knew. Sylvain was amazed each time he heard the Illuminé master speak. In his early days, he wondered what a powerful, world-class man sounded like. This was he.

"Je veux parler avec Le Pater de tous Patres." In asking to speak to the father of all fathers, Sylvain used the Latin word for father and fathers so there could be no doubt it was he completing the handshake. He switched to English. "How are you this fine evening, Elder?"

"Very well, indeed. And how are you, my dear Sylvain?" the Elder replied, not expecting a call on this encrypted phone to be a social one—it never was.

"Elder, I believe we have come to the point where my son is ready to join us. He has already performed well. We have translated our seed money into the universal currency, diamonds. We have made payment to our eastern ally.

"At this point, Jean-Marc is only aware of my personal need for his services. I am looking to you to grant permission to bring him to the next level. I am asking that you grant to him an initiation into formal membership in our brotherhood. Our movement. I call upon you to grant your permission for a grand initiation to add him forever to our supreme cause. I wish him to become *Illuminé*."

The Elder leaned back in his gold and white lacquered chair, which had once belonged to France's final king, Louis the Sixteenth. He wished to dispatch with the relatively lightweight issue of accepting Lalumière's bastard son and move on to the big issue—that being what exactly a significant quantity of diamonds purchased, where it would be taken, and how it would be put to use.

"Sylvain. You have raised yourself up from the masses and have performed brilliantly. And, clearly, you are an aristocrat by bloodline. Of course, I have witnessed your son's successes to our cause and am impressed. He has attained the intellectual standards we require, and he shows no signs of any religious interest."

The Elder had, of course, used covert operatives to keep an eye on everything Lalumière and his son had done and to report back in excruciating detail. Their reports coincided with Lalumière's own account. The Elder could both trust and rely upon the two of them.

"I believe, Sylvain, we should go forth with the ceremony before the end of the year. I am confident you will prepare him well in advance. You know the process through which he will pass. You also know what you can and cannot tell him prior to his initiation. But one thing he *must* know, Sylvain—once inside there is only one way out. The commitment is indelible. For that reason, a wife for him must be chosen with the greatest care. Do you acknowledge all of these things, Sylvain?"

"I do, Elder. I am deeply honored. Thank you from my heart—*de mon coeur*."

"Now, Sylvain. You must bring me up to date on the acquisition of the weapons."

Sylvain Lalumière proceeded to tell Elder of the verified delivery of payment to the Asian and the subsequent embarkation of the weapons. He could tell that the Elder was pleased of the success to this point, but was equally aware of the pitfalls remaining. One thing was certain to both of them: the end game would change France, and the world, for all eternity.

CHAPTER 25

The Dassault Falcon carrying Crayle and Lenny had left Hawaii fully refueled and was over the Pacific just ten hours from its destination, Hong Kong. The flight had been silky smooth as it often is before the inevitable turbulence.

The two men had been able to catch some sleep prior to the refueling stop. Now, Flori rested in the aft cabin, thus allowing Crayle and Lenny privacy in the business part of the plane.

"Lenny, you're right about one thing. I need to know what happened in China and how I was involved. It's the only way I'll understand why people keep trying to kill me."

"Yeah, it seems the amnesia has formed a wall in your mind. Tough luck. Hey, if it weren't for bad luck, you wouldn't have *any*. That's how to look at it."

The onset of one of Lenny's palaverings failed to penetrate Crayle's funk. He felt like a man in a very small boat on a very big ocean ensconced in an opaque fog. He could paddle in any direction, but only as Bob Dylan had scripted, 'with no direction known.'

Lenny interrupted the funk nothingness as he continued, "Well, hold on. What about the chick who saved you? And you got some from her afterwards, huh? The luck's not all bad."

Crayle looked down at the leather amulet Hekka had given him. The white birds, wings spread, symbolized freedom to him. But the woven brown leather ribbons seemed to keep them suspended, incapable of flight. He felt bound up by mental threads composed of Kevlar.

"Lenny, when she put her mark on my heart, she put her mark on my soul. I close my eyes, and I see her. I feel her right here with me." He patted his chest with his fist.

"Wow," was Lenny's reaction.

"I cannot get her out of my head."

"But you were only with her a few hours."

"I try to put my mind on target, but it just goes right back to her."

"Well, I'll be damned," said the P.I.

"What?"

"You, Magus Crayle, are in love."

"Oh, my god."

• • •

Crayle needed something to help settle his emotions. He went to the bar. Lenny extended a pull-out desk and returned to work on his laptop. He pulled papers from a folio, examined them, and just as quickly stuffed them back. Crayle walked by just as Lenny stood. They collided. A page from the folder floated to the floor.

Crayle apologized and picked it up. Lenny knew it was no use trying to stop him. He hoped Crayle would not see what Lenny saw in the paper. He had not transcribed anything for a layman's eyes. But all hope vanished when Crayle looked up at him and asked, "Who's Sammy?"

Lenny wanted to cry. He really wanted to run, but the logistics were not in his favor.

"Now, don't go off on me. He's … he's …" he stammered. He took a deep breath hoping it was not his last. He breathed out the words, "My father." Then his head dropped. His chin came to rest on his chest.

"He's involved in this, isn't he?"

"He's why I'm here," Lenny confessed, shaking his head in disgust with himself. He looked up at Crayle as if to show him how deeply this ran inside.

Crayle's face turned rage red. He yanked the poor man towards him.

"And the part about helping me find my past?" Crayle grabbed him by both shoulders; he shook him. "What about *that*?"

"I … I'm sorry. I'm sorry—I'm sorry—I'm sorry." There was a pause. "Look. I need a drink real bad. I promise, I'll dump the whole thing on you. Then you can throw me to the sharks—just kidding." The last words were not even in jest. They just trailed off, barely perceptible.

Now it was Crayle's turn to catch *his* breath. To regain control. He lifted Lenny like a sack of feathers and put him on his chair. He went to the bar, returning with two glasses and a bottle of Maker's Mark bourbon. He brought along a bottle of tonic water, but no opener—it, like the glasses, was just a prop. They each took a long pull. From the bottle. Lenny began a story so improbable, Crayle concluded it had to be true.

• • •

"My dad and I had a P.I. shop in Washington, D.C. Silberweiss & Son. Private Investigations. We did some cool work for the pols. Then, one day, my dad tells me the business is mine. I thought he was going to retire, but we didn't make that much and he was still in his 40's."

Lenny took another long pull, wiping the bottle mouth with his shirt. He handed it to Crayle, who repeated the process.

"He couldn't keep a secret from me if he tried. He went to work for somebody he identified as *the company*. Later, much later, I learned the company was an insiders' euphemism for the CIA. They put him where he had knowledge and experience. He worked his way up in the Directorate of Administration's Office of Security.

"Near retirement age, he got himself appointed to the Office of the Inspector General. It oversees what everybody else in the company is doing, mainly to ensure Congress didn't find out something the bosses didn't know about. He called them *bad surprises*. They could deny. That was fine. They could lie. Okay. But they couldn't get blindsided.

"Inspector General was the top guy's title. The position used to report to the Director of Central Intelligence, the top spy guy. But someone saw a possible conflict of interest. Imagine that. So the Office became independent. It also became a collection point for deadwood, which offended Dad to no end. He called it a *waiting for exile* posting.

"Anyways, Dad was assigned to clear the desk of some guy that had gotten gone. A *Gone Away* was what he called them. He said the term originated in fox hunting. Someone cried that out when the hounds were in hot pursuit and the hunt was on. The company co-opted the term to replace the uglier sounding *Goner*: someone dead, lost, or past recovery. He didn't know it at the time, but the GA was you and you had been placed in the *past recovery* bucket."

"But why was I gone? They must have told him about the accident."

"Dad wasn't told why. Just gone. That's how they summed up some people's service to their country: gone."

Crayle's tension started to break. He asked, "Where do I come in?"

"The story reads like a novel. There's a lot more."

"Go on. But understand this: the longer you take, the more chum I make." Crayle fought back a smile.

"Something happened while he was boxing up personal stuff from this gone guy. It all had to be checked and delivered out west. Innocuous items were to be boxed and sent to someone who might give a shit. Dad told me all this. He didn't say who was to receive your stuff. It was probably the doctor. Or maybe Jack."

"This needs to get a lot more interesting," Crayle said. "I can still toss you to the seaborne carnivores."

"Okay. Okay." Len held up his hand. "I think my dad found something. I heard from my brother, who lives over in Europe. He told me Dad had gotten onto something real big. He said Dad was going for it. I didn't have a clue what he meant. Then, one day, this guy in a decent suit shows up at the P.I. office. He's wearing shades, and he never takes them off. He tells me my dad is dead."

"This had something to do with me?" Crayle asked.

"Yeah, big time. Sunglasses dude tells me I can help catch whoever did it. He says his government unit has to do with foreign affairs and cannot operate in the U.S. I asked him to finish the thought. He went on that a guy who got injured in a car crash was the key, but that the guy had lost his memory. He said that someone like me, along with some doctor they had, could maybe bring back enough memory to surface the why of my dad's murder."

"And this guy's name was *Magus Crayle*?"

"Magus Crayle—you—was the guy my dad was checking out of the system. Sunglasses figured my dad had found something. But, instead of destroying it, he smuggled it out of Langley. He must have called my brother about it."

"Why your brother? Why not you?"

"After my dad split, it just wasn't the same. I'd see him now and then. I'd plead with him to come back to the business. To make the shop father and son again. He said he was helping the country. That I was just being selfish. We argued, and it got bad. He left. For good. It broke my heart.

"I cashed in the business and headed for the Left Coast. I figured I could start a P.I. business all over again. And make up for what I had lost in D.C. to Hollywood-style debauchery, boozing, and babes. I felt a sense of renewal: I was going to soothe the savage breast.

"I'd heard that Southern Cal had babes popping up out of the woodwork—some with *real* blonde hair. Mensa-challenged, too, the way I like 'em. And only a few of those brunettes like they have back east that think too much."

Both men were past mellow from the alcohol now, and Crayle was no longer a physical threat. This was all new to him and quite a lot to digest at one time. He felt his vacuous memory filling up too fast, the blur of the alcohol making it worse.

"Want to know why they picked me from the perspective of you?" Lenny asked rhetorically. "Finding out the past is what P.I.'s like me do. I'm thinking they believed that, if I started pumping your mind with your past history, you might start remembering on your own. So, in short, I had the chops, and they'd fed me motivation. Aptitude and Attitude, my dad used to say. But, seriously, I think they need something real bad that you might be able to get back."

"So this Jack guy, who owns the cabins and the plane and all, he's the guy who came to see you in D.C." It was a declarative question.

"No. I didn't get a name. This guy was hoity-toity, not like Jack at all. But afterwards, Jack contacted me out here and so he must be hooked up with Sunglasses. Phoebe, I'm hoping, is just a bodyguard."

"Sure. What else?" Crayle did not get Lenny's inference.

"If not, and you do get your memory back, they might figure they don't need me anymore. And the kind of chops Ms. Bransfield has, she's already come close a couple of times. And that was only because she can't take a joke. You missed some real stuff before you got conscious."

"That's a lot in one sitting, Lipschitz. I'm getting some sleep. You, too. We can try to make something out of this for both our sakes. Hong Kong seems to be the place and, right now, it's the only lead we have."

They fell asleep easily, though Crayle's mind continued to work on connecting the dots.

Lenny's mind counted its blessings. He'd come close to permanent sleep. He'd done well in what he had confided to Crayle. However, he had not told him what he'd found in the building at the airstrip.

CHAPTER 26

Crossing the midway point en route to Hong Kong, the plane hit severe turbulence. One violent shake knocked both Crayle and Lenny out of their sleep and onto the floor. Crayle cracked his forehead against a bulkhead, wincing at the pain.

Lenny rushed over and sat him up against a chair. There was not much blood, so the external damage was minimal. Lenny pushed Crayle's eyelids open and the pupils responded to the light. But Crayle's brain had taken a severe jarring, and he was seeing stars.

"*Blackstone!*" Crayle cried out.

Lenny saw something different in Crayle's expression. He looked zombie-like. Just staring. Repeating the same word over and over. "Blackstone. Blackstone. Blackstone."

"Jesus. You're delirious." Lenny slapped Crayle across the face. No effect. Just "Blackstone. Blackstone." Over and over.

A few minutes of the same, then Crayle stopped. He looked up at Lenny like he had regained his senses. His eyes widened. "Blackstone. That's it. That's *why*."

"Why, what?" cried Lenny. "Why, what?"

"It's the connector. It connects everything."

Crayle grew excited, animated, as if he'd just discovered the meaning of life.

"Blackstone is from my past. It's Hong Kong. It is somewhere else, too. I don't know. Only Hong Kong is clear. And a man there. A key for me. Maybe for you, too."

Then, Crayle gripped his head with both hands.

"My God! Lenny, it's coming back to me. I close my eyes and I see an image, a document. It's my father's service record. It mentions Hong Kong and intelligence. There's a commendation. It says OBE, British government. It … it says posthumous. And there's another one. Another commendation. This time from the Republic of Vietnam. Omigod! How am I seeing this? What the hell does it all mean?"

"Uh, I know a little about that," whispered Lenny. He wondered if they were close enough to land that he could swim

Crayle's head snapped up.

"I saw something in the building at the airfield. Uh, you know, when I went in to take a wiz. It said CRAYLE on the top, so I snatched it. Honestly, I forgot about it." He removed a folded paper he had transferred from his old pants to his new and handed it to Crayle. It read,

> Regards CRAYLE. Father: Army intelligence Lieutenant Colonel detailed to Hong Kong during Vietnam conflict. Worked with Chinese liaison. Russians helping North Vietnam; Chinese more than upset—wanted it back. Father to set up Chinese interference against Russian effort. Died in Hong Kong—bullet from Russian Makarov.
>
> NW

He stared at Lenny. There was no look of bewilderment.

"We are in this together, P.I. We need each other. We are like life to each other."

"Don't you think that's a little …" Lenny was mercifully stopped short when Crayle grabbed him and hugged him.

• • •

Later, the pilot advised them over the jet's speaker system, "One hour to touch down in Hong Kong."

They would land at Hong Kong International Airport and would proceed through a customized version of customs. Hotel arrangements had been made by Jack. All expenses were covered.

They changed and freshened up in the lavatories. Neither knew how to dress for Hong Kong, but Flori had layed out a full complement of clothing on the bed for each man. As they made their way back into the business section of the cabin, Flori walked past Lenny, giving him *the look*. He started to follow her, lemming-like, into the bedroom, but Crayle got a firm grip on his collar and sat him down.

Crayle wore his game face. He would obtain answers or people would die.

Flori's soft, sexy voice announced their arrival at Hong Kong International Airport. She also advised the two travelers that it was exactly midnight back at their origination time zone in California. Because it was a new day back there, she observed that it was even newer here. It was, in fact, tomorrow. She wished them a pleasurable stay.

The two answer-seekers were more than ready when the plane taxied to a stop. They descended the jet way and breezed through a faux customs inspection. Crayle experienced a feeling of déjà vu about the place, but did not notice anything in particular. A beautifully polished dark green Rolls-Royce picked them up and transported them to the posh Peninsula Hotel in the mainland city of Kowloon.

They thought themselves special and praised Jack's spare-no-expense approach to things when they learned from the bellman that fourteen Rolls-Royce Extended Wheelbase shuttle cars transported all Peninsula clients. Crayle's room astonished in its splendor. A wall of glass afforded a view across the harbor to the city of Hong Kong. It exceeded spectacular. All he wanted was a hot shower and a soft bed. He got both.

CHAPTER 27

Hong Kong is spectacular on any day. On this particular day, the orange sunset in the west and the view across the bay to Hong Kong astounded. The play of the early city lights on the still harbor waters suggested a reflecting pool created for the gods. The muted glow of a blood-orange setting sun backlit the tall buildings. A postcard moment.

By the time Crayle and Lenny had gotten to bed, it was past 1 a.m. They slept without interruption by maids or anything else until five in the afternoon, Hong Kong time. Some showering, tooth brushing, and dressing later, they ordered a light lunch from room service. It was elegant and delicious. Now, it was time for work.

Lenny had lifted a set of power conversion wall warts from the jet. They divided the ambient 220 volt hotel circuit in half for his laptop. He busied himself picking up intel on navigating Hong Kong. Apropos, he asked the concierge to procure a Rolls for their trip to the nearby cross-bay ferry dock. When the concierge protested, Lenny assured him that Mr. Lipschitz and Mr. Crayle were of diplomatic stature. That translated into large tips.

The ride down Salisbury Road took less than five minutes. They were dropped off at the Star Ferry Company's Tsim Sha Tsui dock. Lenny had learned that ferry service frequency at sunset was every eight minutes, Monday through Saturday, and every twelve minutes on Sundays. No running for the ferry. If they missed one, another would be along soon enough. He filled Crayle in on the non-essential facts.

"Here ya go, MC. Ferry service began in either 1880 or 1898 with a boat called the Morning Star. There was this guy—"

"Skip the history, okay?" Crayle had things on his mind.

Lenny took note of his game face. "We'll board on the upper of two decks before the main crowd gets its shot. I know more, but I'll let the rest be a surprise."

Crayle glanced at the bay waters for signs of a shark presence. He wanted no part of surprises—only answers to his questions.

During his brief encounter with the Internet, Lenny had learned the Chinese equivalent of baksheesh. After bribing the ticket clerk, they crossed ahead of the crowd onto the boat amidships. A very pleasant young man dressed in a starched white uniform greeted them. He showed them to the forward outside deck through a pair of sliding glass doors. There were only two tables, each with three chairs. The young officer offered them seating at the starboard-side table.

Other prime guests were ushered to the port-side table. The three men wore tan uniforms replete with medals and red trim—the universal indication of generals. They seemed curious as to why two non-Chinese had been given equivalent deluxe treatment.

Crayle noticed their interest through the side panel on his sunglasses. He neither needed nor wanted anyone's curiosity. He made a mental note to blend in wherever he had the chance. He would need to lose Lenny.

The rest of the passengers filled the ship's middle interior. They showed no interest in the Americans or the generals—they just peered at the awesome sights through the glass-curtain side walls.

The sound of banter in Chinese and other Eastern tongues stayed within the glass enclosure. The only sounds Lenny and Crayle heard were those of a non-stop, world class harbor. The former British presence endured.

The crossing from Victoria Harbour—named after the 19th century British queen—to Hong Kong Island aboard the Shining Star took eight minutes. The two men walked the length of the old wooden pier to a thoroughfare that paralleled the harbor. The road, more of a highway, acted to separate the harbor area from the city itself.

Driven by habit, Lenny checked to the left and, seeing no traffic, began to cross. He did not realize the British had imposed their will on the unsuspecting Hong Kong Chinese, and he was nearly cut down by high-speed traffic coming from his right. Only Crayle grabbing him by the scruff of the neck saved his life.

"What in Jesus Christ's name drove those crazy Brits to drive on the wrong side of the road?" wailed Lenny, coming up short of breath.

"The French," answered Crayle. "*They* drive on the right."

This time, Crayle laughed alone. He realized it was not his role to be the humorist and followed with, "I apologize for the bad joke."

Having barely avoided a British Racing Green Jaguar sedan clipping along at about seventy miles per hour, Lenny and Crayle crossed the thoroughfare. Crayle summoned a rickshaw boy to take them the several blocks to the *Wan Chai* district. The Wan Chai—Chinese for small bay—was the traditional home to Hong Kong's famous red light district and the impetus for the even more famous film, *The World of Suzie Wong*.

Not to disappoint, there were plenty of bars, nightclubs, restaurants, and a palpable party-down atmosphere. Sailors from many countries wandered the streets in various stages of inebriation, many of them looking to hook up with a *date* for the night. A date was a short-term relationship that might include a trip to the rooftops, a place that put them under the stars, but also at the hands of robbers and other criminals. The rooftops were never recommended in Frommer guides and certainly not by the local police. The local undertakers, however, gave them four stars out of five.

For men who arrived in port after several months at sea, Wan Chai offered one-stop shopping for sex, alcohol, drugs, and hell raising. Sailors *steamed* from bar to bar in groups. Often, they hit the sidewalks with *travelers*—freelance girls that steamed right along and provided a number of deluxe services for appropriate compensation.

The licentious side of Hong Kong was more confined than in the past, but money in sufficient amount could still buy any degree of pleasure a man—or woman—desired.

Along the route, Lenny gawked at the sights. Until something else caught his attention. He tilted his head and sniffed the air.

"Man, this place stinks—but in a good way. I banged a China doll once back in D.C. Yeah. In her dad's Chinese food place. Great food. She was gorgeous. I went down on her like a sailor. Yeah. In the kitchen. It smelled just like this."

Crayle tried not to smell, but it was dinner time in Hong Kong and delicious scents filled the air. He was hungry, but food would have to wait.

Crayle had decided to meet the Chinese contact alone. He did not want to put Lenny at risk, and Lenny could serve no positive purpose. In addition, Lenny had not been allowed to take his firearm off the jet. Crayle sincerely doubted the P.I.'s ability to provide meaningful protection. Had it not been for Lenny's forced disclosures on the flight and their common interests, Crayle would've rather had Phoebe here to watch his back. That was no longer possible. So, he hailed a rickshaw and sent a disappointed Lenny back to the dock. The P.I. could continue his Web search at the hotel.

The twelve-story building matching Jack's address information sheet was not too spectacular at first glance. The outside was made entirely of gold tone, smoked-glass panels, which Crayle noticed produced no reflections. The other buildings reflected the streets, buildings, clouds, and the darkening sky. He reasoned that tempered non-reflective glass panels would be extremely expensive, even for a building this size. The fact that the metal trim was a deep gold color was not lost on him.

But when he entered through the huge and ornately carved wooden doors, he was set agog by the beauty of the interior. It resembled an incredible museum with suits of Chinese battledress dating before 200 BC. The dates were intelligible, but the explanations were expressed in Chinese characters so he did not pause for particulars.

He presented the card Flori had given him to the lobby attendant. He was shown to the special penthouse-only elevator, the conveyance ornate in its artistry and of gold and cardinal colors. He drew a coin from his pocket to test the gold appointments. He smiled up at the elevator video camera while doing the scraping behind his back, then casually turned around as if to admire the furnishings. The gold color did not scrape off. It was real. The heavy weight of the gold provided ballast and stability. It made the rapid acceleration skyward barely noticeable. The car neither vibrated nor shook.

A young woman who wore a traditional high-neck, long dress of black silk with gold designs and replete with slit openings up the sides, greeted Crayle at the penthouse entry. Her face was perfection in that it showed no signs of lines, blemishes, birthmarks, or facial hair. It was as if her perfect skin had been stretched over perfect, elegant cheekbones and then buffed to a luster. He also noticed her sensual, puffy lips formed a perfect 'O' when she spoke.

"Hello, Mr. Crayle. Welcome to the Dragon Building. Please follow me."

Her hair was long and glossy black. In sum, she was quite pretty. A flash of thigh and black stiletto heels caught his eye as she led him to a double golden door embellished with the same cardinal red enamel as the elevator.

As they neared, the huge doors silently slid into the walls on either side. Crayle and the young woman stepped inside. He was startled for a moment as the doors quickly closed behind him. As before, they made no sound.

The large room, oval in shape, was well decorated and, to his right, a man sat at an ornate, carved desk of black lacquer, again with gold detail. As if by oriental magic, the girl disappeared, the room left to the two men. Crayle crossed the beautiful lacquered parquet floor thirty feet to the desk. There sat a man of obvious oriental stock, who looked neither rich nor powerful. Crayle made a mental note not to underestimate this man.

"Mr. Chin?"

The man looked up from his work. He waved the guards out and pressed the *Isolate* button—the American might well expose what Chin had told no one.

"Mr. Crayle. I am indeed Chin. I have heard of your accident and the resulting affliction of amnesia. Please accept my sincerest sympathies for your bad fortune. How may I be of service?"

"Mr. Chin, it is like waking up one morning to find an arm or a leg missing. Regardless, I'm operating on the hope lost memories can be recovered. As I've searched for the keys to those memories, your name has come up. Why? I can't say. Do you know me, Mr. Chin?"

"Eh, Mr. Crayle. Would you have a fine glass of single malt with me? It will help us to relax and free up our minds."

A different girl, this one dressed in emerald green and gold, carried a tray with two crystal glasses and a bottle with the label Bladnoch. She poured three fingers each, then left.

"Try it, Mr. Crayle."

Chin waved the glass under his nose, gathering the bouquet in a single puff-like sniff.

"The vanilla and the almond scents are quite apparent," Chin continued, "and you will find the scent reminiscent of a field of flowers. It brings peace of mind, this one."

Crayle acceded to Chin's protocol and took a sip. The unencumbered Scotch burned as it went down, but left a sweet aftertaste.

"Mr. Crayle, I know you from a couple of years back when I required a particular talent you alone seemed to possess. You were recommended to me, and you helped with a very important—you could say monumental—project."

Chin noticed that recovery from the accident had softened up Crayle's ripped features. It told him the man had not returned to the Spartan regimen that had produced the man he remembered.

"What did I do, exactly, Mr. Chin?"

Chin stood. He wore an elegant floor length robe of purple backing and gold designs reminiscent of the famous French lily of the valley. He shuffled over to a pair of chairs. Crayle followed Chin's lead, and they both sat in the exceptional comfort of padded chairs placed, not facing, but at a slight angle to one another. Chin began his answer, looking directly ahead, past Crayle.

"We were engaged in an international effort of immense proportions. Please let me know if anything I say triggers a lost memory, Mr. Crayle." Chin needed to know if the critical memories, ones he needed to remain in absentia, were forever irretrievable. Crayle had been irreplaceably useful. Perhaps, he could objectively appraise his own plan.

"Mr. Crayle, if I may digress. You had, and may still *have,* qualities I have never seen before. You took the most complex of operational requirements and analyzed them into their natural structure. Then, you translated those components into an array of viable solutions and, in the process, left out nothing of material importance. Where others missed that one essential element that could bring an otherwise perfect strategy crashing down on its makers, you overlooked nothing. Your construct even included flexibility, thus allowing for that which cannot be anticipated. Remarkable. That which could not possibly be anticipated with current knowledge. Beyond remarkable."

Crayle noticed with interest that Chin could throw out superlative after superlative without injecting passion into his discourse.

"You describe me as some kind of planning functionary with an obsessive-compulsive disorder. Mr. Chin, a team of people I don't know have made two very sincere attempts on my life in the last few days. I escaped them by using skills I can't explain. The boring, fastidious functionary you describe would have been easily killed, even by an amateur. There has to be more to my story."

Chin took his glass of Scotch and held it up in the air.

"Mr. Crayle, it takes a thousand activities in my body—some acting in parallel, some acting in sequence—just to hold this glass up without spilling the precious liquid. If any of these activities, any one, were to fail, then—"

Chin turned the glass sideways, and the glistening amber liquid spilled onto the floor.

"That is a $500 lesson, Mr. Crayle. You see, in my enterprise, the risk is extreme. It extends beyond my future to the future of an entire people. I and my associates are forever indebted for your skills and your application of them to our most noble cause."

Crayle made a mental note of *associates* and *noble cause.*

"And what cause could be so important, Mr. Chin?" Crayle felt impatient, the diplomat in him beating a hasty retreat. "No more hand-waving and pontificating, Chin, just tell me … who … the fuck … I am."

"Unfortunately, Mr. Crayle, I cannot go into specifics. As is often true for people of your profession, those for whom you work will seldom tell you more than you need to know. Those facts I kept from you then, I must continue to keep from you now."

That did it. Crayle leaped from his chair. The guards outside could hear nothing. Chin dropped his glass in total surprise. He had not played this well.

When Crayle grabbed him by the throat, Chin managed, "Wait, Mr. Crayle! Desist!"

Crayle spun him around. He might have finished him, but something on the far wall stopped him. It was a full size painting that matched the one in the cabin. The Yin and Yang.

"Jack!" cried Crayle. "He's in this with you! He set me up! When I'm done with you, he's next."

"No, Mr. Crayle, it is not true," choked Chin. "You liked it. I had a small copy made. My present to you."

"That gets him off the hook, for now, but not you."

"Mr. Crayle, there is someone who will provide the answers you seek, but you must see him in person."

The handgrip loosened a fraction.

"You … you must travel to France," Chin gasped. "I will clear things for you, but I must have time. It will take several hours for the parties there to be available." Chin saw his dreams evaporating as he tugged at Crayle's wrists. "Please, Mr. Crayle. *Stop!*"

"When?" the supra-functionary Crayle nearly spat in the man's face.

"It could take—"

Crayle watched Chin calculate.

"—it could take fourteen hours."

"In fourteen hours, you'll be pushing up incense in the Temple of One Hundred Names!"

Somehow he knew about the temple where ashes of the dead with no known families were taken to be honored by the locals to console their restless and implacable ghosts.

Crayle squeezed harder.

"*No!*" gasped Chin. "*It's the difference in time! Please!*"

Crayle lacked a viable alternative. He released his grip and backed off.

Chin grabbed his beleaguered throat and coughed several times. "*Ling!*" Chin called out, straightening his robe and gathering his demeanor.

The young woman who had greeted Crayle at the elevator appeared.

"See to dinner for Mr. Crayle. And entertainment. Have him back by 2 a.m."

The girl bowed her obeisance and turned to her charge. "Mr. Crayle?" She extended her hand to him.

He noticed again the plump, circular nature of her lips as she spoke. It made them, at once, sexy and sexual.

As Ling led him from the room, Crayle realized strangling Chin into the next world would have gotten him nowhere. He could not chance losing an essential link in his search to rediscover himself. He also needed some fresh air and a much higher level of self-control for whatever came next. Still, he had learned a few things from Chin—a few new puzzle pieces took residence in his head.

CHAPTER 28

The mystery woman in black and gold summoned Chin's limousine, which took them three blocks down Lockhart Road, Wan Chai's main thoroughfare, and stopped at an intersection. When they exited the car, Crayle experienced the hustle and bustle of one of Hong Kong's most visited streets. For a few seconds, he lingered on the corner. He marveled at the sight of hundreds of signs, mostly in Chinese characters and illegible to him. His moderate knowledge of Latin proved useless. And the sounds. Myriad sounds of cars and motorbikes, banter and shouts collided, it seemed, in his head, providing him an unnerving ambience. It unnerved him. He wanted to leave.

Ling saw the discomfort in his face. Nevertheless, she had been given direction by Chin and was obliged to obey. She turned him around to windows aglow in neon.

The sounds emanating from within reminded him of the Sugarloafer.

Below the Chinese characters on a sign above the door were the words Monday Club. He'd been here before. But why? And when? Why had the girl brought him here? Had Chin directed her in some kind of silent code? And what had he, Magus Crayle, done here? A meeting? A liaison? Questions begot ever more questions. He looked down in dismay. Once again, he was drowning in enigma.

"Father … uh … Chin owns this club," she said. "We will go here. But only later."

Chin's daughter tugged on his arm. He followed her across the street. A sign indicated an eating establishment with an unlikely name, The Texas Restaurant. As if there were not enough enigmas to go around, here were the Lo Mein Cowboys.

They entered the door for the Texas and climbed stairs to the second floor. Crayle wondered if he had ever been to Texas.

Crayle could not have known, but the Texas Restaurant was *THE* place if you were an American far from home and craved a southwestern-style steak. He chose a seat where he could watch the street and the door while he ate. What he took for a mild dose of paranoia represented tradecraft from a former life. He noticed nothing at all suspicious, but his eyes kept returning to the young and beautiful woman seated opposite him. Had he known her before?

Ling ordered two twenty-ounce T-bone steaks with steak fries. The waiter offered up Lone Star or Pearl beer to wash it down. Ling wrinkled her nose at the suggestion. After the steaks, fries, and two bottles of *Tsingtao* beer, the girl announced it was time to be entertained. He paid in cash. They descended the stairs back down to the street and crossed to the Monday Club.

As they entered, a memory flashed back to him. It was just as the newly-regained memory depicted it—tables hard left, a dance floor straight ahead, and a bandstand past that.

To his right was the bar. He found two stools at the far end to facilitate a view of the entire club and to prevent anyone coming up on him from behind. Tradecraft. He checked out the club. Everyone appeared to belong and no-one gave him any special notice or seemed to recognize him.

Then Ling spoke, leaning close to his ear, in a soft, whispered tone. "Save my seat, please. There is something I must do every time I enter this club."

She crossed the room to the band and spoke a few words Crayle could not hear.

The house band had just finished playing *Honky Tonk Woman.* It was an old tune he recognized by the Rolling Stones. It amazed him that bands all over Asia could not only cover famous American and British bands' tunes, but sing them just like the originals and still not be able to speak a single word of English. Then it struck him: this fact was a memory. He had been right. Memories were starting to return. He smiled.

At that point, the band leader spoke. "Tonight we are honored to have, as our singer for the next number, one of our very own. A young and very talented woman of *mainland* ethnic Chinese origin, so, businessmen from Taiwan, beware."

Laughter reverberated throughout the club.

"Ladies and gentlemen, the beautiful, vivacious, and charming chanteuse, *Ling An-yee*!"

Crayle sat stunned as his escort mounted the stage. She looked incredible under klieg lights. The dress with gold embroidery on a black satin background shimmered. It was apparent that Ling possessed talents he'd not yet experienced.

Crayle ordered two bottles of San Miguel dark beer. Ling returned to the bar, sat next to him, and lit up a cigarette. Her round lips seemed perfect for the task.

A sit-in band of American sailors mounted the stage. One with a white-crow-and-red-chevron emblem on his upper left sleeve took the microphone.

"We're *Drunk As A Skunk*," he chortled, as if their band name and state of inebriation were one and the same. The crowd loved it.

The drummer counted them down, and they tore into *Ina-Gadda-Da-Vida* by a venerable 60's group. A name flashed across Crayle's mind. Pinera. Mike Pinera. Iron Butterfly. More memory. Not bad.

Crayle leaned close enough to be heard. "Where can we talk?"

"Up on the roof," she replied, not taking her eyes off the sit-in band.

"Look. I remember a few things from the past. I've been up on the roof before," he said. "It's where sailors go with their dates. They don't do much talking."

"It's alright. Come."

She took his hand. As they ascended a staircase to the right of the bandstand, the sailor band moved into *Asian Eyes* by an obscure American songwriter. The chorus implied that, as inscrutable as Asian eyes were, they never lied. Crayle wondered. He could be staking his life on it.

CHAPTER 29

The rooftop was as dark as he remembered. But Crayle had not recalled the brilliance and beauty of the stars in the Hong Kong sky. He and Ling stood alone no more than a stairway up from the raucousness that defined nightclubs in the Wan Chai.

Crayle was right about the *talk* up on the rooftop. He looked down from the sky to find Ling unbuttoning his shirt. She began to caress his chest as one hand glided down to his belt. It felt good. Too good. His pants fell to the ground.

"You don't need to do this. I can tell Chin you were magnificent," he whispered as if trying not to disturb one of the most vibrant cities on Earth. As if actually wanting her to stop.

"I intend to be magnificent, Mr. Crayle," she replied.

As the singer-turned-sex-goddess began to work her magic, Crayle thought he saw movement off in the shadows. But neither he nor Ling heard a thing.

She paused to tell him, "Yes, sometimes Chinese men come here to rob sailors and other *lovers*, but they try not to kill them—bad for business. They will not come here above Chin's club. Bad for future." She went back to work.

The men burst out of the shadows with no warning, each dressed in black with hoods much like the Japanese Ninjas. They wielded bladed weapons. Crayle and Ling saw no guns, hence no betraying sounds to attract unwanted attention.

The men attacked in a bizarre form of martial art that neither Ling nor Crayle had seen before. They made wild and rangy attacks with their legs and feet, but threw no punches or chops.

There were four attackers in all. One stayed in the shadows while the other three commenced the assault.

Ling jumped ahead of her charge to form the first line of defense. Crayle tried to help, but his pants tripped him in mid-stride. He hit the pebbled surface hard.

He stood up only to take a hard kick to the chest that slammed him against an air conditioning unit. He *crashed* to the rooftop. Stunned, he looked up to see Ling's prowess in action.

The man who'd leveled Crayle, whirled to attack Ling from behind. Crayle ripped off his pants. Grabbing the cuffs, he slung the improvised lasso at the man's back-spinning kick. He caught it just before it could slam into Ling's head. Crayle twisted and pulled, whipping the man to the ground. The man snapped up to a sitting position.

Crayle, now full in the game, swung his pants by the waist belt over the man's head. The man, blinded by the fabric, yanked at it with both hands. Crayle seized the belt ends, and jerked hard across the attacker's throat. It worked. The impromptu garrote strangled from the killer his last gasp.

As he re-dressed, he saw Ling, three feet away, block both straight and spinning kicks from the two men nearest her. She attacked at just the right moment. The sounds of the pain she inflicted accented the street sounds below. Crayle took note of how much faster and more accurate her hands and arms were than the attackers' legs.

Ling bobbed and weaved like a prize fighter. At times, she crouched low to the ground. At other times, she flew up in the air. The attackers had not dealt with her style of fighting before and proved no match. She poked and jabbed them with straightened fingers and elegant, slender thumbs. The two went down in a matter of seconds.

The fourth man backed away. Ling looked to Crayle and then back. As quickly as he and his associates had appeared, the remaining man dissolved into the night. Crayle caught a glimpse of him. Even with the hood, the shape of the man's face seemed familiar. And then it hit him. The face-painted attackers at the lake. The one with the prominent triangle-shaped jaw. Their leader.

"This is three times for him. I think he's struck out," Crayle said to no one in particular.

"Perhaps this was merely a robbery," Ling offered.

"No. I have seen that last one," he said, pointing after the man who had disappeared. "He and his men attacked me in America. But, why? I still don't know."

Ling did not speak.

He looked at the blank space where the man Lenny called TJ had stood. Then, he turned to Ling. "There must be an answer to this. I have just bits and pieces, Ling. How can I put two and two together when I can't even put one and one together?"

"It is done, Mr. Crayle. Is there anything else?"

"Yes. Something bothers me."

"And that would be, Mr. Crayle?" Ling managed a provocative tone.

"Chin sent me with you, and we were attacked. He would do that to me, but not to his daughter. Who sent these men?"

Ling managed an inscrutable look, but no answer. She checked each of the downfallen for a pulse. She found none.

"I'll try not to become your adversary," Crayle said as he closed the distance between them. His heart had slowed to the point where his breathing seemed normal. "And those moves with your fingers," he added, referring to the pokes to the attackers' bodies that were a composite of disabling and death-dealing blows. "Your hand techniques were something to behold."

"You also seem informed regarding the martial arts, Mr. Crayle. Yes, I am highly skilled with my hands."

Crayle looked at her face, then her lips. He moved to her. He put his hands on her shoulders and leaned down to kiss her. She turned away.

"I cannot," she said. "I belong to Chin and cannot kiss another man." She lied. She could not afford the affection and attachment she knew would emanate from such a kiss. With this man.

Crayle stood but a foot away from her. He felt something for her. Something he knew he could not afford.

Ling knelt down once more before him. It was her duty.

CHAPTER 30

After they concluded Ling's dutiful obligation, Crayle and the fragile-looking young singer-escort-warrior decided it would be best to leave the rooftop for the relative safety of the Monday Club. First, though, they removed the black hoods of the assassins and discovered the attackers were neither Chinese nor even Asian. Their complexions were white. Then, lest other patrons of the club ascend the stairs to salve their romantic needs and discover the bodies, the two pitched the three dead assailants over the alley side of the roof, scoring three perfect shots into a large open dumpster. The bodies would be disposed of by Chin's men before the new day, Ling informed Crayle.

Out in front of the club, a black Mercedes 600—the former British ambassador's violence-hardened limo—awaited them. They slid into the back seat. The car headed back toward Chin's office building.

Crayle remained amazed that this tall, lithe, young Chinese woman could take down several attackers as if she were the master of some highest-order martial art. He also noticed, when it came time for business, she did not smile, did not frown, and did not scowl—she committed death like she committed sex. She was somewhere between habit forming and an addiction. In any rational society, Crayle concluded, she would have been illegal.

Ling noticed his fixed attention on her. "Do you know anything about the Chinese medical art called acupuncture, Mr. Crayle?" she began, as if having read his mind.

"If I did, that memory is gone," Crayle replied.

"Through long and intense study, the practitioners become adept at knowing the key meridians of the body. These are key points and energy channels, which directly influence body functions. By mastering their locations and purpose, the doctor can affect anesthesia and even produce cures using mere needles. They are poked into critical points even in the case of major operations. Patients can rise from the operating table under their own power and go home. It is not yet widely accepted in America, however."

"Amazing," was all he could say.

"It was adapted by some into a most severe form of martial art. You could call it the art of poking."

Crayle started to laugh. But the terminal violence delivered by someone who might blow away in a strong breeze cut short his humor.

"It is so lethal, Mr. Crayle, it is no longer practiced."

"What is it called?"

"A name is never mentioned," replied Ling

"Then how did you come to know it?"

"My father, uh, Mr. Chin, sent me away for training after I was selected."

"Selected? Father?" Crayle didn't understand her meaning. "You're his daughter? And the rest of the girls are also his daughters? I'm totally confused. What do you mean by *selected*?"

She laughed. "We are not really his daughters, but that is what he calls us. He has no wife. He has never married. We were selected by him for this role. It is important. To him." She paused a heartbeat. "To us."

Crayle saw that she was sincere and emotional—almost to the point of tears. He decided to return the conversation to the martial art.

"Please, tell me about the fighting method. How does it work?"

"There are just three steps. The first is to defend against a disabling blow. The second is to choose an attack point. And finally …" She formed her long, slender hand into a fist, resting her thumb across the top. "… the blow—really just a poke—is delivered into the meridian you have chosen. The effect can be immediate and fatal."

She took his arm and poked it. Then, up near the shoulder.

Crayle tried to recoil, but his body refused to function.

Ling pressed a calming acupressure point, and his control returned.

"My God. A couple of pokes and trained combatants just fall down dead. I would not believe it, but I saw it. You said the effect *can be* immediate and fatal. What do you mean *can be*?"

Ling had already said too much. There was something about this man that made it easy to say things. Things that should never be said.

"Ah, we have arrived, Mr. Crayle. I will tell Father of our experience. He will see that his rooftop is made safe once again. The mess we made will be …" She searched for a word. "… sanitized. Cleanliness is most important to Father. He is forever reminding that things must be cleaned up."

The driver opened her door and whispered in her ear.

"The driver has indicated a change in plans. He is to deliver you to your hotel. You will be contacted there. Please have a safe journey, Mr. Crayle."

In a blink she was gone. Gone back into Chin's strange world. Crayle was left with serious questions. Some about the mysterious martial art. Some about Chin. And some about the attraction he felt for this girl-woman called Ling.

• • •

A half-hour after dropping off Ling and proceeding through the under bay tunnel, the black Mercedes pulled up before the Peninsula Hotel. Crayle offered a tip, but the driver only bowed and, without so much as a smile, drove off into the dark, early morning. With Crayle's biological clock out of wack and the toll taken by the rooftop skirmish, he wanted to crash on the ever-so-sumptuous bed provided by the Peninsula. Using his key card, he pushed into the room.

"There you are," came a voice from the desk to his right. Lenny got up from his netbook computer.

"I got stuff, MC. But first I want to hear about your quiet little evening with Fu Manchu," he finished.

"Crap," Crayle thought out loud. "It wasn't quiet. We talked. He sent me out with his daughter. Beautiful girl. Incredible lips. There was a thing on the rooftop. She was incredible."

"You scored the guy's daughter. Holy sh—"

"I need sleep, Lipschitz. We can talk in the a.m." Crayle tossed himself onto the bed.

"No, my man. We are so out of here," Lenny said, waving his finger side-to-side like a second grade teacher. "We are done with the China man and off to points east. Or west. Anyway, I jumped on the Internet and was researching the hell out of *Magus Crayle* when our friend called. You wanna guess who?" Lenny cocked his head in anticipation of an answer to his rhetorical question.

Crayle pulled a pillow over his head. His only thought centered on whether he could muster enough strength to kill Lenny Lipschitz once he woke up again. Where was Phoebe when he needed her? Crap. She'd probably been given a righteous funeral with the guns and all. She deserved no less for her bravery. He knew the memory of her would remain.

Before Crayle could get any further into his thoughts, hands ripped away the pillow and hurled it onto the floor.

"It was Jack. Yeah, that Jack," continued the excited P.I. "We have a flight in two hours on that *big ole jet airliner* bad private air force of his and we are going to … *ta-da*," he sang, "Strasbourg, France."

Lenny was lucky Crayle was exhausted and had fallen fast asleep. Lenny flung his arms up in the air in an expression of "oh, well" and followed suit.

• • •

The two information travelers woke up a little over an hour later. And not by choice. The doorbell chimed, followed by delicate, but persistent knocking.

Seeing that Crayle was half awake and half in dream land, Lenny muttered "Christ on fucking toast," and went to the door. Too tired to check the peep hole, he just flung it open, ready for a righteous one-sided repartee with who—or whomever—had created the cacophonous sacrilege.

His jaw dropped. Standing only three feet from him was the woman of his dreams. He held up his index finger. "One second, please." Then … "Hey, MC. I'm goin' for Chinese," were the words he threw at the near-lifeless Crayle.

"May I come in, Mr. Lipschitz?" Ling An-yee inquired with practiced politeness.

Lenny stepped aside and in she walked. Lenny's radar-locked eyes followed her transition to the center of the room, seeing nothing but her signature lips.

"Hey, MC. The LG is here," Lenny called to Crayle. "You know, the lips girl." He stared at her enhanced, puffy lips. "God has invented the perfect O-ring."

Rubbing the fresh cobwebs from his eyes, Crayle made it to a sitting posture on the edge of the bed.

"Long time, Ling," he croaked.

"Father has directed me to escort you to the airport. I am to be sure you do not miss your flight to France. Instructions for your trip have been given to the pilots. You may sleep on the aircraft."

With that, the Red and Green daughters entered the room to pack the men's things. In less than twenty minutes, Crayle and Lipschitz were delivered to Jack's awaiting jet and bundled aboard with their belongings. Flori herded her two charges into the bedroom. She ushered them into proper sleep attire, red and gold silk pajamas provided by Ling.

The sisters watched the jet taxi and then traverse two-thirds of the runway before lifting off, heading west, chasing the blackness. They had accomplished their orders from Father and could now report their success to him. He would rest easy, knowing his two headaches, especially Magus Crayle, had been dispatched to a location wherein destiny would deal with them.

Several thousand miles to the east, a phone call was placed. The man named Jack called the good Doctor Rorschach to give him the news: *subject* Crayle was headed even farther away.

"Ahhhhh!" the doctor screamed.

CHAPTER 31

General Li considered Chin to be a brilliant businessman and strategist. Still, he did not want to become entangled in any political intrigues, nor did he want to hitch his star to a man who might be a genius bordering on insane. Chin's relationship with his *daughters* seemed more than a little strange. For one, Chin offered them up to his dignified visitors. And two, Li felt certain that Chin saved the best for himself.

But there was no easy way to dig into Chin's backstory, as Li called it. Li's adjutant, if a little on the young side, possessed intelligence and an expertise with computers. He had tried with no luck to track down an acceptable explanation for Chin's behavior. Li was quite displeased by his failure. After suitably chastising the young man, he still felt reluctant to abandon so promising a venture. So, Li concluded a more drastic solution to his intelligence vacuum must be found.

After two more solid days of digging on the Internet, the adjutant came to him with excitement glowing in his face.

"Yes?" Li inquired.

"Honorable General, I have good news. I found it in the medical archives hidden away under cyber lock and key. I penetrated it like a man penetrates a … well. I discovered that Honorable Chin has seen a doctor regularly for the past five years."

"It would be nice to know his medical weaknesses, but I am afraid you have come up short," the General rebuked.

"But these are very special medical weaknesses, Honorable General. The doctor is a psychiatrist."

That made the General sit up. "What? He's in some kind of therapy? That is not good."

"Not necessarily, General. This doctor has seen many in the party's upper echelon. His specialty is to provide a sounding board for matters of conscience and matters of anxiety. It is said that he has enabled many to overcome severe psychological obstacles. Most have excelled greatly under his care."

Now the adjutant tilted his head to one side, claiming a sort of personal victory without exhibiting arrogance.

Li thought for a moment that he himself might seek out this doctor, but quickly refocused. "What do you suggest we do? Kidnap him?"

The young adjutant, Gao Bo-da, said nothing—he merely smiled.

Li, however, missed the smile. His brilliant military mind was already well along on a tactical plan. He would flesh it out to obtain the strategic knowledge about Chin he so coveted. Yes. It would be a kidnapping in place.

• • •

The computerized electronics Chin had provided to Li in their second meeting now came to mind. Of course. He had tried out the device on his adjutant with success. Then the young man had the computer cloned. Li returned the original to Chin, citing inconclusive results. In other words, "keep working on it."

Li now had a knock-off of Rorschach's computer. His mind effortlessly formulated a plan of action. Yes. It was dangerous, but it could provide the key to his very real dilemma: continue with Chin—or not. He explained Gao's role to the young man, his excitement visible. The young man began to set up the situation that would ultimately enable Li's plan.

• • •

It was three days after General Li had received the computer from Chin. The sun had settled in the west three hours past. The legendary city lights were in full review, but proved no distraction for the doctor. Dr. Chong Ming-shu was reviewing audio recordings of the day's psychiatric sessions, something he did each and every day since the start of his practice thirty-four years earlier.

The young man, his new subject, had appeared only that morning and, only at General Li's insistence, did Chong agree to see him. Chong, who knew of General Li, had his own extensive experience with leader types in the glorious People's Republic.

The young man appeared to him in loose-fitting orange attire. He was thin, perhaps as tall as five-foot-seven. He had spoken in no more than a whisper, but the words bore severe impact.

"You refuse the good general's request at my peril."

Chong, adept at the subtleties of his culture, read between the lines and mentally replaced the words *my peril* with *your peril.* He then agreed in short order to hear this young man's laments.

According to Li, the young man had evidenced great promise, but his background as a Buddhist seemed to stand in the way. He had beseeched the good doctor to analyze the young man and lead him to accept the wonders of violence and mayhem. The doctor had bought the story. Gao had prepared well for the subterfuge.

Later that evening, Chong was still in his office when he heard a noise in his anteroom. He called out to his secretary, but to no avail. Then the door opened and the same young man, still clad in the orange robes of his religion, appeared in the doorway with a black box in his hand. It was wrapped as a present in gold and red and tied with a green ribbon. The colors red and gold were royal and were anticipated. The color green, however, was funereal. A mistake by the young man, no doubt. The country's youth, he mused, no longer had the innate sense of depth and honor built into certain traditional protocols as the doctor's own generation.

"I am so sorry to disturb you, Honorable Dr. Chong. The general is pleased that you have accepted me—he wished that I deliver a gift," the young man stated as he bowed deeply in a display of deference to the doctor.

"Oh. It is unnecessary, but I accept it with gratitude and humility from a man of such honor and renown," said the doctor as if reading from a script. In reality, he did not want presents from dignitaries, because they always took acceptance to mean you now owed them something to be defined and claimed later by them. It was some kind of imputed cosmic debt, he supposed. But Chong also knew that to refuse such a gift would be far worse.

The adjutant moved across the room, in a continuous bow of deference, to the side of Chong's desk. He placed the box in front of the doctor.

"Please, you must open the gift so I may report back your expected pleasure to the General," Gao said in an almost plaintive tone.

Doctor Chong decided it was better to continue his charade the sooner to be alone with his own thoughts once again. The young man could close the loop with General Li. And that would be that.

He opened the package with the care warranted by the occasion and removed the black tissue paper—a curious color, indeed. He barely felt the injection into his right shoulder as Li's adjutant stepped back to observe the drug as it took effect. The medication was a modern variant of the drug so successfully used on American servicemen—and others—who had been captured or otherwise taken prisoner in Korea and China. It had enabled the excessive but necessary mind control operations to take place. Graduates of the process came to willfully and defiantly denounce their mother countries. It had been one of China's glorious, though unsung, victories.

The doctor fell into an immediate unconscious state. Gao just caught his head before it slammed against the desktop. Gao placed the syringe into the box and closed it.

New footsteps sounded in the anteroom. Gao knew to whom they belonged. He turned in their direction and began his deep bow of respect.

General Li strode into the room, not bothering to close the door. He felt assured there would be no interruptions. He placed his leather briefcase atop the doctor's desk, careful not to disturb the few items Chong kept there.

From the briefcase, Li removed an oblong device perhaps eight inches wide by ten inches long. It appeared to be a notebook computer display, despite no physical keyboard. A special cable led from the device to a strange looking end-piece that resembled a metallic fan with five spokes. On the ends of the spokes were special sensors. Li placed them against the doctor's temples, into each ear, and the final one at the base of the back of his skull.

General Li powered up the display. Ten seconds later, a series of file folders appeared. None had the usual folder names next to them—the names were not known and not knowable at this stage of the technology. But, on each folder, pictures began to form. The general and his adjutant scanned them as they evolved.

"There!" shouted Gao, stabbing his finger at a folder in the lower right corner.

"Yes!" exclaimed Li. "That is him."

The picture was small, but a clear enough likeness of Chin Yao-wu, the General's new partner. Both men knew they were looking into the memory of the good doctor and into recollection of his sessions with Chin, who, it could be argued, would some day direct all aspects of the People's Republic from the top.

Gao tapped twice on the image of Chin, which moved to the top center of the screen. Beneath it, two more images appeared: one with the English letters ONE, the second with TWO. The adjutant tapped the first image twice.

What they saw next surprised them both. It was an image of an ancient Chinese icon. Li recognized him at once. It was Ch'in Shihuangdi—First August Emperor of China. Born in 259 BC, Ch'in had become emperor in 246 at age thirteen. He'd built a capital in Xianyang and in it an elaborate palace he called A-Fang. He ruled there until his death in 210 BC. Li had studied this man. He knew him to have been a callous tyrant who slaughtered defeated armies. But something much more profound presented here.

Li also recalled that Ch'in had been described in literature as having the proboscis of a hornet and the voice of a jackal. Li caught his breath. The ancient emperor bore a striking resemblance to Chin. Li further remembered Ch'in to have been characterized as a megalomaniac. What on earth had he gotten himself into? What, indeed?

The drug administered to Doctor Chong would be good for only about twenty minutes, thirty minutes tops. In that period of time, they processed the remaining images. Gao took careful notes of their observations. They would retain the files in the display computer to be more fully processed later. What they found in the second image proved far more uncanny than any fiction. It was Chin's soul laid bare. Li had just drawn a new card from the deck, clearly a card to die for. Li knew *to die for* was more than a cute phrase if he were somehow found out. But one could not win a game with stakes as high as this without risk. Substantial risk.

• • •

The contents of the Chin sessions revealed the psychological traumas of his youth, as well as the measures he'd taken in reaction to them.

The computer technology was capable of sequencing the images into a form of psychological slide show. The final processing and analysis yielded the following exposition on the honorable Chin's psychological underpinnings:

Before Chin had even been a thought in the mind of his parents or anyone else, the story started with the marriage of his mother and father. It was clear to the General that these early items had been related to Chin by others—probably his parents.

They had lived in the same village since birth and had known each other throughout their youth. His father had tended a small plot of land, growing the staple bok choy. Li knew about this vegetable from his hobby of studying famous members of the Li clan in history. One, a pharmacologist during the Ming Dynasty, had studied this plant for its medicinal qualities. *Brassica rapa chinensis*—known as Chinese cabbage in the West—had been thus included in Asian diets for many centuries. It was now known to defend against cancer when taken in small quantities, but, in large quantities, could bring about coma. The images further showed Chin's mother, for her part, had prepared meals and kept their small farmhouse in good repair.

They loved each other deeply and talked often of having children even under the repressive constraints applied by Beijing. Surely, no one from Beijing would venture this far south into the hinterlands, but the local government official was said to be a very mean, unattractive man who made regular calls to their village.

The Chins decided to wait to have children, and perhaps destiny would take care of the official. But destiny dealt them both a cruel blow when the official took a liking to the young woman. She did not rebuff him in any overt manner, but she did not return his smile or react to him touching her arm when he talked to her.

After a few months, the official came to the village with news. Several of the men would be required to travel far north to the Great Wall. The official allowed that much-needed repairs were being made and each village in China was required to contribute. That same day, the young husband and several others were taken in a bus to a train station many miles away. The woman was told she would not see her husband again for six months.

The selection of men, of course, was not totally random. The official began to spend much more time in the village than he had previously. His official story was that he had been sent by the government to see to the needs of the work-widowed wives. And this he did. The wives could no longer look directly at other villagers due to their great shame. Everyone knew what was happening, but no-one had the power to stop the evil government representative.

The Chin sessions skipped around, but Li and Gao assembled the puzzle pieces in their minds. They could see that, some years later, Chin had discovered the facts of his parentage, a consequence of his mother's rape and impregnation by a government official. She could not have reported the assault as it would have most certainly resulted in the forfeiture of her life—and that of her unborn child, as well.

After months of torment, she had delivered her baby to the world, but had died before holding the newborn for the first time. Chin Yao-wu was the result. When he was old enough to understand, he was told by a village elder the circumstances of his creation and birth, as well as the great courage of his mother. It had scarred him to the degree that he'd resolved to never have intercourse with a woman. He would never defile a woman in the manner of that official. Years later, the official found out about Chin's birth. When he arrived to claim his son, Chin committed murder. To him, the act felt like justice. It was not the last time he dispensed such justice.

Chin made his way from his village to Hong Kong. Chin knew in his heart that this Hong Kong, industrialized and modern, would be his new home. His wealth, accumulated in the then-nascent stock market, allowed him to indulge his unusual sexual proclivities and to pursue his dreams. But any chance at normalcy in relationships with women were denied him. Forever.

• • •

The two men were fascinated by the revelations of the Chin memory files. But important questions remained. Were they merely the memories of Doctor Chong, which could be materially in error of admission or omission? Or misunderstanding? But then Li and his young co-conspirator quickly put aside those possibilities. Li had personally witnessed the proclivities of the Chin daughters, and they fit hand-in-glove with what he had learned this night.

One more detail remained. While it would be possible to see that the good doctor met with an unfortunate accident, that might present a fatal discontinuity in Chin's therapy. It could be, as Westerners liked to say, *screwing the pooch.* In order to keep the pooch in optimal working order, Li, with Gao's obedient concurrence, decided to use this wondrous computing device to locate the 'Gao drops in unexpectedly with a present from General Li' file and remove it from Doctor Chong's memory, along with any other Gao memories stored there. The good doctor would not remember Gao nor the gift that took much more than it gave. And Li would leave with more than the daughter card in his hand.

He had witnessed Chin committing murder. It explained why he'd taken the name Yao-wu. Li recalled that, at a Red Guard rally, Chairman Mao had given that name to a girl named Bin-Bin. In the context of Chin, it was his motto. It meant *Apply Violence.*

• • •

They made their way out of the building to the awaiting black Lincoln Town Car, disappearing into the night and rather pleased by the ease with which they'd stolen Chin's psyche. Doctor Chong, for his part, awakened not ten minutes later and surmised, quite incorrectly, he had fallen asleep at his desk. He decided, tomorrow was another day. He collected his coat and left, having no idea whatsoever of the game-changing role he had just played. Nor that Li, if caught, could finger the doctor as the source of the very personal dialogs between the doctor and Chin.

That meant, at some as yet undecided point in the future, Li would be able to recite chapter and verse of what only Chin and the doctor should have known. Li would be able to play the Dr. Chong get-out-of-jail-free card, if need be; Chong would, of course, merely forfeit his life.

Li's normally stern countenance gave way to a smile. He now understood the daughters and had, in the process, been given the gratuitous gift of a Plan B. One always needed a Plan B. *Sun Tzu.*

CHAPTER 32

The warm, late Autumn day was unseasonable for eastern France. The temperatures were well above the characteristic sub-twenty degrees Celsius range. The sunset horde of insect activity would normally be diminished as Winter approached. This afternoon, the insects had been given new hope and the activity in the château's manicured gardens exceeded normal. Lalumière viewed the random motions through the wall of windows that made the château's Great Room feel open to the world. But he was not here to observe the abundance of garden life. He had summoned his son, Jean-Marc, from Antwerp for the most important father-son *tête-à-tête* ever.

Jean-Marc arrived on time and let himself in. His height of just under two meters and weight of eighty kilograms provided a visual of an imposing force and stature belying his youth. At six-and-a-half feet, his father thought his 176 pounds not enough. He looked too much like a malnourished De Gaulle. Today he looked good, if a little pale. Lalumière made a mental note: he would have to see to his son's physical regimen, to include a strict diet of fatty foods and expensive whores. Serious female relationships would be out of the question for the next several years.

After a warm embrace, Lalumière sat his son down. While he had hinted before of what might be, he now intended to transition from the conceptual to the specific. The attentive expression on Jean-Marc's face proved the final inspiration.

"My son, today we must talk, not of diamonds or plots or schemes, but of the future. I speak of the path, for you and for the family, you will one day take. It was many years ago during the Reign of Terror that our heritage was set aside. As I have explained to you, it was during that time that our ancestors were taken to the public square in Nancy, the historical center of our region, and they were summarily tried and sentenced to a swift, yet ignoble death.

"It is our destiny to return our home and our family's status to its proper eminence. To that end, I, with your help, have nearly completed the restoration of our ancestral home. The cost has been staggering. I worked long hard hours in places where the heat rises above 120 degrees in the day and the wind blows sand like needles fired from a cannon. But my years in the Middle Eastern lands provided an income the likes of which are unknowable here in our beloved France.

"Which brings me to my point. We are in the third century of the grand republic, yet the so-called socialists' redistribution of wealth dogma has left us with none of the upward mobility of the Anglo-Saxon countries. It precludes the entrepreneurial spirit necessary to create work for the masses, as well as a myriad of new products and services prevalent in countries like America and our eternal foe, England. Do you understand? You are either born to wealth in our country, or you must steal it. Either way, the government wants to take your money and hand it to those who either cannot or will not work.

"Our unemployment rate stands at more than ten percent—in good times—when America's is normally less than half of that. Clearly, that is unacceptable. Our democracy progressed from the socialist thief Chiraq and the conservative thief Sarkozy, but to what end?"

The question was, of course, rhetorical. When Lalumière delivered a soliloquy, his son knew it was best to be a good listener.

"I have taken the lead in joining an organization, Jean-Marc. It is barely known even to our history books. But first, I must know … will you give me your pledge to stand by me and see to its fruition the return to our past? Or do you wish something else?"

Jean-Marc began to formulate a response, but Lalumière pushed his agenda further.

"Over time, we will re-establish the proper leveling of French society. The aristocratic families of yore will be reborn. Lands torn from our ancestors will be restored. We will make the grand decisions and see to the well-being of the peasant class, according to the *noblesse oblige*. We will protect them, and we will reignite in them the spirit imbued in the heart of every Frenchman. And the women, too. We will bring France, by any means necessary, once again to the international forefront.

"Democracy and socialism have resulted in rule by the most unfit. Power and control have corrupted their puny minds. Our leaders live in the land of the self. *Vivre La France* are words of antiquity to them. Not a spirit and a life voice. They must go—to the salt mines, if necessary. They—" Lalumière lost his train of thought.

Knowing an opportunity when he saw one—and they were seldom—Jean-Marc jumped in. "So the diamonds are part of a grand plan you have to fulfill our destiny? I did not know. I only acted as you requested."

"But you have acted brilliantly," Lalumière enthused. "Each operation a success. And no loose ends. You have brought to me a pride that resounds with each beat of my heart."

Lalumière looked upon his son with pride. Pride in his *bâtard* son. Who the hell cared about his legitimacy, anyway? Many aristocrats and royals fathered bastard sons, on whom they bestowed the trappings and powers of the ruling class. Lalumière went off on a new tangent.

"My son, look at what happened in the once world-class *Amérique*, the United States. The corrupt and incompetent politicians have found ways around what their forefathers and our great diplomat, Lafayette, envisioned. Power and control. That is what they now seek. Appealing to the masses for permission is but a walk-through for them. Those greedy for power and wealth fabricate justification for their confiscation of the great American wealth. The current president acts as if he is Machiavelli reborn or, as some of the religious have postulated, the third Anti-christ. He has no heart. He has no soul. He lacks the passion that once defined America. It is so like the situation in our homeland."

Lalumière's vigor and passion had given way to an almost plaintive behest. His diatribe wore on his son, who considered it all too much to digest at one sitting.

"Father," interjected Jean-Marc. "It is getting late. I should go back and attend to my work. I love to hear your insights and will consider them deeply, but when there is work to do …" he trailed off.

"Forget the work, Jean-Marc. Tonight we must travel to the *Rocher*. As you no doubt have guessed, I am not the only one with a heart-deep passion for France. I am a member of a group of powerful men who think and believe as I do. I have made arrangements for you, my son, to be accepted. For you to formally swear allegiance to all that is important. Allegiance to the body and soul that is *La Belle France*. To the restoration of its former glory—a true renaissance. Will you accompany me and embrace our future?"

He wanted the question to be a mere formality. If Jean-Marc said no, then … then he would be devastated beyond measure. He was not disappointed.

"Father, I am indeed ready to pursue that which is much larger than my self-interest. Yes, I will accompany you."

• • •

Sylvain Lalumière and Jean-Marc Desrochers made the trip to the *Rocher* in the family Maybach. Sure, it was German, but there existed no French counterpart to such a super-luxury sedan. In a way, it validated Lalumière's point that modern France had no grand coach. Modern France had no grand anything.

The ceremony would take place at *La Chapelle de Dabo*—The Chapel of Dabo. The father and son drove out their long tree-lined driveway to a winding country road. Lalumière, intent on the dimly lit road, looked over to see how Jean-Marc was handling the pressure. He was not happy to see his son swaying back and forth. Jean-Marc did this whenever he felt stressed.

"It is alright, Jean-Marc. It is the necessary thing to do."

Lalumière's good intentions only intensified the feelings.

Exasperated, the young man spun his head toward his father.

"I can't do this!" he yelled as he grabbed the steering wheel and jerked it.

The car veered right. Lalumière stomped on the brakes. They left the asphalt and spun onto the dirt shoulder, but the anti-skid system worked perfectly. The car stopped. Lalumière turned to his son.

"My son. This is bigger than you. It is bigger than me. Please, I beg you as my only son. Please do this." Lalumière's eyes revealed it all.

His plea caught Jean-Marc off guard. "It is just so big. I am afraid."

"You are strong, my son. Just now, you proved it."

The two men reclaimed their composure. The rest of the trip took only a few minutes, but Lalumière almost missed the turnoff due to the poor signage. They made a left turn onto what appeared to be an unmarked side road that ran deep into the woods.

After a mile, the road widened into a parking lot capable of accommodating fifty or so cars. They appeared to be last to arrive, most of the spaces already occupied with top-of-the-line automobiles. Lalumière drove past the cars to a valet, who stood near a one story restaurant.

Lalumière led his son along a steep path that wound uphill in an arc. It ended at the top of the prominent multi-layered rock known as *Le Rocher*. The top of the rock was flat and perhaps 100 feet in diameter. The modest chapel could hold no more than sixty people.

They were greeted as they entered, and Sylvain and Jean-Marc were escorted to two large thrones at the front. The one on the left sat upon a purple riser, the one on the right positioned higher on a double riser, also of purple. The livery on the thrones was unmistakable in its meaning and significance. The powder blue fabric with gold embroidered symbols established the theme. Everyone knew that the *fleurs-de-lis* represented France's monarchic period. The golden bees symbolized Emperor Napoleon. The bees and the *fleurs-de-lis* were separated by a diagonal gold stripe. *Of Monarchs and Emperors* would have been a suitable label, the post-revolution notation that promised freedom, brotherhood, and equality conspicuously absent.

Jean-Marc noticed, as he approached the thrones, that each of the men lining both sides of the chapel wore a different emblem—placed over his heart—on his purple tunic. He recognized Russia, Sweden, Belgium, and Bavaria from his studies—all coats of arms of former European kingdoms. He guessed, correctly, that he was in the presence of blue blood and future royalty. And then the epiphany of a lifetime hit him: the throne for his dad was no overstatement for some past-his-prime, fantasizing old man. *My God!* thought Jean-Marc. His dad was going for the big one.

Pleasantries and ritual verbalizings were made by various people. But, to Jean-Marc, voices constituted a drone. He could not stop his mind from assembling the puzzle pieces. It all started to make sense. If you went into a nascent, post-modern monarchy as a peasant, you would remain one forever. Likewise, if you started as an aristocrat, there you would dwell for your lifetime as would your heirs and so on. Forget upward mobility. His dad needed to start at the top. *Le Roi Lalumière*. No. *Roi d'la Lumière*—the King of Light. "Holy—"

A voice calling his name jarred him out of his trance-like state. The voice emanated from a man who stood directly before him, a man dressed head-to-toe in white bishop's garb. He cradled a scepter of gold in the crook of his left arm and a gray stone tablet in his right. Jean-Marc's peripheral vision caught the fact that his father was already standing. Jean-Marc stood.

The bishop placed the scepter atop his right shoulder and read text written in Old French from the tablet.

Jean-Marc did not hear a word, his mind wandered. If his father could, would become king, then he, the sole male heir, would become the crown prince—*Le Dauphin*. "*Sainte Merde!*" he muttered under his breath. But he realized there was good news and bad news. The good news boggled the mind. He knew his father would pursue this goal, either succeeding or dying in the attempt. Therein dwelled the bad news. If his father fell prey to the axe, he, Jean-Marc, Prince of Everything French, would be number two in line. Perspiration dampened his forehead, even though the temperature felt like a cool fifty degrees.

Given the intensity of his father's preparation, there was no backing out—*in for a centime, in for a Euro*. Or a *Franc*. On the road, his father had prepared him for the only word he would utter. He must respond "Oui" to the one question he would be asked.

"Jean-Marc Desrochers, do you accept the role established for you by the brotherhood of the blood of blue and gold gathered tonight in this place?" The bishop appeared and sounded as solemn as a massive stroke. "Do you, in your mind, understand the magnitude of this night and what it bodes for not only your future, but for the future of your homeland? Do you, by your heart and your soul, accept that there will be only one outcome for failure and that failure is never an option? Jean-Marc Desrochers, will you now place your life into the brotherhood of the enlightened?" The words speared like lances thrust by a savage warrior. The bishop's fierce green eyes bored through Jean-Marc's irises and straight into his soul.

Then, the bishop held up a purple tunic, adorned with the emblem of royal France.

"Do you accept the mantle of the *Illuminé*?"

"*Oui*," was all that could emerge from the mouth of the dumbstruck son of France's next king. Oh. My. God.

• • •

No anointing or other religion-inspired rite occurred as the ceremony reached its conclusion. The bishop merely handed to the designated crown prince the scepter of the *Dauphin* and the tablet, which Jean-Marc nearly dropped. The ceremony complete, the other participants removed their tunics, filed out of the chapel and walked down the pathway. The sound of automobile engines signaled the end of a ceremony that had lasted a mere twenty minutes.

Jean-Marc had returned to an awakened state, realizing that no one had congratulated him. No one had come forth to shake his hand. He supposed that, among royalty, no touching was allowed. In fact, his father had not embraced him or made any effort at a congratulatory grasping of his shoulder or arm. Nothing.

The trip back to the château was intensely silent. Neither man said a word and even the most sensitive microphone would have struggled to pick up the sound of their breathing. Such was sometimes the nature of so heady an occasion. Perhaps his father would fill in all the blanks at a later time. Prince Jean-Marc could only hope.

While Jean-Marc continued to daydream, his father took a call on his cell phone. Lalumière did not respond other than to offer an affirmation every now and then. The son did not realize that his father was being informed of something quite serious, not in the distant future, but in the very near one. The targets were on their way.

CHAPTER 33

When he met with Chin for the fourth time, General Li was ready for raw meat. Two questions—*What do I do?* and *When do I do it?*—weighed heavily on his mind. The philosophy and history lessons were fine—it was like hearing about a fine meal. It was now time for the recipe.

Li was escorted to a different room this time. The room, though equally beautiful, was of a less comfortable nature. It was decorated with Chinese suits of armor, while the walls were emblazoned with the shields of warriors past.

The one constant was the richly lacquered seats, the ornate and sumptuous cushioning, and the liquor. The latter was a new single malt this time. A Brora. A 30-year-old whisky with a complex aroma that included notions of coffee and licorice. Notably dry and smoky in taste, Li imagined the highlands and fields of Scotland and the coastal namesake town where it had been distilled.

Chin had learned, during a trip to Scotland, the time for this distillery had sadly passed back in 1983. Special bottlings of the notable single malt produced there had been made available only to men of international significance, such as himself. With that as a backdrop, his thoughts brought the old together with the new. He recalled that the Scots were known as fierce, persistent warriors, who never accepted defeat. Perhaps Chin was passing this message on to Li in a subtle way.

"General, tonight I will ask you to listen first and, when I have finished my moderate length monologue, I would like your comments. It is important that you hear everything first. Are you of accord?"

The General nodded in affirmation.

"Fine. You are aware of the several provinces that make up our country. You are also aware of the westernmost province, Xinjiang. Then you must know that the Muslim Uighurs have been responsible for bombings in the provincial capital of UruMagushi. Our struggles with Muslim extremists does not seem to play in the Western media, but the Uighur separatists wage a constant war against the *normal* people of China.

"Our government's dealings with the Islamist government of Iran—nuclear technology for oil—makes it difficult to secure these western territories as we have done with Tibet—our source for uranium. Our first step, in my grand plan, will remove Iran from the equation. Your direct involvement in assuring, controlling, and monitoring our assistance with nuclear technologies makes you a key player. Once Iran is neutralized, I can assure you of the top leadership position in bringing peace and stability to Xinjiang, once and for all."

"Ah. This is the substance I have been waiting to hear," announced Li. "Please, continue."

Chin stood and moved about the room, assured that Li's eyes tracked him at all times. His intel had been exact. Li was a true leader, a patriot without question, and loyal beyond doubt.

"As you know, the Iranians have built hardened facilities far beneath the earth's surface to house and conceal their nuclear ambitions. The facilities have been made so secure and so impregnable, any strikes from above would fail. I have made arrangements with other resources to provide you with the means of instituting a catastrophe from the inside. You, of course, will not be present when it occurs, and no one will ever realize your involvement or that of your men. I have but to make a few more moves before I can provide you with actionable orders. Do you understand what I have said so far?"

Li could only nod. Yes, he was the man for the job. Under normal circumstances, he was not one to pass up credit for his accomplishments. But adulation meant nothing when compared to readying China for its destiny.

"When these last few items have been put in place, I will notify you. I understand that you will be travelling soon to Iran. I expect to have everything prepared by then and will brief you with plenty of time to spare. Do you have any questions, my friend?" asked Chin.

That Li's travel plans were known to Chin was not lost on him. He continued to be impressed by Chin's ability to develop a resource such as himself and to obtain rock solid intelligence. In short, Chin was a man prepared. That, Li adjudged, was a prerequisite for success in an endeavor of this magnitude.

"I have none at this time."

"Fine. Then, if you so choose, you have earned some entertainment and relaxation before you depart."

Li remembered well his last session. He recalled every instant from the girls' singular attentiveness to the time he had re-dressed, travelled home in his staff car, and until the time sleep had overcome his realization of a recurring fantasy come true. He also noted that Chin had never provided him the one in black. The one called Ling. Li felt compelled to succeed at all costs in his momentous task. Then, he would find a way to ask Chin for her as a reward. With that thought complete, he nodded affirmation to Chin. And again, as if by magic, the beautiful young daughters appeared and led him off.

Chin had made his defining move. Now that the General was solid in the fold, Chin would turn to the Frenchman and lock in the remaining piece to what was the first major segment of the elaborate puzzle.

• • •

The time had passed and, as the General prepared for his trip to Iran, he and Chin met again. Chin provided him everything necessary to begin. He had paid Li the agreed amount via secret accounts split between Vanuatu and Vancouver. As far as Iran was concerned, Li knew where to go, whom to meet, and who would provide him with what.

Li boarded his personal transport jet at a high security airbase, accompanied by a team of twenty and set off for the Iranian military airport at Yasd. His navigator routed them away from Xinjiang and the dreaded Uighurs, flying to the south of Tibet and India. Over international waters there would be no unpleasant surprises. He had been assured that neither the Iranians nor the Americans would fire on his aircraft. Someday he would travel a more northern route to the magical Himalayan lake that alleged to heal all afflictions. Perhaps in his later years.

Upon landing, Li's jet was taxied off the runway to a large hangar. Once inside, Li and his small entourage deplaned and were greeted by military dignitaries along with an armed guard. Li felt uneasy about Muslims with weapons, but did not let it show. *Never let them see you sweat*, the Americans would say. Damn! For all their faults, the Americans did have some quite good sayings.

"Greetings to you, General," said the man in charge. "I am Hamid Mohammed. I am general in charge of those items of mutual interest. Please excuse the armed escort. We are quite safe here, and the weapons are not loaded. Your flight was, I hope, uneventful?"

Li noticed the man's English was Oxfordian, which meant he'd probably studied in England. He hoped his technical expertise equaled his linguistic prowess.

"My flight was excellent. The sights along the way are always to be honored though I have seen them a thousand times. And thank you, General Hamid, for this illustrious welcome."

General Mohammed chose to overlook the Chinese general's mistake. He knew the patronymic came first in Li's native language. Hence the Hamid instead of Mohammed.

He guided Li to a room where they could both change into civilian clothes, as planned. Mohammed led him to a bus with Red Crescent markings—inappropriate for either of their intentions.

The bus ride that carried them east along treacherous winding roads took more than four-and-a-half hours. This bus, unlike real Red Crescent vehicles, featured blacked-out windows, air conditioning, and creature comforts similar to Li's aircraft. A section in the rear had been closed off so Li could rest and relax from his long flight. Mohammed's adjutant had seen to the inclusion of two Persian women whose beauty Li would put up against any on the planet—well, except for Chin's daughter-in-black. He made a mental note to conscript them to travel to China and teach the young women back home their man-pleasing secrets.

Li arrived at the destination refreshed in all meanings of the word, ready to commence Chin's plan. Because the bus' windows had been blacked-out, Li saw no scenery along the way. He had only his memory of a highly-classified map he'd memorized prior to the trip to know his destination.

The bus pulled into a garage. Li heard the closing of a large door behind it. He left the ladies in the 'bedroom' and joined the Iranian general and the rest in exiting the bus. Mohammed led them all to a corner office, unusual in that it had no windows. Once inside the room, a metal door slid closed and the cubic capsule began its descent.

For over two minutes the elevator slithered and banged its way into the bowels of the Earth. Li noticed the Iranian glancing his way every now and then, probably searching out clues to take his measure. Li did not like tight places and hated being underground, but he'd learned to control his breathing so as not to panic or alert others to his weakness. After all, generals were always in control.

Li guessed they were just shy of four hundred feet down when they came to a stop. The elevator doorway opened onto a platform. It extended twenty feet from the elevator and was edged by a waist-high steel railing. Mohammed led the way, describing the scene before them.

"As you can see, Li, our vantage point is some twenty feet above the tunnel floor and another twenty feet below the ceiling. You could say it bisects all of the activity you see before you."

Ahead Li saw pipes that stretched off into a tunnel and workers, some obviously not Iranian. The latter group placed and welded bracing for the final pipe sections.

"This, General Li, is our grand project. As you are aware due to your previous dialogs with my predecessor, we have brought water to where none has been before. Above us lies an arid land—much too dry to permit such a creation as that," he said, pointing to a large cement structure to their right.

"We, of course, have brought these copious amounts of water here to build the world's first mini-nuclear plant. We shall demonstrate to the world that we do, indeed, intend to use the atom for peaceful purposes. Up above will blossom an entire city with miles of greenery and a playground for the rich like none seen before. Say goodbye to Dubai, General."

Li smiled, as if in agreement at the wonder of it all. In truth, he knew there would be no city and no playground. Iran would build nuclear weapons at this most unlikely of places. No one would know, they were confident, except their Chinese brethren. We shall see, thought Li.

"It is truly a grand plan, General. By the way, I understand you contracted a French water company to accomplish the extensive tunneling and pipe-laying. I would be most happy to meet their principal leader while I am here. Would that be possible?"

"Why, of course—"

Four of Li's entourage appeared down to their right. They carried a crate, pall-bearer style, toward the cement structure. One of the men nearly stumbled, causing both general's hearts to skip a major beat. They both knew the small, heavy crate contained fissionable nuclear material—for peaceful purposes, of course.

But the man regained his balance and the crate continued on with no further incidents. Mohammed motioned Li to follow him to an office situated to their left. It had been built against the wall of the tunnel and appeared quite sturdy. But Li grabbed his arm to stop him. Mohammed looked surprised. No one would ever lay a hand on him without facing certain and immediate death. Li stepped closer, peered around, and lowered his voice.

"General, I just wanted to re-confirm our agreement. You will authorize the transshipment of the oil-payment carried by foreign-flagged tankers the moment the package I have delivered is verified. The contents are keyed so they will be unusable until we have confirmed delivery at our petroleum terminal. At that time, the *key* will be turned and the contents will go live. Any attempts by men—violating your orders—to override the safety mechanism will cause it to self-destruct."

Mohammed had calmed from his *touching* reaction enough to respond. He knew exactly what self-destruct meant. "Of course. The operability of the contents will assure future shipments of oil in exchange for like payment. In our transactions, General Li, everyone will win."

"As it should be," said Li, turning toward the office.

Inside, Mohammed introduced Li to the Frenchman with overall responsibility for the pipeline. He had not met the tall man before, but he at once noticed his bearing despite the labeled overalls he wore.

"General Li, may I present the man-in-charge? Sylvain Lalumière from France, of course."

The two men traded bows and shook hands to cover the multi-national protocols, and took seats in two of the six chairs. Mohammed did not join them.

"Gentlemen, if you will excuse me, I must oversee the placement and installation of the, uh, package General Li has so thoughtfully provided." With that, Mohammed left them to get acquainted. Their usefulness had passed, while he had some serious fish to fry and Ayatollahs to please.

Once he departed, Lalumière and Li smiled big smiles. Everything was going as Chin had said. And now, Li had finally met Chin's illustrious partner in crime.

"You are much better looking than I anticipated, General," said Lalumière.

"And you, Lalumière. Please, call me Li."

"*S'il vous plaît,* call me Sylvain."

They both laughed. Each knew this was far more serious an encounter than any pretense at mutual admiration. In fact, the repartee was none other than a prearranged *handshake* interchange, designed to verify their identities and to signal that it was alright to speak freely.

"Is all in place, Sylvain? Is the pipeline complete, and are the pumping stations in place and operable?"

"But, of course. Water is to be brought here under the desert for many, many kilometers. All tunneling was disguised at the other end and all work completed underground by remote-controlled robots. And the French, as you know, have many decades experience with peaceful nuclear power generation, which includes all possible means of reactor cooling. Everything is in place and will be operational whenever the nuclear fuel you have brought has been installed. I expect a test within a week."

Both men knew Sylvain's banter was bullshit. Neither of them expected one light bulb to be illuminated by any reactor. They anticipated an event far exceeding any Iranian expectations, and with a far more material impact.

"In addition, since telecommunications by cell or satellite are prohibited by our current location, I have arranged signaling equipment to use the water in the pipe for ELF transmissions. I have a resource at the site of origin. He will contact me when you advise him your oil has been received to your satisfaction. For my part, I will communicate through him when all is in place here. This I will transmit just prior to my departure. I trust you will keep Chin apprised."

Li nodded. "Then everything is in place. I will now help our friend Hamid put things in order, and then I and my team will leave. By the way, how did you enjoy the bus ride, Sylvain?"

The Frenchman smiled.

CHAPTER 34

The flight from Hong Kong took just over ten hours to traverse the 5855 miles at mach .8—the 7X's 576 mile per hour cruising speed. Thus Flori informed her charges as she prepared them for landing. Crayle slept most of the time. Near exhaustion, he'd had little appetite for Flori the flight attendant and her deluxe services.

Strasbourg represented more of a question mark than Hong Kong, the universe of possibilities greatly expanded by their previous encounters with Chin, Ling, and TJ and his gang.

As he wolfed down flight food with a distinct Brazilian twist, Crayle took a mental accounting of what he had learned in Hong Kong. Lenny had slept well there while he'd endeavored not to die. Discussion time, he concluded.

"Lenny, I need to tap into those private investigation talents of yours. I know I shut you out back in Hong Kong and I apologize for that. It's time to get us both on the same page. We must unravel what appears to be an enormous ball of intrigue—layer by layer."

"Apology accepted. It might help if you think of me as the American version of the great French detective, Hercule Poirot," he suggested an accent as close to French as a waffle is to a *crêpe*.

"Poirot was Belgian," Crayle corrected.

"Sure," Lenny said, taking out a comb and rearranging his hairstyle to more closely approximate the fictional detective. "From what we've learned, Chin has—or had—an associate in France, this Lalumière guy. From the martial arts style you encountered on the rooftop, I have consulted the Net and we can conclude it was a form of *savate*—the French foot-fighting style."

"Yes. And the French-sounding words at Big Bear, which Chin did not know about, add up to this Lalumière being the man behind the attempts to kill me."

Lenny perked up, an epiphany at hand. "In fact, he probably ordered you run off the road north of Malibu in the first place. That makes one more attempt on your life."

"Clearly, he knows, or thinks he knows, I possess something very dangerous to him. There's no way he could have known about the amnesia, though, or about Doctor Rorschach's attempts to help me to remember. But he had to know I was staying in Big Bear, in order to send TJ and his crew of killers. But, how?"

"Yeah, you're right. I'll bet he worried that you may be able to get those special memories back. Memories that would cause him severe bum burn."

"Perhaps him and perhaps others, Lenny."

"Excerrent, glasshoppa," replied Lenny shifting gears. "I bet Chin knows a lot more than he let on. These two are up to something and it's huge—and you're the spoiler, MC."

Crayle nodded. "I agree, so we should assume Lalumière knows we are coming. If our assumption is correct, he has tried four—maybe five—times to pull me down and failed. He wants me *gone*."

"Look, this crap from Jack says our fearsome frog lives in a château, probably surrounded by heavy security. We'll need surprise and a small, well-equipped army to get inside and grab his ass. And we have to be extremely careful not to kill the fucker. Not until we've dragged every bit of truth out of him. About you … and about my father."

"We need serious planning, my investigatory friend, and, according to Chin, that is my specialty. We will have to fake the well-equipped army, though I am not sure how," Crayle said.

"We could so use little Miss Fibbee here," Lenny admitted.

"She's dead, Lenny. The firefight was too brutal." He dropped his face into his hands. Then, running his fingers back through his thick hair, he said, "She's the reason we're still alive."

"It's okay. We'll dedicate this caper to Phoebe." Lenny's face took on a sober look.

"Here. Here," Crayle mumbled, closing his eyes and massaging his temples. The loss of Phoebe still bothered him, but he couldn't allow it to cloud his thinking.

• • •

Air traffic was light on the approach to the Strasbourg airport. The tower cleared them for the live international runway. The Dassault Falcon 7X settled into its pattern, their landing letter perfect. Crayle and Lenny both saw that it was light outside, but had no idea of the time.

The pilot did not taxi to the debarkation area for normal European traffic and normal international flights. There was nothing normal about this flight. Instead, he taxied to the west of the terminal building to a large black hangar whose twenty-foot by thirty-foot door opened quickly up into the ceiling instead of the usual sideways. The two men looked at each other. Neither one needed to say, "Jack's been here."

After he brought the jet to a stop just short of the opening, he shut down the engines. The plane was towed into the hangar. The door closed, the entire operation achieved in complete silence. Anyone watching would have thought that strange—and so it was.

The flight attendant and everything girl, Flori, opened the outside cabin door. Crayle and Lenny deplaned.

The hangar felt strange. Crayle's senses heightened. Both men were struck by the darkness of the place. They looked around, taking in the absence of windows to the outside. The entire interior was painted in a flat black. Numerous fluorescent lights glowed, but the black walls, floor, and ceiling seemed to suck the light from the room like a black hole.

Crayle turned by instinct. He spotted the pilots and Flori as they walked to the far side of the hangar. Flori's head turned, as if she felt Crayle's stare.

"Damn," was the word that came to mind. He knew he would like to see her again. He did not know, however, that the plane was not yet empty.

"So, *guten morgen*, *bonjour*, good morning," said an accented female voice. It belonged to a petite, youngish woman, who stood close to five-foot-seven in her four-inch, black satin heels. Her shapely, but strong legs led nicely up to a pair of out-of-context blue denim short shorts. Above that, she wore a tied-in-front, tight black T-shirt with a large graphic depiction of an ancient warrior's head and *Aztecs* written in aggressive script. Despite the poor illumination, she appeared to be quite pretty. The dimples, when she smiled, made her delectable.

Lenny, who had learned some Southern California Spanish, smiled and responded with, "*Buenos tardes, chica*."

The woman cocked her head and gave him a quizzical look. She understood the Spanish, but wondered about his intent.

Lenny had assumed that the well-tanned woman was of Mexican descent based on the Aztec symbolism and her short, black, spiked hairstyle. Once again, he had added two and two and come up with something other than four. In three words, he was on his way to offending someone new. Crayle recognized the trend.

"Welcome to Strasbourg, Mr. Crayle and Mr. Lipschitz," she continued in perfect English, abandoning further demonstration of her prowess in linguistic affectations. She cocked her head sideways again and directed a coquettish smile at Crayle. "Your bags will be *handled* and transportation made available. After inspection, of course."

She spun on her heel, and they fell in behind her. The trio paused before a uniformed officer who wore a blindfold. He resembled an escapee from the movie, *Irma La Douce*. The customs inspector, with physical guidance from the young woman, quickly initialed and placed French 'inspected by' stickers on the luggage. Then, still blindfolded, he was led away through a nearby door.

Crayle and Lenny looked at each other nonplussed. No passport inspection. For the first time since leaving America, they realized they had no passports. They'd flown across the Pacific Ocean, entered and left Communist China, and travelled halfway around the globe without passports.

On cue, the woman turned and handed them each a dark blue passport replete with gold U.S. of A. symbolism. Crayle and Lenny examined them, discovering that their entry visas for France were in order and the proper stamps had been obtained. But when? And by whom? And neither passport indicated they had just been to Communist China.

Before they could ask any questions of the woman, they heard an all too familiar voice behind them. Of course. Jack. Jack was not normally one to smirk, but he wore one now. He did not have to say, "Look what I can do." He'd made his point. In spades.

Jack ordered an associate neither of them recognized to collect their luggage. He then escorted them through a tunnel under the runways to the main terminal and into the *Étoiles* Lounge.

Back in the hangar, the stowaway deplaned.

• • •

A hostess, her dark brown hair arranged into an upswept French twist and dressed for business in a black skirt and white long-sleeved blouse replete with ruffles, ushered them into a corner booth. The scarf at her neck shouted Hermés.

After they sat down, she positioned a tall privacy panel across the opening. With Strasbourg a focal point for the European Economic Community, many dignitaries passed this way. And with them, hundreds if not thousands of closely held secrets: state secrets, personal secrets. The privacy panel prevented interested parties from photographing the men, interpreting their body language, or listening to their conversations.

A man of few words, Jack nodded to the document folder Flori had handed to Crayle before he'd deplaned. "Read that. I'll be in touch later. Got some stuff I need to do." With that, he left the booth.

Inside the folder, there were no verbose analyses depicting strategies and tactics, nor anything regarding local resources or acquisition of needed supplies. The one-page document inside the folder was short and sweet.

1. Take car provided, with driver, to *Hôtel de France.*
2. Reservation under Lipschitz—security.
3. Get rest. You will be contacted.

"I'm so glad Jack has our back." Lenny oozed sarcasm. "Would've been a shame if he hadn't covered each and every fucking base."

"Come on, Lenny. We can get one and two done and improvise a little room service to fill the void until our contact gets in touch. I think Jack allowed for your P.I. skills to fill any gaps."

Crayle's mind and body were not up to dealing with any more fog. He needed a rock solid plan to get to this Lalumière character, as well as to deal with whoever got in his way. He felt closer than ever to substantive answers, yet they could be hidden on the moon for all he knew. The raft of new memories, acquired since he'd regained consciousness in the Fawnskin cabin, were not sufficient. Not by a long shot. His patience had worn to a nub.

They walked out of *Étoiles.* Crayle noticed a tall middle-aged man clad in a chauffer's garb. He held a sign with *Lenny* written on it. Their driver guided them outside to a stretch Mercedes parked illegally in the white zone. The luggage in the trunk and Crayle and Lenny settled in the back seat, the limo exited the airport.

As they drove toward town, they passed through a section of Strasbourg where all the car dealers dwelled. Lenny leaned forward, peering into each showroom they passed.

"It's just like the states, but French. *Come to zee kilometre of zee cars,*" he said, affecting a French accent with the accuracy of a late-night comedian. "You know, cities keep all the red light stuff and all the car dealers quarantined in their own sections of town. All to protect the children. *Wait!* I see that we are being followed."

Crayle straightened up. "You're kidding!"

"I'm catching the reflection in the showroom windows. An old P.I. trick. If you look right at 'em—I mean the perps pullin' the tail—then they know that you know."

Just then the BMW following them turned into a BMW dealership.

"Of course," Lenny continued undaunted, "coincidence can also come into play."

Lenny sat back. He didn't notice the replacement car in the tag-team tail.

According to Lenny's stopwatch, it took just short of twenty-seven minutes to reach the hotel. A large square sign identified the square across the street as *Place Kléber.* Crayle considered that Jack had put them in the center of Strasbourg for a reason. He hoped it was a good one.

CHAPTER 35

The *Hôtel de France* was decorated with a modern design palette. The foyer, registration, and the room itself conveyed a modern Germanic, rather than French, essence. Crayle had no idea how that occurred to him, but he felt sure of it. A short hallway led to the living quarters, a bathroom on each side. Crayle focused ahead into the living area, half-expecting to see someone he knew. In doing so, he tripped over a metal wastebasket left in the hallway.

"Sonofa—" he yelled as the trash can top banged into his shin. He grabbed the can, carried it into the living quarters, and placed it next to a desk, where it belonged.

They settled into the room, both appreciating the two double beds, the couch, and two chairs and a coffee table. There was an additional desk and chair against the wall where daylight would backlight the work surface. Nice for a business traveler, but how would it be for planning an assault on a château?

They were not in their room twenty minutes when a knock sounded on the door. Lenny answered it, responding to a courier in an unknown dialect of French. He handed the young man a ten-dollar Hong Kong note worth about $1.28. He closed the door on some creative, but destructive French from the courier. He carried a plain brown envelope down the hall and into the room.

"Well, this should answer all of our questions, MC," Lenny said.

"I'm starting to be impressed with Jack's style. He does what he says and doesn't waste a lot of time in the doing."

"Yeah," Lenny retorted. "He got us into the Strasbourg Ritz, the one with the large Best fucking Western sign out front. Hoop-de-fucking-do."

"Be quiet and order us some food and drink from room service, will you?"

Crayle opened the plain brown envelope, pre-ignoring Lenny's expected remark about French porn, and found several items of interest. An 8.5 by 11 brochure, extolling the virtues of sightseeing in Strasbourg, and a city map. And a silver key. And a list of names and phone numbers. And a Sim internal phone card.

The last item was a *Kümmerly + Frey* area map. Unfolded, it depicted the Alsace region around and about Strasbourg and the forested Vosges territory in the region west of Alsace known as Lorraine. The map cover and text were in German. Crayle half-expected to open it up and find a battle plan for Germany's next foray.

Then, Lenny, après-room-service-call, said, "I told them I wanted food and water, but they had a problem serving water with food, so I just asked for two of whatever passes for food around these parts and a bottle of the best wine they grow wherever they're not raising pigs. I think my French needs more work—the chick sounded upset."

Crayle restrained from comment. What would be the point?

Both men, famished when the meal arrived, enjoyed the excellent regional food and wine.

When they finished, Crayle declared nap-time. He could not function with so little sleep. Three hours later, he awoke to a vigorous shaking by the P.I.

"It's time for business. Let's plan," Lenny said, mustering unexpected enthusiasm. "Let's *git-r-done*."

Crayle ignored Lenny's attempt to invoke Larry the Cable Guy as a muse for military action. His mind drew focus on how he and any resources he could muster would attack a château and not all die trying. Their assault needed to be a surprise to provide advantage.

But what if their earlier conjecture proved accurate? What if Lalumière already knew of their presence? Worse than that: what if he knew exactly *why* Crayle and Lenny had come and what they planned to do? There was no doubt in either of their minds that this part of France was Lalumière's home turf—his ancestral tribal grounds. Crayle felt the need to bounce his concerns off Lenny, since the P.I.'s life would be on the line, too.

"Things are about to get serious. There are things I need to do, and I have a gut feeling that people are going to die. If one of them is me, then my unanswered questions are of no consequence. But your life is on the line, too. You had better think long and hard about what is at stake."

"I appreciate the waving of the warning flag, MC. I really do, but I haven't come this far for just *moi*. Sure, I need to get answers about my dad's death. His murder. But whoever stuck a knife in his back needs to come down the hard way. And anyone in the command chain who set him up. He and I had our differences, my dad and me, but I won't be able to rest until I apply some *extreme prejudice*, as they say in the spy game, to the cocksuckers who did him. Thanks for the thought, but I'm in—as long as you'll have me."

Crayle looked Lenny straight in the eyes. He saw that the guy was being real. He saw courage and determination, as well. The cause, his father, gave him strength of purpose. Under the circumstances, both strength and purpose would be necessary assets.

"So let's take a look at this. The château is probably more like a fortress, given Lalumière's politics and the fact that he can muster even a small attack force anywhere in the world. The best place to take this guy is away from the château."

"Yeah. Maybe when he goes to the grocery store."

"Lenny, I may be wrong here, but I do not think men who live in *châteaux* go to grocery stores. They have servants for that."

"Maybe when he goes to the bathroom, then. Servants can't do that for him."

Crayle reassessed his positive-trending view of Lenny. He pressed on.

"We have to get some surveillance on him. We need to discover his routines."

"Ah, I have experience in this area—it's what I do," replied Lenny. "I just need to surveille someone who lives in a probably fortified château, whom I wouldn't recognize in a crowd of one, and in a place where I don't know the lay of the land and, *au contraire* to popular opinion, am not exactly proficient in the language. Piece o' cake." He snapped his fingers for emphasis.

"We'll work on the *how* later. We need tools of the trade, and the only person we know who can help in that department is Jack. So, where the hell is Jack?"

"What about the package? Weren't there some names and phone numbers? Let me see." Lenny reached for the list.

Crayle reluctantly surrendered it. Lenny scanned up and down, finally spotting something on the fourth pass. "This has got to be it. Here's our contact." He started to show the item to Crayle, who was exchanging his Sim card for the one supplied in the package.

"What's the number?"

Lenny recited the digits. Crayle dialed. A woman answered, which surprised him. She had a French accent, but spoke English quite well. Her voice sounded vaguely familiar. The woman told Crayle to meet her at a specific location in a section of town called *Petite France*. She told him Strasbourg was a very big city where streets curved this way and that—they did not form a grid as was the case in many American cities. She suggested he have the front desk call a cab. "Oh," she said, "and come alone."

"Lenny, I'm going to make this meet. I would feel a lot more comfortable with a weapon of some kind—I just hope ..." his voice trailed off.

"You need me along for the ride. Two of us weaponless should equal one of us armed." He fixed his eyes on Crayle's.

"No. You need to find your way to the main library. Get anything you can find about this Lalumière and his château. The more we know, the better this whole thing is going to go. I'll be fine. If Jack set this up, we're cool."

"If Jack set this up?" Lenny parroted, turning it into a question. "Who else could get us hooked up to get our stuff?"

"You're right, P.I. Look, find someone at the library to help you, but be careful not to mention Lalumière. I do not want him getting any phone calls. Tell them you are an American—no Canadian—scholar and you wish to research the pre-revolution aristocracy of the Vosges. Pretend to be smart. Meet back here in three hours, no more. Now, let's get going. And, Lenny, I will be fine. So stop frowning."

Outside the hotel, Crayle decided against taking a cab. According to the map from the package, they were just a few blocks from both the library and *Petite France*. They turned left and walked down the narrow *Rue du Jeu des Enfants*. Crayle reckoned only the French could name a street to honor the Joy of the Children.

They reached the end of Happy Kids Street, paused, and then found places to stand in the large throng at the trolley stop.

"Lenny, do you know where you're going? Are you sure you can find the library?" Crayle was concerned he might later have to search for the P.I.

"Hey, no problem. Right on *Kageneck*, right on *Kuhn*, and *voila!*" Lenny replied, ending in a triumphant gesture with his arms. His pronunciation made the foreign words sound even more foreign. "You, when you get to *Petite France*, turn right onto *Fossé des Tanneurs*, stop before you get wet, and—to the right—will be the *Maison des Tanneurs*." His pronunciation this time was more like bad French than bad English. Practice seemed to help.

Lenny checked out a sign proclaiming this the bridge over the *ILL* River.

"I think it means, 'Don't drink the water.'"

Crayle shook his head once again. Need to focus. Every bit of him needed to focus.

"Meet back at the hotel."

As Lenny crossed the intersection and the river bridge, Crayle thought, this will be over soon. No more bad jokes. No more mangled French. No more Lenny. A sudden pang of regret swept over him. Lenny, for all his faults, had become like a brother. He was the one you frequently beat up, but defended to the death against outsiders. Crayle knew he would miss him—if they survived.

Crayle headed west along the *Quai de Turkeim* to the part of Strasbourg known by the French-speaking population as *Petite France.*

CHAPTER 36

It was the old part of town, *Petite France*—the historic center of the tanning industry. The old buildings had since given way to other enterprise. Juxtaposed to the river *L'Ill,* it provided a picturesque setting for a meet. But Magus Crayle was hardly a tourist. The beauty and history of the place were lost on him; he needed and maintained 100% focus on the task at hand.

He crossed the first of the *Ponts Couvert,* the historic covered bridges, and made a left onto *Quai de La Petite France.* The woman on the phone had given him the number 39. He found it in short order. The building, three stories in height, boasted the Germanic-style half-timbering still prevalent in modern Strasbourg.

The building with its two large wooden doors seemed more reminiscent of a barn than a residence or place of business. He noticed a sign nailed next to the right door: *Maison des Tanneurs.* This was, indeed, the House of the Tanners. Given its large size, he guessed it was a building owned by one of the larger, more successful tanners.

He pushed a large button to the right of the doors with no result. He tried knocking, but the heavy timber doors hardly made a sound. When his knock turned into a pound, the door on his right creaked its way open a few inches. Hearing no invitation, he pushed his way inside.

The barnlike smell assaulted his senses. He half expected to be greeted by a cow or a pig. The interior lighting was midway between light and dark. Crayle squinted to locate signs of life.

"Hello!" he shouted into the blackness.

"*Allo*," came the French word behind him. He jumped and then whirled in the direction of the sound. "Holy crap!" There, partially bathed in beams of reflected light, stood the woman he had talked to on the phone. The blonde hair with the little braid and a face filled with attitude—there could be no mistaking.

"Phoebe! For Christ's sake! I don't believe—"

He stopped mid-sentence. His gaze travelled from her face down to her right arm, which was cradled in a blue-cloth sling edged in white binding.

They each stepped forward, almost colliding. They embraced with passion, both careful of her still-healing arm. Then, he stepped back.

"You were hit! But you're here! What the hell do you think you're doing? Where is Jack? What in God's name is going on?"

Phoebe had prepared for this moment on her overnight flight from the states.

"They didn't get enough of me to keep me out of the fight. Just one hit: through and through. Not enough to keep a Bransfield down. Besides, I still have a nagging urge to put a couple in that funny-in-his-own-mind P.I. friend of yours."

"A couple? Not just one between the eyes?" Crayle, still in a state of shock and disbelief, came back with a smile.

"That would be too quick—he *soooooo* deserves to suffer." She laughed.

Her smile was all Crayle needed. He gave her a full-on hug, to which she grimaced and moaned. It was obvious she was not very far into the healing process. But damn, she was a sight for Crayle's sore eyes. The odds against the Frenchman had just gotten a whole lot better.

Phoebe turned around to pick up a black rucksack, but Crayle anticipated the move and grabbed it up. There would be no heavy lifting for Phoebe—that would come later. As they retraced Crayle's route back to the hotel, he could not keep quiet. Seeing Phoebe was a rush.

"I've come all this way for answers. Now I'm presented with a bunch of new questions instead. What happened at the cabin? How did you get here? And why? Why did Jack do this? It's crazy. I love it, but it's crazy."

"At the cabin? I heard the gunfire—I know how it sounds. I switched the Glock to unsafe and took out a pair of them before they could get me. Jack told me later in the hospital the two of you got away. If you hadn't, those bad boys wouldn't have had to chase. They would have come over to the house and finished the job on me. So, thanks." She smiled.

"Forget that. You're the reason we got away. You deserve *our* thanks, Miss Phoebe AO Bransfield." Crayle smiled, too. He realized what he'd done: the AO was so Lenny.

Phoebe noticed, too. "AO? He's still contagious. Where's my gun?"

After a quick laugh, she filled in an obvious blank.

"When Jack told me that it was just a through-and-through, I told him I wanted back in the game. He's a doer, Mag. He didn't try to talk me out of this—no. There's no glass ceiling in the FBI, you know. I get to do what the other boys do. Jack knows I'm as tough as the guys. So, here I am."

"Tough as nails seems inadequate." He noticed she had not just used his first name, but had coined *Mag* as his nickname. He somehow felt closer to her now. Then another thought jumped into his head.

It had been indelible in his mind since Big Bear. He decided not to ask if she knew about Hekka. His thing with the Serrano woman was probably a half-night stand, anyway. And it was best for Hekka that he be just a brief memory. Hekka's dad needed her around to run the ranch. He would just be a complication. A distraction. Maybe a danger. She needed to put him out of her mind. And he, her.

"Hey? Hello? You seem to have wandered off," Phoebe said, bringing Crayle out of his trance. "We have work to do. And where is that slimy little P.I.?" Her hand moved instinctively back to her hip where she normally kept her Glock—not there. Without it, she felt like a naked little schoolgirl, skipping along through the world with no cares. She needed her weapon in case any big bad wolves showed up.

"Let's pick up the pace. When we're back at your hotel, we can get this château invasion thing down and maybe have a little fun. What do you say?"

"Yeah," was all he could summon. He was in no mood for frolicking in the sack, if that was what she meant by fun. He needed to gather together his extended team and keep them focused. And keep himself focused.

• • •

Back at the hotel, Crayle and Phoebe walked in on Lenny. He sat at the table, shuffling papers around as if prepping for a presentation. When he saw Phoebe, his heart almost stopped. He jumped up.

"OMG! My everloving God! The one and only!" Lenny crowed.

"*C'est moi,*" Phoebe came back.

"I thought you had lured the bad guys away with that hot body." He gestured toward her with his hand.

Phoebe's hand moved instinctively for her weapon. It was still not there. Oh, well. She graciously received a hug from the P.I., and responded with one of those adult-burping pats on Lenny's back with her good hand.

"Good seeing you," she lied. "It will be great having you there for backup," she lied again.

Before Lenny could counterattack, Crayle grabbed them both and led them to the table. As the afternoon sun prepared its exit, the eclectic threesome sat down to plot in earnest. Tomorrow would be another day. They needed to be ready for it.

"Here. Come sit with me on the loveseat," Lenny beckoned to Phoebe, while panting like a puppy.

"You wish," she replied. "I tried my hardest not to save both of you, but the excitement caused me to fall back on old habits."

"Look. You're our hero, Phoebe. We owe you big time," was Crayle's remark.

Receiving praise worked for the agent. In fact, it touched a major nerve.

"Look. I think … I mean … Lenny. Can I call you Len?" Her eyes had widened. She wanted, perhaps needed, some validation here.

"Len, it is," the P.I. said.

Then Phoebe head-gestured over at Crayle. "And this here's Mag."

Len looked over at *subject* Crayle, then at her, then back. He opened his mouth to say, "Ohhhhhhhh," but Phoebe held up her good hand to forestall the *so when did you two get so chummy* repartee sure to follow.

"Thanks, Phoebs," as Mag closed the topic.

She tossed her black bag onto the bed and walked over to the bureau, looking for a place for her things. Pulling open one of the drawers, she appeared surprised by the array of togs she found there. The men, too, looked speechless. Both of their apparel bags still sat in the closet, placed there when they'd first entered the room.

Phoebe opened the rest of the bureau drawers. Amazing. She discovered an array of protective clothing replete with forest camouflage, as well as bladed hardware and handguns.

"Jack's a fucking doll!" Phoebe exclaimed. "Dude comes through like General George G. fucking Patton," she added, claiming her signature Glock 30 and initiating the together-again fondling process.

Crayle and Lenny rushed to the dresser and started pulling out firearms as if searching for a favorite. Phoebe took the toys from the boys and replaced them. They both looked a bit saddened by the experience.

"Later," she counseled.

Phoebe then pulled out a pair of olive drab cargo pants and, with her good hand, undid her slacks and let them drop to the floor. Lenny placed both of his hands before his face, palms in, in an effort not to peek. Quickly, though, his fingers parted in a salacious two-handed Spock salute. Phoebe was wearing panties that matched the pants. Both men noticed.

"Little help here," Phoebe called as she wrestled the cargo pants up her legs and over her hips.

Crayle arrived first, shoved Lenny back onto the loveseat, and saw to the fastening of the pants. He stepped back, announcing, "Perfect fit."

"Yeah," came a comment from the loveseat. "Nice ass."

Phoebe's lips flared. Crayle grabbed her in transit.

"How cute," Lenny piped in. "A father-daughter dance."

Crayle tightened his grip on Phoebe.

"We have got to stop the nonsense and plan this out, you two," Crayle admonished. "I promise to put you both in an old Roman amphitheater not far from here, but only after we're finished with Lalumière. Until then, we're a team." He eyed them both. "A team. Clear?"

"Yeah. Team."

"Yeah. Team."

Crayle knew he needed to take the leadership role with his motley crew. He moved to the small table, and the two followed.

"Okay. Lenny, uh … Len, what did you find at the library?" Crayle demanded.

Lenny piled copied documents onto the table. He did not mention he had tried French on the librarian and had, in short order, been escorted out of the building. He segued into teacher mode. "Class? Listen up. Strasbourg is France's seventh largest city. Round about 800,000 folks and covers 86 square miles. Pretty big. A bunch called the Alemanni—the nasty Germans before there were official nasty Germans—settled here …"

"Why do we need a fucking history lesson when we're trying to assault a fucking fortress that is somewhere west of this fine fucking town, teacher?" Phoebe demanded.

"Wait!" Crayle threw her way. "Your approach to things is nuts and bolts. I understand that. We don't know what will help us and what won't."

"The name Strasbourg comes from Latin, which means 'road' and 'cross.'"

Crayle put it together. "A crossroads."

Eyebrows arched all around, then returned to their default positions.

Len continued, "Strasbourg is at the eastern edge of France in the region called Alsace. Southwest of Strasbourg is the Vosges forest, actually a group of forests, and, in it, a little burg called Dabo. It is the birthplace of our friend, Sylvain Lalumière. *Ta-da.*

"Dabo is not, however, in Alsace, but is in the next *département* west. That one is called Moselle, which is in the Lorraine *région,* which is in the Sarrebourg *arrondisement.* And I think it's in the Phalsbourg *canton*, too. Are you all with me on this?" said Lenny as if presenting a treatise on global warming.

Stares all around.

"Small wonder they can't find anything with both hands. Anyways, the mayor there is named Weber, pronounced *Vay-ber.* He can provide directions to Monsieur Frog and his digs. And here's some actionable intelligence. Check this out. The altitude there ranges from 770 feet to 3100 feet, so the Vosges mountains are little bitty mountains and there'll be plenty of air for us to breathe during our attack. Shouldn't be much colder than here, so the clothes provided by Jack will do."

Crayle smiled.

"Enough for today, lady and gentleman. Let's get some food."

"*Yay!*" came the unanimous response.

CHAPTER 37

The trio exited the hotel. Crayle took the point. He appeared confident, so the other two fell in behind. In ten minutes they reached the restaurant, Le Bartholdi. Situated at *31 Rue Vieux Marché Aux Vins*, the Bartholdi was known by the locals to have good food and excellent ambience.

The weather, sunny and not too cool, prompted the selection of a table outside. They needed a sense of this place and its culture. Phoebe wore a crème-colored blouse and a black pant suit. She had decided having her weapon on her hip might attract attention, so she'd strapped a backup piece just above her ankle. She reasoned she would be fine as long as she kept it in her pants.

From their sidewalk table vantage point, they surveyed the pedestrian traffic and acquired a sense not just of what to wear, but how to wear it like the natives. They were here to observe as much as to eat and drink. They had concluded before leaving the hotel that, as they moved about Strasbourg, standing out would not be a good thing, especially if Lalumière expected them.

"*Bonjour*," came the perky voice, which belonged to a diminutive waitress dressed in a maroon skirt topped with a light yellow blouse.

At her neck, she'd draped a colorful gauze-thin scarf. Over the ensemble, she wore a white apron embroidered with the restaurant's name. Beneath the curled and waved hairdo, she smiled with both her red lipsticked mouth and her beaming hazel eyes.

"What a fucking doll," Phoebe whispered a tease. Crayle and Len saw more in her than did Phoebe. The medium brown hair and long eyelashes did not conceal the young woman who had met them at the airport. Anne-Isabel—under cover.

"Perhaps something to drink," she said to them in French-accented English as she handed Crayle the wine menu.

Somehow, he knew what to expect. He opened it and began to read text that had been inserted in place of the usual Bartholdi history. He absorbed the message. Then, he ordered a bottle of Mosel white wine from a Cochem vineyard about an hour north, and he asked for a bucket of Brittany oysters. They would begin with these and follow with a meal, he told the spy-in-waitress-cover.

"Zee *entrecôte* ees *magnifique* thees time of year," she advised with her trademark dimpled smile.

Crayle felt that a buttery *entrecôte* steak was not the only thing that was magnificent. He noticed an undeniable sexiness about this petite woman. Perhaps there was something going on inside him that he did not recognize: a distant memory foregone. He also knew those thoughts would have to wait until later, if at all.

The wine arrived. It was crisp and full of flavor and aroma. The oysters slid off their half shells along with the requisite sea water, the sea salt the perfect condiment to the oysters. All three were starting to enjoy being in France. It was catch-your-breath time and …

A sound.

The trio looked up to see someone astride a noisy moped down the other side of the street from the restaurant. Suddenly, the rider swerved towards them. He passed within a few feet of the trio, tossing something at them. A small bag. A bomb?

They all sucked in air as the bag landed on the table with a bang. In that instant, the moped and its driver disappeared—the sound trailing off in the distance.

They all stared at the cloth bag. The bag did not give away its contents. It did not hum. It did not whir. It did not tick. It just sat there.

Crayle moved first.

He picked it up and opened the top. It did not explode. They all leaned forward to peek inside. Nothing jumped out at them. But, the bag's contents changed the game.

The bag contained nothing more than a tiny scroll. The three-inch-wide paper, obviously parchment, had been rolled and secured with a purple ribbon. Crayle slid off the ribbon.

The text on the paper was entirely in English, which all but removed the chance it was meant for someone else. Phoebe and Lenny both looked at Crayle, waiting to be told, waiting to be included. But Crayle just rolled it back up and replaced the ribbon. He knew what he needed to do, and he needed to do it alone.

"Look, Jack says he needs you two to help put together everything so we can go after the château."

"What about you?" Phoebe admonished. "We can't go leaving you alone in this place. The original rules are still in play, Mag. To protect and to serve," she finished, pointing at herself and Lenny in succession.

"I don't need both of you, and this needs to get done. I am going to secure transportation; I should be able to do that without risking my life, don't you think?"

"Fine. Let the Len-ster do the logistics bit. I'll come with you. We can pretend to be married. We'll be *sooooo* in love." She did her eyelash-flutter again.

"Jack said he needs someone to help Micmac—"

"*I'll go!*" Phoebe volunteered.

Crayle sent her back to the hotel. She would be picked up there, and they would all rendezvous back in the room at 2100. He used the twenty-four-hour clock as was *de rigeur* in France. He did not know how he knew that, either.

Phoebe took off like a shot. Now, Crayle needed to read Lenny in on the real story.

"Listen up. Phoebe's mission is real, but there's more. The menu text was as I described. The meet up with Jack and Micmac is real, but that little scroll turned this whole thing all around."

Lenny's head snapped up. He knew something serious was about to happen.

"Lalumière wants to see me. At a place called the *Chapelle de Dabo*. It's a chapel perched up on a rock called the *Rocher de Dabo*. He says it's the only chance I'll have to speak with him. He's leaving for the south of France in the morning. He felt it necessary to meet with me and to explain everything, but he considers it inappropriate to meet at his home. I'm sure he means the château. He wants me there at sunset, Len. He said 'Come alone,' but, given the situation with your father, something tells me you won't want to stay behind."

"Roger that, MC," Lenny confirmed. "If we have to, we'll each grab an end and wring your information and my confession out of him. Then, he dies. Of course, we'll have to say a few words over his lifeless body, but, hey, what are chapels for?"

"There's more. Jack has arranged for us to pick up a car in Germany. Just across the Rhine. I have a hand-drawn map, but we'll need to hop a train to get there."

"Trains scare me," Lenny intoned.

"It's okay. It's only a ten-minute ride. You'll be fine."

Then Crayle sensed something he had not noticed before. A man down the street at an ATM had been there for about twenty minutes now. And another man—across the street—was still looking in a flower shop window—one that could reflect them to an observer.

As they stood up, Crayle saw three other men stir to life and start their way.

All Crayle managed was, "*Run!*"

They ran west along the street of the old wine market, weaving in and out of the pedestrian flow. Crayle risked a quick look back. He saw that the five men had all broken cover and were now in hot pursuit.

They quickly reached the intersection that separated the new town from the old town. They bore right. This was déjà vu all over again as they raced to the Ill River bridge Lenny had crossed the previous day.

They seemed a spectacle. The normal street chatter raised up a notch. Apparently, it was not typical in Strasbourg for two men to be running full speed with five other men chasing in similar fashion. It was a question of who would win and what would be the consequence. So much for remaining anonymous.

• • •

In no more than a minute, Crayle and Lenny made it across the Ill River bridge and down the two blocks of the *Rue du Maire-Kuss*, which dead-ended at the train station. The building itself was huge. A giant electronic sign listed the constantly changing incoming and outgoing trains. Lenny spotted the next train to Kehl. It was scheduled to leave … now.

"It's okay. French trains are never on time. It's the law," Lenny said, panting as though he'd sprinted only two or three hundred yards. Just then, a train behind them started to move. They whirled around. To their shock, the number on the train matched the number on the giant schedule board above the ticket counter.

Lenny's heart sank, but Crayle immediately began to run for the train. As it picked up speed, Lenny nearly abandoned all hope.

Crayle persisted, reaching a door on the last car. He grabbed the handle and jerked. The door opened.

Lenny, right behind him, dove through the open door, landing hard on the floor.

One second later, Crayle landed right on top of him, knocking the wind out of both of them.

As they stood and began to dust off, their success turned to dust. A man in a dark blue uniform replete with cap—that of a conductor—stood before them. He had heard the open door alarm and, astounded by their lunacy, launched into a French tirade they did not even want to understand. He waved his arms to and fro in the finest French tradition while the two men gasped for air.

Lenny, as usual, was the first to find something to say.

"Uh, I . . . am . . . sorry. We . . . are . . . Americans." Lenny pronounced the words slow and loud to help the Frenchman understand.

The conductor resumed his tirade.

"We … do … not … speak … French," Lenny proclaimed, as if proud of his ignorance.

The French conductor's eyes began to bulge from his head. His face turned a bright shade of red. Disgusted, he threw his hands toward the ceiling, spun on his heel, and bounded down the car, emitting what were most likely lethal threats against the two imbeciles, in particular, and Americans, in general.

Crayle and Lenny let out a sigh of relief. As the train picked up speed, they saw their tail just inside the front doors of the station, looking in all directions as if seeking divine guidance. The boys were safe.

• • •

The sights were magnificent as the train circled around the west end of Strasbourg and proceeded east to cross the bridge over the river Rhine. All of eleven minutes elapsed until they were once again stationary. They disembarked with far less flourish.

Crayle considered that Lenny had not, even with all the whimpering, given up and had not presented a danger during their escape. He reached a conclusion that, perhaps, he had been too tough on the guy. After all, the unmasking and unraveling of this puzzle was just as important to Lenny, who needed closure on his father's murder.

CHAPTER 38

The station in Kehl was much smaller than the one in Strasbourg. It let out onto a pedestrian promenade lined with shops. All kinds of shops. A number of other people either walked or browsed or took a break to sit on benches.

Both Crayle and Lenny had watched the Jason Bourne trilogy at the cabin, so they knew a little about spy tradecraft. They walked a bit, looked into store windows a bit, using the reflections in the windows and their Jack-supplied wraparound sunglasses to full advantage. Neither one spotted a continuance of the previous tail.

They strolled past the east end of the promenade before they turned north. Away from the shops now, and still no sign of anyone following or watching. Feeling comfortable that no one posed an immediate threat, they followed the road around to their left and circled back toward the Rhine. Crayle had the address on the hand-drawn map Jack had supplied. Only a couple of blocks, and they were there. The sign on the one story building read Europcar.

"I go inside. You stand outside the door and watch," Crayle said to Lenny. "You see anything, come inside right away. We'll find a way out together."

"You sure you can handle renting a car all by yourself?" Lenny said, employing the least amount of finesse possible.

"If you say another word, I will take you over there ..." Crayle pointed to a flat patch of dirt. "... and stake you to the ground. Stay!"

Lenny remained outside as ordered. If pouting made a noise, Crayle would have heard it.

The manager told Crayle the car Jack had rented for them was ready, and he promised to have it brought up immediately. Crayle stepped outside to console Lenny, but the car arrived ahead of him. They both exclaimed, "A Volvo!"

"Great," said Lenny. "If we are attacked by a bunch of crazed school teachers, we'll stand a chance."

The car was not just a Volvo. Their attack/escape vehicle was a Volvo station wagon. The visage, layout, and configuration cried out *soccer mom*. The car was, in fact, quite comfortable inside, had the new car smell, and sported a five-speed, manual shift transmission. Certainly no teacher cum soccer mom would drive one of these. This was a man's Volvo station wagon.

They found their way to the automobile counterpart of the nearby train bridge over the Rhine, recrossing into the southern part of Strasbourg. They knew they must be vigilant. Since Lenny's face was buried in the route map, Crayle figured he would be extra vigilant for the both of them.

Lenny's navigation took them onto the Autoroute—France's payway equivalent of the American freeway. They paid the toll with Euros provided by Jack, then headed south briefly, and then west. They bypassed the German-sounding towns of Lingolsheim, Geispolsheim, Molsheim, and Rosheim before exiting the payway onto the N420 national highway that headed southwest.

Lenny's further directions took them to the Schweizerhof turnoff and onto D128. The rural two-lane blacktop continued across the flatland of the Rhine River Valley. They soon saw the eastern beginnings of the Vosges forested hills in the distance. They both felt they were getting close. And both experienced an excitement tinged with nervousness about the reception they might receive at *Le Rocher de Dabo*.

They passed through the little towns of Niederhaslach and Oberhaslach. The lower and upper Haslachs would have been fun to visit. Perhaps another time.

Crayle had cranked up the speed a notch as they sped under a bright yellow banner stretched above the road, welcoming them to the annual lumberjack festival. Somehow, the thought of running into big, beefy men carrying large sharp axes appealed to neither one of them. Forcing that thought to the backs of their minds, they began their climb into the forest that would lead them to *Le Rocher*—and their quarry, one Sylvain Lalumière.

The road became snakelike. Straight stretches that would allow Crayle to relax his grip on the wheel and his attention to the road were few and far between. He kept checking his rearview mirrors for any signs of someone tracking them.

"Navigator to pilot," Lenny piped up. "We're on a departmental highway, it says here. It's either the D218, the D143, or the D45," he advised. "On course."

"On course?"

"Well, these damn roads change names as fast as this country changes conquerors. I noticed that in Strasbourg. Every 40 yards or so, the streets changed names. Seems they'd celebrate one guy by naming a road after 'im, then forget about him and honor someone else a little farther on. Either they have too many heroes or not enough roads. I swear, they change names faster than their buds, the Italians, change sides."

Crayle mentally slapped the label 'Ignore' on Lenny's comments. He wondered if *ignore with extreme prejudice* was possible. The P.I. was now trashing political correctness on an international level. Crayle forged on.

For its part, the Volvo wagon performed surprisingly well. The tractability of the five-speed transmission and a not-for-export-to-America suspension kept them glued to the winding ribbon of asphalt. This was a driver's Volvo.

Ten miles in, Lenny looked up from the map and spotted a sign. "*There! There!*" he yelled.

As they drew nearer, they spied a small town ahead. A sign identified it as the thriving miniature rural metropolis called Dabo. Another sign announced the change from highway D45 to the street *Rue Saint-Léon IX*.

Downtown Dabo consisted of a town square that resembled a large parking lot bordered on one side by the two-lane blacktop and on the other three sides by one- and two-story buildings butted together in rows. That was it. The rest of the town was residential, the place laid out in what would appear from an aerial perspective as an 'X' with downtown on one of the legs rather than at its center.

"Population 278.5, give or take. But that would be in the eighteen plus square mile metropolitan area. There can't be more than fifty people in the downtown area at any one time." Lenny was only off by a factor of ten, mistaking a fly-speck for a decimal point.

"Lenny. I need you to stay here and check the map again. *Rocher de Dabo* can't be far, but we could spend days in this forest on these tiny roads trying to locate it. I am going to find a local—I'm sure we are the only people in eighteen square miles who don't know where this rock is."

With that, and before Lenny could formulate a complaint, Crayle exited the Volvo and headed for what appeared to be the main village building. Only two stories tall, it looked at least three or four hundred years old.

Crayle spun around twice as he crossed the parking lot to the building. No one in sight. And no sounds. It made him feel somewhat antsy. Was the entire village at the Lumberjack Festival?

He replayed the situation in his mind. The opposition had followed him in Strasbourg. The message scroll, delivered by moped, had proposed—no—commanded a take-it-or-leave-it meet with the Frenchman at a place known as *Rocher de Dabo*. It should be nearby, and it seemed rational Lalumière's men would have the town under surveillance. If not surveillance, then to try to take him out. But it reminded him of a lazy drive in the mountains around Big Bear. Then, he remembered the downhill death race.

The first building he came to sported the sign: *Camping Du Rocher*. Below it, he read *10, Place De L'Eglise 57850 Dabo*. A peek inside the window convinced him this was not the spot for tourist information. He saw tents, portable stoves, and other camping gear. He moved on.

The very next building in the row was labeled *Mairie, Hôtel de Ville*. He decided to try the hotel—they always knew all of the local sights. He opened the door, setting off a tinkling bell. Not high tech, but it was simple and cheap. He stepped inside.

He was greeted inside by a very nice older man, who sported gray hair and wore a medium brown suit that had seen better days. Wrinkle-free suits had not yet made it to the forested hills of eastern France.

But his smile was warm and genuine.

"*Bonjour, monsieur*," he said. Then, continuing in English, "I can see you are *not* from here. How may I be of service?"

"*Bonjour*," responded Crayle, trying hard to emulate the older man's pronunciation—it came out *bo joo*. "Are you the hotel manager?"

His eyes alight with the circumstance, the man laughed.

"In France, the *Hôtel de Ville* is not a hotel, it is city hall. And I am the mayor of Dabo."

Crayle felt stupid.

"I am here as a tourist. I have driven today from Strasbourg, and I am looking for a site called *Rocher de Dabo*. Since I have found Dabo, I expect that my search is nearly complete."

"But, of course," responded the man. "You have come to exactly the right place. As I am the mayor of this fine town, I know where everything is. I can help you, although I am afraid you have travelled too far."

Crayle thought of navigator Lenny. He considered asking if Dabo had any torture chambers left over from the Middle Ages, but did not. Instead, he said, "If you could please direct me, I would be most grateful."

"Ah, yes. We do have a charity event for area children. Perhaps …" The mayor's voice trailed off.

Crayle reached into his pocket and handed over a 100 Euro note—the smallest of Jack's money he had left. The mayoral eyes opened wide. He briefly examined the bill, stuffed it into his jacket pocket, and turned to walk away.

"Excuse me," Crayle called to him, trying hard to keep his cool. "The *Rocher*?"

"Ah, yes. The rock. I am sorry. I am getting old, it seems. Go back three kilometers. Watch for the sign on the right. It is hard to see. The *Rocher* is not far from the road."

With that, the mayor continued to amble toward the back of the room to what Crayle assumed was his office. Crayle, in possession of what he needed, made a hasty retreat from the mayor's office. Out the doors, he broke into a sprint to the car. Within a minute, they were back on route D45 and headed east.

The mayor heard the front door close and reached for the phone on his desk. He would use it to buy some good karma from the unofficial lord of the realm, Monsieur Lalumière. The 100 Euros from this *tourist* would just be a little extra spending money.

Retracing their route on the D45, Magus and Lenny searched hard for the small sign on the right amongst the bushes and trees indicated by the mayor. A sixth sense made Crayle glance into the rearview mirror.

"They're here!" he yelled at Lenny.

"What?"

"From the lake. Two black cars are coming up fast from behind."

Lenny did not bother to turn around. "Paranoia strikes deep," he parroted the 60's song by Buffalo Springfield. "Into your life it will creep. Look, homeboy, there ain't no way. Besides—one of them went down a really steep hill," he trailed off as if asking a question.

Crayle looked again. "Two black Chargers coming on like mother—"

Lenny twisted around to verify. "Jeeesus! The frogs can't fit a hemi into a Poo-joh, so they bring over the Deeetroit iron. Crank it up, MC."

Crayle did. They fairly flew around the twists and turns, sideswiping a Citroen Deux Cheveaux and sending it careening into a ditch.

"Jesus!" screamed Lenny. "You nearly killed Snoopy!"

Finally, they came upon a stretch of straight road. Crayle used the opportunity to check the mirror again.

"They will catch us, Lenny. Get your gun out now!"

"Shit!" cried Lenny.

Up ahead loomed two orange tractors, each occupying a lane. As they drew near, Crayle and the P.I. made out a round-bale spike fitted to each. The spikes were a good four feet long, at least two inches in diameter, and made of hardened steel. When not trying to spear cars, a farmer would poke the spike into a round hay bale, lift it, and transport it where it was needed. No mistake here. These two drivers were looking to impale the crap out of Crayle and Lenny.

Just then, an opening to a side road appeared amongst the bushes and trees. Crayle flung the Volvo to the right with a gnawing screech of the tires. The Volvo complied.

"This station wagon is for mom and pop and the kids, for Chrissake!" Lenny panted. Crayle could tell the P.I.'s heart rate was pushing its limit.

The turn was onto a very narrow dirt road. They flew past a sign reading, *Route du Rocher.* The road spiraled around a hill like a backward 'at' sign before it dumped them into a paved parking lot.

As they slid to a stop in the parking lot, they saw the top of the hill ahead. Above that, they spotted the pile of rock strata known as *Le Rocher*. They could see a charming-looking chapel perched upon the flat topside of the rock.

They ran across the empty parking lot which ended at a restaurant on the right and a pathway leading up the rock on the left.

"Lenny! Get inside the restaurant! Call the police!"

"No! I gotta protect you! We'll take 'em on together!"

"Trust me!" Crayle pleaded with Lenny. "I'll be fine. It's just like Hong Kong, but we'll need help."

A reluctant Lenny darted into the restaurant. Empty. He searched for a phone.

Crayle looked back as the two Chargers blew into the parking lot and aimed right for him. He needed to lead them away from the restaurant. He spun around to his right and dashed up a pathway that hugged the *Rocher's* side. He could see the top of the chapel spire. He would find a way out of this up there. He hoped.

The two Chargers screeched to a stop near the restaurant. Eight men, all dressed as lumberjacks, piled out of the cars. The one shouting orders stayed with the vehicles. The rest gave chase.

When Crayle reached the top of the pathway, he stopped. The chapel ahead looked small, certainly able to hold fewer than eighty people at a time. Carefully restored, it looked near new. At the front and to the left of the entrance stood a tall bell tower.

The *Rocher* itself was flat as a board on top. Besides the church, there were two tables with chairs. Perhaps for visitors to take a lunch break.

Crayle thought of the view the site commanded over the surrounding hills and valleys when he heard sounds behind him. He turned. His pursuers had split up. The five who faced him were armed with strange weapons.

Tools had been left in a box on the pathway, probably by those performing the renovations. They were tools fashioned in a bygone era, perhaps a requirement when renovating French landmarks. Now, each killer had in his hands a craftsman's tool of yore, each one with lethal potential. There would be no loud firearm reports to alert anyone, just death. The killers fanned out. They did not look friendly, and they came straight for him.

CHAPTER 39

Crayle backed away from the advancing hit team as they fanned out. Right now he *really* wished he had Ling's martial arts skills. He wished he had Phoebe. He wished—where was Lenny? No time. No more wishes, either.

He turned and ran past the wall of the church toward the back. As he did, the sharp drop off at the edge of the *Rocher* became obvious as a containment. Jumping off as a means of escape was not an option. He was trapped.

One of the assailants yelled orders to another. That man charged after Crayle, while the others headed toward the chapel door.

Crayle made it around to the back of the chapel, slamming his back against the wall. He gulped for air. However his body had been before his accident, it was not like that now. The oxygen seemed to be coming in teaspoon-sized amounts—not enough. Not near enough.

His peripheral vision caught his first assailant's arms as they flew out from the corner of the chapel a few feet away. The two-by-four he was wielding was already accelerating. Crayle could not move. The lumber caught him across the stomach and forearms. Hard. He went down like a lead weight.

On his back, he clutched at his wrenching stomach as his attacker raised the six-foot-long board straight up, like an executioner readying for the final blow. The man smirked as if he were a superior being about to destroy vermin. And then he brought the board down with all of his strength, squinting his eyes shut as if to increase the force of the blow all the more.

Crayle, with no other option, rolled toward the man, stomping his heel into the man's left knee just as the business end of the two-by-four smacked the ground behind him.

"*Merde!*" screamed the assailant as his knee went out and he collapsed to the ground.

Crayle quickly pulled out the four-inch Cold Steel flipper knife he'd found in the hotel room bureau and rolled atop the man.

The man, still in pain, managed to get his two husky lumberjack's forearms between them. He held Crayle just far enough away that the point of the knife barely penetrated the man's shirt.

Crayle leaned all of his weight on the butt end of the knife. Then, with one last knee to the groin, he forced the knife into the man's heart.

This assailant no longer posed a threat. Crayle lay sprawled on his back, struggling to catch his breath and regather his strength.

Again, he wondered, how did I know exactly what to do? Why am I able to move and act with such speed and confidence? It was as if his self-defense mechanisms could tunnel through to memories and skills that his conscious mind could not. Would he always react precisely in the right way without any conscious connection? He felt no control and it tore at his mind, feeling at once the victor and, at the same time, the ready, defenseless victim.

Crayle stood, not bothering to remove the knife from the corpse. Where were the others? Why had they not followed? Where was Lenny? More questions.

"Lenny!" huffed out a breath.

He turned and moved with caution around the side of the church. He needed to get down the path and find Lenny.

As he neared the front, he stopped short. He needed to take care—he was no good to Lenny dead. He continued to the front corner of the chapel. Quietly. Slowly.

There they were. They'd exited the chapel and stood in front. One called out to a compatriot. The dead man, who was quite beyond hearing.

Then they saw him. Crayle stood at the corner of the chapel with nowhere to hide. Just him and four thugs who wanted him dead. Perhaps there was a reward; perhaps they just hated people named Magus Crayle.

The men moved quickly, blocking access to the path back down the hill.

Crayle glanced around. No sign of anyone coming to his rescue. No sirens. Nothing. And what of Lenny? He yelled his name into the breeze. Nothing. Running out of options. Think, Crayle commanded himself.

Then, weapons raised, the assemblage charged, screaming what sounded like some sort of French battle cry.

Crayle knew he was outmanned. Weaponless. And outgunned. He turned and ran to the door of the church. He pulled the heavy iron ring as hard as he could. The heavy oak door, designed for a diminutive priest, was amazingly well-balanced. It flew open, nearly dragging Crayle along for the ride.

He was just able to step inside when the first Frenchman reached him. The man swung at him with a heavy mallet, just missing. Crayle grabbed the man's shirt and the door's inside ring at the same time. He jerked on the shirt and then the ring. Though he was running on empty, he pulled the door ring with all of his remaining strength. It slammed the attacker's head into the doorjamb so hard, the door bounced back. Crayle heard the thud of a body dropping at his feet.

Two down.

Crayle turned, scanned the chapel's interior, and saw two sets of pews separated by a middle aisle. He ran toward the front. He saw an altar ahead and, in front of it, a wide board laid across two sawhorses. Next to it was an ablution basin. Then, it hit him.

The first man had not intended to kill him, just to subdue him. The others had not followed in the attack, but had come inside to prepare a much slower demise for him.

The board awaited someone, namely him. He would be bound to it, and the holy water—it would be used in a religiously medieval forebear of modern water torture. Swell.

The three remaining assassins stepped over their fallen comrade, who still lay in ignominious repose on the doorsill.

The one who had before issued orders, did so again.

Crayle couldn't understand the words, but the actions spoke volumes.

A lone man stalked down the aisle while the other two moved several paces behind. Watching.

Crayle no longer expected the catch, torture, and kill scenario. Just kill.

He looked around the unfamiliar surroundings. And then made his move. He ran to the right side of the church, then left down the outside aisle toward the entry.

The leader could not permit him to escape. Not again. He shouted another order. One of the other men ran back to the doorway to bar any escape plan their quarry might have envisioned. Then, the man decided to improvise. He ran along behind the last pew to intercept their target.

Crayle stopped. His heart threatened to pound right through his chest. He could not get enough oxygen. And he had no weapon.

Just then he saw on the wall next to his head an iconic plate, no doubt of porcelain. The painted image of the Holy Mother, the rays of sun, and the angels seemed appropriate.

He yanked the round plate off the wall and dashed the edge against the stone. He Frisbeed the very lethal end product at the man who blocked his escape.

The man had obviously never seen a Frisbee. He took it in the neck. The jagged edge cut his windpipe and severed his jugular vein. The blood poured rather than spurted. He made a god-awful noise through the gash, then collapsed. Dead.

Three down.

Crayle had seen the doorway to the bell tower on his side of the church. He darted inside the small space.

He heard the pandemonium of the other two, and more orders coming fast and furious from the leader.

Inside, he found a spiral staircase. It only headed up.

Crayle, beyond exhaustion, hurled himself up the stairs as the gang of five-minus-three ran into the tower below.

He was high enough that they could only swing their weapons at his legs. There were many swings, but only a few hits. In his deteriorating state, Crayle was slowed to pulling himself up the steps with the remaining strength in his arms.

He exceeded their reach. They scrambled onto the stairway, looking like a reprise of the Marx brothers.

Crayle looked up and the top of the stairs seemed unobtainable. Now, he realized what the advisory sign at the bottom of the stairway meant. He'd only picked up the 50 from it. Fifty steps. Omigod!

The fight at the bottom of the stairway had been resolved. The leader let his last minion go first, a decision designed to tire their target even more. Before TJ would arrive at the chapel to finish him off.

Crayle struggled out of the bell tower stairs and onto the chapel roof. It was flat, devoid of any new threat to him. He ran to the side, searching out a possible exit. A glance down assured him of a thirty foot drop to the ground. A jump would probably disable him. Or kill him outright.

He heard a sound. He turned around to see the remaining minion emerge from the tower. The man, too, was trying to replenish his lungs. Gripping a long chisel in his hand, he began to stalk.

As Crayle moved sideways, the assailant moved laterally, cutting off Crayle's plan to get away from the edge.

He remembered the rooftop in Hong Kong. Feigned vulnerability might work here. He reached to his waist and dropped his pants. The minion charged.

Crayle crouched, grabbed the waistband, but, instead of standing up, he rolled into the legs of the chisel-wielding killer.

The man tried to pull up. Too late. Crayle's bizarre move was a complete surprise. He flew over Crayle and then over the edge. The loud thud from below told Crayle the man was out of the game.

Four down.

The leader stood just outside the bell tower doorway. He was not amused. He waited for Crayle to refasten his pants. Then, he closed in.

His weapon of choice was called an adz. It looked like a hatchet with the blade turned ninety degrees. It was a small hoe-like device that could easily cave in a man's skull. Or rip out his guts with one swing.

The leader had been right. Crayle was now a man with no wherewithal to fight. He looked like someone resigned to death. The man swung his medieval weapon, trying to break parts of his target's body, piece by piece.

Crayle barely avoided the swings. Then he stopped moving. He stood up straight, his hands at his sides.

"I'm done. Just get it over," he panted.

This took the attacker by surprise. But he quickly adapted. He took one final step toward Crayle. He extended his weapon back behind him, as if to complete his mission with a single blow.

Crayle stepped in and jabbed his thumb into the man's midsection. An expression of stunned shock came over the man's face. But he did not fall down.

Crayle knew he did not have any where near mastery of Ling's deadly martial art, but he expected at least something.

The adz still raised behind him, the leader of the attack force fell like a sack of Normandy apples to the rooftop. But he did not die like Ling's victims. He lapsed into convulsions, still grasping the weapon. Then, in one final violent twitch, he went still.

Five down.

• • •

The heavy howl of the late afternoon wind on *Le Rocher* had given way to a gentle early evening breeze. And so the battle of wills and bodies had given way to peace. Crayle surveyed the damage in his mind—five bodies. It was clear Lalumière had never intended to meet with him; he only wanted Crayle killed. Again. Any chance of a non-violent meet with the Frenchman had just gone down in flames.

So, where was Lenny? Crayle looked down from the chapel roof. He saw no signs of Lenny, but, from his vantage point, he could not see the bottom of the curved pathway or the restaurant. Perhaps Lenny had called the gendarmes and was struggling with the necessary French. More likely, he was hiding in the restroom. Crayle's jaw clenched at the thought.

Crayle heard what sounded like a scuffle in the parking lot below. Then two men came into view from the direction of the restaurant. They were dragging a man toward a black Mercedes *Geländewagen*—the German equivalent of an über-SUV with dark-tinted windows. Crayle stumbled down the spiral staircase and out of the chapel. He reached the top of the pathway at a full-out run.

"… your mama!" he heard their captive scream from down below. Crayle knew that voice. *Lenny!*

One of the men turned and looked up toward Crayle as the other threw the trussed-up man into the vehicle through an open rear door. Crayle knew that face. He knew that wicked smirk.

TJ!

Crayle descended the path as fast as his body would allow, but the car sped away, spewing a blast of gravel in its wake. *Now what?* was all he could come up with.

He ran past the two parked black Chargers to the Volvo, key in hand. He blew out of the lot as if he were driving the Cobra.

After he had unwound the spiral road that had delivered them to the rock in the first place, Crayle saw the Mercedes SUV turn right onto the D45. Back toward Strasbourg. He was only a couple hundred yards behind.

The country road was as twisty on the return as it had been coming. Turn after turn, it was now you see him, now you don't. After what could not have been more than ten minutes at breakneck speed, Crayle came to a run of over a mile during which Lenny and his captors were out of sight entirely.

Finally, Crayle passed a tourist sign for the *Château de Hohenstein*. He remembered he had seen it going into the forest and realized he would soon emerge from the Vosges with no captors—or Lenny—in sight. As he passed once again beneath the lumberjack festival banner, his view ahead provided no hint of the Mercedes. In fact, the entire vista was vacant of tail lights. His heart sank.

Crayle had to pull the car over and think. Just think. There had to have been a turnoff. *Of course! They took him to the château!*

Not for a second did it occur to him that he had no army of Jack, Phoebe, and Micmac. He spun the Volvo around and retraced the last few kilometers. To no avail. There was no sign of the big black Mercedes. There was no sign of any driveway. There was no sign of Lenny.

Now completely exhausted, he fought back the tears of failure. He turned around for the last time to drive back to Strasbourg and the hotel.

Crayle realized he had won another skirmish, but he had not won the war. There was some good news. The fact the men had not killed Lenny, but had kidnapped him instead, indicated the war remained an on-going enterprise. In other words, the game, in which he was a player and that he did not understand, was still on.

Crayle parked the Volvo in the underground parking beneath the *Hôtel de France*. He was sure Lalumière and his cohorts knew where to find him.

CHAPTER 40

When Lenny awoke, everything was dark. He could make out no shapes, but his P.I. senses captured the odor of wood, metal, and something rubbing against his face that smelled like wet cheesecloth. Then there was the musty, damp smell one would ordinarily associate with dungeons. He sensed no vibrations from a nearby highway or airport.

His body complained in the areas where he'd been struck while being wrestled into the car at *Le Rocher*. And he had another gripe to air if someone wanted to listen. Lenny always slept on his side, yet he found himself lying on his back—face up—unable to move. Beyond the smells, the silence about him felt stark and eerie. Then, a voice.

"Good morning, Mr. Lipschitz. Or should I say, Mr. Silberweiss?"

The accent was French. Lenny had no doubt whatsoever that it belonged to his favorite Frenchman, Sylvain Lalumière. Apropos of his P.I. tradecraft, he feigned ignorance.

"Who is that?"

No answer.

"You know my name. It's Lipschitz. Silberweiss was my dad's name, so that means you knew my dad. You—"

"I did not know him personally, Mr. Silberweiss. He was not a serious player as, I am afraid, neither are you. I could play games with you, but, as I am sure you must have concluded, you will soon achieve the same unfortunate end, also at the end of a blade."

Lenny lost it. "The only game I want to play with you, Frogface, is a game of Whac-A-Mole on your testicles."

The P.I. struggled, but was bound hand and foot to what felt like a wooden bench. Only his mouth was free. He utilized his only available weapon.

"I understand from the library docs that you have a son with a different name. If you're going to call me Silberweiss, then you gotta call the little bastard Lalumière. Them's the rules."

"If you can dispense with your wry sense of humor for a moment, I will fill you in on what actually transpired regarding your father."

Lenny went silent.

He needed to know.

"It seems your father had been enlisted to deal with colleague Mr. Crayle's personal effects, I believe you call them. Within the personal effects, he found a very interesting device. It, in turn, contained some information highly pejorative to me and to my associates. Your father, Samuel Walter Silberweiss, determined the intelligence contained therein had a very high potential worth. He then parlayed that find into a blackmail attempt. All went well—perhaps I should call you Lenny—until the moment he died. You must understand, our project was just too important to let anyone derail it. Sorry. Really." Lalumière sounded somewhat sincere.

Someone pulled the cheesecloth sack from Lenny's head. The sack took with it the variety of odors, save the smell of wood. The air in the room was fresh, and Lenny breathed deep. The bright light of a large crystal chandelier overhead caused his eyes to snap shut. In a few seconds, he was able to look around.

He was on his back and tied to a wooden bench all right, hence the smell of wood. When he looked to his right, he could see beyond a wall of windows to a carefully manicured garden laid out in squares of foliage. A gardener, blissfully oblivious to Lenny's dire plight, was clipping an outlining hedge to a proper height of eighteen inches or so. Lenny assumed the glass was one-way.

A scan to his left gave Lenny the impression he might be in an eighteenth-century furniture museum. Chairs and sofas of glossy off-white lacquer framing embellished with gold trim. Louie-the-someteenth or other, he concluded. Then, he looked up. His heart jumped.

"The uprights you see, Mr. Silberweiss, are constructed from trees felled in the Vosges, specifically the *Forêt Domale de Dabo* in which you find yourself as our guest. They support the block of similar material which holds your neck securely in place. They also provide a guide to the razor-sharp blade currently positioned above as it inevitably shall slide to *its* destiny and, in its unique and subtle way, send you to yours. We all have a destiny, Mr. Silberweiss. Your father's mistake, his last, was to interfere in mine."

Lenny, his eyes fixed about four feet above his head, had never before had this perspective of the instrument of certain death invented by surgical doctor Joseph-Ignace Guillotin. His mind flipped through Sun Tzu with alacrity. *If the enemy is superior, run like hell!* Lenny jerked at the ropes binding his hands and feet, but to no avail. Next page.

"My destiny is close at hand now," Lalumière continued with his soliloquy. "Mr. Magus Crayle remains as a major roadblock. He can connect me to Chin and to others, who likewise wish to remain anonymous. He will arrive soon, I believe, to rescue you and to interrogate, or should I say interview, me. You may take comfort in the fact that he will die here, too, Mr. Silberweiss."

"Yeah, with him gone you won't need me anymore, will you, Frogface? Your gardner got a place for me, Monsieur Le Fucknuts? I got a bulletin. Mag and me have beaten your guys four times. Four fucking times. You just don't know when you're licked. I would be happy to accept your habitual French surrender at this time."

Lenny was correct about the four failures of TJ and his gang. Technically, though, Lenny had not participated in the Tack Store fight nor the rooftop battle in Hong Kong, but he allowed that Sun Tzu might have said, *'Intimidate your enemy, even if you have to lie.'* Yeah, and if he didn't say that, he should've.

"He'll be here with helicopters, lots of really big guns, and enough troops to end your destiny long before mine." His heart rate picked up the pace.

Lenny was now on the offensive, at least in his own mind, from a former position of extreme, futile weakness. Sun Tzu had conveniently left out such a hopeless state of affairs.

Lalumière laughed one of those arrogant little laughs men like him do.

"If he had anything other than this pitiful two-man army, he would have brought it at *Le Rocher*. At The Rock. Hmmm? I am afraid, Mr. Silberweiss, I have for you good news and bad. The good news is that my man—the one you call TJ—attempted to bring in reinforcements to both assure my survival and Mr. Crayle's lack thereof. It seems that, when an American was mentioned, it conjured images of smart bombs and endless resources, so it seems we have come up empty on that account.

"The bad news, however, overrides the good. The force I already possess is very much similar to that of royalty before me. It is the sort of imperial guard that does not fight for money. Rather, it fights to the death, if necessary, for a cause. And that cause is me. It turns out we are better off with this force than a much larger, but paid and therefore far more unreliable one. I am afraid that spells, how would you say, *curtains* for the two of you. Do you wish to make further comment while your head is still connected to your body, Mr. Silberweiss?"

So, the Frenchman did not know about Phoebe. Or Jack. Or Micmac. A surge of courage coursed through Lenny's veins. He knew he would be kept alive until Crayle was dead. This Lalumière creep would need to have him available for proof of life. He pushed the offensive.

If your enemy is superior, irritate him. Sun Tzu.

"Row-shay, shmo-shay. You ought to do what all other Frenchmen have done since that Napoleon guy. What does *Liberté, Egalité,* and *Fraternité* mean, anyway? Eat, Drink, and Surrender?" Lenny laughed hard at his lame joke, as usual. Only his restraints kept him from rolling onto the floor.

Lalumière was not amused. "Mr. Silberweiss. I also have in my possession an exceptionally old Guillotine blade a farmer near *Saverne* unearthed in his field. It is quite rusted, and the blade is the furthest thing from sharp. In fact, there are several notches where it repeatedly struck bone and the metal itself failed. I can arrange to have the razor-sharp blade above you changed out should you continue to provoke me. With a modicum of reflection, it occurs to me that Mr. Crayle may choose, wisely, to leave you to me so that he might be rid of you for once and for all. I may need to rethink my strategy. Alas, for you the outcome shall be the same. Gentlemen, move Mr. Silberweiss upstairs. We will hold him in reserve."

In compliance, Lalumière's men hoisted the guillotine and bore it up a stone staircase to the château's main level. The ride for its passenger was far from pleasant. Lenny now hated this man more than he had ever known he could. Although, at this point, Sun Tzu was running a close second.

But Lalumière was right. A one-man assault on a guarded château was doomed. An assault by a force four times that size—not much better. Lenny's spirits took a nose dive, befitting his circumstance. He took a deep breath. He let it out slowly. He closed his eyes, initiating a prayer that Crayle would call the whole thing off and just find a place to hide.

Pick your battles. Sun Tzu.

CHAPTER 41

The man known to those around him as *the subject*, Magus Crayle, made his way back from the forested hills of the Vosges to the Hôtel de France. He had done his best, in his battered visage, to enter the hotel and ascend the staircase without arousing notice from the front desk staff. At least, the hotel's staircase proved more accommodating than the steep spiral at the Rocher Chapel. Had he been in better shape, it would not have been such a struggle. He made a mental note to secure a first floor room next time he went to war.

It took his last vestige of strength to drag open his door. He stumbled down the hallway and ducked into the bathroom on the left. Exhausted and aching from the pummeling, he washed out the cuts on his arms and body and treated them with the hydrogen peroxide he found.

As he staggered toward the main chamber, he tripped over the wastebasket. He placed it next to his bed, just in case, and collapsed across the mattress.

With external trauma in temporary abeyance, his mind delivered to him a situation report on the state of affairs. It had switched into self-preservation mode. It pointed out that Lenny had been captured and that Phoebe, Jack, and Micmac were nowhere in sight. It prevailed on Crayle's sensibilities—any that remained—that there were exactly no chances in hell he could assault a guarded château, sans weaponry and bodies, to capture and interrogate his nemesis, Sylvain Lalumière. His mind replicated the word 'hopeless' into the myriad vacant memory cells of his brain. It demanded that he be reasonable and take his wretched body and quasi-vacuous brain home for serious rehabilitation.

But his body spoke loudest, caring not about the harsh realities. It did not care about people whose lives were dedicated to helping him and whose own lives were on the line. It did not care because, in its present state, it could not. As his body demanded, his eyelids turned out the lights.

The door creaked.

He should have jumped to the ready, but had no hidden resource to tap. No nerves to jangle. Synapses fired blanks.

He knew he had closed the door. Tight. Now, he heard the distinct closing sound.

As footsteps padded softly down the hallway toward the bedchamber, he imagined the assassin and his stealthy moves.

Then …

"Yo, hero. It is I, your protector-in-chief," came a woman's voice. When she stepped into full view, Crayle did a double take. The short jet black hair curled forward at the bottom and the short black French dress threw him.

"Who the—"

She pointed her finger, mouthed *pow*, and, with a soft sexual puff, blew the fantasy smoke from her fingertip.

Crayle sat up with a start.

"Holy crap!" Crayle laughed out loud. The one-woman cavalry had returned. Then, his mind went random.

"I could have used you, Agent Bransfield, an hour ago when five of Lalumière's goons tried to autopsy me alive. And how the hell did you get orders to France in the first place?" he asked, suspicion heavy on his voice. "FBI jurisdiction ends at our borders."

It did not matter. The overriding truth won out. The joker was back in the deck.

At Le Rocher, he had counted down the assassins: one, two, three, four, five. With Phoebe, his side had gone from one up to two up. Trend: positive.

Then, Jack walked into the room. And then, Micmac.

"Four up, for Christ's sake!" Crayle sang. Tears welled in his eyes, the other three staring at him as if he'd lost his mind.

Then, the stowaway. Ling. "*Ni hau*, tough guy," she said. "Five up."

• • •

Jack walked to the entertainment module and inserted a CD Anne-Isabel had provided. As was standard tradecraft, he raised the volume to make listening devices in the room ineffective. The use of a CD by the French rock group *Téléphone* was intentional—loud French music would be *de rigeur* in France.

He told Phoebe and Micmac to position the table next to the bed. They all grabbed chairs and sat down to plan the attack.

Jack began, "We will have to come at this from several directions, guys. Since we only have five, everyone is key. We can't afford to lose any of you … of us."

That little blunder by Jack caused a noticeable silence all around. Was he really operational in this or not?

"You three," he said, pointing to Mag, Phoebe, and Ling, "will leave here at 0400 hours. There are G-shock watches for all of you in the bottom drawer. They're synchronized to each other and to ours and set to local time."

Micmac retrieved the watches and distributed them.

"MacKay and I will head out now and make preparations at staging area Charlie just outside the forest. We'll meet up at Charlie, which you will discover under Favorites on the portable GPS unit, also in the bottom drawer. Once in the car, you fire up the GPS, touch Favorites and then Charlie. Then Go after that. The GPS will guide you to our rendezvous. Whatever you do, do not remove the SD card from the GPS. It has the map layout for France on it. Everyone down with what I've said?"

It was straightforward. No one commented.

"We'll roll into the forest before daybreak. It will give us cover and an element of surprise."

Crayle had a question. "I believe Lalumière knows we—or I—will come after him. We can assume he will have force superiority, too. How can we compromise the odds, which all seem to be in the Frenchman's favor?"

"Yes. And—" began Phoebe.

"I'll answer all questions regarding specifics about your—there, I did it again—*our* assault when we congregate at the Charlie rendezvous. That way, if any of us are captured prior, they won't know detail."

The trio watched Jack and Micmac beat a hasty retreat out the door. Questions grew in their minds at the task soon at hand, and even more so with Jack's verbal faux pas. Crayle did not speculate aloud, but he had been sent to Hong Kong by Jack—and attacked. And he remembered the painting in Chin's office and in Jack's cabin. If Jack was playing on the wrong side, this time would be Crayle's last.

CHAPTER 42

A light snowfall greeted them the next morning. Crayle took the driver's seat with Phoebe riding shotgun. Ling sat in back, knowing that, no matter how good she was at Chin's favorite *chore*, she was nonetheless expendable. She needed to succeed for him here.

She punched in the GPS selections supplied by Jack, hoping the unit knew its route and destination. They caught little traffic heading southwest from Strasbourg and across the Rhine Valley plain. Turning right off the main road, Crayle proceeded toward the Vosges. The distant forested hills, and the danger they held, made the butterflies dive-bombing in their respective stomachs real.

As they reached the sibling villages of Oberhaslach and the smaller Niederhaslach, the GPS directed them off the main road and onto a dirt driveway. Up ahead stood a single-story farmhouse with Germanic half-timbered sides. No matter whether you were French, German, or other, one always seemed to be on borrowed ground in Alsace.

Light emanated from the farmhouse, but not the large barn a short walk away. The team members observed pock marks stitched into the stone exteriors. Micmac greeted them at the door. Crayle followed the women inside, and Micmac closed up. Inside, they found a setup unlike any they could have found except in war-time when troops of one side or the other might have occupied it. The furniture showed severe damage and shards of window glass remained along the walls. The prospect of live enemy fire tattooed itself into each mind.

"Welcome to Garrison Upper and Lower Haslach," Jack greeted.

Anne-Isabel, who had met Crayle and Lenny at the airport, was in the kitchen, a cigarette in her left hand as she brewed what smelled like up-all-night French coffee. Both Crayle and Micmac took in her little body, moving this way and that.

"Put 'em back in their holsters, guys," said an annoyed Phoebe. "I've got more than that over there." She nodded toward Jack's European underling.

Anne-Isabel tossed one of her looks over her shoulder at the men, and they were toast. Phoebe's expression said she had searched her memory for an agency policy that permitted homicide in foreign countries. Finding none, she plopped down on the country-style couch. The guys snapped out of their trances and followed suit. Ling took a chair to their right.

Jack began. "This house is more than it seems. It will be our ops base until we win, are dead, or give up. Anything goes beaucoup wrong, we meet back here. Alright. The doors, walls, and windows are everything-proof. The windows have the further enhancement of disallowing visual incursions from snoopers or snipers. We could all run around naked in here and no one would know."

Phoebe felt on edge. She glanced at Crayle, then Micmac, then the diminutive agent. Her lips pursed outward at the thought.

Anne-Isabel, for her part, leaned against the kitchen counter, coffee cup and cigarette at the ready. She'd seen Pheobe's reaction to her. She couldn't help it. She took a draw on her cigarette, pushing the smoke out and up toward the ceiling. With her eyes still on the agent, she put on enough smile to deploy the dimples. Then, as though issuing a challenge, she slowly ran the tip of her tongue along her upper lip.

That did it. Phoebe surged upward, but used the wrong arm for leverage. She cried out in pain and collapsed back onto the couch.

Jack looked at them both. He decided to let sleeping dogs lie. Anne-Isabel would stay behind to man their base of operations.

"I have chosen weapons for the tactical advantage they offer and for the fit to the individual. Phoebe, you're used to the buck of .45 caliber weapons that go boom, so here is an extra pair of Glock 30's, belt-clip holsters, and ten extended clips. Nine-rounds each. Their carry pouches strap around the top of each thigh—you won't be able to cross your legs in a feminine way."

Jack dropped a forest camouflage duffle at her feet.

"I'll take the first ninety of those bastards, then," she said with a smile.

"Micmac gets an under dash Uzi in 9 mil and a Beretta Px4 *Storm* subcompact 9 mil backup complete with ankle holster."

"Shouldn't we all use the same caliber?" Crayle asked. "The ammunition would be interchangeable."

Jack seemed a little peeved that his experience and expertise would be challenged. He handed the pistol and holster to Micmac. Then, he answered Crayle's question. "This will all happen so fast, any interchange of ammo would occur only after one side or the other is dead. Lalumière will be kept alive if we win this, of course."

"And Lenny," Crayle added.

"If he is still alive, we'll save his sorry ass, too. Crayle, you will fight with an M4 carbine in caliber .223 a.k.a. 5x56. Backstory on you says you are qualified on that piece. And speaking of pieces, try to stay in *one* piece. I have it on good authority ole Doc Rorschach wants you back intact—with all parts properly connected. Your ankle backup will be Lenny's Walther PPK in 7.65 mil."

He handed Crayle what was essentially an M16 carbine with a broom handle front grip—good for control on side sweeps of full automatic fire. Then, Lenny's Walther.

Finally Jack came to Ling. Her mano-a-mano prowess would not be of much use here. He handed her a forest-camouflaged ballistic nylon case shaped as if it contained a crucifix. It did not.

"Ling, I know you're familiar with and favorable toward bowed weapons, so here's a treat. This case contains a rifle-stocked PSE *Reaper* crossbow in Mossy Oak camo. Its compound split-limb bow system has a 185 pound pull and delivers a twenty-inch carbon fiber *Charger* bolt at 310 feet-per-second. Sighting is through a *Viper* Series 3 Red-Dot scope—point and shoot. I also understand that you are stealth-trained as a Ninjutsu adept, among other things, so you will remove any lookouts from the game up front. And with the crossbow, no one will know."

He tossed her a duffel. "Inside you're gonna find a Ninja outfit, complete with split-toe Tabi footwear, in matching camo, and a full quiver."

Ling bowed her head in silent acceptance.

"One last item," Jack said, opening a cardboard box. "These are formfitting gloves. You will need to use them to keep prints and sweat off the weapons. They are special material that fits like procto gloves, tight and flexible, but they are not plastic. In addition, they contain a coating inside that will scramble any DNA you leave when discarded. A word of warning—do not wear them for over two hours at a time. If you do, they will start scrambling *your* DNA. Not good. *Comprenez*?"

All nodded.

"Now, bring your gear and follow me." He lead them through the kitchen and out the back door. Anne-Isabel stayed with her coffee and smoke. She surveyed each passing member of the strike team with interest. Phoebe, the last out, gave her a look. Again, Anne-Isabel opened her mouth a bit and traced the bottom of her upper lip with her tongue. Phoebe started toward the petite spy, but—

"Bransfield, get your ass out here!" from Jack put her back on course.

Jack led them through the barn door into a completely darkened interior. Only when they were all inside and he'd shut the door, did he flip a switch. Spotlights concealed in a loft lit up the place like daylight.

"It's okay," said Jack. "None of this light leaks outside. For all the neighbors know, the barn is as black as before."

Before them was a well-worn flatbed truck that looked like its best days were long behind it. On its bed lay several twenty-meter logs held in place by vertical stays at the edges of the truck bed and by four link-chain tie downs. It was an old French logging truck, pure and simple.

Micmac took over.

"It is, and it is not, what it seems. It can definitely tote logs around and it, along with its Alsatian license tags, looks right at home in this neck of the woods."

"We going to ride these down some river and surprise them from behind," Phoebe asked, her lashes fluttering.

Micmac was all business. He ignored her, motioning them to follow him to the rear of the truck. Hanging on the log ends were three thick flannel shirts in lumberjack plaid. He grabbed two of them.

"Put these on." He tossed the shirts to Crayle and Phoebe.

He gestured at the truck. "We took a page out of World War II. The Germans disguised ships to look like freighters, but hid cannons behind moveable panels. They called them Q-ships. This truck is also not what it seems."

He pointed at the truck bed.

"These appear to be regular logs. They are not. The ends have been hollowed out and these end caps put back on. Inside are two silenced M134 miniguns and enough ammunition that we won't be running out. A/C from the truck cab keeps them cool. They are activated from the console in the truck. At 4,000 rounds per minute each, they will literally erase anything in their paths of fire. This gets us inside and sweeps down the area. We will be careful not to sweep the château. That, we'll need to take with small arms."

"I have a question," Crayle said, looking around. "Where is Ling?"

Jack looked miffed again, but he kept his cool when he spoke.

"She has gone ahead to perform surveillance and to act as a spotter going in. She'll *fix* any sentries just before we light this sucker off. Don't worry. She'll join us when we hit the château. So, the three of you hop inside this beast. Micmac will drive since he created this wonderful monster. Crayle rides shotgun. Bransfield, you're in the middle of this little ménage. Keep the Glocks on either side of you and be ready at all times. And I mean, be ready. When hell breaks loose, the Devil don't take prisoners."

They climbed aboard. Micmac fired it up. The whistling sound at idle told them that this was no ordinary logging truck engine. The turbo diesel he had loaded into its engine bay could pull them, the truck, and the logs well in excess of 100 miles per hour. And they needed to hang on tight. He hadn't had time to upgrade the brakes.

Jack doused the lights before he opened the barn doors.

While inside, Ling had handed Crayle the GPS, which displayed a destination designated *Château L.* He pressed the Go button and the French-accented voice led them out to the main road. Phoebe winced every time the device spoke, thinking of the phony, twerpy, little—she couldn't find the proper word—female back in the farmhouse.

Jack followed them in his own special vehicle with his own special armament. As a project manager, it had been a while since he'd seen action. This was going to be a hoot.

CHAPTER 43

Ten minutes after the unlikely warriors departed Charlie, they passed under the logger festival banner. Lumberjacks, taking down the banner, gave them quizzical looks. Logging trucks didn't carry logs *into* the forest.

The Q-truck climbed the two-lane into the hills of the Vosges. The forested slopes carried with them this morning a hard-earned peacefulness. In a very short time, it would be broken by a scaled-down replica of its former incarnation, and the cacophony of war.

The two men in the cab kept their eyes dead ahead. They were on their way to battle. Phoebe did not have on her game face for the assault. She was pinned in the middle of the cab with Crayle on her right—whom she had known in the biblical sense—and Micmac—her best new prospect for biblical knowledge—on her left. The three were separated only by two Glocks acting as heavy metal spacers. She unclasped her hands and slid them across her thighs to begin a love affair with the new pair of .45s. She slid her fingers sensuously along the receivers, incidentally stroked the men's thighs as well.

Crayle was immune. He stared straight ahead with laser-like focus. Micmac, however, turned and gave her a smile she took to be interest. Later gator. Her game face appeared. She would move heaven and hell to get this done. Only then would she kindle up a fire with the gadget man.

• • •

Ling had arrived ahead of them. The sign Crayle had seen and driven past in his failed effort to catch TJ and Lenny swung away from the road to reveal a narrow driveway. They were close. The logging truck trundled away from departmental highway D218 and into the forest. Off to their left, a dirt bike sailed through the trees like it was on the open road. How a guy could drive that fast through a forest was a question to be answered another day. And so quiet. Mag assumed it was electric.

The thought the biker could be a sentry nagged at him. Was he heading back to the château to sound the alarm? Worse than that, they could be running into an ambush. And where the hell was Jack?

Crayle felt they had an offbeat approach at surprise, but TJ and his crew would be smart enough to have lookouts posted just in case. He hoped Ling had both the chops and the intention to take them out.

The rider veered away from them, disappearing into the greens and browns of the forest known as the *Forêt Domale de Dabo*—the land of Lalumière.

They broke into a clearing and saw the château ahead, surrounded by a ten foot wall and a vineyard. A twelve-foot-high ornate, iron, double gate twenty feet wide guarded the entrance. From Lenny's intel, they knew the building to the right just inside the wall was the château. The stables were to the left. They saw an armed guard on each rooftop.

Micmac pulled the truck up to the gate. Two guards, one tall and one short, approached.

Micmac rolled down his window as the thin, mustachioed taller sentry approached his side of the truck. The diminutive sentry stationed himself on the passenger side.

"Bonjour, monsieur. C'est la maison de le général en chef du forêt?" Micmac used a working class accent, one that would be typical of a French lumberjack. He knew the guard would simply tell him "No. This is not the forest manager's home. Beat it."

The spat out words of the guard to that effect displayed his obvious annoyance that this idiot and his idiot truck had interrupted his daydream. A third guard stood back near the gates, paying little attention to the admonition being given as he took another long drag on his Gitanes cigarette.

The tall guard directed them back to the main road and west past Dabo to Haselbourg. "Everyone zere know heem, hees nem ees *Monsieur Faubourg*."

Micmac backed up the truck and made a 'K' turn. When he had the truck facing the way they had come, he cried, "We're on!"

From the direction of the vineyard came a brief zip sound. Then, another. The two impaled rooftop guards fell in place.

Micmac flipped the transmission into reverse and floored the accelerator. Phoebe popped up through the sunroof and shot the guards. Her arms fit nicely into indentations in the sides of the now-vertical glass. The log trailer blew open the iron gates and slid to a stop.

The three gate guards were down, but, up ahead past the stables, fifteen men, hell bent, burst out of a security force bunkhouse. They fired automatic weapons at the truck's cab, but the bulletproofing Micmac had done was impenetrable as was the sunroof lid that protected Phoebe.

Micmac punched a steering wheel button labeled Increase Volume, and the two miniguns blasted through the false ends of the logs.

He moved the truck slowly now, using the rearview mirror and the steering wheel to wiggle the truck's fanny back and forth. The net effect was to mow down the château's defenders and dismantle the bunkhouse at the same time. When the return fire stopped, so did he.

He wheeled the truck back into a jack-knifed configuration so its tail now faced the château. The staff, upon hearing the din outside, had rushed to the windows. When they saw the business end of the truck being turned their way, the scene turned into a French fire drill. Terrified people scrambled out all doors with no destination in sight—just *pas ici*—not here.

Micmac was on a roll. He was ready to rake the château, but Phoebe yelled, "Lenny is inside!"

The three of them jumped down from the truck and made their way, weapons drawn, to the château doors.

The assault was going better than any of them had expected. They'd breached the castle gates, and there were no casualties on their side.

CHAPTER 44

Crayle, Phoebe, and Micmac moved with caution to the château's steps. Phoebe spoke first.

"Hey, where the hell are Jack and that Chinese chick?"

The men scanned behind and to the sides. No sign of them.

"We do not know why Chin sent Ling. Be extra careful if you see her," Crayle said. He considered the possibility that Chin, as Lalumière's partner, might have sent her to lead him into a trap. Crap! He liked Ling. And what about Jack? Since he'd seen Jack's painting on Chin's wall, he had been suspicious of him. The fact was, in an instant, any one of the team could become a fatal surprise.

"That son of a bitch," Crayle seethed. "Jack's verbal missteps at the farmhouse, the ones that didn't seem to include him, were Freudian. Look, we're on our own. Or—I am on *my* own. You two do not need to do this. I have no choice, so I'm going in."

"The FBI never quits," Phoebe assured him.

Micmac ended the dialog with, "Let's rock!"

The doors ahead were massive and closed. Expecting resistance, the three threw their shoulders into them. To their surprise, the eight-foot tall obstructions opened easily.

Crayle and his strike team entered. They expected a bloody room-to-room battle. The foyer was empty of any signs of life. All they heard was the sound of quiet. To their left was the nearest doorway. Phoebe moved to check the room while Crayle and Micmac covered.

"Clear!" she shouted when she found it—the wine tasting room—to be abandoned.

Crayle remembered hand signals. He motioned Phoebe and Micmac ahead to what Lenny's sketches had depicted as the Great Room, where throngs of aristocrats had partied the night away over two hundred years ago—comfortable to have been born into the power elite. With extreme caution, they stepped up to a ten foot wide entryway.

When they entered the room, they were not greeted by gunfire, but instead by a soft voice, in English. "Welcome to Château Lalumière," it said.

The speaker, a well-dressed man unruffled by the intense combat outside, stood in the far left corner of the room beside a device with two tall uprights and a bench protruding to the rear. There was a basket in front on the floor. A closer look revealed a diagonal blade perched at the highest extent of the uprights.

"Omigod!" Phoebe yelled. "A guillotine!" Then, "I recognize those ugly pants!" She pointed at the prone figure on the bench. "He's got Len—"

The body trussed to the bench struggled against its bonds. Its voice yelled muffled curses through a cheesecloth head sack.

"Stop where you are," the man commanded softly. He held in his left hand a lanyard from the device. "She is right. This," he said, motioning to Lenny's prostrate body, "is one of you, *non*?"

No one moved.

"Yes, lady and gentlemen. Or should I address you: *Les Trois Mages—à la mode moderne.* The Three Magi. I am your host and master of this house, Sylvain Lalumière. This is the grand house of my forebears. And that …" He gestured to the device. "… is not just *any* guillotine. It is a model 1792 guillotine. This particular one was used to behead the early landlords of this estate. My aforementioned forebears, as it turns out."

"We don't care a nit about your ancestors or what happened to them. We are here for Lenny Lipschitz, whom your men kidnapped at the Rocher," Crayle said with force and urgency. He did not wish to dick around with this pseudo-highbrow, sociopathic Frenchman. "Set him free now!"

"And what then? We all adjourn to the wine tasting room and talk history?"

"Then I get answers, one way or another."

Lalumière laughed a smug, evil sort of laugh as he walked to the center of the room. Crayle yelled at him again to release Lenny, but Lalumière ignored him. He reached a table and picked up a TV remote control.

"Do you know what this is, Mr. Crayle? Of course, you do. But it is not just any television remote control, this one is universal in capability." His emphasis was heavy on the word, *universal.* He released the lanyard. "Put away your weapons, or I shall press *Play.* Then that razor sharp blade will give you back your friend in two distinct, though less talkative, pieces."

They saw he was serious. No choice. The heavy blade would complete its fall from top to bottom in a fraction of a second—far too short a time to free Lenny.

"Please, sit down in my Louis XVI chairs. Poor King Louis fell victim to the peasant class. The peasant barbarians severed his head and that of Marie Antoinette. They were good people. Noble people. Like my own ancestors. After they died, the Reign of Terror by the republican *Girondins* and the extremist left-wing Bretons, the *Jacobins,* killed many more. Nobility, it seems, had gone out of style."

Crayle wanted to tell Lalumière where to stick his history lesson. But one click and Len would have to tell his jokes in Heaven. God would not be pleased. They did as their host directed. And they listened.

Lalumière walked to a fifteen-foot buffet along a near wall. He stopped, raised the remote, moved his finger from *Play*, and pressed another button. A ten by six foot section of off-white wall above the buffet turned into a video screen. It had been there all along, but had just displayed in high definition the off-white wall color framed in the gold trim used elsewhere.

The Frenchman pressed another button. A still picture filled the screen. As he worked the volume button, the sounds of the French national anthem, *La Marseillaise*, played up. A state-of-the-art 21.5 sound system, twenty-one high end speakers and five 12-inch subwoofers, shook the walls. Then, for effect, he brought the sound back down to background level.

The screen showed a desert valley, its sides defined by tall mountains. The entire picture bore no color other than sepia tones.

"Mr. Crayle, you have by now killed all of my pitiful defense force. But that is as it must be. Natural selection, you would say in English. My only weapon is this simple device and a logic I believe you will find profound."

Lalumière walked toward the team—he paused just out of reach.

Crayle felt the need to strangle. Phoebe was pissed. She fondled her Glock. And Micmac kept his eyes moving, always aware. Lenny continued to struggle and emit muffled sounds. Lalumière looked directly at Crayle.

"You should know me, Mr. Crayle, but you do not. You came to me three years ago and I, along with Mr. Chin, gave you a dilemma to solve. Perhaps riddle would be more accurate. Do you remember at all?"

Crayle was stuck in a dilemma. He needed to rescue Lenny while he still had a head, but feared that Lalumière was not bluffing. Since he had concluded that Lalumière was a madman, he decided his only recourse was to play him. His language became precise and unemotional.

"Mr. Lalumière," Crayle began, "I have found and met with your associate, Chin. He provided a few pieces of a large puzzle. He gave me your name and told me where to find you. My surprise is that *you* are not surprised. He must have told you so you could do the dirty work—finish the job your men failed when they tried to kill me in America and in Hong Kong. If you choose to use your power and kill me now, please first let me know how I came to be a man with no history. I need the who, the what, the when, and the where. I need ..." Crayle drew in a deep breath for effect. "... more than anything, to know *why*."

Lalumière pondered the statement, and then moved toward the guillotine. Crayle, Micmac, and Phoebe jumped to their feet. Lalumière raised the remote up to shoulder level—his index finger on the *Play* button—his head tilted back and his eyes wide open, signaling alert.

They stopped in their tracks. Lalumière reached down to untie the rope around Lenny's feet. Then, his hands. Lenny flailed even more with his arms and legs free, but his head remained ensnared by the neck-blocks of the guillotine.

"A move of good faith, Mr. Crayle. You were the linchpin in an enterprise founded of necessity by Chin and myself. He and I met at a high-level meeting in Scotland. It was a summit of sorts—a gathering of the world's leading, behind-the-scenes players for the consumption and, dare I say worship, of the finest Scottish malt whisky.

"There, we—Chin and I— found common ground, in that we both find our own well-being and that of our respective countries endangered by the mediocrity of socialistic politics and by the followers of a bizarre and violent faith. We soon realized that each of us had the other's means of resolution at hand. You, sir, made it all possible, Mr. Crayle.

"My contact in America, who will benefit from the project every bit as much as I or Chin, served you up. He told me you were the only man who could pull this off. I know it seems trite, but perhaps we were ill-advised to attempt to make you, and your detailed knowledge of our plan …" He hesitated, searching for the right words. "… go away."

Crayle, under control until now, lost it.

"I worked for the government, dammit. I am a mathematician. The US government does not loan out its employees, mathematicians or otherwise, to international maniacs."

Crayle's voice bespoke his seething hatred for this man, not simply his own soul-deep frustration. Answers begot more questions.

"Tell me, Lalumière. *Who* would give me up to your crazy scheme? *Who* would have the power? And why? Still, *why*?"

Lalumière smiled.

"You would not have been told. But since the tide has now receded for any attempt to thwart my destiny, I will tell you. It is all very simple, Mr. Crayle. The masses see their elected officials as their leaders. No, Mr. Crayle, not even close. Those of us who run this world are not elected by anyone. We are chosen. Not by people, but by talent, by genetics, by birthright. We are chosen by fate."

Phoebe nudged Micmac, whispering, "He's fucking nuts."

"There need be no new world order brought about by members of secret societies, Mr. Crayle. The new world order is already in place. And it is you who have enabled the necessary cleansing of its cancers. It is happening right now. Someone above you in the chain of command is taking orders—from us. Chin's daughter, Ling? She is just ensuring an outcome." He motioned with his head to their left.

Crayle's head turned. There she was. Making no sound whatsoever, she had entered the château and had moved in close behind them. She pointed an automatic at the three of them.

Though he had half-expected it, the betrayal was now official. It hit Crayle hard.

"Look at that incredible machine over there." Lalumière nodded toward the guillotine. "It was built over 200 years ago, yet it still stands strong. With one just like it, the slovenly commoners took the lives of our King and his lovely lady. I purchased mine from a little museum just outside of Paris."

It sounded as if Lalumière was drifting off into his imagination—succumbing to his lunacy.

"My ancestors, rulers of the *Forêt de Dabo*, were the real France. Peasants, never fit to rule, killed them. Those peasants became the masses who, in modern times, have elected bad governments across the globe."

He gave Crayle a rhetorical "don't you agree" look. He continued.

"Ah, but unknown to them, the elected now work for *us*. Our next step will return the noble elite to full power. We will resurrect the commitment of *noblesse oblige*, but we will keep the small people where they belong. The masses, Mr. Crayle, will be happy enough to eat *'ot dogs* and watch meaningless ballgames. We will demonstrate our superiority in leadership by eliminating every remaining threat to peace worldwide. In so doing, we will accomplish what no religion, since time began, has *ever* done …"

"Hitler thought that. Stalin thought that," Crayle said. "They scoffed at religion, too, the Austrian and the Georgian. They both had outsized dreams that turned into nightmares. So will yours."

While Lalumière pondered a retort, Crayle seized the opportunity to survey the situation. It was clear he had two threats now—Lalumière with his clicker and Ling with her gun.

Then a *snap!*

Crayle turned to see that Phoebe had drawn down on Ling. Better, but the Frenchman still held the trump card. One click by the madman, and Lenny was gone.

Lalumière turned back to the large Louis XVI buffet against the far wall. Caught off guard by Crayle's comment, he became flustered. Then, he lifted the remote. He had decided what to do. He pushed *Mode* once, then *Play*.

Breathing stopped.

Mouths dropped open.

Heads spun to the guillotine.

But the guillotine did nothing.

Then a movement on the wall caught everyone's eye. A video began with the same desert scene. As the camera dollied back, they saw more of the valley ensconced by barren mountains on both sides. A graphic was overlaid on the picture. It gave the time and date in a scientific-looking font.

Crayle checked his G-shock watch. It was today's time and date. It was not a DVD. It was a video streaming from a totally barren location. It was eerie with not a sound in the room and no sound from the theater system.

Then came a rumble like distant thunder or the first convulsions of a massive earthquake. The Great Room shook as the sound crescendoed into a god-awful roar. Eyes in the room were all over the place as Lalumière's priceless paintings were flung from the walls. Antiques fell from the table tops, smashing hard upon the floor.

On the big screen, the valley floor erupted. An intense glare of light. All eyes snapped shut, though the brightness of the flash was muted by the video system's constraints. A cloud-like structure swooped up from the valley floor where the village had stood moments before. As the mushroom cloud ascended skyward, jagged shockwave lines squiggled to either side.

Lalumière pressed *Pause*. He savored the moment.

The stark reality of what they were watching swept over the team.

"A nuclear weapon! Of course! Chin!" Crayle looked at Lalumière, astonished by what he and Chin had accomplished. But something else grabbed his attention. He realized that the French lunatic had pressed the *Play* button on the remote. To start the video—and the bomb, he had taken it out of guillotine mode.

He lunged at Lalumière. Something heavy and hard crashed against his head from behind. He slumped to the floor.

Phoebe heard the commotion. Without taking her eyes off Ling, she yelled, "You alright, Mag?"

The same heavy weapon buckled her knees and sent her to the floor, her Glock hitting the wood with a thud.

Crayle did not lose consciousness. He rolled onto his back. Phoebe followed suit. They first looked at Micmac, who had been knocked unconscious. Both gazed up at the man who towered over them. Not Lalumière. TJ.

Phoebe tried to reach for her fallen gun. TJ anticipated the move and kicked her hard in the ribs. She rolled onto her stomach—her cries of anguish and pain almost led Crayle into a suicidal attack on the henchman.

Ling had turned her attention to Micmac, who had just regained consciousness. She seized his weapon.

TJ bent down to jerk Phoebe's arms behind her back. She yelled out when he pulled the right one. Then he stood and handed a pair of comealong tie-wrap cuffs to Ling. Chin's daughter obeyed, silent as she secured Phoebe.

TJ covered the two men while Ling cuffed them. Ling grabbed an antique cotton doily from a table, pressing it to the back of Crayle's head to staunch the bleeding. He held it in place with his hands.

Crayle felt certain they would die here. With Ling's betrayal and Jack a no show, it was over. He asked a final question. Not of Lalumière, but of TJ.

"What happened the first time you tried to kill me? Before I die, tell me what happened at Malibu."

"Malibu? What ees Malibu?"

"You know what I'm talking about. The coast road in California. With the toboggan."

"Only ze two een Beeg Bear and zen Hong Kong and Le Rocher. I only failed zose four time. Not five."

"The crash you caused, you lying, mutant piece of crap."

"Crash?"

"Enough," interrupted Lalumière. "No more talking. Get on with it," he instructed his gunman.

TJ rolled Phoebe over with his foot. As she fell onto her back, her hands pinned beneath, he put his heel on her solar plexus and jammed down hard. She moaned a sound of defeat, totally spent. He picked up Crayle's gun. Just for fun, he kicked Phoebe again. She sobbed at the fresh explosion of pain.

Lalumière's pet killer gave a snarl of a laugh as he kicked Phoebe's gun toward the guillotine.

"Zare. Maybe ze leettle man weel come to your rescue." TJ's words emphasized the hopelessness of their situation.

Phoebe tried to roll back over. TJ slammed his booted foot into the middle of her chest, re-igniting her pain.

Crayle pushed up to his feet and staggered toward TJ, who pointed his gun and motioned him back. Then, he returned his attention to Phoebe.

He rolled her over once again with his foot, clearly savoring the pain she experienced each time. Leaning down, he grabbed a handful of blood-spattered hair. Standing astride her, he lifted her to a sitting position and forced her mouth against his crotch.

The others saw the bulge growing beneath the fabric of his pants.

"Eet was you who keeled my men at Beeg Bear," he yelled before he waved his gun at Crayle and Len. "Eet was you who gave zem time to escape."

Without warning, he shoved her back to the floor and spat on her pain-wracked body.

"Your time, blonde woman, *est finis*." He pointed his French Manurhin semi-automatic pistol at the side of Phoebe's head. Dead silence.

Across the room, Lenny had heard Phoebe cry out. Despite the cheesecloth, he also recognized the sound of TJ's snarl.

Phoebe's cries of agony gave him a fix on her location. If he could just grab her gun. It had slid across the floor. He had heard it hit the hardwood foot of the guillotine. If he could just …

He used the tips of his fingers to edge the gun closer, then grabbed it. He swung it back alongside the French death contraption and pitched it bowling style in Phoebe's direction—toward the sound of the voices. He prayed for a miracle. His bowling style was the lob ball.

Phoebe tried to grab the gun as it flew over her head, but her bound wrists caused her to miss it. Instead, the heavy weapon struck TJ full-on in the groin.

He yelled out in low-grade French, his head arching upward as if to communicate his misery to a sympathetic God.

The Glock fell to the floor between his feet. Phoebe rolled to her side and grabbed it up behind her.

She flipped up—supported by her knees and head.

Resembling a giant black-haired inch-worm readying for a step, she jammed her weapon up between TJ's legs, pressing the barrel hard into the flesh between his aching balls and his ass hole.

She fired once.

Her weapon boomed.

The .45 caliber Hydrashock slug expanded immediately as it bore up through the man's intestines and abdomen, cutting a quarter-sized tunnel through his upper torso. The mangled bullet blew out TJ's head and ricocheted off a ceiling beam in an inverted shower of blood.

Death overtook the henchman in that instant. His lifeless body dropped like felled timber.

Lalumière attempted to retrieve TJ's gun. Crayle reached it first. Lalumière tried to flee.

Crayle didn't risk trying to wound him. He took a run and fell into a slide, knocking the Frenchman down. Lalumière was no athlete. The fall ended any fight or flight capabilities he possessed.

With great effort, both men pushed their way up to standing. Lalumière put up his hands in submission. The game was *finis*—he had lost.

Just then, there was a loud *crack!*

Everyone turned toward the source of the sound … toward the guillotine.

The ricocheting bullet, that had flipped TJ's life switch to OFF, had clipped the tether on the guillotine's blade.

Phoebe—hoping against all hope—spun around, her arms still cuffed behind her.

The razor-sharp blade fell, lusting for the soft flesh of Lenny's neck. Phoebe fired once.

The slug hit the frame just below its path. The destruction jammed the blade in its tracks—inches from Lenny's neck.

Crayle breathed out, his gun and his concentration still on Lalumière. Phoebe managed to work her cuffed wrists down under her feet and to the front. Still in great pain, she stood.

With the Glock still comfortable in her hands, Phoebe saw a movement to the side. She spun in its direction to face down Ling. She adopted an aggressive leaning-toward version of the Weaver grip. Ling, her weapon retrained on Phoebe, engaged in the side-to-side hypnotic sway of a cobra charmer.

An antique table clock on the buffet counted the seconds. Who would give in first remained the only question.

It was Ling. With Lalumière and his gang out of the equation, she could not take out Crayle and Phoebe. She lowered her weapon. Phoebe followed suit.

"Hey!" came a voice from the corner of the room.

The two women holstered their weapons, ran to the guillotine, and untied the remaining ropes at Lenny's waist and freed his head. Just as they sat him up, the blade broke through the splintered channel and crashed down.

Everyone jumped.

Phoebe and Ling caught their respective breaths and pulled the sack from Lenny's head. The two tough-as-nails women had tears in their eyes.

Lenny looked up at them both. All he said was, "*What?*"

Ling bent down and kissed him atop his head. Phoebe followed suit.

Then Lenny, totally in character, blurted out, "Did I miss something?"

Even Lalumière laughed.

• • •

Just five minutes later, the bell-like sounds of the gendarmes pierced the newfound silence as they arrived in force—just past the moment of need. Behind them, in strode Jack, the silenced, scoped sniper rifle slung over his shoulder. Neither Crayle nor his crew recognized the tall thin man with Jack, the latter's old friend from France's intelligence agency, the *Direction Générale de la Sécurité Extérieure*—DGSE.

The gendarmes hooked up Lalumière with a pair of the finest outsourced Chinese handcuffs money could buy. Lalumière's final comment was, "I'd love to answer your remaining questions, Mr. Crayle, for surely I know the answers you seek. Pity. There is much to tell, but, as you Americans say, I must now lawyer up. *Désolé*—I am so sorry." Then he laughed as if *insane* was his middle name.

Crayle made a move toward him. A gendarme with epaulets stepped into his path.

"You Americans always wish to solve the problems with violence," he said to Crayle in excellent English. "This man will be of no further harm. Please …" the French cop said.

Crayle eased back.

Lenny, however, could not let it go. The man who had his father killed was about to leave the scene unscathed. He pieced together a sequence of French words, pointed at the Frenchman, and said, approximately, "Hey! He told us gendarmes suck! Big time!"

The two men holding Lalumière by either arm looked at each other. As they walked him out, they suddenly swerved him headfirst into the doorjamb of the giant double doors. Apparently, they understood a bit of bad French. From the blood spurt and the shrieking wail, the team knew the insulted men had broken Lalumière's nose. They felt better now.

Lenny, feeling empowered by the positive change of circumstance, walked over to TJ's body, rolled it over with his foot, and could not believe the quarter-sized hole in the man's forehead.

"Annie fuckin' Oakley," he observed. "Right between the eyes."

They all shook their heads—except Phoebe. She was not surprised at all.

After the gendarmes had taken the mad and bloodied Frenchman away in handcuffs, the four combatants had a chance to regain their respective bearings.

Phoebe started in on the private investigator, who was happy to have his head still in place. There was attitude in her voice.

"So, Lenny, what happened to you at the Rock? You know, *Le Rocher*?"

"When faced with overwhelming danger, I chose to live to fight again another day. Sun Tzu," Lenny said with only a vague notion of anything Sun Tzu. "If you really want to know, I was trying to work a freakin' frog phone in the restaurant. It didn't work. So, I ran down the driveway to get help." He folded his arms across his chest, looking belligerent.

"Oh? Where did you intend to find help? Were you going to run all the way back to Strasbourg?"

"Break it up, you two," Crayle interjected. "This was a good landing. We are all walking away from it. We will take a breather for a day. Then we will mount up and get back to the States." He looked at Chin's daughter. "Ling, you will be taken home from there. I am thanking you from my heart for what you have done for me. I do not know what won you over, but I am grateful. I still have a long way to go to reclaim myself. I may never really get there, but I am not going to give up. Not ever. You can tell that to Chin."

"You heard him," cried Lenny. "Phoebs and I will get the wine and cheese, Crayle and Ling, crackers and bread. WGP, folks. *We gonna party!*"

CHAPTER 45

The next day brought a cool morning at the château. The war was over, at least for now. Crayle had found his way into the master's chambers. He had slept late and was awakened by Lalumière's chef, who stood just inside the door. A hot brunch would be served in the château's buffet area, *s'il vous plaît*. The chef handed him a note.

> Magus,
>
> Micmac and I had to leave—some business to take care of. Enjoy yourselves, don't burn the place down, and make sure Ling gets to the airport and doesn't stow away anywhere. Chin has sent a jet to retrieve her and would be upset if she didn't show. See you back in California.
>
> Jack

Crayle was hungry if he was anything. He jumped up, ran through the shower, and tossed on some of Lalumière's casual attire. It fit him just enough.

He made the rounds of each of the guest rooms to roust his comrades-in-arms.

The rooms were laid out along one side of an upstairs hallway. The wide corridor was painted a neutral blue with all of the off-white and gold accents characteristic of the downstairs room. Crayle opened the first door he came to and stepped inside the threshold.

This room's décor was feminine by any account. The walls, a light pink, were adorned with paintings of women, probably Lalumière distaff gentry. Each had an ornate gold frame with a notable light background highlighting each. The queen-sized bed was adorned with mauve draperies replete with strips of gold and gold *fleur-de-lis*.

Phoebe sat before a Louis XVI vanity that would have suited Marie Antoinette. She seemed different to him—pensive, not coiled. Then she spoke to him, but softly. "So how do you like my French girl look?" she asked, a dash of subdued coquette apparent.

Crayle surveyed the short cut, the shade as dark as coal. He had hardly noticed before and fought for words. "I'm not sure I like the French look."

Phoebe's eyes fell to the floor between them.

"But I know I like the girl."

She looked up, grinning from ear-to-ear. She jumped to her feet.

"Hug?" he asked.

After a hug that seemed to hang on for several minutes, he felt he had to speak his mind.

"Phoebe, that girl at the farm—Anne-Isabel—I noticed your reaction to her. I know you by now, and I could see how easily she got under your skin. She's out of your life now. She means nothing."

Crayle meant it one way, but Phoebe took it the other. She tilted her head slightly to the side as if to say, "How well do you know *her*?"

He started to clarify, but instead concluded that cat fights between women aren't totally physical. He wished he could help her with her demons, but knew he had to exorcise his own first.

With that, he invited her to the brunch, put any other thoughts or comments on hold, and showed himself out.

• • •

Crayle knocked at the next room. As he entered, he noticed the craftsman who'd rebuilt the château had built into it even the sounds of old wood creaking. This room was painted green. He found Ling inside.

She sat on the floor in front of a lighted fireplace, the light flickering on and off her perfect features.

"Are you okay?"

She did not respond, so Crayle knelt down on the rug next to her.

She turned her head to look at him. The tears welled up in her eyes were her only expression.

"Ling, I've changed my mind. Don't go back. Come stay with us. Start a normal life. You know, meet guys. Date. Fall in love. Don't go back. Chin sent you here to take care of business and, look, we're all still alive. He might—"

"I must go," was her solemn reply. "There is no honor if I stay. If I must die, it is my destiny."

"Stop this *daughter* thing. Come be my sister." Crayle immediately regretted the implication.

She looked at him, brow wrinkled—not understanding a real relationship. And what did Crayle mean by *sister*? Did it really matter what one was called?

"No. Not for that. I mean like a real sister. Phoebe can teach you—it's not about sex."

Ling forced a smile.

"You are a good man, Mr. Crayle. Look." She pointed at a scattering of thin sticks on the floor before her. "I have looked into the future, and it has portended my death. It also says we will meet again. Mr. Crayle, both events must happen."

"So, we will meet again before you …"

"Yes." She smiled. "But I must return to Hong Kong tomorrow."

He returned her smile; he understood.

"And one final thing, Mr. Crayle. In America, you would not call me Ling An-yee. So, since we have touched and must meet again, please call me Annie."

"Annie? I am not sure I can handle two."

She gave him a quizzical look.

"Breakfast is served, Annie. See you there."

He backed out of the room and slowly closed the door, marveling again at the realistic creak.

• • •

The third bedroom was another knock and enter. Crayle walked in to find P.I. Lenny fiddling with the TV remote. He had found a set of instructions in a drawer, but they were all in French. He tossed a look at the doorway, said "Hey," to Crayle and returned to his current dilemma.

"Lenny, I just wanted to thank you for taking the kidnapping for the team and for staying alive."

Lenny looked at him. Confused. It was not usual for someone to express their caring for him—at least not in his presence.

Crayle continued, "Thanks for the super move with the gun. Look, something did come from all this. Now you know why your dad was murdered. And who did it."

"You are most welcome, kemosabe, but I still have some questions about this whole thing. Like, how much did Jack know about this Chin guy and the Lalumière character? And what did Jack and Chin know about your accident? I mean, *all* the details. The who, what, where, when, why, and how? And who did my dad contact regarding the memory card from your shit? I could go on, but I think I'd have even more questions than we started with." He laughed. "I'm starting to sound like you."

Crayle shared the laugh. "I know what you mean. Well, all I can suggest at this point is we start making a list of questions, but not until after breakfast, which is presently being served downstairs. See ya there, LL."

And Crayle left the room, talking to himself the entire way down the hallway and down the stairs. It was more of his Rorschach-inspired internal dialog. And it felt good.

• • •

Following a French-delicious repast, they all moved to the Great Room and settled onto a surviving sofa. Having nothing better to do, Lalumière's manservant Robert provided the service. The team proceeded to drink great German Mosel wine and great French Moselle wine, to eat copious amounts of regional cheeses, and were all around feeling good.

Crayle asked the women if either would like to take a walk in the garden and, to his surprise, both Phoebe and Ling said yes. They each took an arm, and the three exited out the double doors on the north side of the Great Room into the garden.

Left out, Lenny just murmured, "Oh, that's okay. I don't really want to go. I'll just debrief the wine room."

He walked into the room off the entry, selected what he thought to be the most expensive bottle, and opened it. He began a lengthy interrogation of its contents, which got him a little drunk.

Outside, the three walked arm-in-arm between the foot-high hedges that lined the pathways and protected the meticulously-kept gardens. Lalumière had been able to achieve the restoration of the gardens even though the bulk of the estate remained overgrown. There was no visible sign of damage to them even after the small war that had just been fought.

Since the gardens were laid out in squares, the trio could not simply stroll straight to any one spot, but had to walk north, then west and so on. A breeze picked up as they turned left and headed west toward the sunset.

Their path dead-ended at a gardener's shed. Crayle pulled open the weather-damaged door with a loud creek, and they stepped inside. The space was dark save for the light entering through cracks in the slatted walls. Phoebe reached up and turned Crayle's head toward her. She stood on her tiptoes and gave him a longer-than-friendly kiss. On the lips. He responded without thinking.

"Perhaps I should leave?" Ling suggested, not wanting to be a third wheel.

Crayle caught himself. He remembered Hekka. He remembered how perfectly they had fit together, if only for a short time.

"Perhaps we should all get back."

As they headed back toward the château, a fine drizzle began to fall. Crayle ducked under a nearby shade tree. The women followed. It was mostly dry with fine mist sifting through the tree's foliage. He lay down on his back on the soft bed of leaves. The girls took his cue and sat down beside him. Ling seemed to be calm enough, but Phoebe was still at the edge of emotion, near the edge of control.

She moved atop him, applying heavy kisses to his lips. Ling responded, her hands deft as she readied him. She felt heat and hardness stiffen his sex. Ling parted Phoebe's legs and unleashed Crayle's dragon. As she did, the back of her hands rubbed against Phoebe. Phoebe moaned. Ling pushed Phoebe's panties aside and hooked up the re-united lovers.

As they moved together, Crayle and Phoebe could each feel gentle but knowing fingers heighten their pleasure. His hands framed her face, and Phoebe's were firm on his chest. With eyes at half mast and only faint smiles, they acknowledged to one another the subtle, but severe sexual impact of the young Chinese.

Phoebe sat up, allowing Crayle's hands to move to her breasts. She arched back just enough and began to move up and down, but slowly.

As the rain sifted through the leaves of the tree, striking each of them with tingles here and there, Ling moved up behind Phoebe. She pressed her body tight against Phoebe's, their bent legs interlocked. Ling reached around and, slipping her hands under Crayle's, felt the agent's breasts.

Oh, Phoebe was not into threesomes. No. She was a traditional … Ling softly kissed the back of Phoebe's neck. And she never … "Oh!" And at that moment, Phoebe loved it all. She loved Crayle. She loved Ling. She knew now that the Indian woman was not even a distant memory in his mind. She felt sure he had forgotten her altogether. "How fucking wonderful," she breathed into the moist air.

By the time the *orchestre-à-trois* reached a crescendo, a bond between the three had been created that would endure through the trials and tribulations ahead. They would be tested to the point that one or all might not survive. Only time would tell.

• • •

Completed and depleted, the trio walked back into the château to find Lenny, who stood swaying in the middle of the Great Room, a glass of wine in one hand and the television remote in the other. He had been able to power up the system alright, but the screen just held the same still picture of the desert valley—just as Lalumière had left it.

The wine seemed to befuddle the focus he attempted to bring to the situation, but at last he cried out, "Voila! This must be the button here."

"No!" the trio yelled in unison.

He pressed the button with an exaggerated motion toward the screen. The result was immediate. The screen faded to black, and then the words:

Au revoir.

EPILOGUE

By the time the Crayle, Lenny, Phoebe, and Ling made it back to the Hôtel de France to collect their belongings, they could tell there was major buzz in the air. At first, they thought word of Lalumière's downfall had gotten around. He was important in the region, and it was reasonable that news of the battle and his ultimate capture would be on everyone's lips. But, no. That was not it.

The explosion they viewed on the screen at the château had been real, having occurred in a barren valley in central Iran. From the early accounts, there had been an explosion at a secret underground nuclear facility that none of the intelligence agencies would either admit or deny knowing about. It appeared that the Iranians had used other more likely locations—ones with the necessary available water supply—as red herrings to attract the attention of the media and intelligence agencies. They had done that well.

But something had gone wrong. The explosion had been picked up by satellites. There were reports that moderate radiation had been detected as nuclear dust wafted east into Afghanistan. There was panic in the streets of Tehran and other Iranian cities, as well. Journalists guessed that the Israelis had located the facility and bombed it. As was not unusual in the period directly following a cataclysmic event, none of the guesses and exaggerations of guesses came anywhere near the truth.

Thousands of miles to the east in the stylish and modern city of Hong Kong, two men observed the entire event on their Chinese *Pana-Sony* TV, the smell of victory in their nostrils. Chin and Li toasted their first major success. Clearly, the mini-nuke, replete with the innovative radiation sponge casing and delivered to the Iranian facility by Li, had gone off, so to speak, without a hitch. Clearly, Lalumière was a man of his word. Time to celebrate. The Scotch would be of a very rare cask. And there would, of course, be the daughters.

• • •

Jack had just received his phone debrief from Phoebe. She related what he had missed in the Great Room while he guarded the driveway. He smiled an inside smile, popped open a bottle of Bud, and got Neil on the line. He uploaded the château intel, thankful that his ward, Magus Crayle, far beyond his own control, had survived the heavy odds at both ends of the Earth. Jack saw the exceptional qualities this man possessed, especially without the underpinning substance of long-term memory. Incredible. Neil had called to make sure Rorschach had been kept in the loop. Jack lied and said he was about to call him. Jack just wanted to savor the moment before having to talk to the sociopathic doctor of psychiatry. Just the thought of it, at telephone's length, gave him a chill. But he needed to stay on Neil's good side. He set his enjoyment of the moment aside and made the call.

• • •

Rorschach was seated in his office, the door open. Other personnel in the vicinity could not know Jack had just related to the good doctor the warlike events that had occurred at the château. All the staff could hear was the wailing, "Ahhhhh!" that emanated from the doctor's office.

It was clear to all who worked with him, Rorschach was an obsessive man. He had hung up the phone and paced his office—impatient at the time it would take to get *the subject* back into a suitable environment to perform some *routine* debriefing himself. He was only finishing step one with Magus Crayle—many more would follow. He had learned much from previous patients and the seminal work of his predecessors. He also knew that this patient, too, could end up a dead end—in both meanings of the words. After all, failures became loose ends. And loose ends became dead ends.

• • •

Chin Yao-wu continued to implement Crayle's elaborate work of genius—*The Blackstone Perfection*—to rescue his beloved country. Given the 100% markup on Lalumière's three nukes, he and Li had obtained three more for their own nefarious purposes. With them and with General Li's committed help, he was convinced he could lead his country out of the near and present dangers it faced, as well as onto the path of its true destiny. He would see to it with other people's blood, as necessary.

• • •

Sylvain Lalumière had been taken into custody and swallowed up by the French judicial system. He had gone off the reservation in a major way and would have to forego dreams of a return to his great aristocratic past. Even the powerful and connected Illuminé would have trouble saving him. Whatever he had done with the other two nuclear bombs he had purchased from Chin remained a mystery.

• • •

Before he had left with the others, Crayle had secured a moment of privacy. He sat in the château library after pouring himself Armagnac from an eighteenth century decanter of fine Baccarat crystal. He did not realize he was less than twenty kilometers from the little French town that gave the legendary crystal its name. And all the magnificent books. Camus, Voltaire—the list went on and on. Somehow he knew that philosophy was special. It overarched the rawness and rough edges of societies. It made sense.

But sex, raw sex, also made sense. He had now the memories of four incredible episodes. The first had been with the FBI agent. He had been a knowledge-wise virgin with the skills of a craftsman. And then with Ling. A girl who had perfected a tiny corner of sexuality. And then with them both in the fantasy setting of a French château's gardens. But these memories were two-dimensional. There was more. Much more.

He knew it because of the fourth experience. He beheld the Serrano amulet on his wrist. He didn't know if he was superstitious, but it had brought him through the cabin and downhill battles, the rooftop attack, the street chase in Strasbourg, the Rocher, and the château. He needed to find Hekka. If she would have him, they would begin again.

But, no. He firmly shook his head and pushed the heels of his hands against his eyes. There was too much to learn about the things he had done—too much risk for someone like her to bear. *Damn!* In just one day, she had gotten inside him and put her mark on his heart. And now she would have to remain a part of his new … his present past. Someone else would be right for her.

The next day found an exhausted and depressed Magus Crayle with Lenny and Phoebe on Jack's Falcon 7X jet and headed home. Flori had concocted a Malibu rum and Rockstar cocktail. Crayle downed several while he and the others recounted their individual and collective bravery during the previous week.

The trip was long but, chasing the sun, it had been completed in less than one calendar day. Jack provided transportation up the hill from his *private* airport and left promptly, citing yet another personal audience with Monsieur Wohlford. Phoebe and Lenny opted for the multi-bedroom big house. And Crayle walked the short distance to *his* place.

When he entered, to his complete shock, the cabin had been completely repaired. No artifacts of the gun battle remained. No broken glass. No bullet holes. No crashed in doors. Micmac?

There was one thing Magus Crayle was sure of: he needed time alone. But, as a result of Flori's bartending magic, he felt mellow, yet wide awake. What to do now?

He had just set his things down when he saw it. It took him back to his experience two weeks ago. *It* was the fishing gear from what seemed like years ago—his sporting adventure with the P.I.

"What the hell," he said to the empty dwelling.

He picked up his share of the gear and headed for the dock. It was a beautiful day at his Fawnskin residence, and he was going to catch dinner. A fish dinner. All this would be in honor of Lenny Lipschitz. After all, it was the little P.I.'s last-second Hail Mary that had kept them all alive.

It only took him a few minutes to get settled in on the dock. He tossed the baited hook and float, commencing the fisherman's wait. He savored the crystal clear mountain air in his lungs, devoid of the smell of burnt gunpowder, and finally felt back to a relative peace—both outside and in.

His eyes gathered in the late afternoon sun and its reflection on the breeze-swept water of the lake. Then, he laughed. Not big. Not small. Just a laugh. The sparkles thrown off by the waves and reflection caused the water to sparkle all over. He had his own—

"Water diamonds."

The voice came from behind. Adrenalin gushed. He slipped his hand down next to his leg. His fingers fastened around Lenny's filleting knife. He turned.

"Hekka!"

She smiled her minimalist smile.

He let out a gasp. "What the hell next?" he stammered.

Indeed.

ABOUT THE AUTHOR

A native Californian, Dennis Bowen has a long-standing commitment to international affairs, has traveled to more than 40 countries, and is a member of the World Affairs Council. Add to the mix his classified defense and intelligence community background, martial arts training, sports car track-racing, service with military amphibious forces in a war zone, and playing in rock bands, and it's not surprising that this eclectic writer pens International Thrillers. When not traveling the globe to conduct book research, he resides on the Southern California coast.

Website: http://www.DennisBowen.com
Twitter: www.twitter.com/DBowenThrillers
Facebook: http://www.facebook.com/Dennis.Bowen.90

The Blackstone Perfection

Book 2:

International Thriller Series

Chapter 1

The smell awakened him. The vanguard drop of water had pushed along the block wall's seam. Those that succeeded it had propelled it to the edge. It paused a moment, as if having second thoughts, and then plunged over the precipice, falling 192 times its diameter. The drop accelerated the entire twenty-four inches until its obliteration against the smooth flesh of an aquiline nose. The man attached woke with a start. His eyes snapped open, but the darkness defeated any detection of the source of his rude awakening. The nose, expert at sniffing the finest fragrance of a well-balanced Bordeaux, deftly dismantled its component scents.

The single drop signaled that late Autumn had not yet turned to early Winter with the first snowfall. The drop's odorless nature had been adulterated by vehicular essences as it seeped through the asphalt streets of the modern world and down into the dungeon. Although his new residence had existed more than 630 years, no lingering manifestation remained above ground. The head, shoulders, and torso of the Bastille had been razed more than 220 years before, after its fall in 1789. Its bowels, the stone block encasements and ironworks underground, had been left to rot.

Constrained by a bed no larger than his 6'6", 220 pound frame, he rolled over just as the solid iron closure on his 18" by 12" window to the external world screeched open. Since he had pinched out the desk candle after making a diary entry, his world had been pitch black. The sconced gas lamps in the gallery outside his cell provided morning light. The man who peered into his quarters was clothed head-to-toe in Eighteenth Century dress, no doubt intended as an insult. In spite of the lofty title, *Compte de Cièrges*, his jailer provided no concierge services, as the antiquated title implied. The fact that the man opened the portal every morning before breakfast and closed it again after the evening meal enabled the prisoner to count the days. Today made eight since being captured. He could thank the American, Magus Crayle, for the assault, and those in the hierarchy above him for the betrayal. And the humiliation.

He dwelled on his transition from a member of France's elite to a mere captive devoid of any semblance of control over his remaining years. Suicide presented as his most attractive option, but his captors denied him the resources for even that. A brief length of charcoal stick and a writing pad disafforded that option.

One man had done this to him. Magus Crayle, sent to him by American intelligence, had led him to believe there was a pathway to his goal. To replace the hideous, self-destructive socialism, the monarchy of old would be restored. Part of a strategic plan devised by the genius, Crayle.

What had gone awry? The Illuminé's man-in-the-CIA had provided Crayle for the purpose, yet must have been the one who'd given the assault orders. And Crayle—a mathematician. How could such a man have led an assault capable of obliterating his vaunted, seasoned defense force? Perhaps the years of training and experience in the Foreign Legion no longer provided the human resources he required. He pushed aside the enigma. He knew he would die in this place. The French government, having destroyed the economy, needed their greatest detractor incommunicado until death. They had chosen the perfect venue. With its historical significance, the Bastille oozed symbology. His deep thoughts of remorse were interrupted by a now familiar sound. Breakfast.

• • •

She was late. The guard had just begun his shift and already something was wrong. It was feeding time for the prison's sole inhabitant and, of all the uninteresting aspects of guarding someone in lockdown security, meals were the high points.

Ah, there. He heard the light footsteps nearing the cellblock hallway. She would deliver the food and leave. At that point, the guard would call his girlfriend once again and tell her, in a convincing manner, that he would soon leave his wife. The man deprived of all freedoms moved to the side of his cell door, straining to catch a glimpse of this woman, of any woman.

At four meters distance, she emerged from the shadows. Without patience, the jailer watched the period-attired, petite young woman step into view and move toward him, tray in hand. She wore a dress of white linen, her shoulders covered by a dark, heavy mantle secured by a satin bow at the neck. A white scarf draped to each side of her face completed the picture. The prisoner took notice as she deployed her magic. A slight smile came to her face and point dimples to her cheeks. They juxtaposed the words darling and precious with the words sexy and sexual. She was much more alluring than either the jailer's wife or his girlfriend. No words were spoken.

She set the tray and its undisturbed contents next to the rust-red, iron door and moved her delicious body against his. His newborn lust turned to physical action. Within three seconds, he lifted and embraced and pressed her against the cold, moist stone wall. She locked her legs tight around his waist.

He pushed his lips onto hers. He brought both hands to bear on his masculine appendage, now also imprisoned. She jerked at her dress. They engaged with seemingly equal passion.

The young woman breathed hard for effect. She thrust herself at him with intensity. But, behind his back, she slipped the long, conical thimbles hidden in each palm onto her thumbs. She bit hard into his upper lip. He tried to jerk away, but she held fast. With all her strength, she drove the pointed ends up each side of his spine and deep into his brain.

The girl pulled her thumbs from the thimbles and held the guard as tightly with her arms as with her legs. As he slid to the floor, the motion scraped her back on the rough stone, but her emotions were on fire. She felt nothing.

They sat entwined on the floor for seconds. Her breathing slowed as quickly as his breathing ceased. She kissed his forehead, released her grasp, and fell away.

She crawled to where he lay and, with care not to bloody her fingers, retrieved the heirloom murder weapons. She looked up into the flat-iron barred opening that the prisoner called a window. She looked directly into his eyes. She lifted the thimbles, one at a time, to her lips. She licked them dry, removing all traces of red.

But the young woman's goal was not seduction into cold-blooded murder. It was, at this time, not her sport. She operated under the strictest orders. They required no witnesses to that which was to follow. There could be no finger pointing to her or to those who orchestrated the plot. And there could be no trail as she affected their escape.

She had come for the Bastille's lone captive. She had come for France's number one prisoner.

www.ingramcontent.com/pod-product-compliance
Lightning Source LLC
Chambersburg PA
CBHW020257030826
48979CB00026B/1379/J

* 9 7 8 0 9 8 8 1 8 4 1 0 7 *